Yu
D0535570

SORREL MOON

SORREL MOON

COTTON SMITH

FIVE STAR
A part of Gale, Cengage Learning

GALE
CENGAGE Learning°

Detroit • New York • San Francisco • New Haven, Conn • Waterville, Maine • London

GALE
CENGAGE Learning·

LIBRARY OF CONGRESS CATALOGING-IN-PUBLICATION DATA

Smith, Cotton.
   Sorrel moon / Cotton Smith. — First edition.
     pages cm
     ISBN-13: 978-1-4328-2811-0 (hardcover)
     ISBN-10: 1-4328-2811-8 (hardcover)
     1. Ranches—Fiction. 2. Brothers—Fiction. 3. Outlaws—Fiction.
    4. Frontier and pioneer life—Fiction. 5. Texas—Fiction. I. Title.
    PS3569.M5167S664 2014
    813'.54—dc23   2013040875

First Edition. First Printing: March 2014
Find us on Facebook– https://www.facebook.com/FiveStarCengage
Visit our website– http://www.gale.cengage.com/fivestar/
Contact Five Star™ Publishing at FiveStar@cengage.com

Printed in Mexico
1 2 3 4 5 6 7 18 17 16 15 14

In memory of Chief Swift Eagle

CHAPTER 1

Cole Kerry reined his big sorrel outside the clapboard saloon. A frantic tumbleweed scurried ahead to reach the boardwalk first. Pale moonlight glittered off the brackish water in the trough next to the hitch rack. A saddled bay horse, tied there, snorted and sidestepped away from his powerful mustang's advance. The other two horses laid back their ears.

The settlement was a sad cluster of unpainted clapboard buildings with a string of gnarled and splintered boardwalks a few miles southwest of Uvalde, Texas. Pitch was the name on the weathered signpost. The young gunfighter couldn't recall being through the settlement. From the look of the boarded doors, only the saloon, a general store and a livery remained open.

The lone street of Pitch was a mass of hardened wagon ruts from years past. Autumn was usually a time of hustle and bustle in most towns as ranchers and farmers sought supplies for readying their cattle and harvesting their small crops for the coming winter. Not so here, it appeared. More like a hard winter had arrived a long time ago and never left.

Cole Kerry's head was thick with the loss of his wife, Kathleen, and he had been riding since the funeral. It didn't matter where. Away from her death. Away from well-meaning friends and family. Away from their words, their sympathy, their sadness. He only wanted Kathleen. Pneumonia had taken her from him, leaving blackness. Their time together had been oh so short. With her, his loneliness disappeared.

He wanted whiskey. A bottle to mask the ache, for a few hours. He would buy a bottle and ride on, to drink it in the darkness, somewhere on the plains. He couldn't think beyond that as he swung down from his horse and whipped the reins around the rack. The rangy sorrel snorted and yanked his head up twice, a challenge to the other horses tied there.

Cole was dressed in the clothes he'd worn to the funeral. He had ridden away right after the service. The empty words of the region's new preacher had followed him for miles. Cole's black broadcloth suit was dotted with trail dust, as was his white shirt. Somewhere along the trail was a discarded white paper collar and tie. In his coat pocket was jammed one of his ivory-handled, silver-plated Colts that had been in his saddlebags. His two-gun holster rig was packed in there, along with the second gun. He rarely rode without them. A habit from his days of hiring his gun to cattlemen and riding the outlaw trail.

He stood beside his big sorrel and looked back at the dark, empty land. One time he had had the impression someone was following him. Didn't matter, he told himself, and headed for the saloon.

His spurs clanked as he stepped inside and pushed his black wide-brimmed Stetson back from his forehead. Icy blue eyes had seen both sides of the law in the days after the great war. Even the anguish in his face couldn't hide his boyish charm or the deep cleft in his chin. Or the once-broken Roman nose, courtesy of his older brother, Ethan, when they were boys. Cole had returned the favor.

The stale smell of beer, tobacco smoke and old sawdust reached his nose and he shook his head. The gray room was crowded with two scarred tables and a billiard table in the back, propped up by a board. Grimy oil lanterns, hanging from the walls, tried to brighten the room but failed.

Eight men glanced at the stranger, then returned to their respective poker games, four to a table. All appeared to have been at it for awhile. He didn't know anyone in the room and didn't expect he would. They were likely men wanted somewhere. Cole Kerry looked around the smoke-laden saloon. Within him was building a need for violence. It wasn't the first time. He hoped someone would challenge him. Or just meet his gaze. Anything to give him an excuse to vent the ache in his soul. Anything. Fighting triggered something inside of him, an unseen force that took over his body and mind.

No one met his eyes. The eight men at the poker tables avoided his stare with controlled discipline. Three men at the bar studied its somewhat smooth surface, or the grubby oil painting of fruit and a naked woman on the back wall. None were talking. A plate of old cheese and crackers occupied the far end of the bar.

The bartender was a large, heavyset woman. Wearing big hoop earrings and a soiled dress that had seen better days, she had a heavy belly, thick thighs and large breasts. Standing behind the bar, next to the cheese plate, she made no attempt to acknowledge his entrance, continuing to read a wrinkled newspaper probably left by another passing stranger.

Cole strolled to the bar, his hard face defying anyone to meet his unspoken challenge. "I want whiskey. Irish, if you've got it. A bottle."

The lady bartender didn't move from her study of the yellowed sheet.

"I said I want a bottle of whiskey." Cole's voice was louder this time.

A man at the poker table said something to the man in the derby hat next to him and both left by the back door.

"Guess she didn't hear me." He turned to a cowboy with a scruffy beard and a scruffier hat. Weary batwing chaps were held in place by rawhide strings.

"Yeah. Helen Mae's funny that way sometimes," the cowboy's response was hesitant and he kept his eyes on his own glass of whiskey.

Annoyed, Cole asked, "Where's the good stuff? The Irish."

Surprised at the question, the cowboy hesitated, then pointed. "Uh, under . . . there."

"Thanks."

Cole walked behind the bar, pulled up a new bottle with his left hand and examined it.

The bartender dropped her newspaper. "Hey, you can't do that!" She started toward Cole.

The young gunfighter's intensity stopped her. Cole tossed a gold coin in her direction and headed for the door. He had guessed the purpose of the two men who had left and looked forward to the encounter. Holding the neck of the whiskey bottle in his left hand, his right hand slipped into his coat pocket as he moved through the saloon door.

Outside, a lanky outlaw in a dirty long coat and a bowler with a bite out of the brim stood off to the right, holding a Winchester. His partner, a stocky man in a calfskin vest and a derby hat, was untying the reins of Cole's horse.

"Believe I'll jes' be takin' him fer a ride, mister. You don't mind, do ya?" He grinned at Cole with yellowed teeth. "Maybe I'll jes' keep him. Mighty fine hoss."

The outlaw to the right levered the Winchester. Its "click-click" was heavy in the night air. Cole didn't move; his right hand remained in his pocket and his left, lowered against his side, tightened around the bottle.

"Fact is, Orville, why don't you see if this fine gent has any spare cash on him," the stocky man said as he jammed his boot into the stirrup and swung into the saddle.

"That be a fine idea, Billy. How 'bout it, mister? Let's see

what yur a'carryin'. Maybe we'll let it go at that. If'n yur polite."
The long-coated thief with the rifle sauntered toward Cole.

At the tie rack, the sorrel stood motionless and the man
kicked him with his spurs. "Come on, Red. Damn you. Come
on."

As if possessed, the sorrel burst into a wild fury of leaps and
swirls. His hat soaring from a balding head, the horse thief
grabbed too late for the saddlehorn and flew into the air. He
landed awkwardly on his left leg, screaming as it buckled
beneath him. His derby hat settled a few feet away.

Taking advantage of the distraction, Cole spun toward the
second man and fired the Colt from his pocket.

"I'm *carrying* lead."

Three times orange flame tore through the fabric and drove
bullets into the surprised holdup man. His Winchester exploded
and the bullet sang into the darkness, past Cole's shoulder.
Cole walked over to the downed robber. He was dead. Removing the Colt from his smoking pocket, Cole Kerry shoved it into
his waistband and turned toward his horse standing quietly in
the street.

"Good boy, Kiowa."

The young gunfighter walked to his sorrel and led him back
to the hitch rack. He flipped the reins over it, ignoring the horse
thief lying near the red horse and moaning about his broken
leg. The other horses were agitated and stomping their hooves.

The patrons and the bartender hurried outside the saloon;
two examined the long-coated robber and pronounced him
dead. Helen Mae swore.

"Ya shoulda tolt me that were a killer hoss!" The would-be
horse thief said through gritted teeth. "I'm gonna shoot that red
devil."

He reached for his holstered pistol.

Cole took one step and slammed the whiskey bottle into the

side of the man's head. Glass and whiskey exploded, sending both all over him. His hand fluttered from the gun handle and flopped on the dirt street. Soaked in whiskey and bleeding from a deep cut in his skull, the man groaned and fell over.

"Got a sheriff around here?" Cole growled and tossed the rest of the broken bottle onto the boardwalk.

"No, sir. None since Ol' Man Kinson up an' died," Helen Mae said with new interest in the stranger, as she watched the shattered container bounce once and shiver against a warped plank. "No need though, mister. It was self-defense. Orville and Billy, they were asking for it."

"I already know that," Cole said. "Where I come from, horse stealing is a hanging offense."

"Yah, reckon so." Helen Mae glanced at the small man with a graying goatee and wide eyes, standing next to her.

The small man pulled on the lapels of his worn coat and bowed. Striped pants disappeared into his mule-eared boots. A faded orange vest was spotted with food and whiskey.

"Sir, I think there has been a mistake," he said in a surprisingly deep voice, his eyes blinking with every other word. "I am Winston Burlington Lunes the Third."

"Good for you."

Nodding, the short man continued, "Although we have no sheriff, the fine citizens of Pitch, Texas, have seen fit to bestow upon me the titular responsibility of mayor. I also serve, without compensation, as justice of the peace—and attorney at law. At your service, sir." His eyes continued to blink as he spoke.

"Other than two men trying to steal my horse, steal my money and kill me, what's been the mistake?" Cole growled.

"Sir, we are a peaceful community. No longer a part of the cattle drives headed north, we find ourselves enjoying a quiet sort of living." Mayor Lunes responded. "I apologize sincerely—on behalf of the entire community—for the irresponsible behavior of these two men."

"Irresponsible behavior? That's an interesting way to describe it." Cole yanked his Winchester free from its scabbard and levered it into readiness.

Three men flinched at the guttural sound of the cocking.

Ignoring the mayor, Cole turned his attention to the remaining customers strung across the dilapidated boardwalk. "All right, boys. One at a time, toss your guns in there. I want them nice an' wet." With his gun, he motioned toward the trough on his left, just beyond the hitching rack.

Winston Burlington Lunes the Third glanced at the men on either side of him, then at Helen Mae, and declared, "I don't believe that is necessary, sir. We wish you no harm." His eyelids fluttered rapidly.

"I'll decide what to believe. I told you to toss your guns in the trough. We'll start with you, Lunes . . . the Third."

"I carry no weapon, sir. I am an officer of the court." He held out his coat with both hands to demonstrate.

"You'd better be telling me the truth, *Third*. It would be a shame to put lead into someone with so many responsibilities."

Several snickers followed from various men straddling the boardwalk. Helen Mae told them to be quiet.

Cole Kerry pointed his Winchester at the man with a grimy face and torn trousers on the far right. "We'll start with you. Yeah, you."

Gulping, the dirty-faced man drew a short-barreled pistol from his back waistband, glanced at the others and threw it into the water. He shook his head as the gun splashed and sank.

"Here's what we're going to do next. I'm giving you ten seconds for you and your friends to get rid of those hideaways, too," Cole snapped. "If not, I'm going to empty this rifle into the whole sorry-ass bunch of you. Your call, boys. I didn't start this. But I'll sure end it."

The man with the torn trousers pulled another gun from his boot and tossed it into the trough, then turned around. "I ain't dyin' fer ya, Johnny . . . or ya, Rufus . . . do it. He ain't bluffin'."

Mayor Lunes waved his arms as if to disconnect the threat, but no one paid any attention. Two other men hurriedly yanked handguns from strapped-on holsters and coat pockets and tossed them into the trough. One pistol hit the edge of the trough, teetered and popped into the street. Startled, the closest horse snorted and stomped its feet. Fearful, a fat man looked at Cole for approval, retrieved the gun and dropped it into the water. He said he operated the livery, had no weapons and stepped back to the others.

"I ain't carryin' neithur, mister. Honest." The cowboy shook his head and held up both hands and kept them there.

"Millard, come on, man. He knows yur holding," the dirty-faced man leaned over to look at a lanky man on the other end of the ragged line of stunned men.

Cole swung his rifle toward Millard, slouching at the far end. "There's one in your boot, too, Millard."

Sneering, Millard, slump-shouldered with a droopy mustache and a hat with a bullet hole, walked over, ceremoniously dropped a large Walker Colt into the trough, then leaned over and pulled a derringer from a boot holster and threw it into the roiled water.

"And the other one," Cole demanded. It was a guess.

Millard shrugged his shoulders and lifted a Smith & Wesson revolver from his back waistband. He added the weapon to the trough, thought about it for a second, withdrew a Bowie knife and tossed it toward the water.

"Now, you boys are going to join me in singing 'Rock of Ages.' " He choked back emotion that wanted free. "Just heard it this morning. Need to hear it again. So, come on . . . 'Rock of

Ages, cleft for me' . . . come on now, I want to hear you. All of you. 'Let me hide myself in thee . . . let the water and the blood, from thy wounded side which flowed . . . be of sin the double cure . . . save from wrath and make me pure.' " He couldn't remember anymore and ended the dirge with a splattering of trailing words.

Helen Mae and Mayor Lunes sang loudest, enjoying the opportunity. Cole guessed the strange little man would probably add another title, choir director, to his list. Satisfied, Cole loosened the coiled lariat from his saddle and tossed it at the feet of the cowboy from the bar.

"You can use one of these, I reckon. Put the loop around Billy's feet. Both of them."

The cowboy grabbed the rope and scurried off the boardwalk toward the unconscious man.

"Just above his boots. Yeah, there. Tighten it."

Cole retook the reins and swung into the saddle, holding his rifle in his right hand and extending his left. "Give me the rope. Good."

"If any of you bastards try to get your iron from that trough," he growled. "I'll start shooting. Yeah, I'll be watching."

Helen Mae stepped forward, thrusting out her large chest. "No one will. I'll watch 'em."

Letting out enough lariat to allow the outlaw's body to drag ten feet behind his horse's back legs, he looped it around his saddlehorn and began to lope away. The body bounced along the street behind horse and rider. Gasps followed from the onlookers.

Mayor Lunes waved his arms and shouted, "A hearing in such matters is customary." He swallowed and declared in a high-pitched voice, "I declare the evidence warrants a trial." He folded his arms and looked around at the others. "These matters must be conducted legally, you know."

Millard frowned and stepped toward the trough. "I paid good money for those guns. I'll be damned . . ."

From behind, Helen Mae slammed into him and sent Millard tumbling across the boardwalk. Rufus was a step behind. Two others joined in keeping Millard from reaching his weapons.

Fifteen minutes later, Cole returned to the saloon and pulled up in front of the tie rack. No one had moved, except Helen Mae. He was certain no one had attempted to retrieve a gun either. Barely visible at the far end of town was the swaying silhouette of the would-be horse thief hanging upside down from an oak tree.

Mayor Lunes folded his arms and said loudly, "I declare William Finley guilty of attempted horse stealing." He swallowed and added, "And Orville Pinkens guilty of attempted robbery."

"You boys can cut down Billy or whatever his name is after I leave," Cole said. "Tell him that's better than he deserved. And tell him if I ever see him again, I'll kill him. Nobody messes with my horse."

Amid the muttering of agreement, Helen Mae stepped forward and held out a new bottle of Irish whiskey. "Uh, here . . . here's a new bottle. No charge." She smiled. "I sleep in the room in the back. Door's not locked."

"Uh, sir, I haven't pronounced the sentence, sir," Mayor Lunes said, looking peevish.

"That's your problem."

Cole accepted the bottle with his left hand. His right held the reins and the Winchester with his finger on the trigger. He studied the saloon customers and the bartender. "Any of you want to follow me, have at it. Texas would be better off without you."

Rufus cocked his head and asked, "Who are you, mister?"

"I'm Cole Kerry."

Cole Kerry's reputation with a gun had blossomed after his

single-handed fight against Victorio Gee and his gang in the streets of Uvalde two years ago. It was there that the mad bandit king had taken his wife, Kathleen, as a shield to escape. Cole had wanted to be a cattleman like his two brothers, but those battle images had struck a nerve in this part of Texas. He was mentioned in the same breath as Wes Hardin, Clay Allison and a handful of other pistoleros. Tales of his prowess, both real and imagined, had hopped from one saloon to another.

The fat livery operator shook his head. "Damn. Thought so. Told Billy not to mess with you. Saw you in action against that Victorio Gee bunch. In Uvalde, it was. Couple of years back."

"Were you riding with him?"

"Oh, n-no sir. I was workin' for Squeaky Winston. He's the smithy there."

"Squeaky's a good man. You shoulda stayed there." Cole nudged his sorrel with his legs. Helen Mae waved vigorously at him, hoping her jiggling bosom would look interesting.

As he disappeared, the tall man said, "Damn, boys. That there is a pistol-fighter to beat all hell. We're lucky he didn't open up on us all."

The cowboy shook his head. "I'm gonna throw up."

Mayor Lunes looked at him. "I will cut Billy down. I will tell him that he has served a sufficient sentence." His eyelids blinked rapidly.

CHAPTER 2

A few hundred yards from town, Cole Kerry eased his horse onto a faint deer trail that led through a thicket of heavy brush and into a grouping of old oak, elm, pecan and walnut trees. An owl warned him as he passed a tall post oak and rode into the darkness. Letting Kiowa have his head, he rode through clusters of catclaw, mesquite, prickly pear, over fallen limbs and coarse bunch grass and around sharp boulders, and through thick underbrush. The trees gave way to a small meadow cut by a some-time creek.

He glanced over his shoulder to check his backtrail as he crossed the shallow water and clambered up its far slope, entering a tight stand of cottonwoods. He paused, didn't like what he saw and urged Kiowa on. After a few more minutes of riding, he let the big sorrel stop and drink from another pencil-thin stream that wasn't going to make it through the winter. When the horse was satisfied, they moved on and finally reined up among a cluster of scrawny pecan trees and alder bushes, the advent to a thicker stand of cottonwoods and oaks. Nearby was a squatty bowl of land where buffalo once rolled.

It was good enough. No one from town would likely find this place, especially not at night. And if they did, he could hear riders approaching from any direction.

He swung down, unsaddled Kiowa and brushed the sorrel's back with a handful of weeds. The big sorrel whinnied. After a second, easy watering, he returned the horse to the little clearing and tied the reins to a low branch of an unhappy cotton-wood. The bridle was left on, in case he had to move quickly, but the reins were tied long enough for easy grazing.

He looked around. It was dark and one could see shadows of concern everywhere. His Irish father would have seen faeires and otherworld mystical activities in every black corner. Cole was part Irish, that of his father. Due to his English mother, none of the sons carried the sounds of Irish in their voices or the superstitions—but the oldest son, Luther, favored images of faeries in his mind. However, Cole carried darkness and mystery deep within. His father had pronounced it as the way of ancient Celtic warriors. His oldest brother, Luther, agreed.

Whatever it was, he was comfortable in the shadows and darkness. At ease with its overwhelming feelings of loneliness. Perhaps it was the confidence that came to a man of the gun.

Satisfied Kiowa was grazing and content, he took the bottle of whiskey and sat with his Winchester beside him. He cocked the gun, eased the hammer down for safety and laid it beside him. Leaning against the closest cottonwood, he was silent and the night drew close. He took a drink and his mind wandered away.

Minutes passed before he realized a tiny bird was looking at him. The chickadee was inches from Cole's boots. He watched the bird. Something was wrong with its right wing, something that prevented it from flying. The little bird would be a snack for any predator nearby.

"Howdy, little friend. Looks like you're hurting. Are you hungry?" Cole said softly.

The bird cocked its head to the side and shivered.

"Got some grain in my saddlebags. It's Kiowa's, but he'll be happy to share," he said, laying the bottle against a tree root. "I'll get it. You just wait."

He rose as slowly as he could. Reacting to the movement, the chickadee jerkily retreated into the shadows, flapping its left wing awkwardly, but leaving the right wing against its side. Cole was certain the bird was injured enough that it couldn't fly.

"No need to hide, little fellow. Guess I'd like some company. Company that'll just listen—and not try to tell me Kathleen's in a better place. She may be, but I'm not there."

He walked over to his saddle, yanked clear a small sack from his saddlebags. Years ago, his older brother, Ethan, had taught him the importance of carrying vital items all the time. As the youngest Kerry brother, he had listened well. He had planned on riding away after the funeral and had packed for it. A quick search brought another sack of cornmeal dodgers, and a piece of jerky that he stuck in his mouth. One bag contained his rolled-up gunbelt and second revolver. The other bag contained more trail items, including a can of peaches, another of beans, a small box with tinder and matches, an old tin cup, loose cartridges, a small frying pan, some wild onions, and a few wrapped pieces of candy. The can of peaches he carried for his good Chinese friend, Shi Han Rui, who loved the fruit.

Carefully, he laid some grain on the ground then added a broken cracker, not far from where his boots had been when he was sitting. He remembered he hadn't reloaded his Colt and proceeded to do so.

"There's a nice supper for you," he said, chewing on the jerky and shoving new cartridges into the gun. "We'll talk after you eat." He chuckled. "Well, I will." He looked at the bird. A shadow defined it as a darker shape. "Don't know how long those crackers have been there, though. You'll have to decide if they taste good." He shoved the reloaded Colt back into his coat pocket.

Finishing the strip of jerked meat, he remembered the tin cup. Returning to his gear, he grabbed it from the bag, empty-ing four cartridges into his hand and shoving them into his pocket beside the revolver. Retrieving his canteen, he took a long drink, filled the cup and tossed the canteen back with his other gear. He set the filled cup close to the food, cradling it between two exposed roots so the chickadee could access the water easily without it tipping over.

"There you go, little buddy. I know the stream's close by, but this'll be handy when you want to wet your whistle after supper," Cole said softly and returned to his sitting position beside the tree. He took another drink from his bottle. The distraction was a relief from the pain in his heart.

"Hey, I understand. Look it over," Cole said. "I could use the company."

With an energetic skip, the chickadee reached the grain and tasted a kernel, then another. Glancing around, it hopped onto the root, drank from the cup and returned to try the cracker. Cole smiled, enjoying the quiet activity. His mind eased to an earlier time when Kathleen and he had encountered another chickadee on one of their quiet walks away from the ranch. She loved birds and they seemed to sense it. In his memory, he saw the tiny bird fly around her head, almost cooing.

Was this chickadee a sign from Kathleen? He shook his head. That was nonsense. Kathleen was dead. Dead. He bit his lower lip and concentrated on the little bird. The tiny creature was enjoying the meal and becoming less frightened with his closeness. After savoring a piece of the cracker, the chickadee hopped onto Cole's outstretched boot and chirped. "Chick-a-dee-dee."

"You're welcome," he muttered and couldn't help but smile. Kathleen would have been ecstatic to see this.

His reverie was interrupted by Kiowa snorting and stomping. A warning! Within the black bushes, yellow eyes appeared from the far trees. Cole picked up his rifle and eased back the hammer on the readied gun. This time, the little bird only cocked its head at Cole's movement, oblivious to the waiting danger.

"Coyote, not here." Cole swung the rifle toward the staring eyes. "Go or you will die tonight."

The eyes disappeared.

Kiowa snorted again, then was silent and began to graze.

Cole looked down at the tiny bird, eased the hammer down and laid the rifle beside him. "Better stay close," he said. "You're not in good shape right now."

As if understanding, the chickadee tiptoed up his leg, pausing halfway on his thigh, and sat.

A whoosh within the trees caught Cole's attention. An owl looking for supper! It could sweep down and snatch the little bird in one fierce dive. A hungry owl would not be afraid to attack so close to a human, especially with its speed and agility. He had seen an owl grab a chicken in a ranch yard while a person fed them.

Instinctively, Cole's hand blurted downward and grabbed the chickadee. The tiny bird chirped fear and wiggled in his tightened fist. A half second later, a dark shape zoomed in front of him. His right hand, holding the tiny bird, felt the cutting grasp of talons.

Pulling away, he swung his left fist and it slammed against the breast of the large owl. The blow drove the attacking bird backward, tumbling into the night. He listened to massive wings flapping to regain balance and it, too, was gone.

From a nearby branch, Cole heard, "Hoo, hoo-hoo, hoo-hoo."

Cole rubbed the soft head of the chickadee in his enclosed fingers. The back of his hand was bleeding from the owl's attack, but the talons hadn't touched the little bird.

"It's me, that's who, you big bully. Me an' my friend here. Next time, try somebody your own size. Move on—or I'll put a bullet in your chest instead of a fist." Cole held the chickadee close to his chest and waved his other toward the unseen owl.

Night sounds began to return to their gentle symphony. A soothing breeze crossed Cole's face and reminded him again of Kathleen. He blinked away emotion and turned his attention to the trembling bird in his fist, stroking its head again with his finger and ignoring the blood running across his hand.

"Settle down, little buddy. Let's have a look at your wing. No, I'm not a doctor, but I've had to treat a few wounds, you know."

His examination of the bird's right wing revealed the problem. Somewhere, the chickadee had gotten heavy wagon wheel grease on its feathers and the substance had stuck there, preventing them from expanding. Without letting go of the bird, he pulled a handkerchief from his pants pocket, laid it on the ground and poured a little whiskey on the cloth, then on the back of his hand. His strokes on the wing brought blackness onto the handkerchief. He laid down the cloth again, poured more whiskey on an unused portion and stroked the wing several more times. After an hour of cleansing, he gently pulled on the wing and it extended normally. In the dark he couldn't be certain, but thought the grease was gone.

A final washing should finish the task and the wing would be good as new again. He stood and moved his Colt from his coat pocket to his waistband, where it would be easier to reach. He walked back to his saddle, talking with the now quiet bird, and retrieved his canteen and a pair of socks. Sitting again, Cole wiped clean the wing with a dampened sock. A testing of the wing showed no signs of stickiness or stiffness.

"There. You're ready to fly again," Cole said quietly, stroking the bird's head. He released it to the earth and saw the chickadee fly into the night.

"I'll miss you, little buddy. I'll miss you, Kathleen. Forever." He wiped the back of his right hand with the sock to clear the blood.

Sweet images of Kathleen began to fill his mind. Not the tormented pictures of her dying, but happy memories of their time together. Cole slumped beside the tree and was soon asleep with the sock wrapped around his injured hand.

Three hundred yards away, a lone rider cursed and turned back, not realizing how close he was to his target: Cole Kerry.

CHAPTER 3

Early morning found three riders entering the settlement. Beside them, stride for stride, was a large ugly cattle dog named Blue. Cole's oldest brother by six years, Luther Kerry, was in the middle with Elijah Kerry, the twelve-year-old son of his blind brother Ethan, on his right. Cole's best friend and Bar K rider, Peaches, was on his left. Both men were armed with rifles and belted handguns.

Peaches was a short, stocky Oriental man and a fairly new hand hired by Cole. His real name was Shi Han Rui. The stocky Chinaman had only one apparent weakness—a fondness for peaches, fresh or canned. Fresh peaches were difficult to find in this part of Texas, especially in November, so he put up with the canned variety. He usually carried two or three cans in his saddlebags and purchased more whenever he found them. The Bar K riders called him "Peaches." The Chinaman accepted the nickname with silent understanding.

Although he looked like a fugitive from a railroad construction gang, the Chinaman was a man to avoid crossing. His clothes were plain and his shirt worked hard to cover a powerful chest and muscled arms. His black hair was long, touching his heavy shoulders, and only occasionally worn in a ponytail. A gray hat had long ago lost any vestige of shape. From his left ear hung a small gold earring.

Blue, the gray beast with a white muzzle, was totally loyal to Eli and mean to just about everyone else, except Eli's sister and

25

his mother—and Cole and Kathleen.

Eli was given permission by his father to carry a rifle. He was never called Elijah and certainly never Elijah Wayne. The scratched stock proclaimed its appearance from the scabbard under his right leg. He was growing into a young man; his light blue eyes and light brown hair were the same; his freckles, gradually disappearing.

The third Kerry brother, two years younger than Luther and now blind, had wanted to come, but Ethan's wife had insisted he stay. It was Claire's idea to send their son instead. Cole would have a difficult time resisting the boy's plea to return. Ethan was a hard man who had built the Bar K from wild Texas prairie and was dealing with the more terrifying prospect of not seeing it anymore. As an untamed mustang, the magnificent horse Cole rode had kicked him in the head and caused his blindness three years ago.

In a high-crowned black hat, red suspenders and thick, droopy mustache, the oldest Kerry brother was an imposing figure to those who didn't know him. To those who did, he was slow-minded but caring, and especially gifted with horses. He could also keep his brothers working together, and not fighting. Most of the time. He understood his younger brother's agony. Barely a decade ago, he had lost his wife and three children to the fevers and his heartache was still fierce at times.

The three riders pulled up in front of a general store as a sorry-looking man came out, cutting a chunk from a new tobacco plug.

"Any place to get some breakfast?" Luther asked, eyeing the plug and spitting a thick tobacco stream of his own into the street.

"Most days, Helen Mae cooks. In the saloon. Over there."

"Thanks." The right side of Luther's face was more lined

than the other and he always looked like he had slept with his clothes on.

"Sure. You boys ridin' through, I take it. Not law, are ya?"

"No sir. Not law," Luther said; his eyes twinkled and he spat again.

Peaches pulled his horse close to the sidewalk. "You see a man ride through here? Last night? He in black suit. Riding fine . . . red horse."

The man looked surprised at a Chinaman speaking somewhat good English. He was also surprised to see him wearing a shoulder-holstered Webley Bulldog double-action revolver. Distinctive red handles were inlaid with a white dragon. Han Rui's flat face and unblinking eyes gave away little of what he was thinking.

The man on the sidewalk gulped, almost swallowed the fresh slice of tobacco and laughed nervously. As soon as he had the tobacco under control, he waved his arms. "Lordy, Lordy, did we ever!" Without further prompting, he described last night's fight.

Luther looked at Peaches and Eli, then back to the man. "What direction was the boy headed?"

"Wal, he dun rode out thatta way." The man pointed to the south. "Had a bottle of whiskey with him. Helen Mae's best Irish. Good stuff."

"Anybody following him?" Luther's question carried an edge.

"Nobody from here. That was Cole Kerry, ya know."

"Anybody else?"

"Well, there was a fella come through looking for him. A few hours later, I reckon. Said he was a friend. Don't know where he went."

Luther cocked his head to the side. "What'd this fella look like?"

Frowning, the man spat a long stream of tobacco juice. "I'm

studyin' on it. Seems like he were dressed all dark like. Had on one of those serapes, ya know. Didn't see his face. Hat covered most o' it. Ya might ask Helen Mae if'n she saw him."

"Will do. Thanks."

"Oh, I think he had blond hair. Leastwise, it were light, ya know. Might've been short. Or it might've been pulled up in his hat. Couldn't tell. Didn't look close."

Luther looked again at Peaches, who shrugged.

Helen Mae was eager to serve them and even more eager to expand on the evening's violence. However, she hadn't seen anyone following Cole. Breakfasts of steak, eggs and raw-fried potatoes were brought to their table. She had even managed to find a can of peaches for the Chinaman to enjoy. She apologized for not having any milk for Eli and served him a bottle of sarsaparilla.

Before they finished, Mayor Lunes came over, introduced himself in full title and asked they tell Cole that the cases against Billy Finley and Orville Pinkens were settled as far as the law in Pitch was concerned. Eli was fascinated by the mayor's constantly flickering eyes.

Luther wiped his mouth with the back of his hand and looked for a spittoon. "We'll be sure to tell Cole, Mr. Third."

"Oh, thank you very much."

Luther grunted.

"Ah so," Peaches said politely and looked away to hide a grin.

Eli bit his lip and left to give Blue some pieces of steak. Luther thanked Helen Mae, paid and they headed out.

Swinging into their saddles, the three riders talked over the situation as they rode out of the tired settlement. Blue trotted beside them. Around them was a land of low buttes, sand washes mixed with towering mesas and uncluttered prairie, dotted with longhorns and a few antelope.

"Well, at least he's ridin' ready—an' edgy," Luther said. "Those boys'll never forget Cole Keery ridin' through. That's for dang sure."

"Ah so." Peaches chuckled.

Glancing back, Luther said, "You know, I've been through there. Years back. Seems like it were a bigger place. Lots more folks." He spat for emphasis.

"Ah yes. You speak truth. Stage stopped there. I be on it."

"Looks like Uncle Cole left the road here," Eli said, pointing at some bent-over grass on the side of the dirt trail.

"Good eyes, Eli," Luther praised.

"Velly good." A Chinese expression followed that neither Luther nor Eli understood, but Peaches seemed pleased with the statement.

The threesome swung into a thicket of heavy brush, following a faint deer trail with fresh horse tracks. A swarm of birds, resting in a post oak tree, lit up the morning with songs to celebrate their passing. Autumn had touched the trees and bushes with new color. Luther warned them to ride carefully because Cole might think they were from town. He began calling Cole's name, followed by identifying themselves.

"Find Cole, Blue," Eli said and pointed south. The dog disappeared from sight.

No answer came to their calls—and no sign of Blue—so they rode further, passing clusters of catclaw, mesquite, prickly pear, fallen limbs and coarse bunch grass. They crossed a narrow creek into dense woods, continuing to call out. The only responses were the humming of insects, the soft padding of their horses' hooves and the creaking of saddle leather. Overhead, a mockingbird cursed them for intruding on his land. They rode past sharp boulders that had long ago sliced their way toward the sun, splitting buffalo grass and underbrush. A half hour passed as they followed bent grass and an occasional hoofprint. A prairie hawk, munching on a dead field mouse, watched them from a high branch. Other than a few scattered deer prints, only a single horse had come this way recently. They hadn't seen Blue since Eli sent him to find his uncle.

"Do you think Blue's gotten lost, Uncle Luther?" Eli asked. "Should I call him?"

Leaning over in the saddle, Luther spat and said, "Blue's doin' fine. He's probably caught up with your Uncle Cole an' they're just waiting for us." The statement was more positive than he felt. He glanced at Peaches, who said nothing.

Crossing a tiny stream, they reined up among another band of scrawny cottonwoods and alder bushes, the advent of a thicker stand of cottonwoods and oaks. Nearby was a deep indentation of earth. Luther stared at it, thought it was a grave and shivered. A cold wind had intimidated any clouds from the sky. The moment seemed more desolate than it was. Around them, gloom was slowly painting the land.

"This sure ain't no land for beef. Lordy," Luther groaned and wiped his face with his shirt sleeve and spat a brown stream of tobacco juice.

"Look! There's Kiowa. Over there." Eli pointed at the big sorrel grazing quietly between two slender trees.

"Mornin', boys. Didn't expect to see you." Cole called out.

He wasn't visible to any of them.

"We were all worried about you, Cole," Luther peered into the heavy woods.

From around a large, square rock ambled Cole Kerry, brushing himself off as he walked. Beside him was Blue, wagging his tail. The young gunfighter's face carried a lack of sleep and the aftermath of whiskey. But there was a quietness in his eyes that Luther hadn't seen since Kathleen's death.

Cole's gunbelt was around his waist; both ivory-handled, silver-plated Colts were set for right-handed use. One gun rested in a tilted holster on his left side, near the front of his bullet belt, with the handle pointing toward the ground and the barrel parallel to the belt. Some called it a "sidewinder holster." The other matching gun sat in a regular holster on his right hip. It was obvious he had expected to be followed.

Peaches swung down from his horse. "Cole Ker-rie-son, have you to eat?"

"Not hungry. Thanks, Han Rui." Rarely did Cole call the Oriental cowboy by his nickname, but by his personal name. Shi was his family name.

Luther and Eli dismounted. Neither seemed confident about what to do next. Eli wanted to run to his uncle, but was uncertain if he should and chose to remove an invisible burr from his pants. Luther spat into a bush, kicked at the ground amd mumbled something again about this being terrible cattle country. It was Shin Han Rui who broke the awkwardness.

The Chinese cowboy shook his head and walked over to Cole. "Ah so, all of us have lost loved ones, my friend. That why we must be together. Give each other words. Of comfort . . . of friends . . . of family. *Wei*. It is so."

Cole recognized the Chinese word for comfort and re-assurance. They shook hands and Peaches patted his friend on the back.

"Uncle Cole, I'm sorry about Aunt Kathleen. I loved her." Eli wiped his eyes. "I . . . love you."

Cole licked his lips and took a deep breath. "I love you, too, Eli. And I'm all right. Why don't you boys ride on home. Ethan and Claire'll be worried. I'll be along soon." He leaned over and scratched Blue behind his ears.

"We'll ride home together," Luther replied. "When you're ready, little brother."

For the first time, Cole noticed the tear in his right coat sleeve. A moment was needed to remember its reason; he had

31

caught it on a tree branch last night. He thought of the chickadee, but did not mention it.

Instead, he looked up and mumbled, "Had some trouble last night. Little town not far from here. Don't remember the name."

"Heard about it in town. We rode through there this mornin'. Pitch, it's called." Luther supressed a grin.

"Why don't you let me be? I'll be coming."

"Can't do that, Cole." Luther handed his reins to Eli and walked over to Kiowa. His widely bowed legs made it look like the earth was wobbling when he walked.

"I know what you're feeling. I miss my wife an' my kids somethin' awful," Luther said, patting the sorrel.

Cole stared at his brother. "Does it fade? Ever?"

Luther stared back and blinked. He glanced back at Ethan's boy, standing quietly, holding the reins of both horses. "Kathleen'll be wanting you to go on, Cole."

"You didn't answer my question."

The big Kerry leaned over, grabbed Cole's saddle and straightened up with it in his hands as if the burden was barely a blanket. "Depends on the man. I know my April . . . an' Bonnie an' Wendell an' Nan . . . are waiting for me." He swallowed and turned toward his younger brother and said softly, "Kathleen'll be waitin' fer you. I'm sure of it."

Cole studied his older brother as Luther saddled Kiowa, then shut his eyes. In a soft voice, he said, "Wanted to join her last night. Couldn't find anybody good enough."

His mind jumped to Dodge four years ago when Kathleen's weak father was coerced into demanding that she marry a rich man's son instead of Cole. The arrogant son with two friends had attacked Cole with the idea of running him out of town. He had downed the son and one friend with his fists. Both the son and the friends pulled guns on Cole, wounding him. His return shots killed the son and wounded one friend, forcing him to leave Dodge ahead of the businessman's gathered posse—and Kathleen forever, he thought. But she had her own ideas. Fed up with her father's demands, Kathleen had told him goodbye and sought Cole at the Bar K—and his life was new again.

None of that mattered anymore. He shook his head and looked away.

"What's the matter with your hand, Cole?" Luther pointed.

Cole looked at his right hand with the dark spots where the owl's claw had pierced. He decided to tell about the chickadee's visit.

"We'd better get that fixed up," Luther said. "Those claws can be something fierce, you know."

"It's all right, Luther." His statement ended the discussion.

Luther glanced at the silent Peaches, then at Eli, who was watching his Uncle Cole, then told Cole about the man who was trailing him last night.

"Doesn't sound like a friend, Luther. I don't know who that was," Cole said, shaking his head. "Only blond-haired men I can think of are Whitey Simmons . . . and Ernie Belkins. Can't imagine what they'd be doing, trailing me. The fellow in town must've been wrong."

Luther grinned. "Don't think they'd be following you, either. Whitey was at the funeral, though. Haven't seen Ernie in a long spell. Heard he took off for Houston." He looked at Cole. "We can talk while we ride."

Chapter 4

Mid-day found Ethan and Claire Kerry and their nine-year-old daughter, Maggie, waiting anxiously for the arrival of the rest of the Kerry family. Hopefully, Luther, Eli and Peaches would find Cole and convince him to return. Claire kept busy in the kitchen and caring for their two-year-old twins. The tall, blind rancher sat at his rolltop desk, occasionally becoming the source of the twins' activity. Even in his blindness, the desk served as his office for their cattle operation. His long legs were handy places for the boys to play on and around.

Now it was a place for a nervous Ethan to sit and wait. His fingers ran impatiently over the inlaid Spanish carving that decorated the desk. The work had been carefully done by an elderly Mexican who served the ranch as the primary handyman and, occasionally, as furniture maker. Two years ago, he completed a beautiful set of high chairs with Spanish styling for the twins—strong enough to withstand the wear on it by the two little ones.

Ethan was sitting. Waiting. And that was rare. It didn't reflect his drive to build a great cattle ranch. His blindness had only heightened it. The Bar K—and Ethan Kerry—were gaining a reputation. Some called it "the King ranch of Uvalde." The Bar K herds were bred with heavier Eastern cattle, mostly Herefords from England. Corn was grown to supplement the feed for beef and horses, in addition to long acres of tall buffalo grass.

Under Luther's supervision, the Bar K quarter horses were coveted by cattlemen throughout Texas. A new dam had harnessed a stream to create a year-round water source. Advance preparation was the primary reason the ranch had survived the awful drought a year ago—and come out of it even stronger.

Ethan coped with his blindness. Although he had never given up hope for the return of his sight, a lot of the credit went to Claire. She wouldn't let him wallow in self-pity, and secretly believed his eyesight would one day return. The doctors said it was possible. The blindness was the result of a blow to his head and the condition could reverse itself once the nerves in his eyes healed.

Maybe.

Ethan and Cole had shrewdly bought the bank in the town and owned part of a stage line working this part of Texas. Ethan's management of the roundup was unique, creating two separate roundup camps, instead of the usual single entity. Ethan had given financial incentives to his two key men, assuring Bar K beef would be handled well and sold profitably. In addition to top wages, each key man was given a twenty-five percent profit—over a fixed price—of the sale of cattle under his care. Individual houses had been built on Bar K land for these men and their families.

Every Bar K man was working the fall roundup, except for the time taken to attend Kathleen's funeral. Extra hands hired just for the fall had been added to the usual Bar K crew. Neighboring ranches were welcome to join in one or both roundups. This was the second year for his dual-base operation. The Bar K herds were spread out, populating many pastures. Even in the fall, the two roundups were kept separate. Both set in shallow valleys with good water and excellent grass. Ethan believed there was a worthwhile efficiency in his dual operation and, so far, he was right. After the roundup, the horse herd would be turned out for the winter with their shoes pulled except for the everyday mounts staying at the ranch and the horses needed by the hands watching the herds. Wagons, including the chuck wagon, would be stored in the barn. Luther would oversee that step.

"Oh, here they come! Here they come!"

Maggie was the first to see the four riders on the horizon and hurried out to the front porch.

"How many, Maggie?" Ethan called, rising from his chair in response to her gleeful exclamation.

"There are four."

"Good," Ethan answered. "Claire, are you coming?"

She called from the kitchen, "Be right there, dear. Wiping my hands."

Nearby, their twin boys were fascinated by an iron pot set on the floor for that purpose. William Luther, "Will," was standing in the pot; Russell Cole, "Russ," was determined to remove him from it.

Ethan shoved back the desk chair and took a tentative step, then another, toward the front door. His memory told him where everything was placed in the main room. Claire had seen to that. He slid his hand along the wall, knowing just where a coal-oil lamp was stationed, followed by a framed painting of Texas bluebells in bloom. Still, on his fifth step, his knee collided with the edge of the sofa.

"Damn. Who moved the sofa?"

"Hey, cowboy, aren't you going to wait for your best gal?" Claire hurried to his side. The boys lost interest in the pot and hovered around her legs.

"I was doing just fine."

"Sure, you were. But our furniture can't take it."

He laughed and knelt to receive both boys. Neither seemed aware their father couldn't see. He stood holding one in each arm with Claire sliding her hand under his left to guide him. The blind rancher strode out in a proud, commanding way. Lately, he had told her of seeing vague shapes and intense light. She had taken that statement to her heart and kept it there, hoping it might mean some sight was returning. The occurrences were not something they talked about; hope was too hard, if it turned out not to be true.

"Do you have the field glasses?" Ethan asked his wife as they stepped onto the planked porch of their comfortable home. His tanned face carried a trim mustache and a once-broken Roman nose. He was tall, a man comfortable with leadership, even in his blindness.

"Yes, dear." She had learned to anticipate her man.

Ethan's penchant for detail had probably increased, if that was possible, after his eyesight was taken. The anguish and anger had formed into a controlled maturity. Both he and Cole burned with the same fierceness. That had initially brought terrible clashes, but had gradually turned into mutual, and deep, respect. Luther had been a significant part of that.

The three brothers had served in John Bell Hood's Texas Brigade. After the South's awful defeat, they had fought on as guerillas, then as outlaws, attacking anything Union. Claire had fallen in love with him the first time she saw him. Wildly, she had been in the Yankee bank Ethan and his brothers were robbing. His fascination with her was immediate as well. Before leaving, he had walked over, asked her name and said he would be returning to see her. She didn't sleep for two days, alternately wondering if he would come—and worrying that he might. Two days later, he did. Somewhere in her treasures was a folded, yellow arrest poster. Together, they had built the Bar K from the raw prairie.

"Got a rifle?" he asked and let the twins down to run around the porch.

"A rifle?" Claire's question was hard. Crow's feet snapped to attention around her bright eyes. "That's our family coming, Ethan."

As they walked, Ethan cocked his head and looked in the general direction of his beloved wife. "Are you sure? We're expecting four riders, but what if it's four Comanches? Or four bandits? Can you tell from here? I can't." He smiled.

Claire returned the comment with pursed lips. How like her husband to think beyond the obvious. As Cole liked to say, Ethan Kerry could still see better than any man.

"Wait here with Maggie and I'll get a Winchester."

Claire patted his arm and spun away, her ample bosom gently moving with her strides.

Maggie stepped next to her father and took his hand. "Is Aunt Kathleen in Heaven with Grandpa an' Uncle Luther's family?"

"Yes, I reckon so." His shoulders rose and fell.

"Is our horse, Bingo, there? And my turtle, Max?"

"Uh, why sure."

"I want to go there, too. Don't you, Pa?"

"Some day we all will."

The blind rancher squeezed his eyes shut to hold back the wall of sentiment that her statement hurled at him. He eased the twins to the ground and knelt beside her, fumbling to find her face with both hands.

"I'm right here."

"I know, sweetheart. I see you . . . in my mind."

"What's that like, Pa?" Maggie asked, her eyes widening.

"Not sure I know how to answer that, honey."

Will and Russ chirped and bounced against both of them before Maggie could press him for more of an answer. Ethan used the distraction to ask Maggie to study the incoming riders again.

By the time Claire returned with the gun, Maggie had informed her father that the advancing riders were, indeed, Cole, Luther, Eli and Peaches. Tagging along was Blue; his tail wagging. They rode under the big Bar K branded longhorn skull mounted on a crossing pole above the entrance gate.

Ethan asked his daughter if the skull was straight.

She was quiet a moment, then answered, "Not quite. It's a little off."

"Good eyes, Maggie. We'll have Luther fix it later."

"Sure. Is Uncle Cole all right?"

Ethan drew in a deep breath. "Don't know, Maggie. I don't know. Losing the one you love is awful hard. Awful hard."

"We lost Grandpa this spring."

Ethan started to say that wasn't the same, but said, "Yeah, that was hard."

Clancey Kerry was lost years before to whiskey. There was a strange comfort in his passing.

"I miss him. He was fun," Maggie said. "But he had to take his medicine all the time. That was sad."

"Yeah, it was." Ethan held the tiny hands of both boys in spite of their desire to run out to greet the incoming horsemen.

The riders crossed the ranch yard quietly. All of the ranch buildings, bunkhouse, sheds and three corrals were equally silent. All hands were out working the herds, in preparation for winter. They eased past the small stone house for storing butter and milk and a dust swirl danced ahead of them. Blue saw an imaginary enemy and ran barking toward the blacksmith forge near the closest corral.

"They'll be hungry, Claire," Ethan said, standing with his legs apart, holding the twins again as Claire rejoined them.

"They can wait a few minutes. I want to make sure Cole is all right." Claire's voice carried determination and concern.

"Of course," Ethan answered. "Of course."

Cole studied the ranch and the waiting family. He was a lucky man, he knew. Not everybody had people around them who cared so much. Their conversation on the ride back centered on cattle and what needed to be done for the winter. He knew it was his oldest brother's way of distracting him from dwelling on thoughts of Kathleen. This was also Luther's way of saying he wouldn't have time to mope. As they walked their horses toward the house, Cole's gaze took in the foundations of the large buildings, each packed with dirt. Trenches had been dug around them to lead rain water away. Mute testimony to the thoroughness of Ethan Kerry's preparation.

In spite of himself, Cole shook his head and chuckled. Few had seen the other side, the violent side, of Ethan Kerry. Luther had told him of Ethan killing a Comanche war party when they attacked his ranch not long after he and Claire settled here. He had pistol-whipped the last three warriors when he ran out of bullets. Claire had fought at his side like a man. She was some kind of woman. Like Kathleen, he thought, and the sadness returned. He gritted his teeth and glanced at Luther, then Peaches and Eli. They appeared to be within themselves.

He nudged Kiowa into a lope and reined up at the hitch rack, a little ahead of the others.

"Well, afternoon. How are you folks doing?" The young gunfighter's voice popped with forced enthusiasm. The hangover was evident in his face, but Claire saw comfort there as well.

Maggie squealed her greeting while Will and Russ squirmed in their father's arms and wanted down. Ethan told them to quiet down and they did so, for a moment.

With a gasp to hurry her along, Claire rushed to Cole and gave her brother-in-law a warm hug. It was Claire who had believed Cole was alive during the years he was gone. His own sadness met hers and he blinked his eyes. It was Claire who prayed for his return to help save their ranch. It was Claire who had urged Ethan to make him a partner. And it was Claire who helped both Cole and Kathleen deal with the awfulness of the Victorio Gee kidnaping and raping.

After a special moment, she said quietly, "God did not promise us lives without pain and sorrow. But he did promise us love to see us through those times. And the strength to meet every day. Kathleen's love will always be with you. And we love you, Cole. You know that."

Cole nodded and realized Maggie was clinging to his waist. He leaned over and looked into her sweet face.

"I am very sorry, Uncle Cole. I will put flowers on her grave every day."

"Your aunt will like that very much," Cole replied.

Maggie looked into his face. "We will all be in Heaven some day."

Cole bit his lip. "Yes . . . yes, we will."

Claire noticed the cuts on Cole's hand and asked about them.

From his horse, Luther waved his hands in response. "Oh, he doesn't want anybody paying any attention to that. They came from an owl that attacked him—an' a chickadee he was holding."

Cole smiled and repeated the story of the chickadee and the attacking owl. Maggie was intrigued and asked what kind of owl it was. He wasn't sure, just that the bird was big. Shrugging her shoulders, she went back inside the house.

Stepping close to Cole, Claire closed her eyes, but couldn't keep a tear from escaping. "T-That . . . was Kathleen's way . . . of telling you she's . . . happy." She choked on the words. "I'll put some ointment on those cuts. They're deep."

Cole had been thinking the same thing about Kathleen on the ride home. It didn't matter if it was his tortured imagination, the thought felt right.

"My hand's fine, Claire. Really. Done worse working cattle."

"Nonsense. I've got medicine in the house."

Behind her came the joyous twins, bouncing against each other in an attempt to get to their uncle first. Smiling in spite of his heavy sadness, Cole lifted both into his arms. Claire stepped away to greet the other riders.

"Hi, Unc Cole." Will pointed at Cole's sorrel. "Ki-o-waa. Ki-o-waa."

"Hi, Unc Cole. Hoss. Hoss," Russ stammered.

"You're both right." He cradled them in his arms, then swung the tow-headed twins gently and asked if they liked Kiowa. They said yes at the same time and he lifted them onto Kiowa's saddle. Their response was joyful and boisterous. The fierce sorrel lowered his head and didn't move. Cole laughed and pulled them down.

From the porch, Ethan waved his arms and lamented, "Where the hell is my little brother?"

Claire took the twins as Cole said, "He's right here . . . big brother . . . and he's fine."

Ethan turned toward the advancing Cole and held out his arms. "The hell you are. Get up here, Cole. I need to touch you."

In that instant, when Ethan turned in his direction, Cole had the sensation his brother saw him. Was it his imagination? Or was Ethan's hearing that acute?

Blue reappeared and pushed next to Cole as he and Ethan greeted each other with a hug and slaps on the back.

Still mounted, Luther snorted and turned away in his saddle. He spit and tossed the tobacco wad into the yard. Claire wouldn't like him coming into the house with it.

Cole and Luther insisted Peaches stay for supper. Claire brought a small jar of ointment and covered Cole's hand with its yellow cream, then wrapped it with a bandage. She didn't ask and Cole knew better than to challenge her. Ethan or

Luther, yes. Claire, no.

Later, around the massive oak dinner table, they enjoyed Claire's fine noon meal of beefsteak, fried potatoes and fresh biscuits. The chair and place setting next to Cole was empty. It had been done purposely by Claire, to symbolize where Kathleen had sat. As usual, Luther had trouble sitting in his chair; his bowed legs wouldn't move in the right direction. Maggie brought in a leather-bound book and showed Cole a drawing of a Great Horned Owl; he agreed it must have been that. She described the owl in considerable detail.

Both twins were cranky and Claire carried them away for naps. They insisted that Eli tell them a story and he was happy to oblige. Maggie followed, eager to tell her siblings that she knew what kind of owl had attacked their uncle.

After coffee and apple pie, Peaches excused himself to return to the roundup. He and Cole talked quietly for a moment before the Chinaman left. Conversation took on measures of hope, then joy, discussing the roundup. Only Cole was silent, drinking his coffee and staring at the cup between sips.

"That new minister is an interesting fellow," Claire said, looking for a logical subject to allow her to give him comfort. "I thought his sermon was quite nice. Uh, Kathleen would have liked it, I think." She bit her lower lip.

The response was an unexpected one from Ethan.

"His voice is familiar to me," Ethan said, putting down his fork and searching for his coffee cup. "I've met that man. Somewhere. Before."

Quietly, Claire directed him to his cup.

Luther wiped his mouth with a napkin, something he had learned living with Ethan and Claire. "Think he prayed over us . . . during the War?"

Sipping his coffee, Ethan shook his head. "Don't know. Somewhere. It'll come to me. Seems to me, he's quirky as a one-winged duck."

"Enough, Ethan," Claire said.

That subject was left as Eli returned to the table. He wanted to be a rancher like his father and uncles. He wanted to know anything and everything there was about ranching. Right now he wanted to know about the barbed wire fencing he was hearing about, and if they would be putting it across their land, and if it would hurt the cattle. Only Cole remained silent as the men took turns explaining what they thought the role of barbed wire would be. They were in agreement that it was coming and would be the end of open range for free grazing. Now that the big ranches along the Panhandle had strung wire—The Frying Pan, XIT and JA—the race for fencing off owned land was underway.

"It's going to change things forever," Ethan said, fiddling with his fork. "We'll start fencing come spring." He left the fork and found his coffee cup and drank deeply as if to demonstrate the finality of his statement.

Luther wiped his mustache with the back of his hand. "Devil's rope, they're calling it. Gonna bring a lot of fightin' over a lot of land."

"Maybe we need to buy more land. Own it outright," Ethan stated and asked Claire for more coffee.

"What about our trail drives?" Eli asked. His father had promised he could go on the next one.

Ethan thanked Claire for filling his cup and slid his fingers slowly across the table to locate it. He knew well how his statement to buy more land would stimulate the thinking of his brothers; they were in a good cash position. For once. It made sense to him. And it made sense to Claire. They had already talked about it, but there weren't any opportunities right now.

He had wanted the Rocking R ranch owned by Ivan and Evangeline Drako, but hadn't moved fast enough. His hunch that the Russian-born couple were ready to sell and move back East was right, but his timing wasn't. A Scotsman from Emporia, Kansas, had moved in. As far as the Kerrys knew, Heredith Tiorgs had no ties to the Ulvalde region. He was a gruff man with little interest in a relationship of any kind with his neighbors. As far as Ethan knew, all the area ranches, including the Rocking R, planned on joining the Bar K's roundups.

The dead bodies of the Drako family were found by a passing freighter a month after they left. Apparently, Indians had surprised them. Ethan paid for their burial and funerals.

Two other small ranches had changed ownership within the last year. Ethan had grumbled because he had not had the opportunity to purchase the small spread owned by Miquel del Rio when he decided to return to Mexico.

"You didn't answer my question, Pa?" Eli asked, leaning forward on his elbows.

Claire motioned for him to remove his elbows from the table.

"Sorry, Eli, I was thinking about something else," Ethan said, taking a sip of his coffee. "We can drive 'em to Austin and the railroad there. Won't get as much for them, though." His eyelids blinked rapidly. "Or we can map our way north. Around the wire. To Kansas."

"What if we're all blocked?" Eli's eyes were wide.

"We won't be." A finality lay on Ethan's words.

Cole nudged Eli with his elbow to indicate the subject was over.

Eli nodded and asked, "Mr. Sotar is expecting me today. Can I ride out . . . now?" He remembered the sadness of the day and stuttered, "U-Uh, U-Uncle C-Cole, will you go with me . . . us?"

"I would like that," Cole said, pushed back his chair and stood. "Thank you, Claire, for a wonderful meal. Thank all of you for your caring."

He glanced at the room that had been added on for Kathleen and him. "I'll be riding out with Luther and Eli. Don't think I can sleep in . . . our room. When I get back, I'll move to the bunkhouse."

Any response was stopped by a knocking at the door.

"It's the preacher." Eli was halfway out of his chair and headed for the door.

"Maybe his ears are red from us talking about him," Ethan said. "Let him in."

CHAPTER 5

Eli opened the door to greet the new minister, Reverend Paul Dinclaur. Hatless, the minister's face was long and smooth; his white hair, almost touching his shoulders, had little to do with age. He couldn't have been any older than Luther or Ethan. The black ministerial attire fit well on his six-foot frame. Tied to the rack outside was a quiet bay pulling a used surrey.

He was new to the area, arriving only months before, an answer to the town's need for a spiritual leader. Reverend Joseph B. Hillas had passed in his sleep, leaving the Uvalde church without pastoral guidance. Dinclaur had been well accepted; Claire and Kathleen had insisted the family attend regular church services.

Cole had told Kathleen that he thought the man was superstitious, judging from some of his statements and actions. Kathleen had chastised him and told him to keep it to himself and especially away from Claire.

"Come in, come in," Claire called warmly, moving to the doorway.

"Well, thank you," Reverend Dinclaur said with an easy smile, tapping the door frame with his fist three times as he entered. "Didn't mean to interrupt. Wanted to see how Cole was *faring.*" His eyes locked onto the young gunfighter's face, then darted away to Claire.

As the minister eased into the room, Cole noticed a bulge in his coat pocket the shape of a short-barreled revolver.

"Have you eaten?" Claire invited warmly. "We have plenty."

"Oh, that's very kind. Bless you," he said and smiled again. "I've had my meal. But some of that fine coffee would certainly taste *good.*"

Luther jumped up, greeted the minister, and directed him toward a vacant chair Eli was pushing toward the table. It was one of several unused chairs along the wall.

Cole stood to shake hands with Reverend Dinclaur and said hesitantly, "Thank you . . . for the nice service . . . yesterday."

"Kathleen Kerry was a child of God," Dinclaur responded softly. "She is in His *arms.*" He looked into Cole's face. "Know that she is *happy.*"

Cole nodded. Claire's words had been comforting; the minister's attempt sounded contrived. His voice had a distinctive silky sound and a habit of emphasizing the last word in his thought. Cole decided it must be a minister's manner of speech.

Reverend Dinclaur accepted Cole's nod as agreement and turned toward Ethan, standing beside his chair. The minister took the rancher's outstretched hand and shook it while studying Ethan's unseeing eyes. Ethan's left hand remained on the chair back.

After thanking Eli for the chair, Dinclaur sat, noticing Cole was sitting next to an empty chair. He glanced in both directions to assure that he wasn't as well. It was bad luck to sit next to any empty chair, for any reason.

"Hey, the missus just baked an apple pie that was mighty good." Ethan barked, returning to his chair, using his left hand as a guide. "Better have some with that coffee."

"Oh, that's awfully kind, but . . ."

"No 'buts,' " Ethan interrupted, waving his hand, and added, "Eli, take the Reverend's horse for some water—and grain."

"You are most kind. My horse, Benjamin, has been a good and loyal *servant.*"

Eli was glad to have something to do and raced again for the door and disappeared outside with Blue happily chasing after him.

As the white-haired minister sat, Claire placed an ironware cup in front of him and poured fresh coffee into it.

"I'll bring you some pie, Reverend," she said and spun away.

"That would be *wonderful*," he said and looked around for sugar and cream.

Luther leaned over and pushed a sugar bowl and cream pitcher toward Dinclaur who undertook a ritual-like performance of adding sugar and cream and stirring them within the dark brew. He looked up self-consciously.

"I must admit to a fondness for coffee. Hopefully, it is my only *vice.*"

"Well, if that's a vice, most folks I know would be in the same spot," Ethan declared.

"Bless you, Ethan Kerry."

"Haven't heard that too often," The blind rancher grinned and rubbed his eyes without thinking about its significance.

Luther crawled back into his chair, shifting himself to get comfortable.

"Don't mind Luther," Cole said, chuckling. "He thinks every chair is a saddle. Or should be."

"Be a darn sight easier," Luther blurted, finally deciding he was as comfortable as he was going to be.

Leaning forward on the table, Reverend Dinclaur laughed softly and said, "Luther, I've heard you produce some excellent *horses.*"

"The best." Ethan declared and began to roll a cigarette.

Ethan had become adept at the process of making a cigarette. Unlike the first times when a whole sack of tobacco and most of his papers were used to make just one smoke. Ethan struck a match along his jeans and inhaled.

Luther smiled. "Wouldn't argue with my brother."

"We went through a hundred dollars of tobacco before he could do that," Cole teased and leaned back in his chair, trying to hide his unhappiness with the minister's presence.

Frowning at Cole, Claire placed a fork and a small plate with a large slice of pie in front of the approving minister.

Watching Ethan's performance with obvious curiosity, Reverend Dinclaur forked a small bite of pie and put it in his mouth. "My goodness! Mrs. Kerry, this pie is delicious. Absolutely *delicious*."

"Oh, you are most kind, Reverend." She smiled and returned to the kitchen.

Cole sat, watching the minister eat. Inside he was boiling. He didn't need or want another well-meaning statement about Kathleen being in a better place. The better place was here with him. He wasn't churchy, but he was certain she was with God. That wasn't the problem. He wanted her with him. Heaven should have come much later.

Luther's question broke him away from the thought. "Ethan an' me, we thought you seemed familiar. We were wondering if you did some riding with us Rebels. You know, during the War."

Reverend Dinclaur didn't answer immediately, but continued chewing a mouthful of pie, until he washed it down with more coffee.

He cocked his head. "I was a minister during that awful time. With Lee's army in Tennessee, mostly. God's calling has brought me here to bring His Word to . . . you in this wonderful *country*."

Luther looked around, as if searching for a place to spit, then remembered there was no tobacco in his mouth. He shook his head and declared, "That's it then. Tennessee. We were there with ol' General Hood. Had his head up his butt most of the time. Excuse me, preacher." He bit his lower lip. "Pushed us into pure horror. Pure as . . . uh, pure." He rubbed his chin.

"Hood's army almost fell apart. Yes sir. Hard to believe he even had a band playin' 'Dixie,' all while he was sleeping." He motioned toward Ethan. "If it hadn't been for Ethan, Hiram Granburg's whole brigade, a big part of Hood's army, would've been gone."

Cole smiled; his oldest brother was right. Over seven thousand Confederate soldiers were killed or captured in that critical engagement. Hood had promised his key leaders that he wouldn't put his men into a foolhardy situation. Again. But he did. Worse than ever. Men naturally took to following Ethan when times were tough and he saved a lot of lives with gutsy moves while Hood decided everything was going well.

"That was a long time ago, Luther. Let's leave it there." Ethan waved a dismissive arm and the ashes from his cigarette fell into his lap.

Reverend Dinclaur nodded and turned toward Cole. "If I may, Cole . . . there's a passage, a Bible passage, that's always given me *comfort*. May I?"

Cole's eyes caught Claire's urgent nodding from her position beside the kitchen doorway.

"Sure, Dinclaur."

His absence of the title "pastor" made Claire scowl.

Reverend Dinclaur spoke solemnly, " 'Weeping may endure for the night, but joy cometh in the *morn*.' Psalm Thirty-five."

" 'Weeping may endure for the night, but joy cometh in the morn.' " Cole repeated the phrase, glanced again at Claire and added, "Thank you, Dinclaur. That is quite . . . uh, nice." He bit the inside of his mouth.

Returning from the twins' room, Maggie looked at the smiling minister and said, "Will there be enough room in Heaven— for all of us? An awful lot of people have died, you know."

Surprisingly, Cole responded first. "That's a good question, Maggie. I think it's like family. There's always room for more.

In a family."

"Like the twins?" Maggie asked. "And Aunt Kathleen?"

"Like the twins and Aunt . . . Kathleen."

Claire put her hand to her mouth and her eyes fluttered. Luther frowned as if the thought bothered him greatly. Ethan looked like he had been hit with a blow to his stomach.

Silence blossomed and sat in the empty chair next to Cole.

Dinclaur glanced at the fire in the massive stone fireplace across the room. A dark hole within the fire was surrounded by bright orange coals. He nodded. It was a symbol that someone would die. Blinking his eyes rapidly to clear the thought, he returned his attention to the table and cut into his remaining pie with his fork, producing a small bite. After chewing the tidbit, he said, "The Bible tells us God's mansion has many *rooms*. Enough for all of us." He smiled at his observation and put another bite into his mouth. Laying his fork on the pie plate, his right hand moved toward his coat pocket.

Cole saw the move. He was certain the preacher carried a handgun there. What was Dinclaur's intent? No one was armed at the table, except the minister. His own holstered Colts lay on the small table beside the door. He had laid them there upon entering, out of courtesy to Claire. Surely he was mistaken about the intention of the minister's move. Luther said a light-haired man had followed him last night. Could they have mistaken white hair for blond?

Cole dropped his right hand under the table, hoping the move would be enough if the minister had some wild idea of shooting. It had to be Cole's imagination playing tricks on him. It had to be.

Dinclaur caught Cole's eyes and movement. He smiled. "Excuse me. That was rude. I've been carrying a small revolver in my coat pocket. I ride alone most of the time. I think the good Lord wishes us to be *prepared*." He shook his head. "But I forget it's there and at times the weight bothers *me*."

Cole returned the smile. "I know what you mean. The Colt in my back waistband sometimes feels awkward."

It was a lie, but he wasn't convinced the minister's shift was innocent. Kathleen would be angry at such a thought. Dinclaur was nothing but a pompous, superstitious fool. Like some other ministers he had had the misfortune to come across.

Bouncing into the room, Eli broke the uneasiness to report the minister's horse was watered and fed. Blue trotted beside him, then hurried over to Cole for attention.

The minister thanked him warmly.

Marching two little fingers along the table, Maggie continued her quest for spiritual answers as if her brother had never left. "Can Aunt Kathleen see us?"

Claire took a quick step from the doorway. "Maggie, that's enough."

"It's all right, Claire," Cole said.

Without waiting for Dinclaur's response, he rose, walked around the table and knelt beside the little girl. His eyes darted toward the door where he had laid his guns when he entered.

"Your Aunt Kathleen . . . she . . . she's always going to be . . . in your heart." He touched his own shirt, then touched Maggie's heart. "I think . . . she will see you . . . if you want her to." He lowered his head, shut his eyes and gritted his teeth to hold back the ache. Not having a gun was forgotten for the moment.

It was Ethan who ended the sorrowful moment. Pulling the cigarette from his mouth, he said, "Grief is a powerful master. She wants to control everything. A man has to ride on and leave it."

Frowning, Claire went to the weeping Maggie and held both Cole and her daughter. Reverend Dinclaur mumbled something about God's blessing and finished his coffee. Luther pushed away from the table, hurried over to his youngest brother and put his big hands on Cole's shoulders.

His eyes bright, Cole stood, patted Maggie and Claire and declared, "I'm all right. All of us are."

After a few more minutes of excited response from each family member, Reverend Dinclaur excused himself.

"I know you-all have much to do as it is fall roundup. I'll be heading back. Your hospitality was most gracious. Thank you." He stood and looked at Cole. "Cole, I know this is a time of blackness for you—and that words mean little. But please know God is with *you*."

Cole nodded and escorted him to the door. If the minister noticed the Colts laying on the small table, he didn't say. Eli scurried ahead to hitch up the minister's horse and bring the surrey to the porch. They shook hands and the white-haired minister stepped off the porch. Dinclaur saw a small feather lying on the ground, hesitated and leaned over to push it upright in the ground. Cole had seen his Irish father do a similar thing when coming upon a feather. To leave it would bring bad luck.

Cole shrugged. Whatever works, he thought. Ethan joined him at the doorway, holding Claire's arm for support.

Waving as he snapped the reins, Dinclaur's horse trotted out of the ranch yard. Claire said she thought it was very kind of him to come by and see them.

Shuffling toward the door, Luther proclaimed, "Come on, Eli. You an' me, we'll catch up with Sotar. You ready?" He wiped his nose with his shirt sleeve and sniffed.

"Sure."

Cole's shoulders rose and fell. "Ethan, we should ride out and check on the roundup after I change into my working clothes. Unless you need to stay here."

Smiles from Ethan—and Claire—were immediate. Cole always asked his brother to ride with him. Few men could match Ethan's savvy when it came to cattle.

Claire mouthed "thank you" as Cole walked toward the room where he and Kathleen had lived. She guided Maggie toward the kitchen.

"Are you ridin' Kiowa?" Ethan asked and put out his cigarette in his coffee cup.

"I reckon. What are you riding?"

"I'll take the black. Uh, Jake."

He always rode the quiet black horse, but no one commented. It was the only horse Claire would permit him to ride.

"I'll get 'em ready."

Cole stopped a few feet from the room's entrance, turned and said, "Claire, you're welcome to anything in here. I don't . . . want any of it."

Claire rushed to the doorway. A tearful hug followed and more soft words of encouragement, ending with the statement that he would feel different about those things given time.

After changing, Cole walked outside to resaddle Kiowa and ready Ethan's black. Each would eventually carry filled saddlebags, mostly with foodstuffs Claire selected, and a slicker, bedroll and a Winchester. Of course, his blind brother couldn't use the gun, but Cole wanted Ethan to feel normal.

He remembered it was his blind brother who finished off the vengeful Victorio Gee, when Luther, Cole and Miguel del Rios, standing nearby, didn't realize the dying bandit leader was yet alive and aiming to kill Cole.

Minutes later, he drifted toward the large tree stump in the ranch yard, the one filled with the carvings of each Kerry's name. An immense tree stump, it sat four feet tall and four feet wide. Winds had torn away the glorious tree years ago. His fingers touched Kathleen's name and he recalled the day her name was added. It had been a beautiful day and they were deeply in love.

"Cole? Where are you, boy? Got our saddlebags ready!" Ethan

called from the front porch.

"Got cans of peaches for Peaches?"

"Wouldn't dare not to." Ethan laughed.

Cole smiled.

CHAPTER 6

Shortly after they rode out of sight of the ranch, Cole removed the bandage on his hand. He opened and closed it for a few minutes to prevent any stiffness.

Luther asked, "Your hand doing all right?"

"Yeah. Just fine."

Ethan chuckled. "Didn't want to take the bandage off in front of Claire, eh?"

Cole wondered how his brother knew that and glanced at Eli.

"Hell, no. She's the tough one in the family."

They rode easily toward the first camp, exchanging memories of Claire's determination making the difference in a situation. Ethan shared times when he was depressed and she wouldn't let him feel sorry for himself. No one mentioned Kathleen. Time passed quickly and they were soon at the first roundup.

A branding fire was the center of an oval-shaped valley as the four Kerrys rode up. Long shadows were taking control of the land. Dust clouds sprouted in each direction as unseen cowboys worked unwilling cattle toward the roundup camp. This was the larger of the two camps.

Blue trotted between Cole and Eli. The boy leaned down and ordered the ugly dog to be quiet and not disturb the steers. Luther spat and squinted into the dying sun, drawing heavy lines on the right side of his face.

The three older Kerrys wore handguns, even Ethan. Winchester stocks extended from their saddles. Ethan insisted his men wear handguns during the roundup. Not for rustlers, but for their safety. A mean steer, a rattlesnake, even a wolf could leave a man in need of protection. Fast. A downed horse might need to be put out of its misery. Or worse, a cowboy could be thrown by a bolting horse, but hung up in a stirrup. A handgun was the only way to end that problem safely.

Dust, smoke, bawling calves and cursing men turned the late afternoon into a strange symphony of color, smell and sound. A massive herd of grazing cattle covered most of the valley, edged by mesquite thickets, cottonwoods and a wandering creek. Where needed, temporary fences of brush and logs had been dragged together to keep the gathered animals from straying.

Outriders worked hard to bring in the animals and would continue their efforts until it was too dark to see. Heavy leather chaps, jackets and gloves protected them from the ironwoods, prickly pear and mesquite. Most wore tapaderos over their stirrups to keep branches from getting into the stirrups and hurting their horses.

A pole corral kept the calves; another held horses waiting for their turn to work. Any unbranded strays or mavericks—"sooners" the cowboys called them—were kept huddled together, away from the rest of the gathered herd. None were allowed to drift. That would mean doing the same work all over again. It seemed like many of the toughest steers preferred to live and graze in the deepest arroyos among the worst kinds of trees and brush.

The silhouettes of another set of horsemen worked the gathered herd for unbranded steers or animals with apparent health concerns. Cattle carrying brands other than the Bar K were eased out of the herd and encouraged to return to their home ranges or turned over to the reps from neighboring ranches working the roundup. New calves were branded to match their mothers. Over a hundred calves an hour were brought in for branding and cutting. The entire effort was well organized, with each man aware of his responsibility without direction. The fall roundup was different than the spring gathering when cattle were gathered for the drive to market. There were usually many more calves in the spring.

Ethan insisted that calves be branded as quickly as possible. That's why he favored the more expensive, two-camp roundup. Few, if any, calves or steers escaped this layered search. He assigned a full-time tallyman' in each camp to keep good records and to make the decision on which bull calves would survive castration and be saved for building future herds.

Looking up, John David Sotar, the Missouri gunman-turned-foreman, saw them first and waved. His tooled tan-and-white leather vest and black hat had been taken from a dead Victorio Gee outlaw. The vest complemented his tooled gunbelt and cutaway holster at his hip. He would look strange without it.

"Howdy, Boss. Good to see all you boys." His Missouri twang split the air with authority.

He wiped his hands on black-streaked batwing chaps and sauntered toward them. The compact snarl of a man had turned into a key Bar K leader and he received a percentage of the profits from this herd, the southern one. Sotar also had a home on Bar K range and had recently married a nice Mexican woman.

On the far side of the clearing, Loop was riding inside the calf corral with a screaming calf in tow. The young cowboy, whose real name was Josiah Bryanson, was known simply as "Loop." He was as handy, and as fascinated, with a lariat as any man around and wasn't likely to respond to anyone calling out his given name. He was one of only three cutting riders, or "ketch hands," separating unbranded calves from their mothers. A campfire story described the time he had roped a running coyote, just for the fun of it. He had become an accomplished brush-popper and preferred working the hard country to this assignment. Loop was one of the few cowboys who could throw a narrow loop just wide enough to get past the protective woods to a wayward steer.

As he headed toward the branding fire, Loop yelled, "Another Bar K comin'."

One of Loop's best friends was an older Mexican vaquero, Thomas Ramos, who was himself an excellent hand with a lariat. Out of the wooded area came the older man and three more riders, each with a roped cow and calf.

Sotar sauntered over to the four Kerrys, greeted them warmly and suggested Eli help at the fire, and Luther give a hand with any cattle needing medical attention. Eli jumped down and led his horse to the tie-up section and hurried back to the fire. Ignoring Sotar's direction, Luther decided to have a look at the horses in the rope corral. Blue curled up under the shade of one of the remuda trees.

When no one was paying attention, Luther took a handful of tobacco from his makin's sack, whispered some faerie words and tossed the shreds of tobacco into the air. Cole caught the motion and smiled. It was like his oldest brother to feel it was necessary to ask the spirits for a blessing. Of the three boys, Luther was the only one with some of the Irish wonderment in spirits, faeries and leprechauns. Although he would deny it. As long as Cole could recall, his brother had left tributes to the spirits of the land to ensure good luck.

Orville Miller, a sloe-eyed German with long sideburns, was checking selected animals, young and old, for suspected disease, especially lump jaw, sores and open wounds. Three hands helped him; two were new hires and the other, a rep from the small CW Connected ranch. Several medicine bottles, cutting tools and large cans of ointment lay at their feet.

Miller was also in charge of removing scrotums from the

young calves. He was proficient at the unpleasant task, tossing each removed sack into a large pot with an accompanying spit of tobacco in the other direction. For him, it was a significant symbolic passage with some German phrase no one knew accompanying each bloody sac as it went into the container. A supper of deep-fried "mountain oysters" would be a welcome celebration after the roundup was over.

Sweating heavily, the thick-bellied Zeke Ferguson coordinated the branding where grimy men worked diligently and fast over a hot fire. Ferguson was one of the few who seemed oblivious to Miller's constant banter in German. Behind them both, a stern, cigar-smoking Hellis Dorn was keeping tally in a leatherbound book.

Walking next to the mounted Cole, Sotar put his hand on the sorrel's shoulder. "Don't know what to say, Cole. I'm mighty sorry. Kathleen was one special lady. We all thought so."

"Thanks, John David. I appreciate it."

Initially the two men were at serious odds. Sotar's cousin had been killed by Cole in the gunfight in Dodge City and Sotar felt it was his responsibility to avenge the man's death. That vanished after Sotar and Cole fought together to get Ethan's herd through to Kansas.

"Gettin' late. How 'bout you an' Boss stayin' on 'til mornin'?" Sotar asked, patting Cole's horse. His left earlobe was missing, the aftermath of a gunfight years ago.

"Sounds like a good idea. Looks like you've got things well in hand here," Cole said. "Any problems?"

Sotar grinned. "Not so far. The big trick is to keep ol' Miller whar he won't rile up nobody with all his talk nobody understands. German, I guess. Probably callin' us all assholes."

Cole chuckled and turned to Ethan, who rolled a cigarette and began to ask roundup questions. It was hard work, very hard work, finding and herding cattle that had wandered for months.

Sotar responded quickly to questions about the size of the herd, the overall health of the animals, the shape and size of the calves. Range conditions were discussed in detail. Even the condition of Sotar's team of cowboys. Nothing escaped Ethan's concern. Sotar had learned that Ethan Kerry wanted exactness. No, he demanded it. Sotar's answers were crisp, except for an occasional Missouri multisyllable word where it should be just one.

During these times, Cole listened. It was yet a wonderment, listening to his older brother take charge and probe for detail after detail.

"Any problems with our new neighbors?" Ethan took a long pull on his cigarette.

"Well, had some early on . . . uh, discussions about a few calves," Sotar said, grinning. "With that new owner of the Rocking R. You know, the old Drako ranch. Heredith Tiorgs is his handle. Found his brand on a half dozen o' our youn'uns. Still warm they were. Must've been branded while we were . . . at the funeral."

"Damn. Was Tiorgs here himself—or a rep?"

"Both." Sotar turned toward the listening Cole. "Rep is a guy named Aldridge. Wanted everybody to think he was tough. Figure he was the problem with the brandin' though, not Tiorgs."

The Missouri foreman glanced in both directions and quietly told Cole and Ethan that he noticed that the Rocking R was hiring a lot of hard-looking gunmen. From his riding the range, he had encountered many of them. He knew a few from other places and they weren't cattlemen.

Ethan's face turned sour.

"Thought we was headed for serious. But I showed them

where his so-called calves were, standin' with Bar K cows—and that ended it. Tiorgs, he apologized real quick. Got a feelin' some o' his boys did the brandin' and he didn't know about it." Sotar took off his hat and wiped his sweating brow with his sleeve. "We rebranded 'em."

"Where's Tiorgs now?"

"Uh, he left. Maybe an hour ago. His rep's over there, helping Miller. Been just fine since then."

Ethan turned in his saddle toward his youngest brother. "You know him?"

"No, but Miller won't let him get away with nothin'."

"Sure." Ethan rubbed out the stub of his cigarette against his saddle pommel.

Branding the "wrong" calf happened. Sometimes, it *was* an accident. Usually it wasn't. Looked like this time was. He made a mental note to keep his men watching this herd closely. In case it wasn't. And made another mental note to check out Heredith Tiorgs.

"I've sent three pairs o' riders out west to spend the night and circle back in," Sotar said.

"Riding the greasy sack patrol, eh?"

"Yeah. But Rommey fixed 'em up some good stuff. Plenty o' coffee, too."

"How 'bout tobacco?"

Sotar smiled. "Yeah, they each got a plug—or the makin's."

"Good."

Loud scuffing noises, accented by louder curses, from the branding fire interrupted their conversation. A fierce yell burst into the early dusk. A huge, unbranded steer broke away from its rope restraint and savagely swung its horns at anything close. The cowhand bringing the animal to the fire went flying as the enraged beast gored his horse. The cowboy flew into the air and landed on his head, unconscious. His hat twirled on its brim three feet away and plopped over next to the fire.

The steer spun and thundered into a brander who was slow scrambling out of its way. Freed, the steer shook its large head, snorted and pawed the ground, then bounded toward Sotar, Ethan and Cole, scattering the fire's logs and coals as he passed through it.

"Good Lord, that boy wants our blood," Sotar said and pulled his revolver from his holster and stepped away from Cole's horse. "I'll take care of it. Better move."

"I'll stay. Kiowa will hold. You might need some stopping power with that bastard." Cole yanked his Winchester free of its scabbard. He leaned toward Ethan. "Steer coming. Mad as hell. Better get out of the way."

"Yeah. I see a blur coming at us. Figured it was a steer. Are you leaving?"

"No. I'm going to help John David stop him."

"Good. The camp needs some beef for supper. I'll stay." Ethan said, as if discussing the weather. "Give your gun to Sotar—and take mine. His six-gun won't stop him." Ethan reached for his Winchester and yanked it from the boot. He patted his horse's neck and told it to stand.

The beast was thundering toward them, only thirty feet away and closing fast. Cole handed his rifle to Sotar and grabbed Ethan's in one move.

"Here, John David. I'll take Ethan's."

Sotar grabbed the rifle, dropped his pistol, swung and fired, then levered and fired again. Cole's rifle was an instant behind the second shot. Another quickly followed.

The big steer grunted and jerked sideways. Both men levered new cartridges and fired again as the beast continued to roar toward them. This time, the infuriated animal looked like an invisible rope had grabbed its horns and yanked it backward. The animal staggered and fell, heaved once and was still.

Ethan proclaimed loudly, "Guess we're having beef tonight, boys."

Cole glanced at Sotar and shook his head. A mad steer could tear up a man or a horse badly.

"I'd better check on the boys." Sotar picked up his revolver, holstered it and returned Cole's rifle. "Thanks. That could've been worse."

"Yeah," Cole said. "And tell the cook to get over here. There's a carcass to be dressed." He took his rifle and returned Ethan's. "Your gun shoots a mite high, Ethan."

Ethan chuckled. "Ain't the gun. It's the man. Did you reload it—or do I have to do everything?"

CHAPTER 7

Before dawn and after a breakfast of bacon, biscuits and coffee, Cole and Ethan rode toward the second Bar K roundup, where the smaller of the Bar K herds roamed. Luther and Eli remained with Sotar. A long, narrow grassland was home to these cattle, but the surrounding draws, switchbacks and heavy oak and mesquite thickets made it easy for the cattle to disappear. This was the only open land where Bar K cattle grazed that was not owned by Bar K.

A large percentage of shorthorns, Eastern-bred cows and steers comprised much of this herd. Ethan trusted this herd, and the roundup of them, to a long-time Bar K hand. Harold DuMonte was in charge and participated in this herd's profit-ability. He also had a small home on the south side of Bar K land where his wife and three children lived.

When not working, the colored man was rarely seen without a Bible in his hands. The Bar K riders called him "Preacher" and he liked the nickname. He had served the ranch in two other key areas of responsibility—as point rider on several cattle drives to Kansas, and as the roundup rep and tally man when the Bar K was only one herd. Ethan liked having DuMonte responsible for the breeding of new Eastern blood into Bar K beef. DuMonte knew cattle and how to care for them. At this camp, he also served as the tallyman.

As the two Kerrys cleared the uneven ridge that separated the grazing land from a volley of hiccupping hills, Bar K riders looked up and waved. In the distance was another mass of brown animals. Off to the left was the second chuck wagon, branding fire, horse pole corral and unbranded calf corral.

Ethan turned in his saddle and asked Cole if he thought they would be able to fence this part of the land if they actually bought it.

"I'd do it last," Cole said, studying the roundup below. "Going to take a lot of that Devil's hatband down in those valleys. May not be worth it. But you're the one good with numbers."

"I reckon to start fencing come spring."

"Come spring," Cole repeated. "That's gonna bring a lot of hate. You know that."

"It's time."

Cole nodded. "Looks like the roundup's going slow. Herd's small." He described what he saw as they neared a small branding fire and the approaching DuMonte.

"Maybe the beeves are all dug in, down in that heavy brush," Ethan responded. "All that rain might've pushed 'em there."

It amazed Cole what his brother knew about their range, in spite of his condition.

The steady DuMonte was riding fast and reined in his tall bay next to them.

"Mornin', Mr. Kerry—an' Mr. Kerry. Glad you're here." DuMonte's face was a contortion of worry.

Swallowing what he intended to say, the colored drover looked at Cole and said, "Mighty glad to see you out an' about. It was so sad to lose her so soon. Know that Mrs. Kerry's with the good Lord—an' she's smiling." He took off his high-crowned hat and held it in front of him, over the saddlehorn.

"Thanks, Harold. Good friends like you help a lot." Cole started to say Kathleen had come to him in a dream last night, but decided against it.

Pursing his lips as if understanding what was on Cole's mind,

DuMonte changed subjects to the one causing him worry.

"We've got trouble." A heavy frown took over his dark face. "We're missing close to two hundred head. Mostly cow-and-calf. Young stuff."

"Damn," Ethan spat. "You're sure they're not just hunkered down in all those damn thickets?"

"I am now. Just finished a full swing," DuMonte reported, motioning with his hat. "Somebody swept through sometime back." He slammed his hat against the saddlehorn.

"How long ago, you figure?" Ethan asked, shifting his weight in the saddle. Jake lowered its head to graze and the blind rancher pulled back the reins to return the horse to its proper waiting position.

DuMonte folded his arms, still holding his hat, now with a crushed crown. "Well, you remember we rode this range a month ago. After all that heavy rain. Checking that we didn't have beeves bogged down. Haven't been out here since."

"So, they've had a month. Damn."

Cole pushed his hat back on his forehead. "Doesn't matter, Ethan. Nobody's driven a herd of any size to market lately. The whole region would've known. And calves wouldn't be worth much. Not for a few years. So . . ."

"So you think they're holding 'em some place close," Ethan interrupted. "They'll rebrand the cows and mark the calves. Then ease 'em out gradually. That the way you read it?"

Cole pulled his hat back in place. "Right."

"You think it's that new rancher, the one who bought the Russians' place? It's not far from here," Ethan said. "They tried it at Sotar's camp. And he said they were hiring guns. Wasn't high on his rep, either."

"Don't know that. We need to find our beeves first. Besides, we don't know anything about this Tiorgs fellow. John David said he wasn't involved in that, remember?"

Ethan's face twisted into a challenge that didn't voice.

"I was just going to get most of the boys to follow me when you rode up," DuMonte said. "Peaches thinks he's found where they went. The trail, anyway."

Cole studied the men working the animals. "How's Peaches working out?"

"Peaches is a hard worker. Hard-headed, too. Riding with a past," DuMonte said and glanced at Cole.

"Worth keeping on?" Ethan completed a cigarette and snapped a match to flame. He already knew the answer and Cole wouldn't let him fire Peaches anyway.

"Well, he's the only one who found where our beeves went. He's down at the corral, switching horses."

Ethan's back straightened. His demeanor could have easily been during a battle in the Great War again. There was a look to the man. A look of confident leadership. Calm, yet determined. His chin jutted forward. Everything about him read strength and courage.

"Cole, you go with Peaches. Track our beeves. Leave us some signs to follow fast," Ethan said, puffing on the cigarette. "DuMonte, send someone back to Sotar. Tell him to bring six men in a hurry. With their rifles. The rest should stay with that herd." He inhaled the smoke and stared away as if seeing the battlefield take shape. "Have Luther stay with 'em there, too, with Eli. He won't like it, but he'll do it."

DuMonte listened intently as Cole checked his handguns.

"When Sotar gets back, we'll follow you. DuMonte, you'll want to leave a small crew here to keep these beeves close." He pulled the cigarette from his mouth and declared, "We've got to expect they'll be watching—an' take a run at our herds while we're chasing shadows."

"You figure this is well planned, then," Cole said.

"Ain't passing saddle tramps." Ethan's eyes squinted.

"What about sending a rider for Marshal Montgomery?" Cole asked.

"Makes sense. But we won't wait for him." The blind rancher cocked his head. "No. DuMonte, that's a good idea. Send a rider and *you* wait. All right? It's out of Montgomery's jurisdiction, but it'd be good to have him with us anyway. Too damn far to get the county sheriff. He's not worth spit anyway."

"Whatever you want, Boss."

Ethan twisted in his saddle and laid his right hand against the pommel. Anyone watching from a distance wouldn't have any idea the tall rancher couldn't see.

Or was he beginning to see again? Cole watched his brother, letting Ethan's own description of the attacking steer return to his mind: *"Yeah. I see a blur coming at us. Figured it was a steer."*

A blur? That meant he saw something. Something moving. Claire had told him a week ago that Ethan had mentioned seeing shapes. For three years, there had been nothing. The doctors said they could do nothing, that the horse's kick had damaged nerves and that they might heal and they might not. Ever.

"Let's get moving, boys." Ethan's voice was a command.

CHAPTER 8

Cole Kerry and Peaches rode silently with the stoic Chinese warrior leading the way on a short-coupled bay that was a good roping horse.

The tracks of the gathered herd were old but still visible in places and both Cole and the Chinaman could read them easily, as could most men who lived with cattle. At intervals, they stopped to pile rocks in a traditional directional marking. This part of the range had been selectively worked over, for only Bar K steers or cows without young were seen. Calves were missing and so were their mothers.

They eased around a long, low-hatted hill that flirted with a stream and were surprised to see a barbed-wire fence ahead of them. To the southeast were a row of purple hills barely visible in the haze of the day.

"Well, I'll be damned," Cole blurted. "That's where that new guy's land starts. Wonder when he put this in?"

"Do not know, Cole Ker-rie-son. No Bar K rider come this way. No reason. So easy to hide fence."

"Yeah."

Peaches pointed. "There. Herd move through there."

They rode toward a clumsily constructed gate, built from wire and thick tree branches. Cole swung down next to it and studied the empty land stretching beyond the fence. Evidence of passing cattle was apparent, but none were in sight.

"Our beef went through all right," Cole looked up at his

friend. "And they sure didn't do it on their own. You stay here. Ethan and the boys'll be along soon. You can tell them I went for a look-see."

"You go . . . by self?"

"Yeah. I'll be careful."

Peaches shook his head and looked into Cole's face. "No. I no let you, Cole Ker-rie-son." The Chinaman followed his declaration with a statement in Chinese that Cole didn't understand, but assumed it was an affirmation of his intent to go along.

"You probably just called me stupid." Cole grinned.

Peaches's eyes sparkled, but his expression didn't change "I say . . . you warrior. I warrior. *Xiong pi*. Two warriors. I go with you." He motioned toward the ground. "We leave mark for your brother to follow."

Licking his lips, Cole recognized the Chinese phrase for fierce fighters and agreed. The two men prepared a stack of three rocks with a fourth pointing toward the gate. They rode together through the gate, replacing it carefully and trotted across a wide stretch of uneven sandy earth, speckled with mesquite and clumps of buffalo grass. Cole noted to himself that it wasn't good grazing land and that it made sense for Ethan to pass on purchasing this acreage. They eased around a gray knoll, warted with limestone outcroppings and encircled by wild thickets.

In front of them was a small herd of grazing cows and their calves. Within the middle of the animals was a small pond. Afternoon sun reflected from the brown water. Three cotton-woods were coupled with the pond and its life-giving water. Birds gathered in the trees, discussing their next journey. Shadows of sitting men and their waiting horses were evident beneath the trees.

Cole motioned for them to pull back, letting the knoll hide them. After tying their horses to the closest thickets, they

72

unsheathed their rifles, sneaked back for a further look and stretched out behind jagged rocks. Cole carried a Winchester; Peaches, an Evans rifle. The unusual gun carried a 28-shot rotary magazine with an under-hammer that slammed upward when triggered. The army had experimented with the rifle, interested in its rapid firepower, but decided against the gun because of its frequent mechanical problems. If Peaches had any problems with the gun, he had never said, but he rarely spoke of such things.

The closest cattle were only twenty feet away; the men guarding them, forty yards. The herd was beginning to spread from lack of attention.

"That calf is wearing a strange brand. So is his mother. It's been worked over ours. Damn. Some kind of a road brand, I guess. Never seen it before. Covers ours real nice," Cole blurted.

"It is so. Five guard them."

"Five. We'll wait here and see if we lower the odds."

"If you want, I go in, firing."

"Thanks, Han Rui. Let's wait."

Questions came at Cole's mind like a Gatling gun. Questions he couldn't answer. Waiting was the only choice that made sense—and the only answer at the moment. It was the hardest to do. Attacking was always easier. For him.

A few minutes later, a pig-faced man with a big belly ambled in their direction, picking up sticks and small branches as he walked. Obviously, he was assigned the task of building a fire for cooking. In front of him, a jackrabbit spurted from its hiding place and ran toward the rocks where Cole and Peaches watched. The skinny animal sensed their presence and made an immediate left turn and disappeared into a nearby thicket.

As the wood gatherer drew closer to the same rocks, Cole tossed a small rock in the direction of the rabbit. The pig-faced man spun in that direction, more curious than fearful. As he did, Cole slipped behind him. Unable to see anything that could have made the noise, he turned back to look for more wood. Cole's rifle butt drove into the man's round face, crushing his nose and crumpling him to the ground. Peaches helped Cole drag the unconscious rustler out of sight, behind the rocks.

"Well, that leaves four. Let's see if another comes this way," Cole said, glancing at the trees where the men sat.

Peaches nodded and said something in Chinese that Cole took for agreement.

No movement at the rustlers' camp was immediate. Around a wimpy campfire, the four remaining rustlers were relaxing. Good, Cole muttered. A reflection from a bottle told him the men were enjoying some whiskey. Even better.

Fury was climbing alongside Cole's other feelings; the bastards had stolen Bar K cattle. A dark part of him wished for an encounter and he tightened his grip on the rifle. Losing his beloved Kathleen left him edgy. He paused to think through the situation. He glanced back at their horses. Kiowa and Peaches's bay were there. Alert. Ears up. He took a long breath, then another and looked toward the trees where the other rustlers sat. One man was up and had walked away to relieve himself. What Cole wanted was for another rustler to come in their direction, checking on the first. Anything to lower the odds.

A moment later, he got his wish.

From the camp came a loud query. "Hey, Jimmy Joe? Whatcha doin'? It cain't be that hard findin' wood. Come on!"

"Jimmy Joe" had to be the pig-faced rustler lying unconscious behind Cole and Peaches.

Cole cupped his hand to his mouth and growled, "Need some he'p. Lots o' wood."

He froze, waiting to see if his voice deception would work. It should. The other rustlers were not expecting trouble and would likely hear what they expected to hear.

"Billy, go check on Jimmy Joe, will ya? He's either found a mother lode o' wood—or he's got hisse'f a nice red-headed whore out thar."

The command came from a long sideburned man in a high-crowned hat and filthy batwing chaps, as he pushed a stick through the dying fire to encourage new life. The others chuckled as Billy returned from relieving himself. Billy snapped a match to life on his gunbelt and lit the stub of a cigar. The yellow halo of the flame outlined his square face with its scrawny mustache.

"If'n it's that red-haired whore from town, I ain't comin' back."

That brought more laughter as Billy walked toward Cole and Peaches. Passing a large outcropping of rock, the lanky rustler picked his way slowly through the thick underbrush and grass. As he drew near the rocks, Cole cupped his hand to his mouth again and grunted, "Back here."

"Sure. Sure. I'm comin'. You could've made two trips, ya know."

As Billy rounded the rock, the butt of Peaches's rifle drove into his face. The rustler groaned and fell. Struggling with the unforgiving weight, the Chinese gunfighter pulled the body farther behind the rocks as if it were nothing more than a sack of potatoes.

Cole's eyes searched the gathering for signs of discovery. Nothing. He breathed a deep release of battle tension. Grabbing the pig-faced man's derby, he drew his Colt carried in the sideways holster near his belt buckle. He picked up an armful of branches, checking that the gun in his hand was covered, and started for the rustler camp.

"Keep them in your sights, Han Rui," Cole said. "Don't know how close I'll get before somebody realizes I'm not what's-his-name."

The rustlers did not pay any attention to the advancing Cole Kerry. He deliberately avoided looking at any of them, knowing it would bring immediate recognition. Fifteen feet from the camp, he slowed, preparing to drop the wood and declare his real presence.

Releasing the stick he was using to play with the campfire, the sideburned leader moved his hand toward the beltgun at his waist.

"That's not Jimmy Joe . . ."

Cole dropped the branches and fired three times. The camp leader grabbed his chest and fell into the fire. His own handgun fired into the air. The two remaining rustlers were stunned. But the closest man drew a handgun from his belt and fired. The shot missed. Cole, hurrying his own shot, also missed, and stumbled against a long tree root. He dropped his gun and the Colt thudded against the ground as he tried to regain his balance.

Running toward the camp, Peaches paused and fired his Evans four quick times. The rustler jerked and collapsed before he could recock his gun.

In the open pasture, the cattle straightened and began to mill in fear.

Righting himself, Cole drew his second Colt and aimed it at the remaining rustler. "How 'bout you, want to try your luck? We'd like that."

Slowly, the grizzled man with a scrawny beard and a hat with little shape raised his hands. His complexion was a deep crimson from too many years in the sun.

Most of the cows and calves had bolted for the far side of the pasture, but were gradually settling into grazing almost as soon as the shooting ended.

"Not us, mister. We're just drovers, watchin' beeves," he said.

"Hard to believe that. Those are Bar K cows—and their calves."

"They're wearin' our brand, mister."

Cole glanced at the advancing Peaches.

"Yeah, well, I'm going to put that brand on your ass when we string you up," Cole snarled. "You want me to kill one and show you the real brand?"

"I didn't do it, mister. Honest," the grizzled man responded, waving his hands. "You're Cole Kerry, ain't ya?"

"I am—and those are our cattle you've stolen. You boys are going to hang."

"Sumbitch." The grizzled man shook his head.

Peaches strolled beside Cole and he thanked the Chinaman. "Thanks, Han Rui. Check this boy for hidden iron, will you? I wouldn't want him to be tempted. Better check the others, too."

Peaches studied the gunfighter. "You hit, Cole Ker-rie-son?"

"No. Just stumbled. Getting clumsy in my old age."

"De hen," the Chinaman said and repeated it in English, "Velly good."

"Heredith Tiorgs'll get your sorry ass for this!"

"Really? Is he behind this?" Cole said, pointing his Colt at the grizzled rustler.

Hatred poured from the rustler's locked eyes and his fists opened and shut, releasing the anger within him.

"I asked you a question. Is Heredith Tiorgs behind this rustling?" Cole's gaze challenged the man, who looked down.

"Heredith Tiorgs . . . is the owner of the Rockin' R. You're on Rocking R land, ya know."

"I know that. What I want to know is if Tiorgs is behind this rustling," Cole asked. "He's got a lot of answering to do. Where is he?"

"At the ranch, I suppose. I don't babysit him." The rustler shook his head.

"Maybe you should. Safer than stealing somebody's cattle."

"He don't know nothin' 'bout this," the rustler added quickly.

"We'll see."

"No, I mean it. Heredith, ah, he let us go. Fired us. Awhile back. Decided we needed a road stake. Shoulda kept ridin'."

"Guess so."

Laying his rifle on the ground and out of easy reach, Peaches drew his shoulder-holstered handgun, stepped beside the dead leader and yanked a pistol from his belt in back. Satisfied, the Chinaman went to the next dead rustler who had already dropped a handgun on the ground in front of him. Leaning over, Peaches pulled a hidden revolver from the outlaw's back waistband with his left hand. His right held his own gun.

Cole walked over to retrieve his fallen Colt.

Taking advantage of both distractions, the grizzled rustler drew a derringer from his vest pocket. As the man raised the weapon to shoot Cole, Peaches spun and stuck the nose of his Webley Bulldog revolver into the grizzled outlaw's ear.

"Drop it. Or crows eat your dead eyes," the Chinaman purred softly as if he were talking to a woman about her apple pie.

Cole looked up to see the outlaw turn white and drop the derringer.

"Thanks. That's the second time today, Han Rui," Cole said, returning his Colt to its sidewinder holster.

The stocky Chinaman smiled and clubbed the rustler's head with the barrel of the gun.

An hour later, Ethan Kerry, Sotar and the rest of the roundup riders pulled up. The grizzled rustler was tied, as were the barely conscious Jimmy Joe and Billy, still behind the hillside. The other two rustlers were dead.

"Looks like you boys have been busy," Ethan called.

Sotar, riding next to him, had advised Ethan of the situation.

Cole growled, "We need to get the law here. And we need to

find the Rocking R owner. Heredith Tiorgs. These boys say he doesn't know about this. We need to know for sure. They say he fired them a while back. Never seen that brand before, have you? Guess it's a road brand."

Forgetting his earlier question and demand, Ethan said, "Loop went for the marshal. Don't know how long that'll take. That Welshman isn't always easy to find, you know."

"All right. Han Rui and I'll head for the Rocking R ranchhouse. We'll hold Tiorgs 'til you get there with Montgomery."

"No."

Ethan was emphatic. The one-word response caused the riders to turn toward him. Cole looked up, ready to challenge his older brother, but Sotar softened the moment.

"How about Ethan and the rest go to the Rocking R. I'll stay with you, Cole—and Peaches. The riders from the CW Connected and the Bar 8 will also. They'll provide proof if Montomery needs it." He waved toward the four riders repping for the two other area ranches.

Cole glanced at Peaches and said, "Sure."

"Velly good," the Chinaman replied.

CHAPTER 9

"Damn you, Heredith! What the hell were you *thinking*?"

Reverend Paul Dinclaur slammed his fist against a cluttered desk. His white hair flopped along his shoulders in response to the violent move. He should have known trouble was coming when he spotted a cricket leaving the house. Crickets were signs of good luck. When a cricket left, it meant something bad would happen.

Outside, stormy weather matched his mood as he sat alone in his cottage next door to the Uvalde church. He was rereading an unfinished bill of sale for the Bar K ranch. He liked to study it when stressed. As he was now. The contract was his ultimate dream. On it was Claire Kerry's signature, forged from a grocery order he had secured. Ethan's wouldn't be necessary. Of course, she would be dead when it was presented, as would all the Kerrys. Missing was only his own signature and the date. Even two witness signatures were in place—Heredith Tiorgs and his brother, Meken. His stepsister, Jinette Six, would add hers when she arrived.

He read it through three times, as he always did, then folded it carefully and put it away in the middle of his Bible. He loved the irony of the placement and held the book at his side. The white-haired minister had been in his house, adjoining the small church, since learning of the arrest of three Rocking R cowhands for rustling and attempted murder.

They were being held in the Uvalde jail, brought in by

Marshal Montomery and the Kerry bunch. Two other rustlers were brought in, draped over their horses, killed by Cole Kerry and some Chinaman. A perfunctory hearing was over in a half hour. The circuit judge was expected within the week to conduct the trial. The evidence was overwhelming and the town was buzzing about a hanging.

Only a mountain lion and her young walking right down the main street last winter had caused more excitement.

"I told you to be careful taking Bar K beef. Damn you, Heredith! Careful, I said." He shook his head to clear the image of Cole and the blind Ethan Kerry, and their men, riding through town. "They think they're so damn important. They'll *see*." He smiled at the word.

Dinclaur's brother, Meken, had told the fake minister of the bad news. Meken was almost as cunning as his older brother, posing as a bum, wandering from handout to handout, in Uvalde. Stopping at the church was natural and aroused no suspicions. The guise allowed him access to information that would be difficult for Dinclaur to hear otherwise.

It was Meken who found out Heredith Tiorgs had convinced the Kerrys that he knew nothing about the attempted rustling and they believed him. Especially when he added only a fool would try to rustle cattle from the Bar K. It helped that the brand wasn't the Rocking R. He said the men had been fired over a week ago. That statement matched what one of the rustlers had told Cole. Tiorgs had even offered to ride into town with the Kerrys, cursing the rustlers in his Scottish brogue. The Kerrys said it wasn't necessary.

Pacing back and forth, Reverend Dinclaur worried about what the captured rustlers would say if they thought it would save their necks. They might know Tiorgs was his stepfather. And that they, along with his younger brother, Meken, and his half-sister, Jinette Six, planned to kill the Kerrys and take control of the Bar K empire. They might, depending on what Tiorgs had told them.

The agitated minister wasn't interested in ranching, at least not on a small scale like the Rocking R. No, he wanted the Bar K. That would come easier than anyone thought. Eliminate Cole and Ethan Kerry and the operation would fall apart fast. Elimating the rest of the Kerrys would be easy. He planned to make that step look like Apaches had hit the ranch house.

Unfortunately, Tiorgs knew that, too. So might some of his men. Keeping secrets wasn't Tiorgs's strong suit. Dinclaur didn't really like the Scotsman, or trust him, but he needed his stepfather for now. The Scotsman had had a small gang operating out of Emporia, Kansas, when Dinclaur recruited him—and Tiorgs had added additional gunmen as well.

"Why did I think he was smarter than *this*?" Dinclaur bellowed. "Didn't he understand I wanted him to be *careful*?" The hypocrisy of his remark was ignored; it was his idea to peel away Bar K calves and their mothers and put the road brand on them. He didn't think the Kerrys would notice.

His loud comments caused him to look around the small cottage, hoping no one was close outside. He hurried to the one small window and assured himself of the emptiness of his concern. Outside the clapboard structure were some tired lilac bushes and a struggling oak tree. At the sight of two crows resting on a high branch, he relaxed a little. A sign of good luck.

He turned away from the window. This was a perfect arrangement. No one would think a minister would be involved in such a monstrous land grab. Or murder.

Walking over to the front door, slightly ajar, he was pleased to see eight leaves had found their way inside. He smiled. Leaves coming into a house was also a sign of good luck. And eight was also his lucky number. He closed it and left the leaves on the floor. Everything in the universe was reassuring him that the cricket had made a mistake.

His attention turned to a small, waist-high bookcase next to the door. It held an odd mixture of books, including several hymnals. He shoved the Bible into the second row where it was always kept. He used a different Bible for services. A coat rack was draped with a long black robe, worn during church service. The desk and chair, where he sat, dominated the main room. Only an old rocking chair occupied it as well. The walls were unpainted. Two walls were blank. A third had a hard-working fireplace. The fourth featured a framed presentation of the Twenty-Third Psalm.

Reaching to the framed verse, he touched it and mouthed " 'the valley of the shadow of death.' " He was fascinated by the phrase and related it to what he planned to accomplish. A delicious private joke. The adjoining bedroom had a bed and a three-legged dresser, propped with a stone. The bed was arranged so that he could only enter and leave it from the right side . . . for luck.

The church itself was in need of paint, promised by the faithful come spring.

The intense minister's white shirt was wrinkled and sweated-through. Rare for him. He prided himself on his lack of body sweat and odor. His trousers carried spots of dried mud from his walk to the cottage after seeing the arrested men brought into town. Dirt crumbles fell from his high-topped boots. Compulsively, he cleaned up the crumbles and threw them into his quiet fireplace. He was close to becoming a rich and powerful man. So close.

He shut his eyes and envisioned the shadows of greatness forming around him. This he did often. He shook his head and his long hair skimmed across his shoulders. A curse snapped from his thin mouth as he discovered the discolored pants and attempted to brush them clean, unsuccessfully. He would change before leaving.

The idea of owning another ranch was to give him a legitimate reason to visit and learn from Heredith Tiorgs—and gradually to hold stolen young Bar K cattle until he took over that operation. Soon, he would be the "prince of Uvalde," owning the prize ranch in the region. Tiorgs, in spite of his faults, was a good cowman and a good recruiter of gunmen, mostly from Kansas and Missouri. His half-sister, Jinette Six, would likely stay there at the Rocking R. She was coming from Kansas City to assist in the implementation of the grand strategy.

Dinclaur's dark ministral bib was unbuttoned, but his white collar remained properly in place. His suitcoat was flung over the rocking chair and a short-barreled Colt Lightning revolver lay in the chair seat. Both a rare sign of distraction and sloppiness. He noticed them as if for the first time, summarily walked to the chair and picked up the gun as a man does who is comfortable with weapons. The old chair rocked in response to the brisk removal of the Colt. What if someone should unexpectedly visit? he chided himself.

He reloaded the gun with fresh cartridges from a box kept in the desk drawer and shifted it to his back waistband. Unarmed, for him, was like walking around without pants. No one seemed to notice, other than that damn Cole Kerry the other day. Additional weapons were stored under his bed, all well oiled and loaded: a Winchester, a shotgun, and a wrapped pistol belt with a holstered Colt Lightning. Next to the weapons were a canister of gold coins and a valise packed with paper currency.

He took a deep breath and told himself to relax. "There's no way anybody is going to believe Heredith Tiorgs's men if they claim we're after the Bar K. Why would *they*? And if they tell that I plan to kill the Kerrys . . . who's going to believe that *nonsense*?"

A chuckle followed. His manner of speaking, emphasizing

last words, had long since become an established habit, whether he was alone or giving a sermon.

Still, it was something he didn't want known. Even if the idea were laughed at as ridiculous, the Kerry brothers wouldn't laugh; they would be on alert and likely start checking into his back trail. He stood, walked over to the stone fireplace and pushed the ashes with a poker to bring them back to life.

The answer was to break out Tiorgs's men tonight. He would have to kill Marshal Montgomery, or whoever was on duty, but that was a minor detail. The rustlers could hide out in the hills until the time was right to return to the Rocking R.

"Maybe I should wait for *sis*," Dinclaur muttered.

Jinette Six was his half-sister; Tiorgs was her real father. He and Meken had a different father, a drunken railroad executive who left their mother when they were young. Jinette had grown into a beautiful seductress who had secured two fortunes from unsuspecting rich men; she used the last name of her most recent husband. She was expected soon. Dinclaur's loins tingled with anticipation. The two had been lovers since they were in their teens.

Dinclaur went to his bedroom for a fresh shirt. He was calmer now. A planner with much confidence in his abilities, his skill in thinking strategically was exceptional, in his opinion. Almost as good as his skill with a gun. He was adept at turning his plans into real, hard fact. Events seemed to have a way of moving to his favor, because he had created those events, for the most part. His plans envisioned the Bar K ranch becoming the envy of Texas, greater even than what King had done. Or certainly what the Kerrys tried to do. All with his leadership at its heart.

At the right time, after all the Kerrys were dead, he would present the signed bill of sale for the Bar K. He would let the town know it had been his intention to help the desperate family, since the three Kerry brothers were dead, and would explain a recently received trust from an uncle as the source for the necessary cash. The money used to buy the Rocking R ranch was under his bed; he and his brother, Meken, had ambushed the Drakos several days out from their former ranch and resecured their money. A few Indian feathers and weapons were left behind. That's all it took to convince everyone that the Drakos had been killed by Indians. Tiorgs had taken control of the ranch operation a month later.

Dinclaur's real name was Glory Van Camp, one of the most feared gunmen in Colorado and Utah. His brother was Meken Van Camp. Neither name was known in Texas. Nor their faces. Nor was Heredith Tiorgs. "Pastor Paul Dinclaur" was a person he had created. Dinclaur had been his mother's maiden name. It sounded like a thoughtful minister, he figured, and was the perfect disguise to accomplish the first phase of his plan. So Glory Van Camp had disappeared into Pastor Paul Dinclaur. A comfortable role; he had posed as a minister caring for the spiritual needs of the Confederate soldiers while working as a Union spy during the war.

Everyone in Uvalde thought he came from Nebraska. As far as they knew, he was a man of God, a man with a deep and abiding faith, a man who was working with the community. Of course, he had to murder Reverend Joseph B. Hillas to create the necessary vacancy. Suffocation was quick and he was in and out of town before anyone saw him.

His arrival in town a week later, riding a mule, had created quite a stir. He liked the symbolism, recalling that Jesus rode into Jerusalem on a donkey to great crowds. Dinclaur had said he was only stopping for a bite to eat and then "riding on to seek out more souls for the Lord." The town council asked him to stay. He had agreed, but only with the provision he be allowed to serve the entire area, riding from ranch to ranch as needed. It was a calculated response but the town ate it up.

Later, they had made him a member of the town council! Something he hadn't planned on, but accepted as a nice touch to the picture he was establishing of himself.

Now he must be cautious with his own emotions. Sometimes, though, decisions wore hard, particularly if he had a trace of doubt running through the process. If Heredith Tiorgs were here now, he could ask his stepfather how much the arrested men knew, but he couldn't wait for that. The longer the prisoners were jailed, the more likely they would talk. The controlled pastor was most uneasy at having a critical element moving through his strategy that he couldn't control. Misjudgment of people usually brought failure. He wasn't going to stand for this weakness in himself.

As men of the gun in Colorado after the War, and then cattlemen's association enforcers in Kansas, the two brothers had earned good money. A cattleman's casual comment about the growing Bar K and its blind owner had sparked the idea that it could be theirs. Each day the passion grew until Dinclaur decided to act. A stop in Emporia, Kansas, had yielded his stepfather's involvement—and the assets of the bank. He wanted no added obstacles; Cole Kerry was sufficient all by himself. He wanted the gunfighter out of the way soon. Bringing in Jinette Six was smart business, for several reasons. But, to himself, he acknowledged that he wasn't the least afraid of killing Cole himself. How great it would be to have his siblings together again. This time with tremendous power. How great it would be to see his stepsister again, especially in bed.

His laugh curdled the silence. The irony of it all was marvelous. The Kerrys were three brothers—and he had a brother, a sister and a stepfather. And *his* brother wasn't blind.

He laughed again.

Once he climbed the last hurdle and took over the Bar K, he would stand alone as the power to be reckoned with in this part of Texas. Then, most certainly, would come the added dimension of political clout. Such was the vision that drove him daily. He was long through working for some high-handed cattleman like Ethan Kerry, or some silly town council, or some power-hungry politician, hiring his ability to kill, but wanting nothing whatsoever to do with him personally. He had become deeply angry at such people with their superior-acting ways even though they feared him.

But he would have the last laugh. He would be richer and more powerful than any of those bastards. All he had to do was follow his plan. Becoming a "minister" wasn't difficult. His superstitious nature fit well with the image. God didn't care; he favored the powerful and the rich.

He decided his pants needed changing, too, lit a candle beside the bed and carried it to his small closet, letting his mind flow to a passage in the Old Testament's Second Samuel that he had underlined: "How are the mighty fallen." He decided it was God's way of telling him that his pathway was actually the true one.

Once, after the war, he had portrayed a minister again. In Leadville, it was. For almost a year, he and his brother, Meken. Together, they had bilked three widows of their considerable wealth and left town before the law wised up. But, even before he had pretended to be a preacher, he had studied the Bible, repeating passages to himself. Besides the Second Samuel passage, he particularly liked a passage in Joshua, "The sun stood still, and the moon stayed." He didn't know what it meant; but it sounded special. His sermons were never long, for which the men were grateful. Most of the time they were built around themes of peace and love. And family.

Somewhere along the line, he happened across a book designed to aid ministers in planning their services and it had been most helpful. Besides that, he loved to hear his voice. It was always a treat for him.

He was careful not to weave personal superstitions into his sermons, even though such thinking was very much a part of him. Honest god-fearing folk might be offended. That took careful preparation because it would be so simple to say toppled-over boots were a sign that a death was near, or the flame of a lit candle turning blue meant a spirit was near, or seeing the first white butterfly in spring meant luck for the coming year. But he was always careful. Always.

"Waiting for Jinette isn't a good idea," he corrected himself. "Neither is breaking out Tiorgs's men."

After changing his pants, he left the candle on his bed stand and walked into the small kitchen to fix some coffee.

It had been his stepfather's job to hire the right gunmen and keep them ready at the Rocking R. Some had been a part of his Kansas gang. The two brothers and sister worked apart as well. Most recently, Meken was involved in a swindle and murder in Houston, leaving town before the law could bring him to justice.

A breakout would prolong his concern, he decided. Cole Kerry and everybody else would be after the escapees and wouldn't stop until they were captured again. That's when Heredith Tiorgs's men would jabber like little girls.

No, the rustlers must be eliminated. Tonight. Tiorgs could replace them and the threat of death wouldn't be lost on the new recruits.

Absentmindedly, he turned up a gas lamp in the kitchen. Dark was coming soon and he would head for the jail, letting shadows aid his assault. The brighter light seemed to pull him back again to his missed chance to eliminate Cole Kerry on the trail after the miserable man left the cemetery. The failed opportunity clung to his mind like a cockle burr. No one would have linked the killing to him. No one. His attire had been a worthy disguise.

Leaving the not-yet-boiling coffee pot, he returned to his bedroom, knelt beside the bed to retrieve a second handgun and checked its loads. Smiling, he noticed the candle on his bed stand had gone out. A sign that someone would die.

A knock on the door broke into his thoughts. *Who the hell?*

Irritated, Dinclaur walked to the front window and peeked out. Of course, he should have known. His brother, Meken Van Camp, was at the door. Two years younger, Meken had mastered the role of a penniless, slow-minded street person for their schemes. The disguise was perfect; Meken could walk in and out of saloons and stores no one caring. No one suspected that he was better with a gun than even his brother—and meaner. Both were better with a gun than Heredith Tiorgs and their stepfather knew it.

Meken had come to town a week before Dinclaur arrived. It was logical for the new minister to provide occasional comfort for this poor man, even giving him a place to sleep in the church or an occasional meal. The two brothers were close.

"Evening, Meken. Have you *eaten*?" Dinclaur said and glanced around the street to see if anyone was looking.

Before him stood a man slightly shorter with a dirty face and stringy brown hair, wearing ill-fitting, wornout clothes. Boots were worn at the heels and the right toe was partly torn. Both men had tiny feet with squared toes, a physical pass-along from their mother. More like a boy's than a man's. Meken's pockmarked face was a contrast to Dinclaur's long and smooth countenance. With no physical resemblance between them, Dinclaur was not worried that anyone would discover their relationship

"What are you gonna do about the men those damn Kerrys brought in?" Even Meken's voice was different in tone and style to his brother's. When out on the street, he pretended to be scarcely able to speak. Neither sounded like Heredith Tiorgs, who spoke with a thick Scottish accent.

Dinclaur pointed at the cupboard. "I'm going to kill them. Tonight."

"Good. I saw the Kerry bunch ride out about an hour ago," Meken said. "Heard the blind one say they needed to get back to their roundup."

"Excellent."

Meken strolled into the small house. "Coffee smells good. Got any whiskey?"

CHAPTER 10

Thin clouds festered in the night sky as the town's saloons kicked into high joy. The day's stormy weather had left the area hours before. Carefully, the minister worked his way across the town, gliding through the shadows. Somewhere a door slammed shut and a woman laughed. Three dogs were engaged in a verbal fight.

Under the minister's coat were his guns with towels wrapped around the barrels and tied in place. They would muffle the roar of gunfire; saloon rambunctiousness would help, too. Ten feet from the jail, he stepped on a black beetle crossing the planked sidewalk. That meant rain. That was fine with him.

Meken trailed his brother, also keeping to the shadows. As usual, he carried a Smith & Wesson long-barreled revolver under his coat.

Knock! Knock! Knock! Knocking three times meant the spirits living within the wood would be awakened to grant him his wish.

"Marshal, this is Pastor Dinclaur. I want to visit the jailed men and pray for them. Please open the *door.*" Dinclaur's voice was clear in the night with his oratorical style of emphasizing last words and phrases.

"Well, it's late, Pastor. How about tomorrow?" Marshal Montgomery said from the other side of the door.

"From what I've heard, these men should be talking to the Lord *tonight.* Please, it is the decent thing to do. I won't take long. God hears even the shortest *prayers.*"

"Oh, sure. Wait a minute."

The heavy oak door swung open to the office. A lone gas lamp on the wall showered the room with streaks of yellow.

Inside, Dinclaur pushed the door closed again and swung toward the unsuspecting lawman. Flame spat twice from the gun in his right hand and Montgomery staggered backward and slid down the side of his desk. Dinclaur stepped closer and put a third bullet in the downed marshal's forehead.

"Thanks, Glory. Knew you'd come." A rustler called from his cell.

Dinclaur shivered at the use of his real name. The rustlers expected his arrival. He realized his hunch that Tiorgs might have told them about the plot was right—and so was what he must do.

"Where's he keep the *keys*?" Dinclaur growled.

"In the right-hand desk drawer. Yeah, there."

The grizzled rustler bubbled with enthusiasm, watching Dinclaur search the drawer.

"Praise the Lord! I sure was hopin' you'd come. Heredith filled us in on the plan." He paused, grinned and recited, "Now I lay me down to sleep . . . that's all I know, preacher." His chortle was long.

Dinclaur emptied both guns into the waiting rustlers. Looks on the three men ranged from total surprise to abject terror to fierce anger as they dropped inside their cells. As the echo of the last shot was swallowed by the room, Dinclaur spun back to the door, cracked it open and listened.

Outside, Meken leaned against the building. If someone came to investigate the gunfire, he would act like he, too, had heard the shooting and had hurried over; a word to Dinclaur would prepare him for a similar alibi.

"No one's coming. Hell, the saloons are louder than ever,"

Meken reported.

"Then get inside and give me a hand," Dinclaur ordered and laid both of his guns on the floor to free his hands. His long white hair was moist from the tension.

"Should I put out the lamp?"

"No. I need the light," Dinclaur said and touched the fresh blood from Montgomery with his finger. He tasted it. Good luck to swallow the blood of a conquered foe.

They turned to the task of setting the scene everyone would see in the morning. It would look like the rustlers had died trying to break out; Marshal Montgomery was killed, stopping them. Meken placed one of Dinclaur's smoking guns in the closest outlaw's unmoving hand, after he removed the towel and stuffed it into his ragged coat.

Montgomery's own gun would be left in the lawman's hand to match the shots supposedly taken by the dead lawman. Dinclaur drew Montgomery's holstered gun, emptied the cartridges and thrust them into his coat pocket. After removing the towel from his second gun and shoving it into his waistband, he removed the spent cartridges and pushed them into Montgomery's weapon. The lawman's now-empty gun was placed in his unmoving right hand. It took a few minutes to accomplish.

At Dinclaur's urging, Meken returned to the doorway, watching the dark street. By the time people discovered the killing, both guns would be cold.

"You ready, Glory?"

"No. It's not *right*. Yet," he muttered. "Let's see . . . one . . . two . . . and three. Yeah, *three*." He retraced his shooting of the marshal. "There can only be three shots fired from that *gun*." He pointed at the weapon in the dead outlaw's hand.

Moving quickly, he added three cartridges to the gun and put it back in the outlaw's hand.

"Ready now, Glory?" Meken snapped. "I'm getting cold out here."

"Anybody coming?" Dinclaur hated his brother using his real name.

"No. Looks like the saloon's real busy. Damn. A drink sounds good."

"Just be patient. I'm not *ready.*"

With that, he picked up his remaining handgun and placed it in Montgomery's left hand. "Yeah, that's it. Two guns. *Of course.*"

"Wait. There aren't any empty shells in it," Dinclaur warned himself and replaced the three empty shells taken earlier and put the weapon in the marshal's hand.

He stood and took one final look. "I'm done, Meken."

"It's clear, Glory," Meken said.

"Let's get out of *here,*" Dinclaur looked away from the dead bodies. He didn't like being unarmed, or leaving his gun. But it had to be done.

Shrill laughter couldn't be suppressed as they moved away.

"You're going to have to get me another pistol. I feel *naked,*" Dinclaur said with a wicked grin.

"Got a Colt stuck away. Way back under your back porch, wrapped in an oilcloth."

"Damn. Why didn't you tell me *before?*"

"You would've gotten mad."

"Yeah."

They walked in silence. Halfway back to the parish, an unseen dog began to howl. A hideous sound in the night that haunted them all the way back to the church.

"That damn dog smells *death,*" Dinclaur said as they stopped inside a shadow.

"Maybe he's just hungry."

★ ★ ★ ★ ★

Come morning, Uvalde awoke to a blood-curdling scream. Marshal Montgomery's wife had gone to the jail to eat breakfast with him as they had planned. People hurried toward the awful wailing. Some men grabbed rifles before they headed that way. Words on the street were jumbled and full of fear and angst.

"Vhat *ist* vrong?" Mayor Rinnart Heinrich asked passersby as he rushed from his Cattleman's Restaurant.

"Trouble at the jail," a pale businessman in a tailored suit answered. "Montgomery's dead. Stopped a jail break, though. Those rustlers are dead, too."

"Oh my vord. How awful this be."

"Yeah. And now all we got is that fool Logan." The businessman harrumped, ran his fingers along his trim mustache and continued walking.

By the time Deputy Logan got to the jail, the opened door was jammed with townspeople. Mayor Heinrich was inside, trying to console Montgomery's hysterical widow.

"What's going on?" Millard Logan asked, rubbing sleep from his eyes. He was supposed to have replaced Montgomery at six o'clock, but a late night at the saloon had caused him to oversleep. A frowning townsman with disheveled hair and wearing a wrinkled suit told him what had happened and stomped away, disappearing into the closest saloon. Logan's face turned pale. He had survived the Victorio Gee attack on the town—and now this. His floppy brimmed hat was askew and his eyebrows were jumping as he pushed his way through the crowd. As usual, he wore a three-piece suit that didn't fit well and was worn at the knees and elbows. A deputy badge dangled from his lapel, almost as an afterthought.

Around Logan's waist, outside his coat, was strapped a bullet belt with a holstered revolver carried butt forward. No one could recall him ever using it—or even drawing it. He had accepted the job as deputy when he was let go as a general store clerk.

Swallowing to regain his composure, he reached the dead marshal. He bit his lower lip and shivered. "Oh no . . . oh no . . . this can't be."

Montgomery's wife lay weeping with her head against his chest. She didn't look up when he stepped clear of the packed townspeople. Mayor Heinrich was kneeling beside her, talking quietly, although his use of German phrases had increased with the stress.

Behind him, a deep voice said, "Well, looks like you're the marshal now, Logan."

Logan spun around, yanked off his badge and said, "Not me. You don't pay me enough to get killed like that."

Without waiting for anyone to ask him to rethink his decision, Logan pushed his way through the crowd. The sooner he packed his things and got away from this town the better. His parents lived in Austin; he would head there.

Mayor Rinnart Heinrich watched him leave. Stepping beside him, the steely-eyed postmistress, Wilomina Reid, whispered, "We need Cole Kerry. Send someone to get him. He will help us. Please to God, he must."

Squeezing shut his eyes, the German-born mayor answered, "Ya, ve do."

CHAPTER 11

Early the next morning, Luther Kerry was hard at work in the main corral. This was his favorite time of the year. Unlike getting ready for spring roundup or a major cattle drive, he could work with their young horses—and not feel pressed to hurry.

Young colts were his favorite to work with, usually when they were three years old. He understood the inbred apprehension within a horse, any horse, and that fear had to be quieted before any significant progress was made.

Most of the Bar K horses already had their shoes pulled and turned out to pasture for the winter. Luther felt the animals were more comfortable that way. Of course, each line cabin had its own stable of horses.

Over in the second corral was the "rough string," horses that had acted up during the fall roundup and been pulled out of the Bar K cowboys' individual strings. Most had bad habits that needed correcting, a few were spoiled and some were just plain outlaws who weren't ridable. When a horse was pulled out of the cowboys' string for any reason, Luther was the one who worked with it.

And most often, the animal's bad habit—biting, kicking, pawing, whatever—was cured. Except for a few outlaws. He took such animals personally and would not give up on them. Any of them. Just as he hadn't given up on Kiowa after the mustang had thrown Ethan and kicked him. Cowboys wanted spirited mounts and were comfortable topping them off, but none were interested in becoming a bronc buster during the roundup. With so much else to do during the fall gathering, he usually didn't try to correct the animals then.

Eli was helping and, usually, Cole, too. Luther left the busting to Cole and a few of the other younger riders. Right now, Cole, Sotar, Peaches and DuMonte were riding the range checking that no other rustling problems had popped up.

A third corral contained a lone horse tied next to a mule the Kerrys called "Elizabeth." An extra wagon was centered in the corral. This bay had a scary habit of rearing straight up with a rider anytime it came near a wagon—and, sometimes, falling over. It was a dangerous trait and one that had to be broken or the horse would be no good for ranch work. Luther had discovered that a day with their necks tied together would break most horses into taking a lead and behaving. The mule could kick harder than most. The wagon's presence, hopefully, would help the bay get over its fear of such contraptions.

Luther rubbed his hands all over a buckskin colt to get him comfortable with the smell and touch of man. That was his first order of business with any of the young horses. Eli waved a saddle blanket around a black colt, back and front, then put it on the horse's back. Luther called it "sackin' out" and Eli would do this step many times on each green horse. Both were tied to the corral post and were learning to stand quietly. Later on, saddle blankets would be left on their backs as they were led around the corral. Learning to take a lead would come soon enough.

"Somebody's comin', Uncle Luther," Eli said from the far side of the corral.

"Sure looks like it, Eli," Luther responded and stood up. "Wonder who that is?"

A lone carriage entered the Bar K entrance. Mayor Heinrich looked uncomfortable, yet determined. Nearly bald, the man's remaining hair curled around his big ears, adding emphasis to his thick glasses and beard. He had left his restaurant in the hands of his cook to ride out to the Bar K. His duty, he told himself. Uvalde was uneasy and there was no law in town. At least one overnight burglary had already occurred.

"Well, it's the mayor, by golly," Luther answered his own question, spat a steam of brown tobacco juice, patted the skittery colt and sauntered toward the carriage.

Behind him came Eli, leaving the saddle blanket on the back of the nervous black colt.

"Mornin'. What brings you out here, Mayor Heinrich?" Luther wiped his hands on discolored chaps as he closed in on the slow-moving carriage.

"*Guten morgen, Herr* Luther Kerry *und Herr* Eli Kerry," Mayor Heinrich responded and pulled his carriage team to a stop. "I come to talk with *Herr* Cole Kerry. If he *ist* around. We had a bad . . . night in town."

Eli listened to the night's terror with his mouth open. The mayor apologized for the graphic narration of his news. Eli nodded, looking toward the colts. The possibility of vomiting was a swallow away. Luther spat and said Cole was out on the range and wouldn't likely be back until dark or possibly the next day.

"Oh. That *ist* too bad. I vanted to ask him . . . to become town marshal. Ve need him."

Eli's face was a question.

"What about that deputy . . . Logan, ain't it?" Luther drawled.

"Deputy Logan quit and left town."

"Didn't like what he saw, huh," Luther said and spat again.

"Ya. He rode out of town. *Var* fast."

"Where are my manners? Why don't you come inside fer some coffee?" Luther's invitation was warm. If he was surprised by the mayor's purpose it didn't show in his face. "You are welcome to wait for Cole."

"Oh, thank you for coffee. It sounds most *gut*. But I must get back to town after one cup. Much unrest *ist* there, *du* know."

Heinrich drove his carriage to the house, stepped out of the vehicle and tied the two horses to the hitch rack. Eli had already disappeared inside the house. At the doorway, Ethan appeared. No one missed that he held a rifle.

Surprised to see Ethan standing by himself, the mayor wondered if his sight had returned. He glanced at Luther who missed the question in the mayor's expression.

"Well, mornin', Mayor," Ethan said with a forced smile. "Surprised to see you out here. Come in. Hear you want to talk with Cole about taking over as marshal."

Heinrich realized Eli had told his father of his visit. The tall rancher didn't quite look at the restaurant owner as he stepped onto the porch, but his eyelids blinked rapidly as if trying to clear his eyes.

Maggie peeked around Ethan's legs and asked who it was.

"Maggie, this is the mayor of Uvalde, Mr. Heinrich," Ethan said with a smile and introduced the girl to the German restaurant owner.

"So pleased to meet *du, Fraulein* Kerry," Heinrich said and bowed.

Maggie giggled and said, "Why are you here, Mayor Heinrich?"

Ethan rubbed her blonde hair. "He wants to talk with Uncle Cole." He added, "I think the town's heard we're going to start fencing come spring." He chuckled.

Before Heinrich could answer, Luther blurted, "Your pa's spoofin' you. The mayor wants Cole to be the town marshal. Marshal Montgomery was shot last night. Killed those three rustlers before they got him, though."

Maggie's eyes widened and she tugged on her father's shirt sleeve.

"Not now, Maggie." Ethan snorted and backed away, using his hand to help him find the rifle rack. The tall rancher had been quiet this morning and had spent most of it standing outside in the back. Luther wondered if his brother was seeing some again, but didn't ask. When the time came—and Ethan did see for good, if he ever did—his brothers would share in that wonderful news.

From the twins' bedroom, Claire entered the main room, wiping her hands on her apron and greeting their visitor warmly. It always seemed like she was prepared for visitors or anything else. Soon everyone was seated around the table and Claire was serving them coffee along with a plate heaping with freshly baked cookies.

Heinrich related the terrible events of the past night. The Kerrys listened without responding. They made no attempt to send either of their older children away; bad news was a fact of life and they were rarely shielded from such. The twins were still sleeping.

Finally, Luther shifted in his chair and said, "Mighty sorry to hear about Marshal Montgomery. He was a good man."

"Ya, he vas," Heinrich responded and sipped his coffee and tasted one of the cookies. "Ah, this *ist* much *gut, Frau* Kerry. I should be so lucky to have same in *mein* restaurant."

"Montgomery was a good man. A little too nice, maybe, but he was straight up. Killing those rustlers saved the town the cost of a trial and a hanging," Ethan growled. "You say the deputy quit too?" Ethan asked and rolled a cigarette. "Never thought he was cut out for the job."

Eli and Luther took more cookies.

"I am hoping *Herr* Cole Kerry vill take the job. As our marshal," Heinrich said nervously, repeating his earlier statement. "That *ist* vhy I came today." He licked his lips. "As *du* know."

"Well, Cole's out checking our range for more rustlers," Ethan said and put the completed cigarette in his mouth. "Like the ones Montgomery gunned down. May be more trouble coming, Mayor."

Heinrich was fascinated with Ethan's dexterity.

An awkward silence came to the table. Claire broke it by offering Heinrich another cookie and asking if he would like more coffee.

"Oh, that vould be most nice, *Frau* Kerry." He selected a cookie from the offered plate.

"Well, none of us can speak for our brother," Claire said, standing. "But this is a slow time of the year, isn't it, Ethan . . . Luther?" She turned and went to the kitchen for the coffee pot.

Both men realized that was Claire's way of supporting the idea.

"You're right, Claire," Ethan lit his cigarette and grinned. "We'll tell him about it when he gets in. If that's all right with you, Mayor?" He paused and added, "Tell you what. If Cole won't do it, I'll ask John David Sotar, our foreman. He's good with a gun—and smart about it. That way you'll have somebody there until you can get another lawman."

"That *ist* a most fine offer, *Herr* Ethan Kerry," Heinrich responded immediately. "But I hope Cole vill say yes."

"You know, so do I." Ethan smiled and inhaled his cigarette.

CHAPTER 12

Two days later, Cole Kerry rode uneasily into Uvalde, Texas. He wouldn't be coming at all if it weren't for his family's insistence, especially Ethan's.

Uvalde had come to depend on Marshal Montgomery's quiet strength so they needed a strong man to replace him. And quickly. The town was without any law enforcement. At all. Uvalde needed a marshal and Heinrich knew of Cole's reputation with a gun—and the savvy necessary to go with it. Indeed, the whole region knew of his prowess.

Both of his older brothers felt it was important to help the town. So did his friend, Peaches. Cole had finally agreed, but only on a temporary basis until a real peace officer could be hired. Ethan generously insisted that Cole's salary be paid by the Bar K and not with town funds.

How the rustler had gotten a gun was speculation running through the town. The prevalent thought was that another rustler had slipped it to him through the outside window bars. That seemed unlikely to Cole.

November was cold and his long black coat felt good as both his face and his big sorrel's nose were surrounded by breath-smoke. Riding down the main street of Uvalde, he felt every eye was on him from frosty windows, slightly opened doors and the few people scurrying along the sidewalks. What wasn't clear to him was how many were happy he might become the town's peace officer and how many were not.

"Hey, Cole Kerry! You gonna be our marshal?"

The piercing question came from postmistress Wilomina Reid, as she opened the door of the post office. Her face was a spider web of wrinkles and her hair was mostly gray. No one could recall it ever being out of a bun. Her opinions, especially about the town, were frequently sought—and, if they were not, she stated them anyway—loudly and often.

Cole waved and said, "That's up to the council. I'm here."

His trailing smile came easily. His taut face didn't hide his boyish charm or the deep cleft in his chin. Light blue eyes didn't miss much.

"About time that bunch knows what's good when they see it." She grinned, waved and returned to the warmth of the post office.

He smiled. Wilomina was the kind of person good towns had for a foundation.

A cup of coffee at Rinnart Heinrich's Cattleman's Restaurant sounded good. Maybe a donut, if the owner-cook had made any today. That would also give him the opportunity to check with the mayor and see when he could meet with the council. He reined in front of the unpainted building, swung down and flipped his reins over the rack.

"Stand easy, Kiowa."

A tan dog with a long tail wandered out of the alley and greeted him enthusiastically.

"Hey, good to see you, too, bud." He leaned down and scratched the dog's head. The mutt licked his hand and Cole told him to wait.

Entering the warm restaurant, the young gunfighter greeted Rinnart Heinrich, the Prussian-born cook and owner. The Regulator clock in the back of the room was pushing nine o'clock.

"Morning, Mayor!"

"*Guten-morgan* to *du, Herr* Kerry." Heinrich bowed as he delivered plates of hot food to two cowboys. A massive beard and mustache cut low under his nose almost looked like he was wearing fake hair. Heinrich was slump-shouldered and his glasses were thick, but his smile was genuine.

The only other customers were a stranger and a farmer and his wife in town to buy supplies. Cole recognized the farming couple and nodded a greeting.

"Just plain Cole." The young gunfighter smiled. "And I'm looking for a good cup of coffee. Know where I can find one?"

"Ah, come in. Come in." Heinrich turned his back, strutted to the closest open table and pulled away a straight-backed chair. "May I interest *du* in some fresh donuts? Just came from the oven."

"Sounds great. Make it two."

Cole Kerry took off his long coat and laid it over the back of the chair. Mexican spurs sang on the floor. Black broadcloth pants and vest matched a flat-brimmed hat. Across his vest was a silver watch chain that held a Swiss watch with a photograph of Kathleen in the lid. A fresh white shirt covered well his hardened chest and arms. A new paper collar showed off the black string tie and his boots were polished. His attire was Claire Kerry's idea, a proper response to the office he was seeking. His response to her had been that he wasn't seeking it. That didn't change anything. He knew it wouldn't. Claire was harder to refuse than either Luther or Ethan.

Sitting, he adjusted his heavy gunbelt. Light brown hair hung nearly to his shoulders. As was his custom, he withdrew the sidewinder-holstered weapon and laid it in his lap. An old habit.

The bearded cook ignored Cole's offer of informality. "*Herr* Kerry, it *ist* coming up."

Returning with a cup, a coffee pot and a towel draped over his forearm, Heinrich poured the coffee and offered his observation on the new day. As always with him, it was to be a good one. Seconds later, he returned with a plate holding four donuts.

"*Du* need more than two." He smiled and laid the plate in front of Cole.

A series of expectant *hmmm*s accompanied Heinrich's study of Cole eating his first donut.

Cole was quiet for a moment, looked up and grinned. "Best donut I've ever had!"

"Ah, *Herr* Kerry, *du* make me *var* happy! *Danke.*"

Heinrich's eyes twinkled his appreciation for Cole's enjoyment of the donuts. He knew of the youngest Kerry's reputation, riding both sides of the law in Kansas, before returning to his brother's ranch and helping lead a cattle drive to Kansas that saved his ranch. He knew the young man's courage and had seen him save the bank from being robbed. At great personal cost. The escaping Victorio Gee had taken his wife as a hostage.

Cole took a second donut, dunked it in his coffee and bit into it. He wished Kathleen were here to enjoy the treat.

The German mayor glanced again at Cole's heavy gunbelt. "May I ask *du* a question?"

"Of course."

"I hope . . . uh, did *du* come to be . . . our town constable?" Heinrich wiped away an unseen smudge on the table with his towel.

"Well, if you want me, I'll stay on until the town gets a regular lawman," Cole said. "The ranch'll be needing me come spring, though."

Heinrich looked up and his dark eyes locked onto Cole's face. "Ve need *du.*"

"Thank you, Mayor. That's very kind, but I'm not a peace officer. I'm a cattleman."

"*Du* are a man of the gun. Please, no offense."

"Don't know how to react to that statement," Cole said, narrowing his eyes. "I *will* protect my family, my land, my home—and my town. But I'm no gunman."

"Of course. Of course." Heinrich smiled broadly and said he would call for a council meeting this morning at eleven. He glanced at the wall clock as if to confirm his pronouncement. In a whisper, he said one of the saloon owners had been pushing for them to hire his nephew. Supposedly, he had once served as a deputy in some small New Mexico settlement and was currently working in the saloon.

Adjusting his collar, he cleared his throat and explained, "Come to the back room of Saloon No. 6 at eleven. Vill that time be *gut* for *du*?" He rubbed fat fingers lovingly across the table.

"Thank you, Mayor. I'll be there," Cole reached for another donut and remembered the dog outside. "Say, do you have a little stew—or something with meat? There's a tan dog outside that looks like he's in need of a meal. I'll pay for it."

"Ya. That vould be Cooper. He comes around every day or so." Heinrich waved his hand in dismissal. "I vill give him a nice meal. Do not vorry."

"Great."

A few minutes before eleven, Cole Kerry entered the back room of the saloon as directed by the mayor and presented himself to the assembled townsmen, explaining that he would accept the job as town marshal if they wished, until a permanent peace officer could be hired. He didn't feel the need to explain his experience for the job.

Pastor Dinclaur endorsed the proposal. The response from the rest of the councilmen was positive and one of relief. Except for the owner of the saloon where they were meeting. A wolfish-looking man at the far corner of the table, Prem Judleport, took the cigar from his mouth, looked at the long ash and tapped it onto the floor. His nephew was the only other candidate for the post.

"Tell me, Mr. Kerry, is it true you are wanted for murder? In Abilene, Kansas?" Judleport asked, his eyes snapping with agitation.

Pastor Dinclaur blinked and a smile followed for an instant before disappearing into his stony face.

Without hesitation, Cole Kerry explained, in terse sentences, that several years ago he had faced three men intent on killing him. He had killed one of them and wounded the other two. The witnesses had all agreed that it was self-defense. To avoid a lynching party arranged by the influential father of one of the men he had killed, Cole had left town in a hurry

Judleport grinned and returned the cigar to his mouth. "So, a *wanted man* is asking us to hire him as marshal."

"Not exactly," Cole said. "First, if you had checked, you'd find that charge has long been dropped. Second, I didn't ask for this job. I'm here at the request of many in this room. If the council has other plans, I'll be happy to head back to the ranch. There's much to be done there."

Standing in front of the six-man council, Cole looked at each man and asked if there were any more questions. He was trying to keep his anger from showing. He was tempted to leave the room and forget this silliness. He wasn't a lawman and had no intention of becoming one.

Mayor Heinrich held up his hand. "Pardon me, *Herr* Kerry, but I vould like to read something to *mein* friends here. With your permission."

Cole frowned and shrugged his shoulders.

The German restaurant owner pulled a folded telegram from his coat pocket and began to read: " 'TO MAYOR HEINRICH . . . I ENDORSE COLE KERRY FOR UVALDE MARSHAL . . . STOP . . . CHARGE AGAINST HIM DROPPED . . .

STOP . . . SELF DEFENSE AGAINST THREE ARMED MEN . . . STOP . . . RESPECTFULLY . . . ALFRED BASIN, MUNICIPAL JUDGE, ABILENE, KANSAS.' "

When he finished, Heinrich looked up at Cole and said, "Mr. Judleport brought this to *mein* attention and it did not sound . . . right."

"It was a tough time back then." Cole stared at Judleport. "You gentlemen deserve to know Abilene isn't the only trouble I've seen. I was angry about the South losing and still wanted to fight. My guns were for hire. This is not the only man I've killed." He paused. "But they were all armed and facing me."

Several councilmen nodded, including Heinrich.

Dinclaur muttered, "Amen."

A timid-appearing, pinched-faced man, owner of the men's clothing store, held up his hand and asked if Cole had ever been a peace officer before. The question brought a few chuckles.

"Well, Mr. Knudson, yes, I have," Cole said, "after a friend of mine was murdered. He was the marshal in Leavenworth, Kansas. I wore his badge until the murderers were brought to justice. About three months, it seems to me, then I rode on. You can check it."

A loud knock on the door halted the meeting. Hurrying into the room came a thin clerk with a huge Adam's apple that bobbed with every word.

"Big Red's at it again. He's beating up some poor miner at No. 12."

Judleport cocked his head and took the cigar from his mouth. "Maybe you can show us how good a lawman you'll be, Mr. Kerry. Big Red should be arrested for disturbing the peace."

Mayor Heinrich waved his arms. "Vait! Vait! That is *nein* fair, *Herr* Judleport, Big Red *ist*. . . . really, nobody has been . . ."

Cole held up his hand to silence the concerned mayor.

"Seems to me that's why you need a lawman. I'll handle this fella . . . but only as your marshal. Otherwise, I've got things to do at the ranch."

CHAPTER 13

Taking a deep breath, Cole Kerry eased into the smoke-laden No. 12 saloon. On his vest was pinned a marshal's badge. Four customers remained, mesmerized by Big Red Clanahan and the poor man he was beating. The man's face was a bloody mess.

Behind a long bar of uneven planks, a gray-haired bartender looked as if he was going to vomit. Only a fool wouldn't be afraid of facing this large Irishman. Especially when he was drunk and enraged. In the corner table, nursing a free beer, sat Meken Van Camp mildly amused by the scene.

"Let him go, Clanahan," Cole commanded.

Meken looked up, surprised.

The big Irishman turned toward the door, one fist cocked, the other held up the battered man by his shirt.

"I said let him go."

Ignoring the order, Big Red hit the man again with his massive fist.

Cole's own temper was rising. Judlport's attempt to smear him had started it, combined with the fact he didn't really want the job as marshal. Anyway, he'd seen too many bullies, like Webster Stevenson's father. And would-be toughs who thought their sheer size would win any fight. Maybe some would, but Cole grew up defending himself against older brothers and, later, against all manner of dangerous men and those who thought they were. Hard muscle had long been packed into his arms and chest.

He smiled. This would be a time when Ethan would attack. Hit first. The first punch was important. The first punch. Without speaking, Cole headed directly for the Irishman. Big Red released the man and he thudded against the floor.

The bartender shook his head and mumbled.

"You're under arrest, Clanahan. For disturbing the peace and assault," Cole said, closing in on the big Irishman. "Is that your real name . . . Red? Or is it Agnew . . . or Timothy?" He flashed a smile that didn't reach his eyes.

Big Red spun around, cocking his fists. "Jaysus, a foolish man ye be. I be standin' for no arrest. He be calling me a stupid Mick. Asking for such, he were."

Cole's response was to hit him in the stomach with a vicious blow that produced a loud grunt and arched eyebrows.

The four remaining patrons gasped and one started to pray. Meken's eyes widened in appreciation of Cole's aggressiveness.

Wincing in pain and gasping for breath, Clanahan swung a haymaker that Cole avoided easily and slammed a left-handed strike into the Irishman's stomach. Cole knew he had guessed right: Clanahan was a brawler, not a fighter. He was accustomed to his size and reputation dissolving the will of his opponents. But the Irishman was a powerful man; one blow might down the young gunfighter and that could end in his own death or permanent injury.

Cole slid to his right, tattooing the bigger man's face with three lightning-quick jabs. Left. Right. Left. Clanahan's nose and right corner of his mouth were bleeding. Big Red threw a massive roundhouse that Cole managed to stop with his left forearm. The blow sent a vibration through Cole's body. He countered with a right uppercut, thrown with all of his strength, at the Irishman's chin. Clanahan's head snapped backward as if on a hinge. The big Irishman stumbled backward, crashing into one chair and falling over another. He laid there for an instant, then started to get up.

"That's enough, Red. I've had all the fun I want today. Get your hands up."

Cole drew the Colt from his sidewinder holster and pointed it at Clanahan. His own hands were raw and throbbing with pain. One of the scabs of his owl-talon cuts had been knocked off and the cut was bleeding.

Shaking his head, Clanahan staggered to his feet. He felt his chin. "Jaysus, I think ye broke me jaw."

"Sorry. I gave you a choice." The young gunfighter motioned with his gun. "Now march out of here."

Over his shoulder, Cole said, "Get the doctor over here to look at that man. He's hurt bad."

At the same table, Meken swallowed the rest of his beer; his brother would want to know that Cole Kerry had taken the job as marshal—or did he already know? Of course he did. Glory was on the town council.

"Yessir. I will." The bartender said. He shook his head and added, "Nobody's ever done that to Big Red before." He stared at Cole. "Are you the new marshal?"

"I am." Cole nodded and pushed his revolver into the staggering Irishman's back. "Come on, Clanahan. You know where the jail is."

"I be goin', sir. Ye be packin' a hard punch." Clanahan's shoulders rose and fell and repeated, "I dinna be startin' it. He be callin' me a stupid Mick."

"You said that. Doesn't give you the right to kill him. You're a good man. You need something to do and I've got an idea."

"A job I be needin' . . . sir."

"You're going to have one. The jail needs cleaning."

"My real name be Michael O'Reilly Clanahan."

"Nice to meet you, Michael O'Reilly Clanahan."

"Folks be callin' me Big Red an' that's all right, if they be nice about it."

"I know."

They walked down the planked street, talking quietly. Townspeople stopped to stare. At the jail, Mayor Heinrich was waiting.

The German restaurant owner smiled, nodded and held out his hand. "It *ist* a *gut* day for Uvalde, Marshal Kerry."

"Well, thank you, Mayor," Cole said. "Big Red's going to work off his sentence. He's going to clean up the jail."

Biting his lower lip, Heinrich shrugged his shoulders. "Whatever *du* think *ist* best. No one has been in the jail since . . ."

"I know."

"Any time *du vant* some supper, it *veel* be ready."

"Thanks. Michael and I will be over in a little while."

"Michael?"

It was Cole's turn to smile. "Mayor, I'd like to introduce you to Michael O'Reilly Clanahan. Sometimes known as 'Big Red.' "

Shyly, the big Irishman held out a large hand and the mayor accepted it. Cole told him that he was returning to the ranch tonight to get some clothes and other personal things. He intended to take a room in the hotel and stay there unless something came up at the ranch. The town needed a full-time lawman and he was ready to be that.

"I'm going to need a deputy."

"Ya. Some be thinking *du* might hire Mr. Judleport's nephew." It appeared difficult for Heinrich to vocalize the statement.

"Tell them thanks, but no thanks. I've got my deputy." Cole slapped Clanahan on the back. "If he'll take the job . . . Deputy Michael O'Reilly Clanahan." He added, "Bar K will pay his salary."

Neither Clanahan nor Heinrich knew how to respond. The

big Irishman spoke first in Irish, then in excited English. "I-I b-be m-most proud. Me mithur, she would be proud. Bless her sweet soul. On her grave, I give ye me word . . . I will be a good deputy for . . . Uvalde."

Heinrich wasn't sure what to say, but managed to nod.

From down the street came Pastor Dinclaur, noting the activity at the jail. He hurried to the small gathering and said, "Good to see you already at work, Marshal. Uvalde is in good hands." He acknowledged the mayor and met Clanahan. "Marshal, are you staying the night in town?" Dinclaur asked. "I'm sure arrangements can be made at the hotel."

"No, I'm going home. I'll be back tomorrow," Cole responded. "But I'll see what they can do for me at the hotel before I go. On a regular basis. 'Til you boys get a real lawman."

"Oh sure," Dinclaur said. "Well, I've got to be going. I'm needed at a prayer *meeting.*"

"Of course. Before you go, I need your vote. Or rather the mayor does," Cole said.

After explaining the situation and getting Dinclaur's approval, Heinrich promised to get the rest of the council's approval. Both men hurried away while Cole and Clanahan entered the jail. The floor carried dried stains of blood where Marshal Montgomery had been shot and where the rustlers were killed. Dust covered the desk and lay across a cold pot belly stove.

"All right, Deputy Clanahan. You're in charge of cleaning up this place," Cole announced. "I'm riding back to the ranch. I'll be back tomorrow. Probably midday."

"The place will be clean when ye return."

Cole laid his hand on the bigger man's shoulder. "I'm counting on it. Wouldn't want my first decision as marshal to be a bad one. Your pay will be thirty a month and meals when you're on duty."

The big man's face finally voiced the question. "Do I get to wear a badge?"

"Of course."

The Irishman grinned. "Me mithur would be proud, she would. Bless her sweet soul."

"Raise your right hand and repeat after me."

CHAPTER 14

It was late afternoon when Cole Kerry left town. Lamps from Uvalde disappeared as he rode into the darkness. The road to the Bar K led through broken hills, laced with mesquite, arroyos and little water. During the day, the road was well traveled. Now it was empty. Except for an old mossyback longhorn wandering across the road in front of him, as wild as the rest of the creatures inhabiting this stretch of unworkable country.

Cole took a deep breath and let a thick white puff of frosty air escape from his mouth. He wasn't certain if he should feel happy or put upon. Either way, he was now the town marshal. With the agreement that he wouldn't have the responsiblity for more than six months. Hopefully, it would be shorter.

As promised, Mayor Heinrich had secured Clanahan's appointment as deputy with the understanding that it was a temporary appointment to be guided by his performance. Cole had left him in charge of the jail. The Irishman was excited about the opportunity and was hard at work washing the floors when Cole left.

"Nobody's going to mess with him," Cole chuckled to himself.

Kiowa's ears twitched in the direction of his statement to determine if it was a command of some kind.

"Sorry, Kiowa, I was just jabbering." He patted the sorrel's neck, then turned up his collar against the cold.

The jail break and the subsequent killing of Marshal Montgomery lay heavy on his mind. "Never saw Montgomery use two guns before. Never saw him even carry two. Why then?" He asked himself and answered, "Maybe he added a backup because he was guarding rustlers.

"Maybe. But why did he kill those other two when they weren't armed? For that matter, why weren't they?" He glanced ahead at the dark hillside and the trees sprouting from the elevation.

He tugged on his hat brim. "Who knows? Gunfights don't happen in set patterns. Probably didn't take the time to see who was carrying and who wasn't. I wouldn't."

Cole cocked his head to the side. "How'd that one bastard get a gun? I know damn well they weren't carrying when we brought them in."

His voice was barely heard over the clop-clop of his horse. Night completely controlled the land now. "Somebody slipped it to him. A visitor. Or through the window bars."

Shaking his head, he continued reviewing the situation. "Wouldn't Montgomery be watching any visitor that came to the jail? He wouldn't let anybody close without checking first. And it wouldn't be easy to slip a gun through the outside window bars. At least not without making noise.

"Could be done, though. Especially when it was dark." Cole rolled his shoulders. "Maybe one of them sang to cover any noise.

"That many gunshots would've drawn attention. A damn war inside that jail." He shook his head. "Why didn't anyone hear and come to see?"

He shifted his weight in the saddle and leaned forward. "I remember one time we sneaked up on that Yank patrol and took them out. Ethan had us wrap our guns with our jackets. So the rest of those Yanks wouldn't hear us firing."

Cole looked up at the thin sliver of a moon. "If that's what happened. It wasn't a jail break. It was somebody afraid of what those boys might say."

He rode for several minutes without talking to himself.

As he rode, Cole described a possible scenario to himself, with Montgomery being surprised and shot first, then the rustlers killed, and the guns left after everyone was dead.

"Does that mean it was somebody from town?" Cole asked as he watched an owl begin a journey for its evening meal, sweeping silently over the uneven land. "Well, it definitely had to be somebody the late marshal knew—and trusted. He wouldn't open that door at night. Not for strangers." He made a fist of his gloved right hand to bring warmth. "Nobody saw anybody coming or going. Nobody who wants to talk anyway," he continued and added, "Damn, it's getting cold. Gonna put on my slicker."

As he turned to reach the rolled-up slicker, a gun flashed from the highest point of the parallel hillside. Moonlight danced off a rifle barrel.

He felt a sharp concussion against his head and his hat went flying. That was followed instantly by more shots. The impact of the bullet jerked the gunfighter from the saddle and the big sorrel galloped wildly into the night. With five more shots trailing him, he hit the ground hard and it stunned him. Realizing the grave danger he was in, he had the presence of mind to roll to the right where the land broke off sharply from the road. A thin waterfall dropped straight down fifteen feet. He slid down the steep, smooth rocks, guided by the water.

Cole Kerry hit the shallow pool of water and lay there.

CHAPTER 15

Cole Kerry's head was thick with pain. And fear. Whoever shot at him would be coming to finish the job. He must move. He must. If he remained where he was, he would be shot to pieces. His head was spinning from the bullet that grazed his head—and from his falls, first from his horse and then down the watery slope.

Moving to get his slicker had saved his life for the moment, but he had to move. Had to move. Had to move. Everything in him screamed as he forced himself to his hands and knees. His clothes were soaked and torn. Breath wouldn't come fast enough. Like a wild animal, he managed to crawl away from the water and into the surrounding brush. His head ached and so did his left shoulder from landing on it. His left hip was bleeding from the second bullet. A long scratch cut across his right cheek where a sharp rock had caught his face on the way down. Along the left side of his head was a bullet burn. It had been that close.

He sat up, leaning against a moss-draped elm tree within a tight cluster of saplings and older trees drawn to the water. His guns were still in place and only the Colt carried on his hip had been in the water. He slipped the loop from the hammer of his sidewinder-holstered Colt and drew it. The motion made him dizzy. For a moment, he thought he was going to vomit.

From where he sat, Cole could see the trail above. He could also see the only approach down the slope. Pulling away his waistband, he yanked up the blood-soaked tail of his shirt to look at the wound on his hip. Just a cut of flesh, but it would bleed heavily. He shifted the Colt to his left hand and pressed against the bleeding area with two fingers of his right. The wound wasn't deep, but the steady loss of blood could be severe if he couldn't stop it.

Everything in him wanted to sleep. Just for a few minutes. But to sleep was to die. His body was rushing to heal the impact of his two falls and his wounds. Most likely, he was suffering from a concussion. And he was soaking wet.

Think.

That's what Ethan had drilled into him. Think through a situation. Panic was for others. Fear was a normal reaction. Without it, a man was likely to make a foolish mistake. But fear had to be controlled so a man could think—and then act. The shooter would be coming to make certain. He had to assume that. He could stay quiet and hope the man assumed success—or wait until he fired again and try to return it. Or he could spray the hillside above him to tell the gunman that he was alive.

Yes.

He could hear the crunch of approaching boots above. It sounded like two men. Likely they wouldn't know exactly where Cole had fallen and would need to look over the edge. When the crunching sounds stopped, he pointed his Colt toward the dim ridge. He sprayed four bullets along the ridge, not expecting to hit the ambushers, just make them wary of advancing. Checking on a possible dead man was one thing; trying to get another shot at a wounded man who was ready to shoot back was something else.

As soon as he fired, Cole forced himself to move again. This time to a rock outcropping that looked like giant molars twenty feet farther west. Time had cut out a hollow against the slope where once another boulder had stood. The rock shelf would protect him somewhat from any return firing and make it harder for the ambusher to locate him.

Settling into the hollow, he listened for any more sounds of movement above while he reloaded. His hand shook slightly. A cartridge slipped from his hands and pinged off a rock. He covered his mouth with his hand to diffuse the breath smoke as he exhaled. Probably it wasn't visible from any distance, but this wasn't the time to gamble.

Sounds of boots scraped the ground above where he had fallen, followed by a soft curse.

Had he actually hit one of the gunmen? Not likely, but possible. He considered shooting again, but realized it was foolish and would only alert them to his new position. His point had been made. He would wait. If the gunmen had nerve, they would descend and try to finish the job. But they also might leave. It would be obvious that any chance of surprise was gone. Equally obvious would be the realization that their would-be target wasn't hurt badly.

From above came the roar of two rifles spraying the pool and the land where Cole had been a minute before. Faint outlines of the two men were fleetingly highlighted by the orange flames of their guns. Both weapons finally clicked on empty. He couldn't distinguish any details of the two and it was again dark.

Cole couldn't resist. The bastards had tried to kill him. On his knees, he leaned away from the hollow and fired at the silhouettes, holding his Colt with both hands to hold down the shaking. After firing, he ducked back into the hollow.

More cursing followed, but no more shots.

After a few minutes, Cole heard the faint sounds of a horse trotting away. He waited. It might be a trick, although there was no way he was going to try scaling the hillside. At least not tonight. His body was aching all over and his eyesight was blurry. He thought the bullet wound at his hip had stopped bleeding.

He shut his eyes and the gun slid from his hand.

Suddenly, he jerked awake. Behind him were the soft sounds of a horse walking toward him. The gunmen *had* circled back. Trying to be quiet, he eased himself around to face the oncoming threat and retrieved his fallen gun. The dark shape was close enough now that he could see the shape of the animal itself and breath-smoke filling its face.

Wait!

It was Kiowa. Kiowa!

The big sorrel had returned to find his master. Just as he had when Cole was ambushed chasing the Victorio Gee gang. Kiowa was loyal to him, like he was to no other. In many ways, rider and horse were alike. Warriors. Lone warriors.

"Over here, boy. Over here." Cole tried to stand, pushing against the ground. He fell, then grabbed a large rock and inched himself upright, using it for balance.

Kiowa's ears snapped to attention and he began to trot toward the injured gunfighter. One rein dragged on the ground; the other had been stepped on and snapped off. Nearing him, the big sorrel nuzzled against Cole and he returned the greeting by patting his nose.

"Not sure I can get on without finding something to stand on, Kiowa."

False dawn was teasing the land when Cole Kerry reached the Bar K ranch. No lamps within the ranch house windows welcomed him. Both horse and rider were relieved to be back. Ethan and Claire had chosen well. The location of the ranch house itself was sound defensively; no one could move against it without exposing himself to rifle fire from the house.

Cole took a deep breath and let a thick white puff of frosty breath escape from his mouth. He had tied the long rein to the short one and created one combined control. His body was so stiff he wasn't certain he could dismount without falling down. Several times during the night he had fallen asleep and Kiowa's steady walking had awakened him before he fell off.

As he cleared the overhead crosspiece above the entrance gate, his gaze took in the Bar K–branded longhorn skull centered on the split log. In the heavy morning light, it seemed illuminated. There were strong memories here, many he hadn't been involved in. To Cole's left was the long low bunkhouse; two pairs of socks, a shirt and long underwear hung over a rope tied between two young trees. He rode up to the barn and swung down, standing against the sorrel to steady his balance.

Only a handful of horses were kept shod and in the main barn for work. A black horse with a white face whinnied its welcome. Jake was the horse Ethan always rode, at least since he had lost his sight.

Cole's hip was bleeding again, although not as much as earlier. Every bone in his body ached from the falls, but he didn't think anything was broken. His head screamed for sleep. His tired mind reworked the ambush. Had the shooter simply been a stranger seeking a quick kill for what money he carried? If not, why was he targeted? He couldn't force himself to follow that question with more analysis. Not now.

Three quick barks were followed by Blue's appearance from the darkness.

"Hey, Blue. Good to see you, too," Cole said and leaned over to greet the beast. "Guess everybody else is sleeping, huh?"

After unsaddling Kiowa and giving him water and grain, Cole moved slowly toward the ranch house. Blue tagged along. Each step brought a new ache and he fought the dizziness.

From the porch came a voice like no other. Ethan's.

"Hey, glad you're back. How did it go?" he asked, sitting

alone in a rocking chair on the porch. "Thought you'd be home earlier."

Lately, he had taken to sitting on the porch at night. Only Claire knew if it was related to his returning sight or not. Cole could barely see his dark silhouette against the house. How like his brother to be waiting for him. Perhaps a little worried. Cole figured his brother had found his way by himself. That would be like Ethan, too.

"Well, your brother's a lawman." He held the pinned badge away from his vest. "And I got ambushed on my way home. Great way to start the job."

"You got ambushed? Damn, are you hurt?"

"A little."

Ethan stepped back into the house, using the door frame as a guide, and yelled, "Claire! Luther! Cole's back—and he's been shot!"

Minutes later, the wounded gunfighter was in his bed with Claire and Luther, wearing only longjohns, tending to his wounds. Eli and Maggie stood next to their father. The teenage boy was silent, studying his beloved uncle. Maggie was asking questions as fast as they occurred to her. Ethan didn't know answers to any of her questions and said so. From the other room, both twins began to cry.

"Eli, go check on the twins. Please," Claire said, looking up. "I'll be in shortly."

Dragging his feet, Eli turned and left the room.

Cole put his hand on hers. "Claire, go to them. I'm fine. Just a little weak."

"You've lost a lot of blood, Cole." She patted his hand with her hand and continued wiping away the dried blood from his hip. "You were lucky. A fraction more . . ."

"I know. But I'm all right. Just tired."

Luther's face was dark, a mixture of anger and alarm.

"Can you tell us what happened, Cole?" Ethan asked.

After a deep breath, Cole described the events in town and then the ambush. Eli returned to the bedroom, carrying both Will and Russ. Both wanted down to see their uncle. Claire turned them away, saying they could see him later.

"No. No. I'd like to see them. Please," Cole said, trying to sit up, and failing.

Luther lifted the two youngsters onto the bed and they crawled next to Cole, patting him and laughing.

Cole grimaced, then tried to grin. "That makes it all better."

Claire laughed and pulled Will, then Russ, from Cole and onto the floor. "How about we find some breakfast."

"Yay, break-fast! Pan-cakes. Pan-cakes." Both began to recite.

Claire led them out of the room, telling Eli and Maggie to join them.

"Seems like I've been gone a long time. How's everything?" Cole asked.

"Everything's good." Ethan said and rolled a cigarette. "We've got riders patrolling all of our range."

The blind rancher gave him a detailed rundown of the ranch's activities. This was the slow time of the year. Even so there was work that needed doing. So far, they had been blessed with little bad weather and no snow. They were ready for both, if that was possible. Cole folded his arms; no one could be more prepared than Ethan. Of that he was certain. He reminded himself that he and Luther had probably cut enough wood for the winter. If not, they could cut more or buy some from one of their neighbors. He was tired. Very tired.

"Just got another milk cow from the Johnsons," Luther said and straightened the blanket around his youngest brother. "Little Will wants to call it 'Milky.' Russ said it should be named 'Kiowa.' Figures, huh?" He became lost in a thought of his own, then added, "Never seen two young'uns get so worked up about getting another milker. They are somethin'."

He excused himself and went to the stone fireplace out in the main room, banked for the night with its belly of coals whispering to each other. Adding two new logs, latent embers responded to his nudging and soon flames sprang to life and warmth began to take renewed control of the room.

In the bedroom, Ethan glanced toward the kitchen. "Hey, how'd you think Eli did on the roundup?"

"Like he was born to it. He'll be pushing all of us, you watch," Cole answered, taking a deep breath. "After I sleep a little, I've got something I want to talk with you about," he continued. "It's about Montgomery and that attempted jail break."

Ethan took a long pull on his completed cigarette. "You don't think it was a jail break."

"How'd you guess?"

"Been chewing on the same idea."

"Figures," Cole said and shifted his weight in the bed. "Uh . . . I've got to get back to town. They're expecting a marshal."

"You aren't going anywhere for a few days," Ethan growled.

Cole Kerry was asleep.

Chapter 16

Dawn was in full control when Dinclaur returned to the Rocking R, after dropping off his younger brother the day before. A day had passed since their ill-fated ambush of Cole Kerry. His stomach burn was an ever-present reminder of a very close call.

Meken would eventually return to Uvalde, whenever a wagon was headed that way. His frequent absences went unnoticed by townspeople. Most preferred to ignore him and hoped the disreputable man would simply go away. Like his brother, Meken was nursing a bullet burn across his right forearm, thanks to Cole Kerry.

Both had misjudged the ability of Kerry and should have known better than to try closing in on him. Kerry was too good to be given any kind of a chance. To each other, they excused the failure, believing no one could have survived a shot to the head.

Yesterday Dinclaur spent visiting area ranches, then dropping by the Bar K. There, he learned that Cole Kerry had been shot, but not badly enough; his surprised reaction at the news was among his best performances. He had expressed his concern. He had been checking with "the faithful" around the area and hadn't heard. But the young gunfighter would be up and around in a week or so, according to the other Kerrys. Disappointed, Dinclaur had spent the night, sleeping in his carriage, midway between ranches.

"Aye, an' a guid mornin' tae ye, Reverend. Ye're a sicht fir the eyes. How be ever'thin' out an' about?"

The greeting came from the hatless, fat-jowled Scotsman in mule-ear boots and a half-opened shirt, Dinclaur's stepfather. Within his stretched waistband was a Smith & Wesson revolver. Heredith Tiorgs was the owner of the Rocking R and his Scottish heritage was evident on most days. Dinclaur counted on Tiorgs to provide pressure on the Bar K until the transference was accomplished. Dinclaur hadn't decided if he was going to let Tiorgs live after that or not. Eighteen other men were on the ranch now. All were gunmen. All recruited by Tiorgs, but they could be bought, he was certain.

"Good day to you, Heredith. How's the ranch? Where's Meken? Any trouble from the Kerrys?"

"Nah, dinna bin seein' any of thaim bastirds," Tiorgs rubbed his chest. "Oh, I daursay it be guid enough herd we be havin'; but we dinna have thae youngsters we be needin'." He looked around. "Meken, he went tae town. Yesterday. Wilson went for supplies an' Meken went with 'im."

"Jinette arrive yet?"

"Naw. 'Twill be guid tae see me daughter again. She be a pretty one, ya know."

"Hadn't noticed."

Dinclaur climbed down from the carriage, letting his cramped legs feel the solidness. He was certain the Scotsman had no idea of the relationship between himself and Jinette. If he did, there would be gun trouble between them. The old Scotsman had few good qualities, but the love of his only daughter was one of them.

"I'm hungry. How about some breakfast?" Dinclaur asked.

"Aye. Aye. An' a muckle o' fresh eggs we haff," Tiorgs's face showed he was glad to be talking about something else. "Got a wee whiskey tae be sharin' too."

"Good." Dinclaur growled and pointed at the corral.

"Where'd that gray come from?"

Tiorgs grinned. "Weel, got himself just yesterday. Traded a guid nuff bay for hisself. Hellva guid hoss. Doesna he look so?"

"I'm surprised at you, Heredith. Grays are unlucky. You know that. Get it out of here," Dinclaur said and continued toward the house.

Tiorgs was stunned. "Hauld a wee, Glory. Wad ye be wullin' tae listen tae a wee thought I be havin'?"

"Get rid if it. Now . . . now!" Dinclaur waved his hand and went inside.

Minutes later, he heard a gunshot, then another.

Nothing more was said about the matter. After eating Tiorgs's cooked breakfast of eggs, raw-fried potatoes and coffee, Dinclaur checked on the burn across his stomach. The bullet wound was raw and red, but not infected. He applied some salve kept in his carrying bag and sat down at his table. A little whiskey would be nice and the lanky Scotsman anticipated his thought and brought him a glass half-full of whiskey.

"Weel, come this spring we weel be needin' tae sell beeves," Tiorgs said, almost wincing. "A muckle o' money we be needin'. These gunslicks do not be comin' cheap, you know."

"Yeah, I know. A lot can happen in a few months." The white-haired minister downed most of the drink and told him to leave Bar K cattle alone for now. There would be plenty of time for that later.

"Aye, that it can."

With that, Tiorgs excused himself with a Scottish expression Dinclaur didn't understand and went outside.

Dinclaur was pouring more whiskey when he heard a knock at his back door and yelled, "Coming."

He shoved the whiskey bottle and glass into a cabinet in the tiny kitchen and headed for the back door. His sour expression turned into a giant smile. Standing at the door was Jinette Six and she was smiling back.

"Well, Jinette. Good to see you. I was wondering when you'd get here," Dinclaur said, opening the door. "Want some breakfast?"

"Already ate. Hope you got some whiskey, though. Good whiskey. It's been a damn long ride. Where's my old man?"

"He's around. Just went outside."

"That's too bad. I was hoping we could get reacquainted, brother dear." Her eyes sparkled.

Jinette Six stepped into the kitchen. She was a stunning woman by any measure. Long dark hair caressed her shoulders. Large violet eyes studied her half-brother and the room. A simple dress barely hid an exceptional figure. The only thing that looked out of place was a large purse. In it, Dinclaur knew, was a Colt Lightning and there was a special holster attached to her lower leg that carried a derringer.

They kissed for a long time.

"How would you like owning this part of Texas?"

"Just tell me who I have to kill."

Dinclaur laughed.

CHAPTER 17

Awakening, Cole Kerry pulled on his pants and boots and shoved a Colt into his waistband. He walked into the quiet main room and saw the stone fireplace had succumbed to the night and its belly held only a gray stillness. Should he start a morning fire? He wanted to be up, considered it for a moment and decided the new warmth would be nice for the others to enjoy when they awoke.

Cole concentrated on the fire, adding two new logs. Gray embers responded to his nudging and soon flames sprang to life and warmth began to spread. He added one more log for the morning. No one else was up yet. Had he slept through the day and night? He had to get to town and assume his job as marshal. Assuring himself of his readiness, he touched his forehead where the bullet had passed. It was sore. So was his hip. He was weak, but feeling much better. His right hand had been covered with Claire's ever-ready ointment and the claw marks, even the scab that popped open, were nearly healed.

The young gunfighter stepped outside. Evidently Ethan hadn't needed to sit on the porch. Diamonds of dew were spread throughout the land. Only the first brushes of rose and yellow touched the horizon. Breath-smoke hovered around his face as he slid into friendly shadows. He studied the land for glimpses of unwanted company. It was clear someone wanted him dead. Methodically, his vision examined the swells of land around the ranch, looking for a sense of movement, a shadow that shouldn't be there or the glint of metal. His mind jumped to alertness; no one could move against the ranch without exposing himself to rifle fire from the house and the bunkhouse. Of course, a sharpshooter wouldn't attempt anything so foolish; he would fire from long range.

Cole took a deep breath and let a thick white puff of frosty breath escape from his mouth. Patience had been a learned skill; impatient men died young. The only movements were from the horses Luther still had in the corral. Kiowa and Ethan's black horse were now among them. He guessed Luther had turned Kiowa out last night instead of leaving the sorrel in the barn. That was so like his brother.

He strolled counter-clockwise around the house to eliminate any blind spots in his vigilance. In spite of that readiness, a faint smile sought his tanned face as he recalled Maggie reminding them of the need to plant corn. He shook his head. Neither he nor Luther had ever planted anything. But they would learn. Maybe one of the neighbors could give them some tips. Funny, he couldn't remember thinking in terms of seeking help from others. Keeping to the uneven shadows, he moved around the perimeter, ever alert.

For the first time, he realized his mind had been free of sadness about Kathleen. She was there. Always there. But somehow the gut-wrenching ache had dulled. He wasn't sure why. Even the new ranch rooster, young and full of strut, had not yet welcomed the day; the proud bird and six hens occupied the ranch, thanks to the purchase from their farm neighbors, Wesley and Virginia Johnson. Maggie had taken charge of feeding the new arrivals. He recalled Luther telling him that the Johnsons had also parted with a black-and-white milk cow and it was becoming comfortable with its home in the barn. Eli had been assigned the task for caring for the animal and the milking.

This was the way life should be, Cole thought, as he paused

to study a gray hillside. His mind danced away from the examination of his questions. Was he meant to be a lawman? Who wanted him dead? Why? The attempt had to be connected to the Rocking R and the recent rustling. Yet the owner there had been convincing in his claim of innocence.

The early morning silence gave him time to think. Whoever killed Marshal Montgomery and the jailed rustlers had to be the same men trying to kill him. Nothing else made any sense. With that, he circled the house, came to the corral and acknowledged Kiowa's welcoming whinny.

"After breakfast, we'll head for town. They'll be wondering what happened to their marshal," he said. "You saved my life, you know." He stroked the nose and face of the sorrel, who stood quietly next to the railing. The horse whinnied softly and lowered his head.

The sun had not yet topped the land, but the brightening glow signaled momentary arrival when he heard footsteps behind him and turned around.

"Well, good mornin', Cole," Luther declared, walking toward him in his usual bowlegged sway. "Mighty glad to see you up an' around." Walking beside him was Ethan, holding onto Luther's arm for direction.

"Yeah, I didn't mean to sleep that long. Guess I slept through the day an' night."

Luther stopped and chuckled.

Ethan growled, "Try again, little brother. You've been mostly sleeping fer a week. Only woke up when one of us fed you something."

"A week? Can't be." He stared at his brothers.

With Ethan still holding his arm, Luther strolled next to Cole and Kiowa and said, "Can be—an' is. Ethan sent John David to town to act in your stead. He's to tell them what happened."

135

He spat a long stream of tobacco juice. "Have you seen our new rooster?"

Stepping away from the corral, Cole's one-word response to himself was so soft it was almost a whisper. "Haven't."

"Ever since we got him, I ain't been havin' any more nightmares about roosters," Luther folded his arms and spat again. "Ain't that something?"

"Yeah." Cole shook his head to clear it; his older brother complained about nightmares where a giant rooster chased him. His mind was stuck on the length of his recovery. A week? No wonder he felt stronger.

Ethan called for his horse and Jake came whinnying over to greet him.

"Hey, Pa! Uncle Cole! Uncle Luther! Breakfast is on!"

Cole was jolted from his thinking by Eli's warm greeting as he hurried toward them.

"Well, good morning, Eli. It's good to see you," Cole said and slapped the teenager on his back.

"Ma told me you were up. I'm mighty glad. I—I . . . was w-worried."

In many ways, the youngster reminded him of Ethan, but his face was Claire's. Together, the four Kerrys returned to the house and its warmth. Ethan, Luther and Eli went to the table and Cole stood in the middle of the room, taking in the comfort and caring of the entire house.

Pine floors were already freshly swept. The house had the feel of a woman's care. The stone fireplace was dominant with its happy fire. A large brown sofa was centered in front of the fireplace in the living room, along with a table flanked with four unmatched wooden chairs. In the center of the table was a white circular tablecloth trimmed with lace. A blue flower vase sat in its middle filled with carefully dried wild flowers, saved from the autumn. Off to the side was a small room where

Ethan's work desk stood.

A cast-iron stove ruled the kitchen. A large standing pantry contained white ironstone plates, heavy iron tableware, pots, pans, two buckets, a large copper double boiler, and a dozen empty canning jars. On its open, flat area was a large china water basin and a second lamp.

Framed pictures of family set atop a cabinet in the corner, along with a coal-oil lamp. One picture was of the Kerrys when the brothers were just boys. His gaze lingered on the cabinet photographs, especially the one from their childhood. Long-ago swirls of memory followed. He recalled his mother proudly taking them to the photographer's studio. His mother and father stared back at him, smiling stiffly. As he recalled, their father was sober that day, at least until the photograph was taken. Luther looked the same as he did now, only much younger, and smiling awkwardly. Ethan was handsome and smiling confidently. A young Cole was looking at Ethan.

For a moment, an old memory rolled through him. Once more he was outside of school and four older boys were shoving and pushing him. He was alone. Gritting his teeth, eight-year-old Cole Kerry ran at the tallest kid, knocked him to the ground and hit him with both fists. The other three were stunned by his attack, then jumped on Cole and began pounding him. He could still hear Luther and Ethan yelling and pulling each older boy off of him, and both older Kerrys slamming each one with their fists. Minutes later, the four bullies were running away, crying. The three Kerry brothers were laughing and hugging. Never again did the four bullies come near Cole.

Those pictures haunted him when he stared, but still he couldn't resist. The years that followed hardened the young man and eventually earned him the reputation as a dangerous man. He wasn't certain it was a reputation he wanted. Kathleen hoped he would put away his guns and become a serious cattleman like Ethan. Now he wasn't certain that would happen.

Will and Russ waddled over to him from their own exploration and held up their arms to be carried. Cole lifted both and spun around with them, bringing joyous laughter to the twins. Claire peeked at them from the kitchen and smiled.

"Hot cakes are ready, boys," she said.

"Sounds good to me. How 'bout you two?" Cole said and laughed. It felt good.

During breakfast, described by Maggie as "better than yesterday's," Claire told Cole that Reverend Dinclaur had come by almost a week ago, was surprised and concerned to learn of the shooting and said to give you his best wishes.

"That was nice of him. Say, I hear Sotar's handling marshal duties," Cole said, sipping coffee. "Imagine the town was talking about that."

Ethan laughed. "Yeah. Figured they needed a little wake-up. Haven't heard anything since they left. Guess Uvalde is getting along with a Missouri boy—and that Irishman you've got as a deputy."

"Not sure they'd have any choice with those two," Cole said. "I appreciate your doing that."

"They aren't you, Cole, but no one will mess with the town," Ethan rubbed his chin.

Ethan and Luther laughed. Filling coffee cups, Claire frowned and scolded her husband to remember the children were at the table.

But it was Luther who apologized. "Hard tellin' what a town will take to. Most folks just don't want be bothered," Luther said, red-faced. "I reckon if their lives ain't changed by having those boys in charge, they'll find a way to think it's passable."

"Except when it comes to folks of color," Luther added, obviously not noticing Claire's renewed frown. "They draw the line there, I reckon. Guess they don't know DuMonte."

Chuckling, Cole took a bite of pancake and realized he wanted to be the town's marshal. A strange sensation pushed away the aches of losing Kathleen and the lingering pains of the ambush. He wanted to find the man who had tried to kill him. He must . . . before his luck ran out.

Eli told him about the current condition of their range. Nothing had changed since Cole and the others had made a swing around their land. Or so Sotar had reported before leaving for town.

Taking advantage of the following silence, Luther was eager to tell about a new bay colt he'd been working with; Maggie had decided it should be named "Socks," because the young horse had three white stockinged legs. Russ and Will wanted Cole's attention and Eli wanted permission to ride with "Preacher" DuMonte to check the range again. Ethan approved, if DuMonte was agreeable, and told his oldest son to take the buckskin. Claire told him to take his coat. Smiling from ear to ear, Eli left.

Looking up from her plate, Maggie asked, "Have you seen Milky—and our new chickens, Uncle Cole?"

Cole smiled. "Heard about them, Maggie. Hope to see them after breakfast."

"Aren't you going back to bed, Uncle Cole?"

He chuckled. "Well, no. Think I'd better be headed for town. I'm their new marshal, you know."

"Mom thinks you should rest more. Should you?"

Claire looked embarrassed as Ethan and Luther laughed.

Maggie's face was mostly a frown. "Do I ask too many questions, Uncle Cole?"

"Of course not, Maggie. You are a very smart young lady. You can always ask me anything." He glanced at Ethan. "Of course, I probably won't know the answer." Cole reached for his coffee cup. "And I appreciate your mother's concern about me. But

139

I'm feeling fine."

"Why did those men shoot at you, Uncle Cole?" Maggie asked, leaning forward with her elbows on the table. "Who are they? Did you say something to make them mad?"

"Those are very good questions, Maggie." Cole licked his lower lip. "Like I said, I don't know any of those answers."

"That's enough, Maggie." Claire's voice was stern as she returned to the kitchen. "Come and help me. Now, please."

Rubbing his finger around the edge of his coffee cup, Ethan said, "Speaking of questions. Sounds like we've got enough grub to last the winter—an' then some. That right?"

"Well, I think we're going to need a few things. Maybe Cole can bring them from town." Claire answered as she guided Maggie toward the kitchen.

Cole glanced at Ethan, then said, "Well, I plan on staying." He explained that he had decided to take a room at the hotel while he was the town's constable. They deserved a full-time lawman, he said.

"But if you give me a list, though, I'll see that John David brings the goods back with him."

Claire's face showed surprise at Cole's intention to stay in town. She worried about Ethan's younger brother; he was a good man, but a little more wild. And he had just lost the woman of his life. In such a state, Cole Kerry might be inclined to be reckless. Someone wanted him dead and no one knew who or why.

"No, no need. I'm sure we'll want to take a trip to town when we get closer to Thanksgiving."

President Lincoln had declared Thanksgiving as a national day of giving thanks in 1863, just after the Union had won at Vicksburg and Gettysburg. In spite of its Union history, the Kerrys had celebrated the holiday with gusto, inviting all their hands and neighbors to a joyful feast.

"Sure."

"And we'll need your help, too, Cole—if the town can spare you." Claire smiled.

Ethan gave voice to her real concerns. He pushed his chair away from the table. His low growl belied his own worry.

"Remember, little brother. There's some sonuvabitches out there who want you dead. Being lucky has its limits. You've been lucky. Once." He looked away as if seeing something no one else did. "And they're the ones who shot up the jail. Count on it. Find them and you've got your shooters, Cole. Unless they find you again . . . first."

His head swung back toward his younger brother. "And the bastards have something to do with the Rocking R."

Cole had the distinct impression that Ethan saw him.

CHAPTER 18

Cole Kerry rode slowly along the road that had brought bullets at him. His rifle lay across his saddle in readiness. It was silly, he told himself, there was no way the ambushers remained. Still, it was wise to be prepared. Ethan's words echoed in his head.

Maybe he could learn something about his would-be assassins if he revisited the ambush site. He hoped the shooters had been in too big a hurry to worry about what they might leave behind. Even if they returned later, there might be something. Anything.

He reined up on the road where he had been shot. Kiowa seemed especially alert and he told the horse it was safe. His gaze took in the empty ridge and its waterfall descending into the shallow pool where he had fallen. No boot prints remained. Not even his. The area appeared to have been wiped with a branch or something. The road itself carried many tracks and offered little encouragement for finding the clues he was hoping to find.

However, a small wagon or a carriage had stopped here, then moved on. Perhaps to enjoy the view? Perhaps to destroy evidence?

Of course, the shooters could have returned to see how badly hurt their target was and to see if they might be able to track him. After tying Kiowa to a thick mesquite bush, he climbed the highest point of the parallel hillside where the shots had come.

Again, the area behind the high rocks and around them had been brushed clean. Too clean.

He turned back when a thought hit him like the bullets from a week ago. Where did the shooters leave their horses that night? They wouldn't have kept them too close because the men wouldn't have wanted to take a chance that their mounts might have whinnied when Kiowa approached.

A short ride to the other side of the narrow line of broken hills produced an interesting story. His would-be killers had ridden in a carriage. Both of them, it looked like. A one-horse carriage had been tied to a cottonwood. Tracks cut the earth around the tree where the animal had been tied. There were no signs of another mount. The carriage horse had a rear right shoe with a deep crack in it. He would recognize that anywhere. Carriage tracks came from town and then continued to the southwest. Boot tracks of both men were unusually small as if the killers were boys. One wore boots with badly worn-down heels.

"I'm going to find you bastards—and you'd better have guns in your hands when I do."

He swung Kiowa in the direction of what he guessed was the shooters' escape route a week ago. Uvalde could wait. Some of the carriage tracks were readable in the early winter's hard ground, probably because two men weighed down the vehicle. It looked like the carriage had been driven hard for a good half hour, then stopped. The assassins had stepped out of the carriage, probably to relieve themselves and check their back trail, then returned to the carriage and eased the horse into a walk, keeping to the same direction. No one else had been in this part of the country for awhile. Not even roving cowhands. Away from the ambush hillside, a rough prairie took over, spotted with mesquite, an occasional creek bed and sparse grass. This wasn't Bar K land. Might be Diamond T's. Most likely, it was free-range country nobody wanted. He rode through scattered grazing cattle. Most were older animals carrying a Diamond T, the brand of a small ranch on the outskirts of the Bar K holdings. Here and there were CW Connected, Rocking R and Bar K beef. None were young.

Across his path was a new trail of unshod ponies. Eight, it looked like. Apaches or Kiowas, he thought. All tribes had been reduced to reservation life, but small bands continued to roam the land, looking for trouble.

He reined up, levered his Winchester and studied the calm land, knowing that an Indian was not going to be seen unless he wanted to be. Even so, he scrutinized the area around him, looking for anything that shouldn't be there. Apaches, in particular, were expert at hiding in plain sight. A true gift of patience and courage. Satisfied there was no immediate danger, he eased the hammer down on his rifle and resumed his search of the carriage. Returning to Uvalde and his job as a lawman there was forgotten for the moment.

But passing cattle had obliterated the carriage tracks. Finally, he dismounted and led the sorrel, looking for any sign of the direction the carriage might have taken.

A mossy horned longhorn eyed him suspiciously.

"Not looking for trouble, my friend. Trying to find some men who wanted to kill me. That work for you?" Cole said to the hard-eyed animal as he passed. "I'm headed that way." He motioned toward the west as if to assure the longhorn that he wasn't headed in his direction.

Remounting, Cole kept an eye on the beast until he and Kiowa were well past him. "Don't know about you, Kiowa, but I just as soon not mess with that ol' boy."

The big sorrel snorted as if he understood and agreed.

At a small creek lined by cottonwoods, pecans and alder bushes, he dismounted and let his sorrel to drink. He was surprised at how weak he felt. A piece of jerky and a hard biscuit tasted good. He leaned his Winchester against the closest tree while his light-blue eyes scanned the horizon again for any sign of a returning Indian war party. Hopefully, they had left this part of the country. At least for awhile.

A soft song turned his attention to a low-hanging cottonwood branch where a chickadee had just landed.

"Well, good day to you, my friend," Cole said gently and wondered if this were the same bird that had appeared to him the night of the funeral, outside of Pitch. "Are you the same fellow who came to cheer me up?" He smiled and pushed the thought of Kathleen into the back of his mind. The chickadee responded with a familiar chirp.

"Well, thanks. Good to see you again." He decided to think it was the same chickadee. Kathleen would have liked that idea.

After a long drink of water from the creek himself, he said goodbye to the little bird, grabbed his Winchester and remounted his horse.

Over the far ridge was the distinct silhouette of a horse and rider headed his way. Cole levered his rifle and waited. This was as good a place as any to fight, if necessary. So far, the rider was alone or seemed to be. Not an Indian, Cole knew that by the way the man sat on his horse. The man was following him, judging by the way he rode. Had one of the assassins been hiding and slipped behind him? It didn't seem likely, but Cole stepped away from the sorrel and knelt with his rifle readied.

A hundred yards away, the rider saw Cole and waved. The horse was a dun with black mane and tail. The rider was short, powerfully built and wore a shoulder-holstered revolver. Sunlight bounced off the gun. Red handles!

It was his friend, Peaches.

"Han Rui! What the hell are you doing here?" Cole blustered to himself, stood and waved back.

In minutes, the stocky Oriental cowboy reined up. His eyes sparkled with the success of finding Cole. Across his saddle, he carried the 28-shot Evans rifle. "*Ni Hao*, Cole Ker-rie-son. Boss-man Ethan send me. Worry you no go to town. Go find men who shoot at you. He . . . tell me to find you. That all right with Cole Ker-rie-son?" He finished his question with a Chinese expression Cole didn't know.

Cole smiled. How like Ethan to send Peaches. His brother respected men who could fight. Always had. It was also like him—and Claire—to figure Cole would try to find his would-be killers, instead of going straight to Uvalde. It was also like his brother to make sure his young brother had solid backup, even if he wouldn't want it. And it was unlikely Cole would refuse Shi Han Rui's valuable assistance.

"*Ni Hao*, Han Rui," Cole repeated the Chinese "good day" greeting. "Get down and take it easy. Glad to see you. Have you eaten?"

"Me eat. Morning."

"Then you need to eat. Got jerky and biscuits."

Peaches looked relieved to be received well, as he wasn't certain how the youngest Kerry brother would react to his appearance. They shook hands and Peaches accepted the jerky and biscuit from Cole. He ate silently as Cole briefed him on what he had learned and told him that he had lost any signs of the carriage tracks.

"Aiie, too many beeves."

"Looks that way."

As they ate, Peaches suggested they ride straight to the little town of Pitch, instead of looking further. The would-be assassins might have gone there, either to eat and ride on—or they were staying there. He reminded Cole of the trouble the young gunfighter had there after his wife's funeral; the story had spun through the Bar K men during the roundup.

"Why not it be two from there?" Peaches asked, studying Cole's face.

CHAPTER 19

It was hard dark when Cole and Peaches reined up in front of the Pitch livery. The town was even more quiet than before, if that was possible. No carriage was parked anywhere along the short main street. Peaches asked how they would know the killers. Cole admitted that he wouldn't, unless he found the carriage or the horse with the cracked shoe and found who owned it.

If they had no luck finding the ambushers in Pitch, Cole had already decided to head for Uvalde and had asked Peaches to ride with him. The Chinaman would become his deputy, along with Big Red Clanahan, if he agreed. It didn't make sense to ride around the country looking for ghosts. He didn't like the idea of giving up the search, but he didn't like wasting time either. His only real option, if he couldn't find the shooters, was to be ever alert. Easier said than done, he told himself.

"Well, howdy . . . you're Cole Kerry, ain't ya?" The friendly call came from inside the livery. "Prob'ly don't 'member me. Joe. Joe Chinum. I own this pissant place."

"Good to see you, Joe," Cole replied, dismounting. "Anybody you don't know been around here in the last week? Could've been five days ago."

The thick-bellied livery operator removed a misshapen hat and scratched his matted, sweaty head. "Uh . . . no. No. Nobody new to town. Not since you an' your kin came through, ya know. Man, that was sumthin' to see!" Deep lines on both sides of his mouth defined his dirty face.

"These fellows were riding a carriage. Horse had a cracked back shoe. Right rear hoof."

The livery operator frowned. "No suh. Ain't got no carriages in hyar. No hosses wit bad shoes neither. Friends o' yurn?"

"Tried to kill me. Ambush. About a week ago."

"Damn." Joe shook his head and leaned on the handle of his pitchfork. For the first time, he appeared to notice Peaches, then shivered. "Sorry to hear that. Ya git a look at 'em? Ya thinkin' it were somebody from hyar?" He bit his lip. "Billy ain't even up an' around yet, ya know."

"Never saw them. Just the tracks," Cole said. "That's all we've got." He put his hand on Peaches's shoulder. "Joe, this is my friend, Shi Han Rui. Friends call him Peaches. He likes them."

The Chinaman nodded a greeting and the livery owner said, "Howdy. Glad to know ya . . . Peaches." Joe looked around the stable as if to reassure himself that the statement was true before saying it. "Ain't got no carriage in hyar."

"No one in town rides a carriage, I take it."

"No, suh." Joe cocked his head and squinted. "Oh, bin a preacher come through now an' again. Ridin'a carriage. But not recent-like. Woulda bin a month back, maybe more. Another feller came through on a carriage. Maybe two weeks ago. No, it were three. Think he were a cattle buyer. Didn't git his name." Joe rubbed his chin. "Didn't seem like the kind that'd be shootin' at folks."

"Well, thanks, Joe. If you think of anything, let me know," Cole said, motioning toward the saloon. "We're going to see if there's anything to eat. Give our horses a good watering and a bucket of oats. All right?"

"I'll be takin' good care o' em," Joe hesitated and glanced again at the silent Peaches. "Say, that big sorrel won't bite me

149

or nothin', will he?"

"Sweet as the morning dew, Joe. Just don't try to ride him."

"No, suh. I sure won't. Saw Billy try it." He shook his head and smiled a yellow-toothed grin. "Helen Mae'll sure fix ya up good." He shrugged.

"Leave them saddled, though. We'll be riding out after we eat."

"They'll be ready."

After leaving the livery, Cole and Peaches walked down the street to the saloon.

"Don't think Joe would lie to us, do you?" Cole said they walked along the creaky sidewalk.

"No. May be shooters have no been here. Me guess wrong."

"Maybe so. But it was worth a try."

Cole told him about another thought he had. Maybe the assassins have been hired by Webster Stevenson's father, the wealthy merchant in Abilene, Kansas? Could the man who wanted Kathleen for his son's wife be seeking the revenge he couldn't get through the law? Stevenson certainly wouldn't have the courage to face him. Of that, Cole was certain. Or maybe the attempted assassination was related to the Kerry ranch. Did someone think killing him would make it easier to move in on the Bar K? If he did, he didn't know Ethan or Luther. Or Sotar or Shin Han Rui.

"Mystery. Cole and . . . Han Rui find out."

"Sounds good to me."

Stepping inside, the two men stood for a moment to study the handful of tired men gathered there. The last time Cole was here, his mind was twisted into blackness and only a few faces seemed at all familiar. They remembered him, though. Most looked away. A few attempted to smile. Two were playing billiards and stopped to greet him tentatively.

"Oh, how wonderful! You did come back."

Helen Mae waved from behind the bar. She was in the same dress as before and her big hoop earrings danced with her enthusiastic greeting. "What can I do for you tonight?" The question oozed from her big face.

"We're looking for two men. They tried to kill me. Thought they were headed this way," Cole said loudly, hoping someone in the saloon would react. "They were in a carriage. Horse had a cracked back hoof."

No one moved or responded to his statement. An older bearded man, wearing a worn derby and a cane, swallowed and shook his head negatively. Cole was certain he wasn't one of the shooters. Peaches studied the men in the room. His face was unreadable.

"Well, I don't think it's anybody here," Helen Mae offered. "You scared the holy hell outta all o' them the last time. Nobody's been gone anyway." Her laugh was deep and contemptuous. "Nobody ever does."

"Any strangers come through? Within the last week?"

"Ain't been nobody from outta town come through. Since you did." Her smile almost sawed her face in half.

Cole felt weary. He had ridden out of the way for nothing. Maybe he shouldn't have taken the time to track the men, but Sotar would have Uvalde under control and he didn't like the idea of unknown killers after him.

"How 'bout I fix you up with some pork steak an' eggs? Raw fry some taters, too. That sound good?" Helen Mae asked, wringing her hands and wanting to reach out across the bar and touch the young gunfighter. "Your Chink boy kin eat, too, if'n you want."

Cole started to scold her; Peaches touched his elbow and whispered, "Let this go, Cole Ker-rie-son."

"That sounds good. We'll have a little whiskey, too. Irish. Bottle and two glasses."

"Comin' up. Make yourself comfortable." She smiled and winked. "Helen Mae's gonna take good care o' you."

"Look hard for some peaches too, will you?" Cole called after her.

The buxom bartender disappeared into what she called "her kitchen" while Cole and Peaches took seats at an empty table near the front of the saloon. Carrying a bottle and two glasses, Cole glanced around the room, saw no one who concerned him and sat down. He poured whiskey for both, picked up his glass and offered a tribute in Chinese.

"Yung sing."

Peaches smiled, repeated the "drink and win" toast and downed the whiskey. Cole followed with his own swallow. Looking around the room, Cole eased the Colt from his sidewinder holster onto his lap. As if on cue, Peaches did the same with his shoulder-holstered weapon. Sipping their second drinks, the two men discussed the day and what might have happened to the shooters. Likely, it was one of two things: they had either headed for Uvalde or south toward the border.

Humming to herself, Helen Mae brought two heaping plates of food and set them down on the table. She returned with a bowl of canned peaches. She smiled warmly at Cole. "Anything else I can do for you, Mr. Kerry?" Her eyelashes fluttered their sexiest best.

"This looks great. Thanks."

From the back of the saloon sauntered a slump-shouldered man with a droopy mustache. In his filthy hand was a revolver. Cole vaguely remembered him.

"Trouble coming," he said quietly.

"Let this come."

The man strutted toward their table, strengthened by whiskey. When he was about eight feet away, Cole looked up. "That's far enough. My friend and I came in for some supper."

His right hand slid around the Colt in his lap and held it. "We've been looking for two men who tried to kill me. From ambush." He turned his head in the direction of the standing man. "Do you ride in a carriage? You and a friend?"

"What! A carriage? Hell, no. Don't ride in no damn carriage. Think we're some kinda psalm singers?"

"I don't think anything about you—or your friends. Except that you're bothering us right now." Cole motioned with his left hand holding a fork. "Now go back where you came from."

The slump-shouldered man, known as Millard, looked over his shoulder at the three men sitting at the back table. They urged him on.

Taking a deep breath, he said, "You're the one who kilt my friend, Orville. I didn't like that."

From behind the bar, Helen Mae announced, "Don't worry 'bout Millard. He's always yellin' 'bout somethin'." Her smile, this time, didn't quite reach her eyes.

Dropping his left hand to the table, Cole looked up again. "I didn't like him an' his buddy trying to steal my horse . . . an' trying to rob and shoot me." He looked down again and took a bite of meat with his fork.

"This time you don't have the drop on me, mister," Millard declared, taking another step closer and pointing the Walker Colt at Cole. "I ain't afraid o' you none atall."

Helen Mae hesitated, then dropped both hands beneath the bar.

"Mister, you're not very good at this, are you?" Cole said. The cock of his Colt held under the table was sinister. "Your gun's not cocked—and if you try it now, I'm going to have to put a bullet in you. I'll say it one more time . . . go back to your table."

Peaches turned slightly toward Millard. His red-handled revolver was pointed at Millard's groin. The Chinaman spoke with his mouth barely moving. "I hungry. So is my friend, Cole Ker-rie-son. Go away. Now. Or I put first bullet through your balls."

Willard looked down at himself and turned pale. He lowered the gun and started to turn away.

"Leave the gun on that table. Right there. Yeah," Cole said. "Oh, and leave that Smith & Wesson there too. You know, the one you carry in your back waistband."

Slowly, Millard dropped both guns on the empty table, avoiding the gaze of his friends and Cole and Peaches. He kept his eyes on the floor as he slowly walked back to his table.

"When you get to your table, tell your friends you almost died today. Tell them you were smart." Cole returned to his meal, uncocking the Colt and leaving it on his lap. He looked at Peaches. "Good pork, isn't it? Haven't had a pork steak in a long time."

"Aiie, good. Yes." Peaches turned to watch the man walk back to his table. Millard's friends glanced in the Chinaman's direction, then quickly looked away. No one said anything.

From the bar, Helen Mae's hands returned to the bar's surface. She was pale and sweating, but tried to act calm.

As Cole and Peaches ate quietly, a familiar man with a graying goatee and squinty eyes came from the back of the saloon and walked directly to Cole's table.

"Good evening, sir. You may recall I am the mayor of Pitch," he said in his forced deep voice, his eyes blinking with every other word.

"Oh yeah, you're the 'Third,' " Cole said, sipping his whiskey.

"I am Winston Burlington Lunes the Third."

"And we're eating supper."

"You reported earlier that you are seeking villains who attempted a foul murder and I thought you could benefit from advice from the mayor's office." Lunes smugly folded his arms and straightened his back.

Cole glanced away, repressing a grin while the short man tried to think of something additional to say. Chuckling, Peaches kept his eyes on his food, then moved his chair so both he and Cole could keep the men in the saloon in their gaze, particularly the table where Millard sat. Resuming their meal, Cole was frustrated, but trying not to show it. He was no closer to finding the men who wanted him dead than he had been. Millard wasn't involved; he was certain of it. Just a man driven by drink and his friends' goading. He was lucky to be alive.

After taking a deep breath, Lunes resumed talking, but Cole didn't hear a word. His mind was retracking the day to see if he could discover what he had missed. Nothing new came to mind.

"How 'bout some apple pie, hon?" Helen Mae was standing near him, pushing Mayor Lunes aside with the brush of her left forearm. It was like watching a horse nudge aside a colt from a watering hole.

"Uh . . . Helen Mae. I was addressing Mr. Kerry about an issue of our township."

"Shut up, Lunes. Go find a corner to jabber into," the buxom bartender growled.

The mayor stuttered, "I-I . . . t-thought h-he w-would . . ."

"Nobody wants to hear you jabber on an' on, Lunes." She put her hands on her ample hips. "If you're not careful, we'll take that damn title away. Now, go on, git."

Laughter rattled through the gray saloon. Lunes looked like a chastised little boy.

Cole motioned toward him. "That's quite all right, Mayor. We appreciate your offer to help."

Lunes swallowed and pulled on his dirty paper collar. "R-Really? I-uh . . . I feel it is my duty to do so, sir."

Without waiting to hear more, Helen Mae stepped in front of Lunes and leaned forward, touching the table with both hands and allowing her scooped neckline to sag open, revealing much of her ample breasts. At the same time, though, Cole looked at his half-empty glass of whiskey, then at Peaches who was trying to control his laughter.

She was undeterred. "Cole, honey, I just remembered. There was a lady stranger who rode through here. Almost a week back." Her smile showed that she knew this would get his attention. She held her position, hoping Cole would look up. Instead, he stared at his glass and ran his fingers around the rim.

"A stranger? Really?" He finally glanced up and she was pleased that his gaze passed her nearly exposed bosom before reaching her eyes.

"Yes. A woman. Kinda pretty, I guess. If you like 'em skinny. She wanted directions to the Rocking R."

Lunes was fixated on her leaning-over exposure, but managed to say, "I remember. Yes. Rode a black horse. A fine walking horse. Rode a saddle like a man. Scandalous, if you ask me."

Helen Mae, now standing, and the mayor continued a few minutes more, discussing what they remembered about the woman. Both attempted to secure Cole's attention. The woman had been dressed in black with a serape worn over her shoulders like a cape and a wide-brimmed hat that almost hid her eyes. Lunes described her as breath-taking and Helen Mae frowned at the choice of words.

"Had a gun." Helen Mae slid into the adjoining chair without being asked, changing the subject slightly. "A long-barreled rascal. One o' the boys tried to make a move on her. She stuck that thing in his nose real quick like." She giggled and shook her head.

"How come Joe didn't remember seeing her?" Cole asked, finishing the last of his whiskey and glancing at Peaches; his face, once again, void of expression.

The woman wasn't the shooter, but Cole was curious just the same. Helen Mae jutted out her chin as if to reinforce the woman being easily forgotten.

Lunes looked at Helen Mae before explaining. "I'm certain she never went to the livery. Rode on after getting directions. Didn't stay to eat. Just a glass of whiskey. I imagine Joe didn't see her. Not everybody did."

"Was she Mexican?" Cole asked.

"No sir. She was 'Merican."

Cole shook his head and Lunes apologized. "I didn't mean anything by that . . . sir. I should've said she was . . . white." He glanced at Peaches.

"Sounds like whoever didn't see her missed a real treat." Cole grinned and pushed away from the table. "Sure do thank you, Helen Mae. That was good eatin'."

"You're not stayin' . . . the night?" she said, batting her eyebrows again and leaning closer. "The night's gettin' cold. I can keep you nice an' warm. Got me a place out back." She rolled her shoulders to emphasize her bosom. "No charge . . . 'course." She glanced at Peaches. "Uh . . . your friend, uh, he could sleep . . . in the other room. Back there." She motioned toward the back of the saloon.

Cole stood, leaving coins on the table and reholstered his Colt. "That's real tempting, Helen Mae, but we need to get going."

Her face blossomed into crimson. "So I'm not good enough for you. That's it, isn't it? You cocky bastard. I'll have you know I've taken care of a lot of men better lookin' than you." She pushed back the chair and stomped away.

Holding back a grin, Peaches returned his red-handled revolver to his shoulder holster.

Mayor Lunes seemed pleased by the exchange. "You're leaving tonight, Mr. Kerry?"

"Yeah, we need to get a head start for Uvalde." Cole shoved the chair back to the table, keeping his eyes on the men in the smoky room.

"But what about these villains you seek?"

"They'll have to wait until I see them." Cole watched Helen Mae tread back to the bar.

"Thought you didn't know what they looked like."

"I'll know them. They'll have guns in their hands." Cole looked over at the table where Millard sat with his back to them. "Millard, you take good care of yourself."

CHAPTER 20

Cole Kerry and Peaches rode fast out of Pitch, keeping off the main road and letting moonlight guide their way. They eased across familiar broken land; Kiowa seemed to know their destination without being directed. Halfway between Uvalde and the pitiful settlement, Cole reined up beside a small pond, fed by a shallow creek. Half-surrounded by trees and brush, the quiet place sat on the southwestern corner of Bar K range. He and Kathleen had discovered the location and had once enjoyed a special picnic there.

"We'll stop here, Han Rui. That work with you?" He swung down and led the sorrel to the pond, but the horse wasn't thirsty.

"I like." Peaches looked around. "No like run hoss at night. Easy to hurt him."

"Agreed."

The Pitch livery man had fed and watered the animals well. Cole suspected he had also given Kiowa a rubdown, then replaced the leather right away. After unsaddling and unbridling, he tied on a picket rope from his saddlebags. Peaches did the same to his buckskin.

They decided having a fire would not be wise, although its warmth would be welcomed. The night was cold. Neither thought anyone from Pitch was one of the shooters, or would follow them, not even Millard or his friends, but being careless was foolish. There was no wind and they were reasonably warm.

"You sleep. I guard," Peaches said, pulling his rifle from its saddle scabbard. If the Chinaman was cold, he didn't act like it.

"Thanks. Wake me around midnight an' I'll take it from there."

"I do so, Cole Ker-rie-son."

At first, there was a comfort stopping where he and Kathleen had made love. That was followed by an ache, a loneliness that cut into his soul. Cole stretched out on his blanket with his saddle for a pillow, keeping on his clothes and boots. He unbuckled his gunbelt and laid it beside him with his Winchester; one Colt was in his hand. A cold, orange moon shivered back at him. A sorrel moon that offered little comfort. Only loneliness. Peaches's silhouette was barely visible against dark trees. Cole stared at the distant orb and his mind returned to the day when Kathleen had come back to him. She had ridden away because she couldn't deal with the shameful rape by the gang.

In his mind, he saw himself telling his brothers and two friends that he was leaving to find her. He would ride first to San Antonio, then wherever it took to find her. The three Kerry brothers, John David Sotar and Miguel del Rios had returned to Uvalde with the captured Victorio Gee gang; six of them were killed, including their leader, along with the stolen bank money.

He remembered Miguel's smile suddenly springing across his entire face, followed by a similar grin appearing on Luther's, who whispered something to Ethan. A faint smile trailed across the blind rancher's face.

"Amigo. I do not theenk you weel have far to ride."

"What do you mean, Miguel?" Cole had looked in the direction his friend was pointing.

Silhouetted against the dying sky Kathleen galloped her horse into view. From the white streaks across its withers and neck, the small paint mare had been pushed long and hard. It was one of the most beautiful sights he could remember ever seeing. Cole yanked Kiowa away from the group and the horse exploded in her direction.

He couldn't remember jumping down from the big sorrel and running toward her. He didn't remember dropping the reins or that, for once, the sorrel remained in place. She had halted her mare, which was heaving hard. A few steps from her, his mind warned him that she might not be receptive and he skidded to a stop.

"Kathleen?"

"Yes?"

"I love you."

"I know."

Her face sparkled with perspiration. "I tried to ride away, I really did. I got as far as that funny little pond. The one where you and I . . . I couldn't imagine living without you. Claire told me where you and your brothers were headed. Can you accept me as . . ."

"I was coming after you, Kathleen. I wasn't going to stop until I found you—to tell you that I love you. That's all that matters to me."

"Are you ready to go home?" Long tears raced each other down her pale, freckled cheeks.

Cole resumed his dash toward her. "Wherever you are is my home."

The memory broke and retreated to a shadow of his mind. Cole stood with a start.

"Oh, Kathleen . . . how could God take you from me? How could He?" he moaned.

Peaches hurried over from his guard position. "Cole Ker-rie-son . . . you all right?"

"Yeah. Sorry. Having a nightmare, I guess."

The Chinaman shook his head. "I know. Have many . . . after sister killed. Take time my friend."

"I know. I know."

"You sleep. Good for you. Shi Han Rui no sleepy. Shi Han Rui watch."

"Thanks. You're a good friend."

Cole walked to a soft spot under the trees. He and Kathleen had been there. He shivered and went to his knees, and his mind was black. How long he stayed there, he didn't know, but finally he stood once more, feeling weak and tired. His wounds were demanding his attention and his head was swimming. The moon had softened into a sweet yellow. He returned to his blanket and lay down, grabbing the handgun as he did, and was soon asleep. But rest was fitful with nightmares.

Peaches stood quietly, enjoying the silence of the night. The night was cold, but he felt alive. He walked every few minutes to keep himself alert and warmer. There would be no rest until Cole Kerry found the two men who tried to kill him. Until he did, they could be lurking anywhere. He looked up at the moon and recalled his mother in Singapore telling him never to point at it because the tips of his ears would fall off if he did.

The moon was yellow now and that was the color of Heaven, he had been told growing up. Did that mean the moon was Heaven? He had often wondered about that.

Somewhere, a coyote howled its own question. Peaches rolled his shoulders to keep them from stiffening. Across the way, Cole had finally fallen asleep. Good, Peaches thought.

The young Chinaman remembered his grandmother telling him and his sister stories of gods and goddesses of old, but only one story had truly stuck in his mind. It was about the Taoist goddess, *His Wang Mu.* She was known as "Royal Mother of the Western Paradise." According to his grandmother, *His Wang Mu* celebrated her birthday once every six thousand years. At this time—and only at this time—magic peaches ripened in the palace garden. During the celebration, all of the gods gathered to eat the peaches to renew their immortality. Since then, he had eaten peaches as often as he could find them. Of course, he didn't really think they would make him immortal, but it didn't hurt to add to his strength.

Movement in the bush caught his attention. Peaches lowered his rifle and walked in that direction. He spoke softly, telling whoever was there to come out or die. A few steps from the dried bushes, a chickadee scurried from its hiding place and flew into the night.

Peaches said, "Go now, little friend. Find place warm."

He was surprised to see a chickadee fly at night, then remembered Cole telling him about his encounter with a wounded chickadee outside of Pitch. He couldn't help but wonder if this were the same bird, looking after Cole.

Chucking at his silly idea, he returned to the trees and rechecked his rifle. The Evans rifle had been purchased in California. He liked the weapon in spite of its tendency to jam. But he was more comfortable with a handgun. The weapon seemed an extension of him. Fighting was what he did best. And fighting—and dying, if necessary—was what he intended to do for the Bar K.

His loyalty to the Kerrys had no limits, especially Cole. No one else would have hired him, not an Oriental seeking something beyond hard labor. Cole and the other Kerrys saw him as a man, a warrior. Not as a Chinaman. Maybe it was because they were Irish and the Irish were looked down upon. His mind returned to the shooters who attempted to kill Cole. Who were they? What did they seek to gain? Was it highwaymen? No, he was sure of that, as was Cole. They had a purpose. But where had they gone? To Uvalde? To Mexico?

Like Cole, he was certain they hadn't left the region. No, they were more likely to live around here. The Rocking R? Was the owner trying to move in on the Bar K? John David Sotar had said he saw twenty well-armed men at the ranch the last time he rode close about two weeks ago. They needed to keep a close watch on that neighboring spread. Something wrong was going on there. This time of year no one, except a big ranch like the Bar K, needed twenty riders. And especially not well-armed ones.

Peaches rolled his neck and walked over to the grazing horses. He patted their nuzzling noses and recalled the story of Ethan trying to break Kiowa and the sorrel throwing him and striking his head with his hoof, blinding the savvy rancher. He couldn't imagine not being able to see. Looking up to the sky, he shut his eyes for a moment, then opened them as if to reassure his ability to see. A Chinese prayer of thanks followed.

His gentle mother had brought her two small children to San Francisco from China years ago. Her husband had died shortly after the boat arrived in America. Determined to make it in the new land, she had worked in a laundry there, night and day it seemed. Her health had deteriorated and she had passed away four years ago. By that time, Peaches's reputation as a fighting man was established. He worked for one of San Francisco's leading saloons, using his skill with his fists and a gun. His small stature belied his strength and skill. He had been paid well for the task.

Peaches woke Cole at false dawn. The intense Chinaman had already built a small fire for coffee and was cooking a little breakfast.

"Thought you were going to wake me at midnight." Cole sat up and rubbed his chin. He was tired, but knew he wouldn't be able to sleep longer. Remmants of Kathleen's return flitted through his thoughts.

"I no sleepy. You need sleep, Cole Ker-rie-son."

"Thanks."

After drinking the last of the hot coffee, the two gun warriors saddled and left. Cole glanced at the ground where he and Kathleen had made love as he rode away. He couldn't remember feeling so alone. Except when he thought he had lost her forever in Abilene.

CHAPTER 21

At the Rocking R ranch, Reverend Dinclaur rose from his bed. He couldn't sleep, even though it was the middle of the night. He paced the main room, keeping stride with the heavy snoring of his stepfather in the next room and a dozen gunmen stretched out through the house. Jinnette was sleeping alone in the remaining bedroom.

The rest of Tiorgs's outlaws filled the bunkhouse. None were watching the meager Rocking R herd. Tiorgs didn't care; the men were hired to help get rid of Bar K riders at the right time. Dinclaur liked the idea of a major ambush, destroying them in one deadly trap.

His left ear itched and that meant someone was talking about him. Maybe it was the lonely widow in town; she wanted male company badly. Or maybe it was Cole Kerry. No, that didn't make sense, he told himself.

He stopped and looked at the gray fireplace and scolded himself for worrying too much. The resumption of the sexual relationship with Jinette Six had been satisfying, even though they had been quiet with Tiorgs and the other outlaws sleeping.

Drawn to the large stone fireplace, he stood next to it, studying the gray ashes. His mother could read divination in ashes, but he never could. His superstitious ways had come from her. He had no idea who his father was, other than he had been a drunken railroad executive. His mother had never mentioned him. She died years ago, leaving him, his brother and sister considerable wealth they hadn't expected.

Taking an iron poker from its stand, he jabbed at the still ashes with greater energy than he felt. Tiny flames responded eagerly and soon he had a good fire going again, with the addition of two logs. Warmth began working its way through the room. He watched the flames. If the fire blazed, it meant a stranger was coming. That could mean Cole Kerry. Only he wasn't a stranger. No, wait. The supersitition was true only if the blaze brightened when a crock was hung. He looked again. If the fire burned only on one side, a stranger was coming. The fire's blaze was even. Still, he watched it. His mother had told him that each orange flame was a different spirit. Each was important and could tell him much. He believed, but never could read, what they were saying. That was his mother's gift.

He turned away from the fireplace and looked about the room. The fire's glow had made shadows retreat to the corners. Nothing had been changed inside the comfortable ranch house since Tiorgs took ownership. Only the family photographs were gone, taken when the Russians left. A large desk, controlling the west wall, was crowded with newspapers. One of Heredith Tiorgs's passions was reading. As long as it didn't interfere with the Scotsman's work, Dinclaur didn't mind.

An old rose-colored sofa and a table for eating governed the rest of the room. Last night's supper dishes were strewn across its uneven surface. The only non-gunman on the ranch was the cook. He wasn't particularly good, but he could produce the necessary quantities three times a day. Unmatched wooden chairs were spread about; all showed signs of wear. A torn spot on the side of the sofa was most noticeable. Someone, probably Mrs. Drako, had tried to sew it together unsuccessfully.

An oil painting of Texas that Tiorgs had found in the barn now hung over the sofa. The corner of the painting was discolored, but it gave the room some color. The house consisted of only four rooms: a living room, kitchen and two bedrooms. Pine floors were in need of sweeping; he planned on telling that to his stepfather tomorrow. Next to the sturdy fireplace was a wall rack of rifles and shotguns. His examination of the weapons brought silent approval; they were recently cleaned, oiled and loaded.

He walked over to the gun rack, stepped around two sleeping men and fingered one of the Henrys. Cole Kerry had shown a cunning ability to survive. Where was he now? In Uvalde? If not, he would be soon; the young man was too damn tough for his own good. How could he set up an ambush the gunfighter couldn't survive?

A sound from outside jerked him into fear. Cole Kerry could be sneaking up on them. Right now!

Grabbing a rifle from the rack and levering it into readiness, he stepped to the doorway and opened it. Cold air rushed to meet him and accepted his breath-smoke as he stepped outside and slid into unfriendly shadows. Everywhere he looked, shadows darted. The concern about a wolf staring at him reached his mind. The beast's gaze brought blindness. He didn't want to be blind like Ethan Kerry. Maybe that's what really happened to the rancher, he mused.

He studied the land for glimpses of unwanted company. Methodically, his vision examined the swells of land around the ranch, looking for a sense of movement or shadow that shouldn't be there, or the glint of metal. The Drakos had chosen well. Good rich soil and ample year-round water. However, the location of the ranch house itself wasn't where he would have placed it defensively; it would be easy to advance unseen without exposing oneself to rifle fire from the house. There was nothing he could do about that now and after he owned the Bar K, he might not even want this ranch to continue operating separately. After all, it *was* Tiorgs's ranch.

Dinclaur took a deep breath and let a thick white puff of frosty breath escape from his mouth. After a few more minutes, he was certain the only thing moving were a few horses in the corral. A frown reached his face as he recalled the gray from earlier. Tiorgs knew better than to have such a horse around. He dismissed any concern about where the horse's body had been disposed.

His carriage bay was there. The horse's back right hoof had been reshod after he noticed the track it was making when he arrived at the ranch today. He began to stroll counter-clockwise around the perimeter of the house to eliminate any blind spots. Keeping to the uneven shadows, he moved around the perimeter. Every six or seven steps, he would swing the Winchester to his shoulder and aim, then resume walking.

As he turned the far corner, a rabbit darted from its night's sleeping place and ran southward. Dinclaur hurriedly ran backward. Letting a rabbit cross one's path before sunrise meant evil was coming. Panting and sweating, he stood with his rifle at his side. That was close.

The night's silence gave him time to think, in spite of its chill. Was he thinking straight himself bringing his stepsister into this? Or was it simply lust? Why not use some of the gunmen he had already hired? Make them earn their money. Why not attack the Bar K with his men and be done with it? No, that was foolish thinking. The Kerrys together were a force. The trick was to isolate and destroy them one at a time. His plan was solid because it was a patient strategy.

He passed the bunkhouse, filled with gunmen. Loud snoring escaped the narrow building. Why not have his brother steal that fancy black horse of Lucius Eister's and leave an easy trail to follow. Some of Tiorgs's gunmen could wait in ambush for Cole. Yes! That was perfect! Perfect.

Happy with his new idea, he encircled the house and went back inside, shivering as he did. His mind worked as he stepped inside and let the warmth of the room greet him. He unlevered the rifle and returned it to the rack. He would talk to Tiorgs in the morning. It was also time to start rustling Bar K cattle again. The roundup was over and everyone would be relaxing. Tiorgs would relish both tasks.

"That you, Glory?"

The strained call came from the bedroom where Jinette Six slept.

"Yeah. Couldn't sleep."

"Damn. You know what time it is?"

"Yeah. Got a great idea to get rid of Cole Kerry."

"I need you. Here. Next to me."

"Sure."

Dinclaur was surprised at her directness. Someone might hear. He yawned and decided he wanted Jinette. Especially now that he had everything under control. Again.

CHAPTER 22

Mid-day sun commanded the streets of Uvalde when Cole Kerry and Peaches entered the town and rode straight to the marshal's office. Wearing the marshal's badge again, Cole swung down and stood still, letting weakness pass through him. Peaches pulled his buckskin alongside Kiowa and swung down, casually flipping the reins over the hitch rack.

Yesterday had been a wasted day. Worse, there were two men out there who wanted Cole Kerry dead and he didn't know who they were—or why they were after him. After checking in with Sotar and Big Red, Cole would check at the town livery and see if any carriages had been out of town recently. That might narrow it down, but he doubted it. Most likely, the shooters were long gone after the attempted ambush. Anyway, shooters riding in a carriage just didn't seem to make sense.

"Hey, Cole! Good to see you!" A hearty greeting from inside the jail caught his attention. "You, too, Peaches. How yo-al been?"

A smiling John David Sotar was at the opened doorway. His Missouri twang laid easily on Cole's ears. His black-and-white calfhide vest looked good on the compact man's fresh blue shirt. The vest was curled on one side like he had slept in it. Attached to the vest was a deputy marshal's badge. He tugged on his black hat and his left hand brushed past the missing lower earlobe.

"Glad you're up an' a-round, Cole. Wasn't sure how much

170

lead yo-al were a'carryin'."

"Let's just say they weren't good enough."

Sotar chuckled. The thumb and forefinger of his right hand rubbed together in a tiny continuous circle, a nervous habit long past correcting. "Got some coffee on. Red's walkin' the town."

"How is that big Irishman?"

"Helluva good man," Sotar answered and deftly rolled a cigarette. "Rates yo-al mighty high. Said he never had nobody hit him so damn hard—and never had anybody give him a job like you did. Trust him to stand, Cole."

"Well, he's a good man. Appreciate your help a lot, too, John David. You're welcome to stick around. I've asked Han Rui to stay for awhile," Cole said and noted the jail cells were empty, except for a cowboy sleeping off a drunk night.

Sotar lit his new smoke before responding. "Naw, I need to get back. Been wonderin' about that there Rocking R bunch. Two weeks back, I saw twenty guns hangin' out there, you know, last time I rode our graze. Don't know why they'd need that many riders this time o' year. Think I'll take a swing 'round our land to make sure all's right. I'll have Preacher and Zeke join me."

Moving to the desk, Cole avoided stating the obvious—that he, Sotar and Peaches wouldn't fit anyone's description of cattlemen either. Sotar beat him to the thought.

"Come to think of it," Sotar said with a grin. "Don't think anybody's gonna think you, Peaches an' me are ordinary cowhands either."

Cole grinned. "Guess not."

He walked over to the occupied cell and studied the sleeping cowboy. Without looking back, Cole continued, "Know anything about Heredith Tiorgs?"

Sotar drew on the cigarette and let the smoke drift away, with his response only a negative shake of his head. He strolled over to the hard-working stove and touched the coffee pot handle. His hand jumped away and he cursed. Looking around, he found a rag on a rickety table near the stove. Using the rag to hold the pot, he poured hot coffee into a mug, also on the table, and asked Cole and Peaches if they wanted some.

Peaches said, "No thank."

"No thanks. Think we'll head over to the restaurant. Haven't eaten since this morning. Han Rui's a good man, but he's not much of a cook." Cole elbowed the Chinaman and grinned.

"Ah . . . Cole Ker-rie-son not appreciate . . . fine Oriental dining." Peaches bowed deeply.

"Reckon it featured peaches," Sotar said.

Cole chuckled and said, "Want to join us, John David? We can find Red and see if he's hungry, too." He explained what they had been doing and his lack of success in tracking the would-be killers, including Ethan's warning that the Rocking R might be somehow involved.

"Your brother's probably right. It's got something to do with the Rocking R," Sotar finished his cigarette and jammed it into a half-full ashtray occupying the same table.

"Something strange's goin' on, Cole. I can feel it."

"I think you're right. But I don't know what they're going to try."

"Think I'll have the men ridin' in pairs and carryin'." Sotar hitched his gunbelt with both hands for emphasis.

"Well, that makes sense, but we don't want anybody getting trigger happy," Cole advised.

"They won't."

Sotar's silver-studded pistol belt was no ordinary cowhand's. Neither was the cutaway holster on his left hip, holding a short-barreled Colt pointed forward for a right-handed draw. The gun's walnut handles were inlaid with a silver star on each side.

Cole shook his head. "I can't believe they would try rustling from us. Those boys we caught were operating on their own. That's what Heredith Tiorgs said and I believe him."

Behind them, the door opened and Red strolled in, a shotgun cradled in his arms. He greeted Cole warmly with an Irish expression that only he thought was funny and grinned.

Cole shook his hand and introduced him to Peaches. "Good to see you, Red. Thanks for the good work. We're headed over to the restaurant to get something to eat. How about joining us?"

"Aye, t'would be to me likin'."

Sotar motioned toward the sleeping cowboy behind them. "I'll let this ol' boy out. He should be sober now. Feelin' like hell, but sober. Think he works for the CW Connected."

"Sure," Cole said.

At the Cattleman's Restaurant, Big Red and Sotar brought Cole up to date on the happenings in town. The onset of winter had quieted Uvalde, even though the weather had been milder than usual. Neither man was aware of any townspeople being bothered by a Missouri boy and an Irishman acting as the community's lawmen. They decided most would have been afraid to say anything and laughed.

Peaches looked around. "No see any Chinamen, do you?"

They laughed.

Cole told them about backtracking a carriage pulled by a bay with a cracked hoof, and that he thought it was the shooters who had tried to kill him. He and Peaches had gone to Pitch, but no one there had seen any strangers, except for a woman seeking directions to the Rocking R. He didn't see how she could be involved.

From the back of the restaurant came Mayor Rinnart Heinrich, the Prussian-born cook and restaurant owner. "Ah, *guten tag, Herr* Marshal Kerry. *Ist* so *gut* to see *du.*"

"Well, it's good to see you, Mayor. Glad to be here." Cole introduced him to Peaches and said he would be staying on as a deputy. Peaches nodded his greeting and continued eating.

If Heinrich had any problem with serving a Chinaman or an Irishman—or having either serve the town as lawmen—it didn't show in his face or his words. Of course, it didn't hurt that Cole, Sotar and Peaches would be paid by the Bar K and not the town. Clearly, though, he was pleased to see Cole and his friends.

The Mayor asked about the shooting and Cole told him what had happened, but that he had no idea who might have tried to kill him. Heinrich thanked Sotar for stepping in and told the big Irishman that he was doing a good job. With that, he returned to the kitchen, promising their food would be out soon.

As they ate, several townspeople stopped to wish Cole well and thank Sotar and Big Red for helping out.

"Any strangers in town?" Cole asked as the last of the townspeople walked away.

Sotar deferred to Big Red because he knew the townspeople better.

"Aye. Only but a few," the Irishman responded, rubbing his chin. "There be a drummer from St. Louis . . . a cattle buyer from, I think he be from Dallas . . . and, oh, and there be a fine-lookin' woman. A real looker she be. Word is she's a widow from Kansas, on the way to San Antonio. Visiting relatives at the Rocking R," Sotar added.

"Sounds like that's the same woman they talked about in Pitch." Cole finished his coffee and wiped his mouth with a white napkin, glancing at Peaches.

"Reckon so." Sotar asked, looking around as if she were near. "Wonder why she's visitin' now?"

"Who knows?" Cole said. "You'd have to ask her. I'm more

174

interested in finding out who those shooters were."

"Ask her yourself. She's comin' in. Now." Sotar motioned toward the door.

A woman stepped inside the restaurant, so stunning she would stand out anywhere. Every man in the room stopped eating to stare at her. She was dressed in a dark purple suit with a plaited skirt and a small, matching hat, composed mostly of feathers. An embroidered vest, complementing the coat and skirt, accented her bosom. A soft violet blouse emphasized her violet eyes. In her hands was a large purse.

She studied the room and her gaze stopped when it came to Cole. He acknowledged her gaze with a simple nod. Her responding smile showed off deep dimples. Long eyelashes danced with him for an instant and she looked away and moved toward a table across the room.

"Reckon she'd like you to ask," Sotar whispered.

Cole looked back at the two men. "That's it? A drummer . . . a cattle buyer . . . and her?"

"She came in yesterday. Jinette Six is her name. *Miss* Jinette Six," Sotar said, emphasizing her marital status.

"Have you met the others?" Cole asked.

Sotar touched his finger to his tongue, then returned it to twirling with his thumb. "Uh, yeah. This mornin'."

They talked a few minutes more with Sotar and Red describing the town as being quiet and that the mines were operating steady again. Big Red was eager to tell about the history of the town he had learned from the talkative postmistress. The settlement was founded by Reading Wood Black in 1853 as the town of Encina. Then, in 1856, it was renamed Uvalde after a Spanish governor, Juan de Uvalde, and was picked as the county seat. Had a lot of Indian trouble until troops were brought in. The mill itself was built by Black and James Taylor in 1858. The post office was opened in 1857, a fact Wilomina Reid was proud to say. Two rock quarries and a lime kiln were started by Black, too. Big Red was filled with the area's history and both Cole and Sotar tried to act interested. Cole guessed the postmistress was interested in the Irishman.

Finally, Cole said he needed to get going, stood, left some coins and pushed his chair into the table.

"Aren't you gonna go over an' introduce yourself, Cole? You're the marshal, ya know." Sotar grinned. "I know I would."

"Some other time. I'm going to take Kiowa to the livery, then see about a room in the hotel," Cole said. "John David, if the Rocking R starts something, come and get us."

"She's lookin' at you, Cole," Sotar whispered.

"Quit it. Let's go."

As they left the restaurant, Cole glanced back to see her watching him. Her smile reminded him a little of Kathleen's.

He smiled back.

After seeing Sotar off and deputizing Peaches, Cole went to the town livery while his two deputies checked out the rest of the town. The livery stable was a mixture of smells: fresh manure, new hay and old leather.

"Lots of nice folks use our carriages, Marshal," the livery owner declared and yanked on his wide, red suspenders, barely able to withstand his ample girth. "Some keep their own here, too, ya know." He spit a long stream of tobacco juice. "You're welcome to try one out." He eyed Cole with a frown. The marshal didn't look like a man who would want to ride in a carriage.

"No thanks, Benjamin. But I'd like to keep Kiowa here."

"Sure. Sure. Fine lookin' hoss."

"Thanks. He is a good one. Don't let anyone try to ride him, though. Or handle him except you. Kiowa doesn't take well to strangers," Cole said.

He walked over to a black carriage with gold trim in the

corner of the barn while Benjamin led Kiowa down the wide aisle between stalls to an open stall. Shadows protected every stall. The big sorrel went quietly; Benjamin chatted with the horse as if the sorrel could understand and Benjamin seemed very comfortable with the fiery animal.

"I came across carriage tracks on the way in. Probably a week old. Maybe longer. They belong to this rig?" Cole asked.

"A week back, yah say?" Benjamin spit again and led Kiowa into the open stall and began removing his saddle. "Gonna take this off'n yah fer a while, big fella. Think that'll be all right?" He spat.

"Yeah. A week back."

Benjamin carried the saddle easily outside the stall and laid it down propped on the front fork. He noticed the rifle sheath was empty, but that wasn't unusual, and especially not for a lawman. He liked Cole Kerry. He had heard Cole was only a temporary marshal, but hoped he might stay longer. Uvalde needed someone with real backbone—and good with a gun if necessary.

"Well, that un was out then, I think. Uh, the preacher likes to go out an' about. Ya know, spreadin' the good word," Benjamin said, returning to Kiowa's stall with a bucket of water and a brush. "Sometimes, the bank president, Mr. Yankison. Triston Yankison, he does, too. Those two might've been. Can't recall for certain."

"Oh. This one had a horse with a cut shoe. Might've had two passengers."

"A cut shoe? Two passengers?" Benjamin poured some water along the big sorrel's back and began brushing. "Naw. Doesn't sound like one o' my hosses. I check 'em regular. An' I ain't had two in a carriage since . . . well, your wife's funeral, it would've been. Several folks then."

"All right if I check your horses?"

Benjamin nodded and spit. "He'p yourself. If'n there is one, I'll git ri' on a' shoein' it." He shook his head. "I know thar ain't. I run a good place hyar, Marshal."

"I know you do, Benjamin. A shoe can crack anytime. Not your fault." Cole lifted the right hind leg of a buckskin, then let it down. The horse's ears followed him.

"Maybe so, but I check 'em close when they come in."

"Good to know."

To make his point, the livery man checked all of Kiowa's feet, picking a pebble out of the left front hoof with his pocket knife. "Like ri't hyar, ya bin carryin' 'round a stone. Thar, that feels better, don't it? Kiowa, ain't it?"

"Thanks. Must've just picked that up," Cole said. "Is his hoof tender?"

"Naw. He's fine. Real fine. Ain't ya, boy?" Benjamin looked over at Cole who was checking the hooves of a bay horse. "Clean feet mighty important fer a hoss, ya know. I always check the frog. Each time. Like it cut a little higher than the rest, ya know. Do my own shoeing." He let Kiowa's hoof down. "What ya lookin' for this . . . carriage for . . . if'n ya don't mind my askin'?"

"The men in it tried to kill me."

Benjamin spit, shook his head and returned to brushing Kiowa. "Damn, that's awful, Marshal. Nuthin' like that 'round hyar, I swear."

Finishing an examination of another bay, Cole stood. "No. I'm sure you didn't know about it, Benjamin. I don't figure it was anybody from town. Pays to be thorough, though."

"Does ya know what they look like?"

"Only thing I know is that they both have real small feet," Cole answered, moving to another stall. "Almost like women's. Or boys'."

The livery operator spat and grinned. "Don' spend much o'

my time lookin' at folks' feet." He looked up, thought about spitting again, but chose, instead, to move the chaw to the other side of his mouth. "Figger a fella'd look kinda weird doin' that."

"Could be. If you think of someone like that, let me know."

"Sure thang, Marshal." This time he did spit. "Mighty glad yur here. Need ya. Yes, suh."

"Thanks. But I'm just a short-timer. 'Til Uvalde gets a real lawman in here." Cole returned the front hoof of a black to the ground.

Benjamin looked at him, musing the statement. "Reckon yur as real as they get, Cole Kerry."

CHAPTER 23

The third day of Cole's officially becoming marshal found Big Red Clanahan sitting outside the jail, relaxing as the morning brought warmth to the November day. From up the street bounded a hysterical Lucius Eister, driving his buckboard with abandon. He almost hit a woman crossing the street.

Eister owned and ran the freight business for the mines. He was rarely seen around town although he and his wife lived two streets over in a well-built stone house. He pulled his horses to a hard stop in front of the marshal's office and jumped down.

"Marshal in?" he demanded, barely pausing in front of Clanahan.

"Ay. He be. Can me be . . ."

Eister hurried past him and into the marshal's office.

"Marshal, somebody's taken my good horse," he yelled as he entered.

"The black one with the right front stocking?" Cole asked as he laid his coffee cup on the desk. Everyone in town knew of the magnificent animal Eister had been grooming and training since he bought it as a colt.

"Of course, that's the one. Whaddya think it was?"

Eister's narrow-brimmed hat was cocked on his head, smashed against hair that demanded freedom in all directions. His bulging eyes were even more extended by the discovery of his stolen horse. His white shirt had seen better days and barely covered his massive chest; his suitcoat was having the same problem with his thick arms. A black string tie had been yanked together around a limp paper collar.

He was filled with his self-worth, having built himself up from a freight driver and expected action wherever he went and usually got it.

The young marshal rose and walked easily around the cluttered desk toward the rifle rack on the far wall. "You still keep him in your barn?"

"Of course I do. Hurry, we ain't got all day, ya know."

Cole stopped and looked back at the freight company owner; his intense blue eyes broke the man's arrogant manner.

"Sorry, Marshal. Sorry. I . . . just . . . I care about that horse."

"I'm sure you do. Won last year's Fourth of July race, didn't it?"

Eister's chest swelled. "Third year in a row."

"That's great. Maybe I'll enter Kiowa this year. Might be fun," Cole said as he yanked free a Winchester and checked its loads. "When did you last see your black?"

"Last night. Wiped him down after a ride out to the mine. Wanted to make sure the wagons were ready for 'em. Can't believe somebody would steal him."

"Me, neither. That horse is known all over this part of Texas." Cole tugged on his hat. "Let's go, Eister. I want to check your barn first."

"Of course. Sure."

As they walked past the big Irishman, Cole said, "Someone stole his black horse last night. I'm going to check out Eister's barn. Tell Peaches when he gets back."

"Ay. That I be doin'."

After a few steps, Cole stopped and turned back. "If Jimmy Waters is sobered up, you can let him go."

Big Red Clanahan nodded, rubbed his chin. "What if he not be?"

"Don't let him go."

"Aye."

"An' tell Bobby, he needs to refill the water troughs. All of them."

"Aye."

Cole went to the saddled Kiowa standing quietly behind the hitch rail and swung onto his back. "I'll meet you there, Eister."

Keeping the big sorrel saddled was already a standard procedure for the marshal. A demonstration of his readiness to react. It had been Ethan's idea, suggested to Cole before he left the ranch.

The freight owner crawled onto his buckboard and snapped the reins.

At the barn, Cole was already inside the structure before Eister arrived. The small barn smelled like all barns, only this one was cleaner than most. The four stalls were empty, except for an older bay who eyed him suspiciously. Cole walked past the ladder to the loft and out the unlocked back door. Hoof prints were clearly evident in the morning's dirt. They headed north.

Who would be foolish enough to steal a horse so easily recognized? It was a rare man who didn't know horses and their brands—and their owners.

"See?" Eister said, running to the back side and pointing at the tracks. "That's where he took him."

"Sure looks that way. Didn't see a saddle anywhere," Cole said.

"Damn. Must've put the leather on 'im and ridden out. Sweet as you please."

Cole returned to his horse and mounted.

"I'll go with ya," Eister said. "Might need an extra gun."

"No. This is what I'm paid for. You stay in town."

"You gonna find Revolver?"

Cole guessed Revolver was the name of Eister's horse. "I am."

Wiping the sweat from his thick brow with a wadded handkerchief, Eister said, "He's got more'n eight hours on you." He seemed more settled than earlier.

"Yes, he does," Cole responded. "I'm going to take a second horse along, so I can keep moving. Might surprise him that way. It'll take awhile, but I'll get him."

Eister nodded. He was impressed with this young gunfighter. He had a way about him that most men did who were good with a gun. Only Cole Kerry didn't seem to need to prove his ability. That had to be one of the reasons the town council thought he was the right choice.

After stopping by the marshal's office and informing Red and Peaches where he was going, he went to the livery, got a second horse and then a few things from the general store. He might be gone several days, so it made sense to go prepared. The horse thief already had a significant lead on him anyway. His movements were swift and he was on the trail of Eister's black horse within the hour.

The horse thief's immediate trail led down and through a narrow arroyo cutting along the far side of town. A good place to come and go without being seen. He rode with his Winchester laying across the saddle. It wasn't likely the thief would stop so soon, but not being prepared was a good way to die.

Chipped marks on passing rocks, an occasional hoof print, kept him at a good pace. He was gradually out of sight of the town and riding into land that was pickled with cactus, rock and only occasional water. His focus alternated between the tracks and the land itself. He knew this rolling land well; it would soon lead into farming country. The horse thief's pace was brisk at first, but slowed down after the initial hours of escape, and actually stopped for awhile. The horse droppings were fresh and occurred while standing. The way Cole read it, the rider waited to see if he was being followed or not.

Late morning, he lost the trail and rode in a wide circle until he picked it up again. If he read the trail correctly, the horse thief realized the uneven ground had left no trail so he purposely backtracked to make one. Why would he do that? The only answer that made sense was that the thief intended to ambush whoever followed him. Cole tightened his grip on the rifle, keeping his right hand in the trigger guard as it lay across the bridge of his saddle.

A part of his mind danced back to his futile tracking of the shooters who tried to ambush him earlier. He didn't like the emptiness of that effort. Attacking was his much preferred style of action. At least, this time, he was going after something known, a black horse. Ethan was the brother who could best combine strategy and its execution. Most people just thought he, Cole, was mean. But he wasn't mean, just determined, he told himself. And he would get Eister's horse back and capture the thief.

Switching his saddle to the second horse, he continued with his big sorrel on a lead rope. Kiowa wasn't tired, but he didn't want the fine animal to get worn down unnecessarily. He rode at an easy lope for a mile, his focus alternating between the tracks and the changing horizon. The lack of cover would make it difficult to ambush someone here. There were no hiding spots.

Soon the land was transformed into dark rows of plowed ground. Beneath the raised ground, cotton plants were being nurtured by the earth. He knew the farmer's family. The Johnsons were good, hard-working people and had sold the Kerrys a milk cow and some chickens. Their land butted against the Bar K and would be the first area fenced off come spring. That would be a relief to the farm family, for their plants were an inviting target for cattle.

The horse thief's track skirted along the farm land and then galloped northwest, headed toward the hill country. Cole was gaining; the tracks were deeper, fresher. Did the thief want to be found? Why did the thought cross his mind? He reined up alongside a shallow creek, dismounted and let both horses drink their fill. A piece of jerky tasted good while he resaddled Kiowa. The big sorrel was eager to go as he tightened the cinch.

His eyes caught something in the creek bed. Boot tracks. New tracks. They were small. Just like the feet of his ambushers. That was too much of a coincidence. Someone was trying to lure him into another ambush. At least he had to assume that was the case until he knew better.

He swung into the saddle. "Yeah, I know you're ready, Kiowa." He pulled on the lead rope for the bay. "Be alert, big fella. We're riding into trouble." The sorrel's ears twitched in response.

They rode over ever-slanted country, passing live oak, pecan trees and struggling mesquite. It was easy to let his mind wander away to Kathleen and to Ethan's happy family. He shook his head to drive away the thoughts and reminded himself to study the land ahead of him. Riding into an ambush would only take seconds. They rode on with the sun sliding toward the horizon ahead of him. The thief knew the country and was headed for a place known to have year-round water, a good place to stay the night.

Daylight would be leaving soon and he must find some place to camp. He rode for another half hour, heading for an area he remembered. The location was off the horse thief's trail to the west and led to another place where water usually could be found. Few knew of its existence because of its foreboding boulders. There should be some water collected in a rock seep, surrounded by the boulders on one side and cottonwoods on the other. Just in case, he approached with his Winchester cocked and held ready in his right hand. The area was empty of life, except for a coyote that slithered away. There were no signs anyone had been here recently.

Soon both horses were watered, hobbled for the night and grazing in the pocket of buffalo grass and weeds outside of the rocks. A small fire beneath the low-hanging branches of a cottonwood would provide heat for coffee. The sticks for his fire were dry and what little smoke they created would dissipate in the tree's leaves.

More jerky, an apple and a hard biscuit were washed down with half a pot of coffee. A November breeze tempted to keep the fire going for warmth, but that wasn't smart. He spread out the remaining coals and moved to a secondary rock shelf overlooking his horses. Kiowa would warn him if anything or anyone came close. He slid under some branches nearly touching the ground, rolled up in his blanket with his rifle at his side and went to sleep.

Sometime in the middle of the night, Kiowa stomped and snorted, bringing Cole awake in an instant. He grabbed his rifle and listened. Night sounds had disappeared. Something was close. Even the bay was nervous now, pawing the ground as best it could with its hobbles.

A pair of unblinking yellow eyes was soon evident on the far side of the area below. A cougar!

Cole aimed at the eyes, then moved his barrel to the left away from the animal. He fired and the eyes disappeared. Killing such a beautiful beast didn't seem right. The shot would be heard for a long way, he knew, most likely by the horse thief. But it solved the immediate problem. The cougar would not return. At least not tonight. Both horses gradually settled down and he tried to fall back to sleep, but couldn't.

After awhile, he got up, stirred the gray coals enough to get heat for warming up his leftover coffee. Finishing the pot, he doused the coals with the remains, followed by a pot of water. He watered both horses, saddled and rode out. Daylight was hours away, but he would return to where he left the horse thief's trail and work his way from there.

His eyes adjusted easily to the night's soft light, supported by a three-quarter moon. In the distance, a tiny light winked at him. A campfire. Likely belonging to the horse thief. Two hundred yards from the fire, he dismounted and tied the horses to sturdy mesquite trees. He didn't want to risk his horses whinnying to the black horse, if it was there and he was certain the animal was. After removing his spurs, he took his rifle and began working his way toward the light.

Cole was surprised at the apparent closeness of the horse thief's camp. He knew he was closing the gap between them; it was easy to read in the horse tracks. But with that great a lead, he hadn't expected to catch up for at least another day. Having two horses had helped, but still the closeness made sense for only one of two reasons: the thief didn't think anyone was following—or it was an ambush set to kill him.

Logically, the thief would expect the person trailing the stolen horse to be Cole. Eister was blustery, but not brave. Of course, Cole could have given the assignment to Peaches or Big Red. Yet it was likely the thief could expect Cole to come himself. He was new and would be eager to prove his worth.

He moved easily through the broken ground, trying to stay away from anything that would make noise. Stepping around twigs and dead leaves. Using the scattered trees for cover. Crouching, he studied the camp ahead. The camp itself sat in a wide spoon of flat land, backed up against a tall embankment studded with rock, trees and overrun with grass and weeds. Eister's black horse was tied to a tree off to the side of the camp, sleeping with its right front leg curled against the ground. The fire itself was banked with three logs. A much bigger fire than made sense, even in the coolness of the night. The sleeping thief was rolled up in his blanket, his hat over his head.

Moving closer, Cole knelt behind a large rock and watched the sleeping thief. Although he preferred attacking to waiting, Cole was an adept and patient hunter. During the War Between the States, Ethan had used him to scout out the enemy's position on a number of occasions. Something about this didn't feel right. He eased back into the darkness and began to examine the area surrounding the camp.

There. A gleam of light from the fire shimmered off a gun barrel within the rocks on the embankment's ledge.

It *was* an ambush.

This time, he wouldn't be surprised; the ambusher would.

Working his way silently around to that part of the ledge, he picked up two rocks and held them in his right hand. His rifle was in his left. He stopped twenty feet from the sprawled position of the thief. To the man's left was a cluster of trees and more thick brush. The man's attention was on the camp below.

Cole stayed to the man's right, nearly behind a sprawling young tree; it would be an awkward move for the thief to swing his rifle toward him. Setting himself, he hurled both rocks toward the far side of the camp, striking the ground not far from the black horse. The animal jumped awake and snorted.

The noise served its purpose: giving the thief something to study closely.

With his rifle in both hands, Cole stepped closer and pointed it at the man's back.

"Mornin'," Cole said loudly.

The thief jerked in response, but didn't turn around.

"Drop the rifle and face me. Real slow," Cole barked. "This is Uvalde Marshal Cole Kerry."

"W-Wai . . . W-Wait a minute, M-Marshal. I . . ." The thief released his grip on the rifle and turned to face Cole. He glanced to his right and faced Cole with a queer smile on his face.

Golden streaks from the campfire couldn't hide his identity. Cole knew the man was the wretched bum from town. Meken was his name. His pockmarked face was dirty as usual; his brown hair, stringy; his worn-out clothes, ill-fitting. Even in the dark, he looked decrepit, but different. For the first time, Cole really studied the man. Had he known Meken from somewhere else? Why was this bum trying to kill him?

"Waiting to kill me . . . a second time. Right, Meken?"

"Huh? I . . . dunno whatcha mean . . . Marshal. I was just restin' here."

"Doesn't matter, Meken. You're going back to town and stand trial for stealing a horse. That's a hanging offense, you know."

Meken's gaze was a mixture of anger and fear; his appearance was no longer that of a homeless buffoon, only of an evil killer. His coat pocket bulged slightly and Cole knew what the bulge meant.

"I want you to reach into your pocket. Use your left hand. And bring out that pistol. Barrel first," Cole said. "Then drop it."

His shoulders rising and falling, Meken glanced again to his left and slowly complied.

Cole watched the gun drop and snarled, "By the way, your boot prints were all around . . . where you and your partner tried to kill me a week ago. On the trail to my ranch."

"Don't know what you're talking about, Marshal." Meken changed the subject and waved his hand in the direction of the black horse. "Hey, I was . . . just taking Mr. Eister's horse out for a ride. It needed exercise. I-I was helping . . . Mr. Eister."

"Is that why you were waiting up here?" Cole said. "Waiting to kill me."

Meken shook his head repeatedly. "Ah . . . no. No. 'Course not. I . . . uh . . . I heard somethin'. That's all. Thought it might be a cougar. Or Indians." His eyes sought the slight movement inside the trees and realized Cole was standing where it would be difficult to get a good shot at him, since he was mostly hidden by a tree. Did Cole Kerry know there were two other men waiting?

"You can tell that to the judge."

Meken's face locked into hatred. "You're playing with fire, Kerry. You and your brothers. You're not going to like the way it ends."

Cole smiled. "Let's see how this might end. We're alone. It would be a lot easier . . . for me . . . just to shoot you. No real need to mess with a trial. Or mess with getting you back to town."

"You wouldn't shoot me, Kerry. You're a lawman."

"So what." Cole fired and drove a bullet through the top of Meken's right boot.

The fake bum screamed and knelt, grabbing his boot with both hands.

"Tell me who else tried to kill me, Meken—or I'll take out your knee next."

"N-No. N-No. Damn, what're you waitin' for?" He yelled. "Shoot him!"

Cole had already seen the movement within the trees to his left. The young marshal's Winchester roared four times as fast as he could lever the gun. Without waiting, he ran toward the trees, continuing to fire at the two surprised silhouettes scrambling to escape. A groan was followed by a curse and one silhouette disappeared.

From the second silhouette came orange flame and its lead sang a few inches from Cole's stomach. He levered and fired three more times and the second silhouette jerked backward and fell. Behind him, Cole heard the rush and spun toward Meken as he brought up his retrieved rifle. Cole emptied his

Winchester into Meken and the horse thief melted onto the ground.

Dropping his rifle, Cole hurried to the dying man.

"Who was it, Meken?" Cole grabbed Meken's bloody shirt and pulled him forward. "Who was with you . . . on the ranch road that night?"

Meken's eyes were unfocused. He gurgled and blood vomited from his mouth. "M-My b-brother."

"Your brother?"

"G-Glory. G-Glory V-Van Camp."

Cole stared at the dead man, mouthing "Glory Van Camp" as a question that wouldn't be answered. He stood and turned to find the other two ambushers. Drawing a Colt, he didn't find what he wanted to find. Another pair of small feet. Neither were Meken's brother. As dawn came to the day, he found the ambushers' horses, hidden deep among the trees.

Two days later, Cole Kerry rode into Uvalde, leading four horses. Two held strapped-on bodies; a third held a wounded man; the fourth was Eister's black. The town buzzed with the news. Meken's body was identified and the gossip took on another dimension. Why would a bum try to steal a fine horse? Didn't Meken understand what stealing a horse meant?

Why did the marshal have to kill him? Wouldn't it have been good enough to bring him in for trial? Who were the other two men? Did they encourage poor Meken into stealing the horse? Was Cole Kerry too quick with his guns?

A few voices steadied the crowd with support for their young lawman. Wilomina yelled out her thanks to Cole for bringing the thieves to justice. Mayor Heinrich joined in with his support, including a few German expressions no one understood. Several others shouted out that Meken had stolen from them, too.

And Lucius Eister met them at the jail, his face wide with joy.

As Cole rode past Jinette Six, she screamed, "Cole Kerry, you're a killer! A killer."

Cole looked at her and said, "So were these boys. Just not as good."

"Oh, thank you, Marshal! Thank you!" Eister patted the black horse as Cole reined up at the hitch rail. He stared at the dead Meken and spat at his unseeing face. Spittle ran down his cheek.

Cole went into the judge's office, reported what had happened on the trail, indicating he would stand for a hearing. Judge Moreland was a youngish-looking judge who grew up in Michigan and every month or so expressed a desire to return. Moreland said it wouldn't be necessary; men who steal horses get what they deserve.

"I would say that's the code of the West, Marshal Kerry," Moreland declared, pushing his eyeglasses back on his thick nose.

"No, a hearing is important," Cole responded. "The people of this town need to know their marshal isn't a gunman."

Moreland pulled on his ear, then agreed. "Tomorrow. Ten o'clock. My office."

"Good enough."

Down the street, Pastor Dinclaur grimaced and held his grieving sister. The next time he wouldn't give Cole Kerry any chance of survival. He dismissed his sister's suggestion that he give a sermon on the marshal's evil ways against a poor homeless man.

CHAPTER 24

As scheduled, the hearing was convened the next morning. Judge Moreland's small municipal courtroom was crowded with interested townspeople, including Pastor Dinclaur and Mayor Heinrich sitting side by side. The rest of the town council were spread out, talking quietly. A tense atmosphere was building with several demanding the marshal's arrest—or at least his dismissal. Most people were shocked at the death of the town's presumed homeless man, troubled by such a mild and humble man being killed. Behind the scenes, Pastor Dinclaur had reinforced the reactions.

At the rear of the room sat the blacksmith discussing horseshoes and shoeing with Big Red. Peaches remained at the jail, watching the prisoner, who would be escorted over later. Nearby was Willomina Reid, talking as usual. This time about how lucky the town was to have Cole Kerry as their lawman. Another couple appeared to be praying. At the front of the room was Lucius Eister, eager to testify and get on his way; he had work to do. The town banker was there and so was the newspaper editor, ready with pencil and paper.

After taking his position behind a lopsided, scratched bench, Judge Moreland opened the proceedings with a simple statement that the purpose of a preliminary hearing was to determine whether sufficient evidence existed for the accused to be bound over for formal trial. If such a trial was warranted, it would be conducted by the circuit judge at his convenience.

Then he added, with his thin, rather high-pitched voice gaining intensity, "This hearing is also to review the conduct of our town marshal—and is being held at *his* request."

The last statement brought a rush of whispered responses throughout the room.

Someone in the back yelled, "How ya gonna git evidence outta some dead man?"

Across the room, a deep voice added, "Should be arrestin' that gunslinger of a marshal, that's what. Killin' a poor ol' man."

Judge Moreland's gavel slammed against the bench and it rattled with the impact. "Another outburst like those two and I'll clear this courtroom. Is that understood? Nod yes—or leave."

Cole Kerry sat quietly at the defense table, already having decided he would act as his own counsel and as the prosecutor. The hearing would, in effect, be two parts. The first part would be to clear him of any wrongdoing in the killing of Meken and the other man. The second part would be to determine if there was evidence to bind the remaining outlaw over for trial.

Johnny Lee Vicker had agreed to act as the defense attorney at the request of Cole and Judge Moreland. He was an older man with a tendency to stutter, but a solid citizen. Most didn't realize he had ambitions of becoming the justice of the peace if Moreland decided to leave for any reason. Not many knew Ethan Kerry had underwritten his legal practice when it was going through a bad time. Both Moreland and Cole expected him to act fairly.

"The issue before this court is twofold: First, did Marshal Cole Kerry act in accordance with the law in shooting Meken and this other man? And second, is the accused man, wounded and in jail . . . to be held for trial for stealing Mr. Eister's horse and attempted murder? Is that understood?"

Judge Moreland studied the room filled with intense townspeople. "Is it further understood that my judgment is the sole determination of whether or not a trial is justified in either matter?" Moreland continued, gaining confidence. "However, a judgment against either the arrested man or the dead men or against Marshal Kerry is not an indication of guilt or innocence. It only means there is sufficient evidence for a jury to decide at a later date. A trial will be held at the time I designate, along with the schedule of Judge Burnett, and a jury of the accused's peers will be selected at that time."

Looking satisfied, Moreland looked over at Cole. "Let us take up the matter of your actions first, Marshal Kerry."

"Certainly, your honor."

Cole motioned for Eister to take the witness chair and was sworn in by the grocery store clerk, serving as the bailiff.

"Mr. Eister, will you please tell the court what happened . . . to your horse."

"He was stole, that's what."

"We understand that," Cole hid a smile. "Has Meken ever cared for your horse? Have you ever let him ride it?"

In his usual gruff manner, Eister blustered, "Hell, no. 'Scuse me, judge. No, sir. I wouldn't let him around my horse. No way. Would you?"

That brought chuckles through the crowd.

"Well, was he ever around your barn?"

Eister leaned forward with both elbows on his knees. "Yas, sir. Once. Four days back, he came to the barn while I was rubbing down Revolver after a workout. Asked me if anybody else ever rode Revolver other than me. You know, was he gentle, or was he like your big sorrel?"

"I take it Revolver is the name of your horse, the one stolen."

"Hell, you know that, Marshal. Everybody in town knows that horse. Best around."

"Go on." Cole folded his arms and hid a smile.

Eister explained that Meken left and he didn't think anything about it until his horse was missing the next morning.

"No other stranger came to your barn?"

"Hell . . . uh, no, sir." Eister fidgeted in his chair, then held up his hand like a school child. "Marshal, may I . . . show you something?"

Cole looked at the judge, then at Jimmy Vicker. "If it's about the robbery, I guess so."

"After you left to get my horse back," Eister pulled a button from his coat pocket and held it up proudly. "I found this. Down the trail a ways. Where that thief went." His eyes narrowed. "This came from Meken's coat. I checked it. When he . . . uh, he came in."

Jimmy Vicker interrupted. "I object, your honor. There is no way anyone can be certain the button was in any way connected to this crime."

"Agreed." Judge Moreland looked over at the transportation manager. "Mr. Eister, you can't expect this court to consider that as evidence. It might have been left at any time."

"That's true, your honor," Cole said, motioning toward the upheld button. "Interesting though, that it was found on the morning the horse was stolen and on the trail where the thief rode Revolver away."

"Anything else?"

Cole nodded. "If it pleases the court, I want to point out something important."

"Proceed, Marshal. The court won't stand on formalities. This is a hearing. My hearing."

"Thanks. This whole thing was an ambush to kill me," Cole said. "Meken and the other two set it up for that purpose. Stealing such a well-known horse didn't make much sense in the first place. Who'd buy it?"

Eister loudly agreed.

"I became suspicious as I trailed Meken. He was leaving an

easy trail to follow and I found his camp much sooner than I expected."

He explained what had happened at Meken's camp and how the other two men were hiding to kill him. Cole said he had hoped to bring Meken in alive, but Meken had attempted to kill him when he was fighting the other two men.

"How will the remaining arrested man describe this encounter?" Jimmy Vicker asked, shuffling his feet at his desk. He didn't like this responsibility, arguing against Cole Kerry.

"Don't know. Depends on whether he lies or tells the truth."

Without waiting for a response, Cole produced two wanted bulletins, identifying the two other outlaws as wanted for murder and robbery in Texas and Kansas. Then he reached into his pocket and withdrew a telegram and handed it to the judge.

Moreland examined the message and asked Cole to read it aloud.

"Certainly," Cole unfolded the paper and read:

" 'TO MARSHAL COLE KERRY, UVALDE, TEXAS . . . MEKEN VAN CAMP IS WANTED ON CHARGES OF SWINDLING AND MURDER IN HOUSTON TWO YEARS AGO . . . STOP . . . CONSIDERED ARMED AND DAN-GEROUS . . . STOP . . . PROCEED WITH CAUTION TO BRING HIM IN . . . STOP . . . HOLD FOR RANGERS . . . B J ATKINS, CAPTAIN, TEXAS RANGER COMPANY B.' "

The audience erupted in response.

Cole waited for the noise to quiet down, then continued, "None of us realized Meken's true nature. We have reason to suspect there are other crimes in his past. Wires to various law enforcement agencies in other states have been sent, but we haven't heard back yet."

He reached over beside the table and held up a boot. "This is one of Meken's boots. Most of you will recognize it is small. This is the same boot print I found around the carriage tracks where the two ambushers tried to kill me two weeks ago."

In the back of the audience, Dinclaur sat listening intently, glad he had taken to wearing larger boots, shoving old newspapers in the toes so they would fit. He had told Meken to do the same, but he hadn't listened.

Cole turned toward the audience, holding the boot. "There were two men who tried to ambush me then. On the day I accepted the job as your marshal, I was returning home to tell my family. One of the ambushers was Meken. He admitted it. The other had small feet, too. Before he died, Meken said the other shooter was his brother . . . Glory Van Camp."

A man sneezed and several people frowned at him. Otherwise the crowd was so quiet, it was scary. The young lawman explained Glory Van Camp was not known in Texas, but Ranger headquarters had informed him that he was well known in Colorado and Utah as a gunman. His current whereabouts, however, were unknown. The young lawman said he thought Glory Van Camp was hiding somewhere in the region.

At Cole's urging, the blacksmith came forward and was sworn in. He responded to Cole's question that he had seen Meken carrying a handgun two weeks ago. The weapon was carried under his coat, stuck in his belt. He had seen the gun when Meken happened to come into the blacksmith's shop to ask if he had anything to eat. Meken had turned to his left when the blacksmith pointed at a small table holding a coffee pot and some crackers.

Johnny Vicker stood. "Your Honor, many men carry guns. How does this relate to the charges?"

Cole answered, "I doubt that anyone in this room thought Meken went around carrying a gun. Much less owned one. I thought it was important to begin to see him for who he really was and not for who he wanted us to see."

"Why did he want us to see him as a . . . bum?" Vicker asked earnestly. "And why did he and his brother want to kill you?"

Cole nodded. "Best I can tell is that he had used the disguise before. It allowed him to move about the town freely and no one suspected him of anything." He rubbed his chin. "I don't know the answer to the last question."

Cole completed his thought. "I don't know this Glory Van Camp. There's no photograph of him that I know of. But I guess it's possible we crossed trails somewhere. Maybe it's some kind of twisted revenge. Wish I knew."

A few minutes later, George Newton, the remaining outlaw, was escorted into the courtroom by Peaches. His right arm was in a sling and he limped badly. He was guided to the witness chair; Peaches whispered something to him as he backed away and stood in the back of the courtroom.

After being sworn in, the outlaw slouched in the chair as Cole approached him. "George Newton, is that your name?"

"Yeah, guess so."

"According to the Rangers, you're wanted for bank robbery and murder over in east Texas."

"Whatever."

From his desk, Vicker raised his hand. "Objection, your honor. Previous crimes are not relevant."

"Oh yes, this is," Cole said. "It proves two things. One, this man is a known killer and wanted. And two, it demonstrates he is inclined to lie."

Judge Moreland frowned. "I agree. The warrant will be submitted to the court. Proceed, Marshal."

Cole laid the warrant next to the judge and turned to pick up two more. "How did you happen to be riding with two men who are also wanted by the law? Meken Van Camp and Oral Grant?" He waved the additional warrants.

"Again, your honor, I object. The other cases are not germane to this concern." Vicker folded his arms and stared at the outlaw.

Newton smiled widely, displaying a jack-'o-lantern mouth of missing teeth. "Thanks, mister, you keep it up."

Jimmy Vicker frowned, his disgust evident.

Cole handed the additional warrants to the judge. "Again, these warrants show the character of the men I was dealing with and Meken was involved with."

"Proceed, Marshal. These warrants are admissible in this court."

Glancing at Vicker, who tried not to smile, Cole walked over to the outlaw. "Tell the court what you and Oral Grant were doing at Meken's camp?" His eyes cut into the outlaw's round face.

Newton licked his lips, scratched on his arm in the sling. "Meken, an' Oral an' me, we were just campin'. Enjoyin' that part of the country, ya know," he grinned. "Heard some noise. Thought it was Injuns. Oral an' me slipped into the trees to wait."

"I see." Cole's voice was even. "Just how did your friend Meken come to have Mr. Eister's black horse?"

"Uh, he said the owner wanted him to give it a workout. Don't know this Mr. Eister, but I hear tell he's a busy man."

"So, why did you stay in the woods after I approached Meken—and you could tell I wasn't an Indian—and announced that I was a marshal?"

"Uh, well, we *was* comin' out and you cut loose on us. Didn't have much choice but to shoot back. We didn't know you from nothin'." Newton straightened his back. "Ya didn't have no authority out thar, ya know."

Cole recognized the story had a certain truth. And in the cold presentation of a courtroom, it sounded like he was the attacker. He smiled to himself, knowing he was.

"Excuse me, Newton, Meken yelled 'Shoot him!'. Isn't that correct?"

"Uh, I don't recall nothin' like that," Newton said. "We ain't gunslingers like you."

Cole ignored the statement. "Before Meken died, he said the other man who tried to murder me on the trail to the Bar K was his brother . . . Glory Van Camp." His eyes tightened on the outlaw's face. "Do you know who Glory is? Where he is?"

"Nope. Never heard o' him."

"Well, then, who hired you to kill me?"

"Meken did. Uh, I mean nobody. We was just mindin' our own . . ." Newton's face twisted at the slip.

"Why did Meken pretend to be a bum?" Cole interrupted.

"Dunno."

"Was it because no one in town would pay any attention to him?"

"Guess so. He never said."

"Why did you kill that couple in San Antonio?"

Vicker raised his hand and objected. Cole nodded agreement.

Johnny Vicker stood and said in an even voice, "Your honor, there does not seem to be any reason to continue this hearing. I recommend the arrested man be held for trial. He will have his day in court." He paused and straightened his chest. "And that Marshal Kerry be cleared of any wrongdoing."

From the audience came enthusiastic support of Vicker's statement. Dinclaur forced himself to agree with the proposal and said so to Mayor Heinrich.

"Ya. *Herr* Marshal Kerry *ist* a *gut* man."

CHAPTER 25

Hard rain had punished the land for most of two days. Luther and some of the men were bringing horses from the corral into the barn out of the pounding wetness. Shorty and Loop occupied the northern cabin; Peaches would join them when he was through helping Cole in town; Orville Miller, Zeke Ferguson and J.R. Middleton had the far western cabin. They would be there for the winter.

Ethan was restless. Even Claire's reading of the newspapers hadn't helped. It was one of his dark moods, brought on by his blindness. He was a man of action, trapped in darkness. Maggie was engrossed in her school studies; the twins seemed to reflect their father's uneasiness, finding little that could hold their attention, but finally succumbed to a nap.

Sotar had returned before the rain started and left to check the herds and the men staying in the line cabins at the edges of their land. DuMonte went with him. So did Eli, after asking his father. Blue had tagged along with his master. Claire was wary of letting her oldest son go; Ethan insisted their son needed to experience all aspects of ranching. Ethan wanted to go himself, but knew it would be unfair to saddle them with his limitations. If Cole were going, that would be different.

The blind rancher was preoccupied trying to reconcile the pieces of information he had about the Rocking R. Two of their men were killed, presumably when trying to escape from jail. Sotar had told him about twenty-some gunmen were occupying that small ranch. What was happening? Were they intending a massive strike on one of the area ranches? Who tried to kill his brother? Why?

Ethan fumbled for his cigarette makings and settled into a ritual preparation. Was the owner of the Rocking R preparing to attack the Bar K with those gunmen? He took a match from the silver cup of matches on the desk, snapped it into flame along his jeans. The flame brought the cigarette to life as he continued to think. Cole could wire the Rangers and find out what kind of man Heredith Tiorgs was. Sure. That made good sense.

He decided to ride to town with Claire and their youngsters in the next day or so. She would enjoy seeing folks while he talked with Cole. That would be a good time to check in with the bank, too. The Kerrys had owned it since the Victorio Gee gang was destroyed.

Running his hand through his hair, Ethan said, "Who do you think tried to kill Cole?"

Claire folded the newspaper, knowing this was a signal her husband needed to talk. He wasn't normally talkative, except with her. He had never kept details about the ranch from her, good or bad. She was as much a partner in the operation as Luther or Cole. When Sam Winslow had tried to gain control of the Bar K by buying the bank and then calling Ethan's bank loan, she knew immediately. It was Claire who endorsed the idea of Cole leading the herd to Kansas with her blind husband with him. If asked, Cole would say she was more indispensable than Ethan himself or either brother. Then he'd smile that boyish grin of his.

"Been wondering that myself," she said. "He has a reputation with a gun. But I don't think it's that. Do you? Some would say you do, too."

Ethan twisted in his chair and leaned forward on his elbows. His answer was another question. "Wonder if it was a good idea to push Cole into that marshal's job?"

"I think so. He needed something. Something outside himself—and us. Something different."

"I miss him."

"It's only been a week, Ethan."

"I know. But I miss having my little brother around. To chew on."

Claire smiled. "I miss him, too. So do the kids. I'd like Eli to spend more time with Cole. Learn some good things."

Ethan cocked his head. "Like how to use a gun?"

Claire shook her head, but was distracted by the stomping on the porch. Luther shook his poncho and hat before entering the house.

"Hey! What the hell is that?" Ethan blurted as sprays of water reached him. "Well, howdy, Luther. You been swimming?" Ethan teased.

"Sorry, Ethan. Claire. Got mighty wet. Really coming down," the oldest Kerry said.

"You think . . . Eli's doing all right?" Ethan stared in the general direction of his older brother.

"Of course. He's a Kerry, ain't he?"

"Thanks."

Luther described the heaviness of the rain and said that he had checked the bunkhouse as well as the barn for leaks. Ethan was glad to hear that the roofs were dry and that the men there were working on saddles and bridles and he put several to work in the barn, wiping down the horses. He reported on the "rough stuff" held in the corral. All but three had been returned to pasture.

The oldest Kerry brother walked over to the fireplace and held out his hands to warm them, checking to see if he was leaving a trail of wetness, which he was.

"Don't worry about it, Luther," Claire said. "Take off your

boots and socks. Leave them on the hearth." She motioned and stood. "I hear the twins. They're waking up."

From the table, Maggie looked up from her book and said, "I'll get them."

Before Claire could respond, Maggie was off to the children's bedroom. Claire followed, smiling. Minutes later, Will and Russ bounded into the main room and headed for Ethan. He knelt and gathered them in his arms and laughed.

Did he see a blur of light just now? Yes, then a brief glimpse of blurred small faces. Was his mind playing terrible tricks on him? He blinked and saw his small sons. Truly saw them for the first time! He blinked again and their images faded. This time, though, they were indistinct blurs and not void. Could it be? The doctors told him that a part of his eyes had been badly bruised; he had forgotten the fancy terms they used to describe the condition or the part of his eyes affected. That didn't matter. The injury had something to do with internal bleeding. What mattered was that they told him there was a possibility his sight would return if the eyes healed properly. It would take time, a long time. He wiped his eyes to remove the dampness swelling in their corners and grabbed both boys.

"That's quite a handful you got there," Luther said as he pulled off his second boot.

"It's great," Ethan responded and blinked his eyes. Only blurred images.

"Where Unc Cole?" Russ asked, looking around.

"Where Unc Cole?" Will repeated.

"Yeah, is he hiding?" Russ asked. They enjoyed playing hide-and-seek in the house with their uncle. Claire explained Cole was working in Uvalde and was staying there.

"Is Aunt Kathleen with Unc Cole?" Will asked, poking a finger in Ethan's right ear.

The question brought a gulped silence to the room.

Maggie bound into the room and answered the question. "Aunt Kathleen is in Heaven. With Grandma and Grandpa. And Bingo. And Max."

"Bingo and Max? Who Bingo and Max?" Will said.

"Bingo and Max, Bingo and Max," Russ hollered.

Maggie frowned, but everyone started talking at once. An almost joyful relief of energy and grief. Ethan let down both twins and they ran around the room. Feeling happy, Luther did an awkward-looking jig, lost his balance and fell. The house rattled with laughter. Ethan was certain he could see the twins running.

Wiping mist from her eyes, Claire asked Maggie to help her in the kitchen and asked Luther and Ethan to care for the twins.

"Cole's missing out on some mighty special times." Luther leaned over and pretended to grab at the passing twins. "Guess I didn't figure he'd stay in town."

Ethan's mind jumped away to the attempted ambush of Cole. He had sent Peaches to guard his younger brother in case he left alone, trying to find the shooters. He knew that would be what Cole would do.

If the rain stopped, he would ride to town tomorrow with Claire and the youngsters. She would enjoy visiting and shopping while he checked in with Cole. His smile curled up his mouth at both corners as Russ and Will tugged at his legs. He squinted in their direction.

There! He could see their shapes. He shouldn't hold out hope, that was foolish. He had adjusted to the sadness of not seeing. He had to assume this was just some strange phenomenon that might disappear and leave him in darkness. He blinked and his sight was clear. Clear!

From the fireplace, Luther said, "Getting hungry. Are you, Ethan?"

Ethan turned toward his brother and saw him.

Saw him! Luther didn't realize the significance of the connection.

"Yeah, I am."

CHAPTER 26

In the middle of the night, Ethan Kerry lay in bed wide awake. At the moment, he was staring at the stars outside their window, then at Claire asleep beside him. Rain had stopped and Luther had moved the horses again before bedtime.

He lifted his right hand and studied each finger. The scar on the fat part of his thumb had turned white. He couldn't remember how he had gotten the cut. Both of his hands were smooth and no longer thick with calluses. He chuckled and muttered, "Just like some damn Mississippi riverboat gambler." Ethan bit his lip, wanting to yell out that he could see. He could see!

After a few minutes of wondrous examination of their bedroom, the framed landscape on the west wall, and his ever-strong Claire, he slipped from the blankets. Easing into his boots, he stood in his longjohns and walked out of the room. Every detail of the house was savored. He had been seeing, truly seeing, for most of the day, but had kept it to himself out of fear that his sight would leave as it had before. But this time, his sight was truly back. He was certain of it.

The tall rancher slipped into the twins' bedroom and gazed, for the first time, at them sleeping. This was the newest addition to the house. During the day after his sight had returned, he had figured out which twin was Russ and which was Will. Will resembled Claire and Russ looked like him, he decided. He studied each sleeping child. Tears swelled and ran down his lean, tanned face. He made no attempt to wipe them away, but stepped back from their beds and went to his knees.

"O God, I-I thank you. Th-Thank you . . . for, for everything," he muttered, grasping his hands together tightly.

After another long look at the sleeping twins, he visited Maggie's room, then Eli's and remembered his son was gone. How the house had grown over the years; a room added whenever it was needed. Over time, the additions gave the home a rather unbalanced and bloated appearance, as if the structure needed a good burp. It didn't matter; they were together.

He walked past Luther's room and grinned at the loud snoring. He thought about waking up his older brother, but decided the news could wait until morning. Cole's and Kathleen's room was empty. So empty. He missed his younger brother, enjoying his ever-present daring, his confidence, his intensity. Stepping inside the empty room, he went over to the tall dresser and picked up the gold-framed photograph of Cole and Kathleen on their wedding day.

"I'm back, Cole. I'm back," he muttered and returned the frame to its place of honor.

The fireplace in the main room had a graying fire. He stirred the ashes with a poke and was amazed at the richness of color he created. Sparks of gold, crimson, yellow and even blue. He couldn't remember seeing anything so beautiful. The image brought vividly to his mind all of the campfires he had been around over the years. Faces streaked by the gold of the fires paraded through his thoughts. Some long forgotten. He saw his brothers, Luther and Cole, during the War. Then he saw his beloved Claire in his mind. As if for the first time. He had loved her from the moment he saw her in that Union bank.

He wasn't sure why, but he wanted to go outside. Throwing on a handy coat, hanging from the coat rack next to the front door, he stepped out on the porch.

"Man, oh, man, if the boys'd see me now, I'd never hear the end of it," he laughed, wearing boots and a coat over his long underwear.

He just wanted to *see* the land. See the beautiful land. *His* land. Bar K land. He stepped off the porch, leaned over and dug his fingers in the wet earth. A small ball of mud was rolled in his hand as he studied the black shape. How amazing the land was, he thought, and tossed it.

November had brought colder nights, but he didn't feel the bite. How long he stood and gazed at the ranch buildings he wasn't certain. Each sight brought its own awe. He even complimented himself on the sturdiness of the structures and the wisdom of digging trenches around them to draw rain water away.

Ethan Kerry walked into the barn. A whinny caught his attention and he strode to the stall where his black stayed. The barn was full because of the earlier rain. Luther thought it wasn't good for the horses to be exposed to raw weather when there was no need. The bulk of the Bar K horse herd was out in the pasture, but Luther didn't worry about them. Ethan never argued with his older brother on matters of horse flesh.

"Well, good evening to you, Jake," Ethan said as the black horse moved over to where he stood outside the stall.

The horse whinnied again and rubbed its nose against Ethan's arm.

"Of course. Of course. I'll pet you." Ethan stroked the gelding's nose and scratched its long neck. "Got a secret, Jake. But you can't tell your buddies. I can see. Again. Yes sir, I can see. Everything!" He laughed and added, "So when we are riding, I won't be aiming you into some tree. Or a hole or something."

Giving the horse several more pats on its neck, Ethan continued his stroll through the barn and around the ranch. A breeze bit the back of his neck and he wished he had remembered to put on his hat. He laughed—and his pants. The bunkhouse was a music fest of snoring. He tried to remember who was there and who had been assigned to the line cabins.

"Let's see, who'd we put in the north cabin? Oh yeah, Loop . . . and Shorty," he recited to himself. "Peaches'll join them when he's through helping Cole." He rubbed his unshaved chin. "That means the west cabin has Orville, Zeke and J.R. Now, that'll be three to draw to." He chuckled and continued walking.

Halfway back to the main house, the front door burst open and Claire appeared in her robe.

"Ethan? Ethan?"

"I'm over here, Honey. Just checking on the horses." He tried to sound calm.

Claire's face was still, then burst into a huge smile and she came running, tears streaming down her face.

"Oh my God, Ethan! Can you . . ."

"Yes, I can see."

They met in an embrace that left the rest of the world behind.

Neither knew how long they had been in each other's arms when a blustery Luther came to the front door.

"Everything all right out there?" Luther bellowed and peered into the darkness.

"Mom? Pa? What's going on?" A worried Maggie pushed ahead of her big uncle and down the front porch steps.

Ethan and Claire turned toward their daughter, both were crying. Claire spoke first, "Your father . . . he can . . . see." She began to blubber.

Maggie ran to them and hugged them both. For once, she had no questions.

Luther lumbered toward them; the big man's eyes were welling with sweet wetness. "Oh my Lord! Ethan, you can see! Hal-

leluyah!" He started jigging and dancing halfway to them.
After hugging each other, they held hands and danced.

CHAPTER 27

Two weeks after the bogus horse stealing and ambush attempt, Cole Kerry walked down the main street of Uvalde, Texas. The arrested outlaw, George Newton, had been turned over to the Rangers for trial on murder charges in Huntsville, instead of trial on attempted murder charges in Uvalde.

Cole had tried to persuade Newton to tell him who Glory Van Camp was, but the outlaw only shrugged his shoulders and bit his lip. It was clear he didn't know. A wire had been sent to Ranger headquarters to see if they could provide any answers. So far, no return message had come.

Wearing a badge as the town marshal still felt strange to him. Rain had finally left, leaving sparkles of dew on the sidewalk and mud in the streets. Today was a typical November day with the town settling into what served as winter for the region. But the streets were still active with people hurrying somewhere. Thanksgiving was only a week away.

Peaches was minding the jail and Big Red was walking the other end of town. Cole greeted townsfolk with enthusiasm as he passed; Kathleen had encouraged him to be friendly, to let people see the Cole Kerry she knew and loved. The town still murmured with the tale of his encounter with three killers and bringing back Eister's horse. Most thought it strange that Meken Van Camp had been one of them and assumed the poor man had succumbed to the money offered by the other two.

Cole's thoughts of Kathleen were constant, but weren't quite as brutal. His attention was centered on the town and that was good. He knew almost everyone on the street and knew the brands of the horses along the various rails. Actually, it felt right to be serving others, even though he would have preferred to be with his brothers and Ethan's family. Especially now that Ethan had his sight back!

Luther had brought the news on a quick trip to town and back to the ranch. Ethan had decided not to tell anyone outside of the family yet. Even the Bar K riders didn't know. How like Ethan to do it that way, Cole mused as he walked. Oh, would Thanksgiving be something this year! That brought a black feeling that Kathleen wouldn't be there. He shook his head.

A stroll down the main street was his twice-daily pattern. The appearance had actually been another of Ethan's. Cole thought it was strange that a blind man would think in terms of the importance of the town lawman being seen, then recalled the wonder of his brother seeing again.

"Morning, Mr. and Mrs. Williams, how are you today?" he said.

"Good morning to you, Marshal. It is a fine day," Mrs. Williams responded with a smile as Mr. Williams touched his hat brim in greeting.

Although he was uncomfortable in the role as peace officer, the town had taken well to him. They liked his even-handed approach. It didn't matter to Marshal Kerry whether a person was a cattle baron, cowhand, farmer, saloonkeeper, lady of the evening or hotel clerk, all were treated fairly. They were surprised and many were repulsed, but gradually most had grown to accept his hiring Big Red Clanahan and Peaches as his deputies.

The town was very pleased that the Bar K was paying for all of them. Outsiders were surprised to see the youthful-looking peace officer and a few unwisely decided to test him. Cole had arrested three when they attempted to rob the general store. Three more spent time in jail for various offenses. Big Red and Peaches had hauled in a dozen drunks; three who tried to fight Peaches wished they hadn't. The idea of finding Glory Van Camp, whoever he might be, had settled into the back of Cole's mind.

"Mornin' to you, Mr. Jenkins. How's your boy's leg?" Cole asked as he strolled along the wooden sidewalk.

"Doin' real good, Marshal. Should be up an' runnin' in a week or so."

"Hey, that's good news."

Cole watched him for a few moments, then continued his stroll. Creaks in the wooden planked sidewalk were comforting. He stepped around a small puddle where the beams had curved. Ethan's family would be in town soon, he thought. How great it would be to see them!

As he passed the post office, Wilomina Reid ran out to him.

"Saw you coming, Marshal. Four bad-lookin' strangers just reined up outside our bank. Ridin' fine horses." Her unruly eyebrows danced with her report and met in the middle of her forehead at its completion.

"Thanks, Wilomina. I'll have a look."

"Could be just newcomers. Wanted you to know, though."

Cole shook his head. "Doesn't sound like it."

The gruff postmistress turned for the post office. "Should I go find your deputies?"

"Yes. Please. Peaches is in the jail. Big Red is checking the saloons."

"You bet."

After leaving the post office, Cole turned toward the unpainted building with the "bank" sign on it. He didn't hear Wilomina tell him to be careful. Four against one wasn't anyone's idea of fun, but that's what the town paid him for.

Looking down at the badge on his vest, he took a deep breath, then removed the hammer loops from his holstered guns.

Down the street and inside the church, Reverend Paul Dinclaur watched from a small window with great interest. He had seen the four Rocking R riders pass the church and had looked to see if they were riding Rocking R horses. They weren't; Tiorgs was too smart for that. None of the men being used for this task were known around Uvalde. This would be a glorious day, he mused to himself. If they got away with the bank's money, the Kerrys would be hurt financially—and Cole Kerry would be killed.

Jinette Six was already in the bank, ready to add firepower, if it could be done discreetly, or more likely to provide a suitable hostage if needed. She was also to shoot the bank robbers if it looked like they would be captured. Two more Rocking R men had checked into the hotel yesterday. They were dressed in business suits and presented themselves as cattle buyers from San Antonio.

Dinclaur's attention turned to the third-floor hotel window overlooking the street and across from the bank. He could see a silhouette behind the third-floor window curtain and knew one shooter was in position. He glanced at the roof and realized, without seeing, that his second man was there as well. Both were armed with rifles and had one target: Cole Kerry. They were to hold their fire until they were certain of killing him.

Outside the church, a black crow flew to the ground in search of food. Dinclaur recited an old riddle about crows: "One's bad, two's luck, three's health, four's wealth, five's sickness— and six is death." He chuckled. "Got five more of your brothers somewhere close? You're going to need them." He looked around the small church. A candle flickered and went out. A sign of death, he told himself. Cole Kerry's death.

At the tie rack in front of the bank, a nervous man in a long coat sat on a fine-looking bay, holding three other horses, equally long-legged and strong. Wilomina had guessed right, seeing fast horses at the rack and supposed they were outlaw mounts. They weren't the kind ridden by cowhands or farmers. Luther would love them, though, Cole thought. The long-coated stranger waiting outside the bank was nervous, casting his eyes back and forth constantly.

It was a bank robbery.

Cole eased into the street, using passing wagons and horsemen to hide his advance. Walking through them would, hopefully, give him the advantage of surprise because he could get close to the waiting outlaw with being seen, unless he turned completely around in the saddle. The young marshal paused to let a freighter rumble by, then two riders, and walked alongside another passing wagon. People, mostly men, were walking in both directions in front of the bank. None were aware of the pending robbery as far as he could tell. And Cole was not aware that his quick movements were being patiently followed by two riflemen hidden in the hotel and on its roof.

He drew the sidewinder Colt, moved it to his left hand and cocked it. As the wagon passed in front of the bank, the young marshal turned toward the waiting outlaw, walking toward him from the man's back. He drew his second Colt with his right hand and cocked the weapon as well.

" 'Mornin'," Cole said as he neared the waiting horseman.

The outlaw jumped in his saddle and turned toward Cole. One eye appeared to be too close to his nose and the stubble on his face didn't quite cover the knife scar along his right cheek. The outlaw's gaze caught the star on Cole's vest and his right hand slid inside his coat. Dark eyes sized up the young man in front of him, glanced toward the hotel, then back to Cole. Did the lawman know what was going to happen to him?

"Mighty good-looking horses you've got there," Cole said,

walking closer. "The kind bank robbers like." His light blue eyes blazed brightly. In this kind of moment, he felt totally alive. Always had. Everything seemed to slow down.

"Wouldn't know," the outlaw answered, turning his head toward Cole, then back toward the closed bank door. His hand remained inside his coat.

"Tell you what," Cole continued. "I want you off that fancy horse. Right now. And if your right hand comes out with a gun, you'll die. Right here. You decide if it's worth it."

Wiggling in the saddle while facing the bank, the outlaw whined, "Wait a minute, Marshal. Me an' my friends are just . . . new to town. Openin' an account. That's what. We're startin' a store."

"Good for you. Get down."

"Mister, you don't want to tangle with us."

"Get down. You don't want to tangle with me."

Shaking his head negatively, the outlaw said, "Oh, you wouldn't do that, would you?" He turned toward Cole, his right hand clearing his coat with a long-barreled revolver.

Both of Cole's guns roared and the lead took the man off his saddle as the outlaw's bullet drove a hole through the brim of Cole's hat. The outlaw's emptied horse reared in fright and bolted. Slamming to the ground, the outlaw groaned and rolled over. A circle of blood on his shirt widened.

At the hitch rack, the three other outlaw horses snorted and stamped. Cole enhanced their fear by waving his guns in the air. They joined the fourth horse down the street, stopping when they came to other horses tied to the rack outside a saloon. A quick glance found the outlaw's loose gun and the young sheriff kicked it into the street. Bursting from the jail, Peaches ran toward the action with his Evans rifle. Farther down the street, Big Red Clanahan lumbered toward him with a double-barreled shotgun.

"Lay still and it won't hurt as much," Cole said to the groaning outlaw. "I'll get you a doc when this is over."

The gunshots would warn the other outlaws inside the bank, but there wasn't anything he could do about it. If they stayed inside and took hostages of any bank customers, it would be a long day, but they wouldn't get away. He had already decided that. Several townspeople stopped on both sides of the sidewalk, uncertain of what was happening.

Without turning his attention from the bank door, Cole told them to turn around and get out of the way.

Seconds later, three other outlaws burst through the bank door. Each carried filled saddlebags. The door slammed behind them. A broad-shouldered outlaw with a wide, blubbery face pushed a woman in front of him, holding her close with his left arm. The hostage was Jinette Six, the woman Cole remembered from the restaurant. In the robber's right fist was a revolver shoved against her back. She was pleading with him not to hurt her. To his left were the two other outlaws with revolvers searching for something to shoot. None were surprised to see Cole standing there.

"Sorry, boys. It's over. Drop your guns."

"We're leaving—or she gets it," the broad-shouldered outlaw growled. "Billy. Sam. Get our horses."

An Irish bandit of undetermined age in an ill-fitting suitcoat and a floppy hat looked at Cole and began shuffling toward the waiting horses down the street. The other bank robber, a wavy-haired man without a hat, sneered at Cole and followed.

"Hurry up! Dammit!" The first outlaw growled and waved in the direction of the hotel.

Cole fired and the bullet ripped into the planked sidewalk a foot from the Irish outlaw; he swung his gun back toward the broad-shouldered outlaw. The Irishman almost fell, trying to halt, and the wavy-haired man collided with him and cursed.

"Move toward those horses and you die," Cole commanded, "All of you, drop your guns and put your hands up."

Nodding excessively, the Irishman dropped his pistol and let his saddlebags slide to the sidewalk. His hands rose and he grinned. The other outlaw didn't move, but his gun remained at his side. He glared at Cole.

"I won't give another warn—"

Cole's words were interrupted by rifle shots from the hotel behind him. One caught him high in the right shoulder; a second drove into him inches from the first. A third shot missed, burning his neck, and a fourth slammed into his back. Cole staggered from the impact of the bullets, then spun away and dived for the water trough behind him. Bullets chased his retreat and one caught his lower left leg.

Laughing, the broad-shouldered outlaw stepped away from Jinette and fired at Cole, hitting him again in the upper shoulder. The hatless outlaw raised his pistol and fired, driving lead into Cole's right arm.

From behind the trough, Cole fired both guns and the hatless outlaw grabbed his stomach and fell.

"Get him now," Jinette whispered. "You'll never have another chance like this."

"Hell, I'm getting out of here! He's dead or gonna be." The broad-shouldered outlaw fired a quick shot in Cole's direction and ran for the horses. Cole propped his trembling right hand on the sidewalk and shot again, sending the outlaw stumbling.

Stopping in the middle of the uneven street, Peaches knelt, aimed his rifle and fired five times; three times at the hotel roof and twice at the third-floor window. The window shooter staggered, grabbed the curtain and fell to the street. Big Red kept running as the blubbery-faced man regained his balance and limped toward the nervous animals. Joining him was the Irish outlaw whose hat flew off as he ran.

Bleary-eyed and trembling, Cole fired twice and missed.

Big Red's shotgun blasted the blubbery outlaw as he rose into his saddle.

Reacting to Peaches's firing, the shooter on the roof spun toward him and fired. Too fast. His bullet snapped at the dirt inches from the Chinaman's boots. A second bullet clipped Peaches's left shoulder. Peaches took his time, aimed and fired once. The roof shooter stiffened as a black hole appeared in the middle of his forehead. His rifle clanged on the roof parapet and flew toward the alley. The shooter disappeared from Peaches's sight. Two cowboys with rifles hurried from the saloon toward Peaches.

From the back of the post office, Dinclaur knelt and fired, holding his handgun with both hands. His first bullet creased Cole's left thigh and the second tugged at his shirt.

Peaches glanced back to see where the shots were coming from, but the minister had already hidden his gun and turned around as if he were looking to see where the shooting had come from. Not seeing anyone shooting, the Chinaman turned his attention to the bank robbers and sent the cowboys to check the post office area. He had an odd sensation that the person shooting at Cole was the town's minister. Couldn't be. He resumed his advance, pointing to the hotel for Big Red to check. The Irishman popped open his shotgun, shoved in new loads and lumbered through the hotel's front door.

Barely conscious, Cole saw the first outlaw stand, gather his gun and aim it at Peaches. Cole slammed three shots at him with both guns. Two struck his left shirt pocket and the third missed. The outlaw's body jerked wildly and his revolver exploded into the sidewalk. He went to his knees, then fell face forward. Cole's Colts clicked on empty and he tried to shove shells into one, but his eyes were bleary and he managed to only get two bullets into the weapon before he collapsed.

Jinette watched as Peaches and some of the townspeople dispatched the rest of the bank robbers, then bent over, picked up the closest revolver and walked toward the unconscious Cole. His shirt was more red than white. She stopped beside him.

"You should be dead." She smiled evilly. "Looks like the only places we missed were your heart and head. I can fix that."

"Get away from Cole Ker-rie-son." Peaches's command was hard and loud.

Jinette froze, looked at the bloody Cole, then back at the intense Chinaman with his rifle aimed at her. He was less than twenty feet away. His rifle was aimed at her head.

"You not be first woman I shoot." A Chinese curse followed.

"Oh . . . I was just going to . . . help him." She smiled. "He is . . . breathing."

"I know. He is Cole Ker-rie-son." Peaches took a step closer without lowering his gun. "Leave gun on sidewalk. Go find doctor."

"You misunderstand. I was going to help." She hesitated, dropped the gun and walked away swiftly. She avoided looking at Peaches for fear he would see the fierce anger in her eyes.

Satisfied she had left, Peaches went to Cole and confirmed he was breathing. The young marshal's breath was slight, but it was there. Peaches laid down his rifle and yanked the neckerchief from his neck. Wadding the cloth, he pressed it against the most serious wounds to slow the bleeding.

"Cole Ker-rie-son, you must live. You have no choice." A Chinese blessing passed from Peaches's lips.

From across the street, Mayor Heinrich hurried toward them, carrying a shotgun. A clerk with a Springfield rifle and two CW Connected cowboys, brandishing handguns, followed. Bank President Triston Yankison ventured slowly from the bank and began retrieving the outlaws' saddlebags filled with the bank's money. He only glanced at Peaches treating Cole.

"The town's money *ist* safe. *Ist gut.*" Heinrich declared as he crossed the street quickly, stepping around the dead outlaws. "How *ist Herr* Marshal?" His eyes were wide with fear.

"He is Cole Ker-rie-son." Peaches didn't look up. "He must live."

"Ja. Ja. I agree, certainly," Heinrich eagerly replied, stopping beside the Chinaman. "Vilomina went for Doc Vright." He handed Peaches a fresh white handkerchief, which the China-man began to use, dropping his own blood-soaked neckerchief.

"We take him to his room. In hotel. Doctor tend him there," Peaches said.

"Should not *ve vait* for the doctor here?"

Big Red came up before Peaches could answer and reported breathlessly, "By Jaysus, the two shooters from the hotel be dead. Both. So be the bank robbers themselves. How be hisself, the marshal?"

Peaches shook his head as he continued to apply pressure to Cole's wounds. "There is one more shooter. He shot from back of post office."

"I'll go look." Big Red straightened.

"No, he gone. You help me carry Cole Ker-rie-son to his hotel room," Peaches said. "Doctor come there." He looked up at Big Red. "This not over. They want Cole Ker-rie-son dead. Ambush. No real bank holdup."

The idea hit Heinrich and the Irishman like a fist.

From all over town, people were coming out of hiding.

Tearfully, the big Irishman moved to help lift Cole. "I swear on me mithur's grave, I will not stop until we find the foul bastirds theirselves behind this."

"I will stand with you, my friend," Peaches said, then looked down in the street.

CHAPTER 28

On the same day as the terror in town, Eli Kerry, John David Sotar and Harold "Preacher" DuMonte returned from their swing through the Bar K range with good news about the herds. Blue trotted alongside his master, happy to be returning home. They reined up in front of the porch where Ethan and Luther stood. Water and grass were holding well and the men were keeping Bar K cattle on Bar K range and out of the lone patch of loco weed that had sprouted.

His chaps heavily crusted with dried mud, the teenage boy was tired, but happy to have had the opportunity to ride with three of Bar K's top men. Zeke had left them when they got close to the line cabin where he was spending the winter. Eli and DuMonte eased out of their saddles and started to lead their horses away to the barn.

Swinging down from his saddle, Sotar reported there were no signs of screw worm. Standing on the porch, a smiling Ethan responded by saying it was too late in the year for the problem, except for two years ago when it was so hot. Sotar agreed, then stopped and stared at the tall rancher with his arms crossed. Luther was standing next to him, smiling.

"Now, wait a minute, Boss," Sotar declared, waving his right hand toward the Kerrys, "What's goin' on? You two are grinnin' like it's Christmas mornin'."

DuMonte turned. So did Eli. DuMonte realized first what had happened to Ethan.

"My oh my, the Lord answers our prayers and when we don't expect it," the sturdy colored man said and leaned over to whisper in Eli's ear, "Your pa's seein' again, Eli. Look at him, son. Look at him!"

Eli spun around and dropped his reins. His mouth dropped open and he ran toward the porch. Dried mud flipped off his chaps as he hurried. Blue followed with a bark. DuMonte picked up the loose reins and smiled.

"Pa! Pa! Is it true? Can you really see again?"

"Well, looks to me like you've spent some time down in a bog, son," Ethan said. "Looks like Sotar was there, too. How's that for an answer?"

Luther clapped his hands together like he was at a hoe-down and sang giddily, "Oh Susannah, don't you cry for me . . . Ethan Kerry's seein' again . . . and that's a big hurr-eee!" He laughed at his own singing and so did the others.

Ethan stepped forward and held out his arms for his oldest son. Eli's face disappeared into his father's chest and they hugged. Blue jumped up to share in the attention.

"You have become a man, Eli. You make me proud," Ethan whispered into his son's ear.

Ethan eased backward, assessing his son as if seeing him for the first time, and said, "Well, did you get that cow out of there? Or did you just decide to play in the mud?"

"He sure did," Sotar said and flipped his reins around the hitching rack. "Had to get down in there and work 'er out. We needed a shovel. She was stuck real good." He chuckled. "Think she's gonna be fine, though. Tried to ram Eli as soon as she got out."

"They'll do that. Looks like you were right there with him," Ethan motioned toward Sotar's muddy chaps.

Maggie appeared in the doorway and ran toward Eli, declaring, "You're all muddy, Eli. Ugh."

"I sure am." He lifted her in the air and nuzzled her cheek with his nose, then let her down. "How are you, Maggie? How are Will and Russ?"

"They're sleeping. Did you know Pa can see again?" she asked. "He's been reading with me at night."

Sotar stepped around the hitching rack and hopped onto the porch, ignoring the steps. "Damn, Boss! This is great. Absolutely great." He held out his hand and Ethan shook it warmly and patted his shoulder.

Instead of leading the horses to the barn, DuMonte tied them to the rack and followed Eli and Sotar. He shook hands enthusiastically with both Ethan and Luther while humming "Oh Susannah." After a few minutes of savoring and discussing Ethan's returned sight, talk returned to the range. DuMonte told the Kerrys that there were some new calves since the roundup. They had also found a dead calf; coyotes had gotten it. They tied and milked the cow to prevent infection and found an orphaned calf in need of her milk.

"I told the boys we needed to brand 'em as we see 'em," Sotar advised. "Don't think we should wait 'til spring."

"I take it you're worried about the Rocking R," Ethan said, refolding his arms.

Sotar hitched up his gunbelt. "Didn't see many Rocking R animals out there, Boss. No Rocking R riders either. None. But it looked like there were plenty at their ranch. We didn't get too close, but close enough. Seems like they're keepin' right to home."

"Let's go inside . . . after you boys shed your mud. I want to hear more." Ethan put his arm around Eli's shoulder.

Sotar and Eli unbuckled their chaps and began pulling off their mud-covered boots.

"We can clean 'em up later," Sotar said.

"Sure. Wonder if Ma's got anything to eat?" He laughed as

Blue squeezed close to him and licked his face as the boy sat to remove his boots.

"Knowing your ma, I'm sure she does."

Inside, Claire greeted her oldest son with a warm hug and a kiss on the cheek. Eli blushed and glanced at Sotar, who nodded. She announced that noon dinner would be ready in five minutes. She told Maggie to set more places.

"Oh, now, Mrs. Kerry, we don't want to put you out," DuMonte said. "I gotta be getting along home to my family anyhow."

Claire turned and put her hands on her hips. "Now listen here, Harold. I won't have you leave here with an empty stomach. Bertha would be most upset with me." She motioned toward Ethan. "Besides, he'll want to hear everything. Why don't you men have a little whiskey while I finish up?" She smiled and looked at Eli. "But no whiskey for you, young man."

"How's Uncle Cole?" Eli asked, watching his mother disappear into the kitchen while Maggie began adding settings to the table.

Preparing glasses of whiskey, Luther told about the attempted horse stealing and ambush, and that the town bum had turned out to be a wanted outlaw and one of the men who tried to kill Cole earlier. His information had come from his recent trip to town to tell Cole the good news about Ethan's returned sight. He handed the whiskeys to Ethan first, then Sotar and DuMonte. The four men clinked their glasses together and toasted the Bar K.

"Do you think Uncle Cole likes being marshal?" Eli asked and sat down on one of the main table's chairs and rubbed his stockinged feet. His right big toe peeked through a hole and he pulled on the cloth to hide it.

"Good question, son," Ethan said and swallowed his whiskey in one gulp. "Reckon he'd rather be here with us, but if he's going to be away, it's a good time of the year for it."

"When can we go see him?" Eli's eyes darted toward the kitchen where Maggie had gone and heard her asking questions about the mud on Eli's chaps. He scratched Blue's ears, sitting close to him. From the kitchen, Claire yelled, "Tomorrow." Ethan poured another round and talked about Meken Van Camp, asking Sotar if he knew of a Glory Van Camp, explaining that they were the two who had tried to kill Cole on the way to the ranch.

"Any idea what this Glory Van Camp looks like?" Eli asked nervously, putting his feet back on the floor and moving his right foot to hide the hole. It felt good to be home, but he didn't want to say it. They had gotten soaked one day before they reached the closest line cabin. But he was proud to have gone and to have done his part.

"Only thing Cole knows is that Meken and Glory have real small feet. Like a boy's," Ethan said and sipped his second drink. "Saw the tracks where he was ambushed. And Meken's feet after he was shot."

"Where do you think this Glory Van Camp is, Pa? Why are they trying to kill Cole?" Eli's face was white.

"Well, it looks to me like they want the Bar K," Ethan said evenly. "They figure to get rid of us, starting with Cole. They aren't worried about me . . . I'm blind." His eyes narrowed.

"Will Uncle Cole . . . be all right?"

"Guess that depends on how good this Glory Van Camp is," Ethan said and frowned.

Sotar stared at his drink. "Think he's connected to the Rocking R?"

"If I was betting, I'd say yes."

The Missouri foreman's eyes flashed. "Let's gather up our boys and ride over and clean them out."

Luther shook his head as Ethan said, "Can't. They haven't

done anything wrong we can prove yet."

"We just gonna wait 'til they go after Cole again?" Sotar's question was hot.

"I don't reckon we have any other choice."

"Damn."

"Yeah."

CHAPTER 29

In the early evening, a special church service was hastily called by Pastor Dinclaur. Word of the service spread through town, thanks to the mayor. It was his idea. The purpose was to celebrate the mixed outcomes of the day, the saving of their bank's money and to pray for the life of their seriously wounded marshal. With the entire town buzzing about the daring of their young marshal and the deadly crossfire, the gathering was a natural sequence of events.

The church filled quickly as Dinclaur watched the townspeople file in and take their seats. He had dealt with his own disappointment over the saving of the bank's money and Cole Kerry not yet dying. Jinette Six had reminded him that even if Cole survived, and that seemed unlikely with all the lead in his body, the gunfighter would be out of action for months. Perhaps forever. He would be no help to the Bar K. That had cheered Dinclaur up.

Tomorrow, as planned, Tiorgs and his men would gather and move a herd of two or three hundred Bar K cattle onto Rocking R grazing land, where they would be rebranded. Tiorgs and his men would set up an ambush to trap the Bar K riders sure to come after them. Crippling the great ranch operation would come in one big gulp.

Just like he planned.

It didn't really matter which came first, the killing of Cole Kerry or Ethan Kerry or the elimination of most of the Bar K riders, or the reduction of their great herds. Any would eventually give him what he wanted: the Bar K. He was more and more certain Cole Kerry would not survive with all the bullets that hit him.

"Good evening and welcome to the Lord's house of *worship*," Pastor Dinclaur announced, his voice filling the room. "Let us begin by singing Hymn 48, 'Onward Christian Soldiers . . .' "

In the back row, Big Red Clanahan opened his hymnal and began to sing. His attendance was Peaches's suggestion; the Chinaman thought the town's law should be present. Two rows in front of him, and to his right, sat Wilomina Reid. Near the front sat Jinette Six. She had shared her confrontation with the Chinese deputy with Dinclaur earlier. The pastor wasn't concerned. Any "misunderstanding" could be dismissed by the tenseness of the situation. He thought she should see Cole and, if possible, talk to the Chinaman.

An old man in the third row began to snore lightly. A small boy in the pew in front of him turned around. His mother admonished him to sit still and face the front. The sleeping man was jolted awake by his wife's elbow.

After another song and the recitation of the Lord's Prayer, Dinclaur delivered the sermon with his usual flair. He stood behind the pulpit for a long moment, as if studying each person in the room. A dramatic way to begin, he thought. His sermon was a mixture of thanksgiving for the day's outcome, appreciation that no townspeople were harmed, that their money was saved, and praise for the young marshal, his deputies, even the mayor and the others who helped prevent the robbery. Big Red blushed when several townspeople looked around at him and smiled. Wilomina lingered her gaze longer than the others. Dinclaur's expression of deep concern for the marshal followed, along with a few sobs among the woman parishioners.

Dinclaur's sermon transitioned into traditional church fare, concerns for the city's vices and earnest pleadings to let the riches of the land be governed by godly men, a statement that would help set the stage for the transition of Bar K ownership to him. All wrapped around the opening to Tennyson's *Lotus Eaters:*

> " 'Courage,' he said, and pointed toward the
> land,
> 'This mounting wave will roll us shoreward soon.'
> In the afternoon they came unto a *land*
> In which it seemed always afternoon.
> All around the coast the languid air did *swoon,*
> Breathing like one that hath a weary moon;
> And like a downward smoke, the slender stream
> Along the cliff to fall and pause and fall did
> *seem.* "

He loved the look on parishioners' faces as he ended, saying this was Uvalde and then, Amen. As he expected, many of the women's eyes were moist. He couldn't help smiling as he spoke.

At least half the audience wouldn't realize his long recital hadn't come from the Bible and most wouldn't understand what this brilliantly written poem even meant. But they would get a sense of a beautiful place. That's what he wanted. His face was rich with practiced emotion.

After the passing of the collection plate, which resulted in an above-average return, Dinclaur closed with a prayer: "O Lord, protect us in times of danger, stand with us in times of need, and comfort us in times of *sorrow.* Look with care upon thy servant, Marshal Cole Kerry, and bring him back to *us.* Give us peace as we work together to build our town and this *region.* Amen. Go in *peace.* "

People began to put on their coats. Mingled conversation

became a sort of garbled song. Many offered statements of prayer and concern for Cole to the big Irishman as they left. Wilomina stood in the aisle waiting for him.

In the hotel, Peaches sat alone with the unconscious Cole in his room. The hotel manager had brought up a rocking chair for him earlier. Dr. Wright cleaned Cole's bloody body and removed the bullets. He was not optimistic about Cole's recovery; the gunfighter had lost considerable blood and was unconscious. Peaches was to coax the wounded marshal to drink water with an eye dropper and applying the liquid to Cole's mouth. At his feet was an opened can of peaches. He used the eye dropper to pull out juice and give it to Cole, along with the water. The idea was his. If his grandmother's story was right, the peaches would help Cole heal. Big Red had brought the can before going to the church service.

He was to change the wet compress on Cole's forehead as often as needed. The doctor was worried about Cole's rising fever as well as his considerable loss of blood. The look on the physician's face was somber and Peaches wasn't comforted.

Tomorrow, if there was one, he could attempt to give Cole some broth and some of the peach fruit itself.

Peaches had barely touched his supper, the plate growing cold on the floor beside him. He wasn't hungry and planned to spend the night in Cole's room. Partly to stay close to his friend. Partly because he wasn't convinced the attack on Cole was over.

In the lobby, two cowboys from the CW Connected stood guard; they had insisted on staying. A third cowboy, a Mexican, had volunteered to ride for the Bar K to tell them what had happened. Peaches expected Big Red to come by after the church service; he would ask the Irishman to stay in the jail for the night. Cole would want the town to know that it was not unprotected. The Irishman could stretch out on one of the jail cell cots himself and sleep.

Rocking in the chair with his rifle across his lap, Peaches reworked the attempted bank robbery and ambush in his mind. Clearly, the main objective was to kill Cole. But why? Had he imagined the beautiful woman ready to shoot Cole? Why? And who was firing from the post office? Why did he think it was the minister?

He wished Ethan Kerry were here. The tall rancher would know what to do.

Who was behind this madness? Why? Peaches lived in the white man's world, but often was surprised by some of their actions. The only white man he totally trusted was lying in the bed across the room. He looked over at the seriously wounded marshal and choked. It wasn't fair. Cole had just avoided an ambush on the trail and been wounded then. He had faced three horse thieves. He was supposed to be the town marshal until they could hire someone permanently. Peaches stood and walked over to the bed; he put his hand on Cole's forehead. The marshal's skin was hot. His wounds were bound in bandages, but two continued to seep blood.

That wasn't good. The young gunfighter's gunbelt sat on the worn chair in the far corner. Besides the bed and chairs, the only other furniture in the room were a dresser with an attached, and cracked, mirror and a wobbly leg and a small night-table next to the bed.

Mayor Heinrich, Wilomina and Pastor Dinclaur had come to the hotel, each seeking to see Cole and to learn of his status. None were allowed into the room; Peaches blocked the door from the hallway outside. Only Dinclaur had protested about being turned away, insisting it was important for God to be with Cole. The Chinaman told him God was already with Cole and didn't need the minister's help in that matter.

Resting on the dresser's well-scratched top were a water

pitcher, a bowl, two glasses, several clean wash rags and an unlit gas lantern. Peaches didn't think it was wise to illuminate the room with light. Sitting in the dark was safer.

Slowly, the stout Chinaman walked over to the chair and pulled one of Cole's guns from its holster. The weapon was still empty. So was the other Colt. He reloaded both guns, returned one to its holster and shoved the other into his own waistband. Whoever was after Cole might try again, hoping to catch everyone off guard. He had no doubt in his mind that this madness wasn't over. Easing next to the single window, he studied the street below without revealing himself. The town was quiet. Even the saloons were subdued.

A groan from Cole jerked Peaches away from the window and he spun toward the bed. The young gunfighter was mumbling incoherently and thrashing his right arm around on the bed. Guessing what he wanted, he went to Cole's gun rig and withdrew the second Colt. He hesitated, then removed the cartridge under the hammer and pressed the gun's handle into Cole's agitated right hand. Immediately, the wounded marshal relaxed and was quiet.

"Rest, my good friend," Peaches said, patting Cole's arm. "They were not good enough. No, they were not." He mumbled a prayer in Chinese.

He studied the location of Cole's bed and decided to move it a bit farther to the south. That way no one shooting from outside could hit him. Then he moved the dresser against the locked door.

Rolling his shoulders to ease the pain of the bullet burn, Peaches poured some water into a glass and returned to the bedside. His own wound was so slight that he had refused the doctor's offer to look at it.

"You need power of peach, Cole Ker-rie-son."

A knock on the door stopped his slow process of dripping

peach juice to Cole with the eye dropper.

"Peaches. It be me, Red. Church be over. Thought I'd come an' sit for a piece, if that be good with you." The voice was the Irishman's.

"Ah so. Could use some company."

Laying the cup of peach juice on the floor, Peaches shoved the heavy dresser away from the door, drew his shoulder-holstered gun and opened the door slowly.

"You be alone?"

"Alone, I be. Bringing some hot tea and donuts. Mr. Heinrich thought it might be tastin' good to ye. Maybe Cole. The tea, anyway." He paused and added, "Brought ye another can of peaches."

"Come in," Peaches said, holstering his gun.

Big Red Clanahan stepped in, holding a tray with a tea pot, three cups, a plate of donuts and a can of peaches. Peaches closed the door behind them and repositioned the dresser. The Irishman stood over the bed and told the unconscious Cole of the praise of townspeople while Peaches poured tea for them. He ignored the Irishman's groans; he knew how he felt.

The Irishman squatted on the floor, eating a donut and drinking tea, while Peaches tried giving Cole some tea from the dropper. Their conversation gradually slid to Marshal Montgomery's murder, then to Jinette Six, then to why Cole had been ambushed. The Irishman had no idea, but agreed it wasn't a simple bank robbery. Clanahan had met with Wilomina Reid after church. She had invited him to Sunday supper. She was downstairs and intended to stay the night on guard with her shotgun. Peaches teased him and the big Irishman blushed.

"You ready spend night at the jail? Cole Ker-rie-son would want us to do our duty." He added that Big Red should have Cole's saddled sorrel taken to the livery. There was no reason for the horse to stand at the jail's hitching rail.

"Aye."

Big Red straightened his back and stood. "Mayor Heinrich hisself be tellin' me after church . . . the council will be needin' to appoint a new marshal." His face looked like he had eaten something very sour.

Peaches looked at the floor. It made sense, but still it was hard to hear.

CHAPTER 30

"Hold up right there, mister. Identify yourself. Keep your hands where I can see them." John David Sotar's Missouri twang cut hard through the darkness.

Juan Histallos reined his lathered horse and shouted, "I come from ze town, *señor.* Marshal Kerry has been shot *mucho* bad. Hees deputy . . . ah, Peaches, he send me to tell you."

"What?"

Patting the neck of his tired horse, Juan repeated his message, talking slower this time, and described the attempted bank robbery and the ambush by the hidden riflemen. He said the Chinaman was with Cole now. The doctor had removed the bullets, but the marshal had lost considerable blood and was unconscious. He added the doctor did not think it would go well for Cole.

"You mean he thinks Cole's gonna die?"

"*Si, Señor.*"

"Damn." Sotar shook his head, then looked back at the weary Mexican. "Thanks for coming. Swing down. Coffee's on. Everybody's up."

Sotar explained that some of their herd had been run off during the night. Two Bar K men had been killed, trying to stop the rustlers. Orville Miller and Zeke Ferguson were dead. The third hand in the western cabin, J.R. Middleton, had been wounded, but managed to get to the ranch. He was in the bunkhouse, after being tended to by Claire and Ethan. All of the Bar K men, even those from the other line cabin, were gathered at the main house and would pursue the rustlers as soon as it was light enough.

Graves had already been dug for the two Bar K men and their bodies laid in the small family cemetery not far from the main house. Ethan's father was buried there last spring and Luther's family before that. It was the Kerrys' way that the men who rode for the Bar K and were loyal, were family.

Sotar and the Mexican rider shook hands and introduced themselves.

Halfway to the house, Sotar stopped. "Say, you should've seen Luther Kerry. You know, the oldest Kerry brother. Big fella. Always smilin'. He was headed to town. The boss wanted Cole and Peaches with us. Reckon we're in for a fight."

"I see no one, *Señor* Sotar," Juan replied softly, leading his horse.

Sotar looked off into the dark horizon as if hoping to see Luther.

"Me hoss ees wore down, *Señor* Sotar."

"Yeah, I see. Thanks for gettin' hyar so fast," Sotar said and pointed toward the barn. "Take him in there. Get that leather off him. After he cools down, we'll give him some water an' oats." He pushed his hat back on his forehead. Sweat beaded on the exposed skin even in the cold night. "We'll switch hosses so yo-al can ride home after yo-al get somethin' to eat. Sound good?"

"*Si Señor.*" Juan's tight face was sad and tired.

Sotar headed for the main house as the Mexican swung toward the barn. In the corral, horses were saddled; each carried a rifle in its boot.

Inside the main house, gas lamps were lit. Armed men stood, drinking coffee and eating bacon, scrambled eggs and biscuits from the plates spread out on the table. Claire was working in the kitchen with help from the brawny roundup cook, Mattis Champlin, and her two oldest children, Eli and Maggie. So far, the twins were asleep.

Ethan stood in the middle of the room, drinking coffee and listening to Harold DuMonte as the steady colored cowman described again what they had found. He figured over two hundred head had been driven away sometime during the early evening. Gunfire in the night had startled them into action. Two Bar K men were dead and one, wounded. The injured J.R. Middleton lay in the bunkhouse.

Ethan's energy was boiling over with the need to get after the rustlers, but experience told him they would be better off waiting for daylight. The news of his returning sight drew curious glances from his men.

The tall rancher pulled men to him in a way some leaders could. He was confident. Strong. "Boss! Rider from town just came in. Bad news in Uvalde. Cole's been shot up real bad. Caught him in a crossfire." Sotar yelled as soon as he entered the house. "Sounds like it was planned."

A tenseness took over the room as every man turned to listen. Ethan's face tightened. "Is he . . . ?"

"Said Cole took a lot of lead, but he was breathin' when he left," Sotar continued as he walked toward Ethan. He explained the bank robbery and the hidden hotel riflemen, ending with the simple statement that the robbery was stopped and all of the outlaws were killed.

Claire appeared in the kitchen doorway, her expression shocked. Ethan walked over to the table, yanked out a chair and sat. His mind was crackling with images. Cole shot again? Who was behind this madness? What was going on?

Sotar turned as Juan Histallos entered and the Missouri gunfighter introduced him. Mumbles rolled across the room as the stunned Bar K men tried to grapple with the news. Du-

240

Monte stepped closer to to the Mexican rider, handing him a filled coffee cup. "What about Peaches? The Oriental fella?"

Accepting the hot coffee, Juan said, "He eez . . . all right. He eez in charge. He send me. He eez with Marshal Kerry in hotel. Ze big Irishman eez there also." The short rider pushed his sombrero from his head and let it dangle down his back with the stampede string around his neck.

Eli and Maggie stood in the kitchen doorway, listening. Shaking his head, Eli turned around and walked back into the kitchen, uncertain of what he should do. Claire held the wide-eyed Maggie next to her.

"Has Uncle Cole gone to be with Aunt Kathleen?" Maggie blurted.

Claire squeezed her eyes, then said, "No, Uncle Cole is hurt, that's all. No more questions, Maggie . . . please. Not now."

The eyes around the room were skeptical of the statement. Ethan himself was silent, staring at the floor, his arms folded. His men stood awkwardly. Silence was heavy as if its presence alone could snuff out the gas lights.

"I want those bastards. They killed my friends and now they shot up Cole." Loop snarled his anger and waved his fist. The young roper's eyes were red.

The bitter statement was quickly followed by the bespectacled Hellis Dorn's own challenge. He, too, raised his fist and growled, "I want all them sonuvabitches. All o' em."

Each man felt his own anger and the room swelled with determination and defiance.

Stone-faced, Claire spoke first. "Ethan . . . what do you want us to do? We're waiting, all of us . . . on you."

Startled, Ethan looked up. Claire was standing with one hand on Maggie's shoulder; the other, on her hip. Nodding, he began to speak, talking slowly.

"Men . . . I know how you feel." His eyes met each man's

face. "Those bastards have put my brother at death's door." He rubbed his chin and his hard stare was enough to cause even Sotar look away. "Whoever they are, they're gonna pay. With everything they've got."

DuMonte stepped away from the others and said, "We'll ride with you into hell, Boss."

The statement from the Preacher surprised every man in the room and the response was emphatic support.

Ethan nodded.

"It's that damn Rocking R bunch, ain't it?"

The question came from Loop, standing in the corner. "They're a bunch o' gunslicks an' owlhoots."

Ethan dragged the forefinger of his left hand along the table. "Yes, I think it's the Rocking R. But they've got somebody pulling the strings. It isn't that owner, whatever his name is."

"Tiorgs," Sotar said.

"Yeah, that's it. But that Scotsman isn't calling the shots. It's a man called Glory Van Camp."

He explained what had happened earlier to Cole, the death of Meken Van Camp and who Meken really was and what he knew of Glory Van Camp, which was little, except for his small feet. Cole was going to wire the Rangers to see if they knew anything about the outlaw. He didn't know if Cole had done that yet or not.

Ethan stood and took a biscuit from the plate piled with them. Adding a spoonful of jam, he told the others to eat up for the day could be long. They would take supply horses carrying food and supplies, in case it took longer than a day. The men eased around the table for more food, eager to have something else on their minds for the moment. Each man was to take a second canteen, rifle, revolver and extra ammunition.

The Mexican rider was handed a plate with bacon, eggs and biscuits, which he accepted gratefully. After finishing, Sotar led him to the barn and a fresh horse. Juan Histallos said again that he was sorry and rode off into the night.

The room grew still again as the tall rancher talked, moving salt and pepper shakers and a plate of biscuits to represent their force.

"Here's what we're going to do," he said. "They want us riding after them, crazy mad and not thinking. They plan to ambush us. Probably not far from here. This isn't about beef. It's about getting rid of you and me."

Like an army maneuver, the tall rancher laid out his plan.

From their room, little Will and Russ cried their interest in joining the group. Claire excused herself with Maggie at her heels.

Ethan finished and was quiet. He didn't want to explain what else was on his mind—the rustling, the ambush, all of it was designed to cripple the Bar K. Had to be. Killing him would be the next step. Whoever was after the ranch thought it would be easy to gain possession of the Bar K when he and Cole were out of the way. Whoever it was didn't know Luther. Or Claire. Or, for that matter, any of his key men. For the first time, he was worried about Luther. His older brother had left for town shortly after they got the news about the rustling. He was supposed to bring Cole and Peaches back to help them trail the rustlers and get their herd back.

The last thought yanked him back to Cole. *My God, is my little brother dying?* His mind jumped to their times together before and during the war . . . the time when Cole rode away in anger after Ethan told him that he was settling down with Claire . . . the wild times on the cattle drive that saved the Bar K . . . the fierceness of his brother's determination to bring down Victorio Gee's gang . . . the utter joy when Cole learned Kathleen was waiting for him . . . the terrible look on his brother's face when Kathleen passed from them.

A rage roared through Ethan that he hadn't felt in a long time. He slammed his fist on the table and stood. Every man in the room jerked.

"Those bastards are going to be sorry they ever messed with the Bar K." His face was dark and his eyes slitted. "They're going to be sorry they put Cole at death's door."

Near the fireplace, Blue barked his support.

Only a few of his men had seen that look. Only a few had known the warrior that was truly Ethan Kerry.

As directed by Ethan, Sotar and two men blackened their faces, rubbing old ashes on their cheeks and foreheads. After taking off their spurs, they removed anything that might make noise on their clothes or from their saddles, then slipped away from the ranch minutes later one at a time, leading their horses. It was a black night. They rejoined northwest of the ranch and began their search of the waiting ambushers. A second team followed, led by Hollis Dorn, and headed northeast. Their objective was the same: find the ambushers and wait for Ethan's orders. Ethan was certain the ranch was being watched and didn't want these men seen.

Both teams were headed in a pincher movement in the direction of the rustled herd and the killed Bar K men. Ethan expected the ambush to be set someplace in that direction. He thought the trap would be set around a wide funnel of land, where ridges of large rock would provide cover for at least twenty men. Signs of the herd moving through there would be easy to follow.

Eli asked to go with his father, reminding him of the story about Uncle Cole and the gun battle against Comanches when he was Eli's age. Ethan said he needed him here, at the ranch, to protect his mother and the others. Claire took him aside and told him the same.

As streaks of dawn lightened the new day, Ethan rode out

with ten men and the supply horses. DuMonte, Mike McCoy
and Rommey were asked to stay at the ranch in case the outlaws
attempted a sneak attack there while the men were gone. Mc-
Coy stationed himself on the barn roof, at Ethan's request, to
allow for a greater view of the land around them. DuMonte
wanted to ride with the others but Ethan spoke to him alone.
He was a man Ethan trusted with his family. The colored man
nodded his agreement.

Claire, Rommey and Eli settled in to wait, distracting
themselves by playing with the twins and listening to Maggie
sing songs. Claire's thoughts rode with Ethan. She knew his
returned eyesight was the blessing both had prayed for. Seeing
again was, for him, a return of his manhood. Yet she was worried his eyesight could blur again under stress. Or worse. The
look on his face was like the old days. Proud. Bold. Determined.
All she could do was pray some more.

They had overcome hardships and tragedies before. Comanches. The death of Luther's family. The first cattle drive to
Kansas. The year of the horrible drought. Sam Winlow's attempt to secure the Bar K by forcing a bank loan foreclosure.
Ethan's blindness. Kathleen's kidnapping by Victorio Gee and
then her death. And now Cole terribly wounded. Or worse.

She wouldn't let her mind entertain the possibility of Cole's
death.

She stood and asked Eli and Maggie to help her clear the
table and wash the dishes. Eli had wanted to go with his father.
"Eli, come now. I need your help," Claire said, taking plates to
the kitchen. "I'm going to check on J.R."

Rommey was already in the kitchen. Claire left to tend to the
wounded cowboy in the bunkhouse. Maggie acompanied her.

Eli rubbed his hands through his hair, yawned and headed
for the kitchen. Maybe Rommey would tell him some more
tales of the old days on the cattle drives. His thoughts jumped

once more to his uncle. This just couldn't be. Cole had been wounded a few weeks ago and he was up and going again within days.

Maybe it would be like that again.

Even as he thought it, he knew that wasn't the case. Cole Kerry was "at death's door." That's how his dad had put it. He sniffed away the feelings and glanced at the dawning sun. How soon would they hear from the men? From his father?

Claire knew there was no way she could keep her husband from going. She told herself not to worry, but that wasn't possible. Something very evil was in their valley and that wickedness wanted the Bar K.

Moving swiftly across the Bar K range, Ethan Kerry led his men through the rich pastureland. The early morning was cold and their breath-smoke surrounded them as they advanced. They snaked their way through soft hills and green valleys, headed toward their planned vantage point. It wasn't long before John David Sotar and his men returned and reported the location of the ambushers. They were encamped on two sides of a narrow valley as Ethan had guessed. Their stolen cattle were grazing there. Hollis Dorn and his men were on the far side, hidden above the waiting outlaws.

Ethan and the Bar K riders pulled up on a fat hill overlooking a narrow draw. A mass of tiny dots gradually became a gathered herd of Bar K cattle. Morning fog danced with the grazing animals. From his field glasses, Ethan studied the land, looking for the ambushers. He saw them. Two bunches. One group hidden on each side of the draw. Some were sleeping or seemed to be. *Good*, he thought. *That's just what I want.* A further examination spotted Hollis Dorn and his men, already in place on the south rim above the outlaws on that side.

Ethan turned toward his men. "Everyone, we'll go over our plan again. This is it. We can always buy more steers. I can't replace any of you."

After they gathered and were silent, Ethan split them into two groups. One group would head for the northern rim and attack the outlaws there. A smaller group, led by him, would continue riding into the draw. Sotar and Dorn and their men, above the outlaws, would strike before they got within firing range. It was important to distract the outlaws so they would not realize his men were closing in above them.

Timing was crucial once the shooting started because surprise was the essence. If they were lucky, the outlaws would give up quickly. If not, it could be a long day.

Satisfied with their understanding, he motioned for Sotar to take a group of eight men and ride to the left. After waiting a half hour, Ethan took the lead and his six men headed down the long incline. They would be seen from a considerable distance and that's what Ethan wanted.

Leading men again felt good. Across his saddle was his Winchester. He blinked his eyes, still marveling at his returned sight. Would it disappear again?

"Please, God, no," he muttered to himself.

CHAPTER 31

In Uvalde, Luther Kerry discovered the news about his young brother from Deputy Red Clanahan at the jail. The big Irishman described the attempted bank robbery and hotel ambush, noting that the bank's money was safe, and the outlaws killed— but that Cole was badly wounded.

Without waiting, the oldest Kerry brother hurried down the street to the hotel. He tossed away the old tobacco chaw in his mouth as he went. A cold November wind was whipping through the town, but he barely noticed. His entrance surprised the drowsy Wilomina and the two half-asleep cowboys on guard in the lobby. He didn't stop to talk, but bounded past the hotel clerk and up the stairs, taking them two at a time.

"Peaches, it's me, Luther. I want to see my brother." Luther shouted between pounds on the door with his ham-like fists.

"You alone, Missa Luther?"

"Damn sure."

A bleary-eyed Peaches cracked open the door, then pushed aside the dresser for Luther to enter. The big Kerry brother nodded and came in. His face was thick with worry. Peaches closed and locked the door behind him and shoved the dresser back into place.

"How is he?" Luther asked, heading for the bed.

The small room smelled of medicine, blood and sweat. Thick woolen blankets covered the unconscious Cole. Carefully, Luther pulled back the covering to see for himself. Cole's chest and shoulders were tightly wrapped, as was his upper right arm. His left leg and thigh were bound from the knee to his groin. Blood stained this bandaging, as well as his shoulder wrapping. A burn on his neck had been slathered with salve and left unbandaged. It looked to the oldest Kerry brother like the bullets had missed the vital areas of his heart and stomach. But his brother had lost a great deal of blood.

Luther's gaze took in the Colt in Cole's hand and he looked up, puzzled.

"Cole Ker-rie-son want gun. Went to sleep after I gave to him," Peaches replied without emotion. "Before . . . he groan and . . . and reach all over bed for gun."

"Sounds like my little brother."

Luther listened to Cole's shallow breathing, then removed the wet washcloth over his brother's forehead to feel his temperature.

"Cole Ker-rie-son has bad fever, Missa Luther."

Luther grimaced. "What does the doc say about that?"

"I am to give water. From this little thing." Peaches held up the dropper. "Put wet cloth on head. I am doing that. All night." He pointed to the can of peaches. "I give Cole Ker-rie-son peach juice. My grandmother tell me story about its power."

Luther looked at Peaches. The Chinaman was weary from the gunfight and the nightlong watch. The big Kerry brother spotted the uneaten tray of food in the corner and knew what that meant. A blood stain on Peaches's shirt, along his right shoulder, told more.

"He is Cole Ker-rie-son. He will live. He will fight again." Peaches's words were hoarse but no less determined than ever.

"Yeah, I reckon so . . ." Luther turned to meet the Oriental gunfighter's intense eyes.

"Thank you, Peaches," Luther said. "You've done plenty. Now it's my turn. You get something to eat—and some sleep.

You didn't eat last night." He motioned toward the tray. "You've been hurt, too."

"It is no thing. Only burn," Peaches said. "I have donut . . . and tea, Big Red bring last night."

Nodding, Luther removed the folded cloth from Cole's forehead and refreshed it with new water from the bowl on the dresser, squeezed out the excess and replaced it on Cole's forehead. Grabbing the dropper from the nighttable, he filled a cup from the pitcher and returned to Cole's bed. Drops of water began to touch Cole's mouth. In his ham-like hands, it was an awkward process. He picked up the peach can and repeated the process with peach juice.

Peaches leaned against the dresser, letting the tension of the night pass as he watched. After a few minutes, Luther switched to using the cup itself, pouring a tiny amount of water on Cole's tongue, then gently closing his mouth each time to stimulate swallowing. This was easier than fingering the dropper and gave Cole more liquid anyway, he decided. He would try the same with the peach juice. It would give him nourishment.

Luther glanced at the stoic Chinaman. "Peaches, are you able to get some breakfast? Take those folks downstairs with you." He reached into his pocket and pulled out coins. "Here. That should take care of it."

Accepting the money, Peaches asked, "Who stand guard while I gone?" His eyes were hard, belying the heavy fatigue closing in on him.

"I'll welcome the chance to put some lead into the folks behind this. You go ahead. I'll be just fine." The smile that reached the right side of Luther's mouth was more of a snarl.

As Peaches turned to push away the dresser from the door, Luther added a comment.

"Oh, if you think on it, bring back some broth for Cole. Maybe he'll eat some."

"Ah so, I will," Peaches said, pointing at the dresser. "Push this behind me after I leave and lock door." He cocked his head. "I think Jinette Six woman try to kill him when fight over. I do not know why—and I may be wrong. Do not let her close, though."

"Not sure I know who she is."

"You will. Very pretty. New to town. Has relative at Rocking R."

"Oh. Well, that explains a lot."

"Oh, Meken . . . the street bum . . . was one who try to kill Cole Ker-rie on trail to ranch. He wanted man. Not bum," Peaches continued. "He say other shooter was his brother, Glory. Glory Van Camp."

"Yeah, Cole told me when I was in town a few days ago. Wanted to tell him that Ethan could see. Again." Luther tried to smile. "Who's this Glory fella?"

"Do not know. Yet."

In his flat voice, the Chinaman explained that the attempted horse stealing was a ruse to lure Cole into a trap. The bank robbery was a follow-up strategy with the same goal.

"I appreciate your telling me, Peaches," Luther said, pushing his hat back on his head. Peaches nodded and left.

After closing and locking the door, Luther pushed the dresser against it and laid his Winchester across its weathered top. He returned to giving water to Cole and realized his night's ride was catching up with him.

"Cole, you have to get well, you hear?"

Cole turned fitfully and muttered, "Wait for me, Kathleen."

"There will be time for that," Luther said. "But not now, little brother. Please."

Down the street, Pastor Dinclaur was drinking coffee in the back of his small house and looked up, eagerness in his eyes, as Jinette entered.

"Luther Kerry rode in," Jinette announced. "The guards in the lobby are sleeping. But I'm certain the Chink isn't. Damn that yellow bastard."

She had spent the night with Dinclaur as usual and had gone on an early morning stroll. She looked fresh and nicely dressed in a gray riding suit with white and blue trim. Her hair was pulled back into a bun and accented with a small gray hat. Dinclaur's gaze took in her heavy purse, then saw the bump under her sleeve. Of course, she had a derringer strapped to her wrist.

"Did Luther come in alone?"

"Yes, Glory, he did."

"Don't call me that. You know better. Someone might hear you."

"There's nobody around, *Glory*. We aren't in your . . . church."

Shrugging her shoulders, Jinette changed the subject, began playing with a long lock of her hair that had come loose from the bun. She asked if Dinclaur had heard anything from Tiorgs and the cattle-rustling trap. The fake minister hadn't, but didn't expect to hear yet. Too soon. If things went right, the Rocking R outlaws would tear up the Bar K riders when they rode into the planned ambush. That would put the Bar K in disarray. Next would come the elimination of Ethan Kerry himself. Tiorgs and a handful of men planned on attacking the ranch after the Bar K riders rode out to recover their herd.

"It can't be too tough to down a blind man. We can even make it look like an accident." Jinette poured herself coffee.

"Don't underrate Ethan Kerry, sis. He's built that ranch into something," Dinclaur said, smiling. "Something we'll enjoy."

She asked if there was any news about Cole Kerry this morning and gradually returned the lock to her pulled-back hairdo. Dinclaur didn't know, but said that he planned on a visit to the hotel that morning to offer a short, private prayer service. His smile was wicked.

"You going to see that goofy mayor, too?"

"Yeah. He's going to need to appoint a new marshal right away," Dinclaur said. "Should be a lot of cotton farmers in town today bringing in bales for shipping. We'll need a lawman. So I'm sure there'll be some kind of a council meeting."

"Not too many choices."

Dinclaur chuckled. "Only one. That dumb Irishman."

"What about Judleport's nephew? Won't he push for that?" Jinette added more sugar and stirred her coffee with a spoon and added, "Or that Chink? He's one tough sonuvabitch. Even that idiot council should be able to walk get his yellow skin— and take advantage of his gun."

Giggling, Dinclaur said it didn't matter who they picked.

"What about George Newton? You worried he'll talk to save his neck?" She licked her lips and smiled. "Are we going to finish the job . . . on Cole Kerry? We can get his dumb brother— and that Chink—at the same time."

"Not necessary. If Cole Kerry isn't dead, he's as good as," Dinclaur said. "No, I'm not worried about Newton. He doesn't know anything."

"So what's next?"

"Wait for the end of the Bar K and then pick up the pieces."

At the hotel, Luther took a nap after deciding Cole should not be moved, at least for now. But he needed Claire's care and a place to recover without the danger of someone trying to shoot him.

Big Red, now the interim marshal, Peaches, Mayor Heinrich, both CW Connected cowboys and Wilomina returned from breakfast to get an update on Cole's condition. Shivering onlookers stood outside the hotel and in the lobby, waiting quietly; some were praying and several women wept. Only Big Red, Peaches and the mayor went upstairs. It was Peaches's suggestion, actually more of a demand. He was edgy about others trying to get to Cole.

Jinette Six slipped in with the crowd; Pastor Dinclaur was a few minutes behind her. Dinclaur made his way around the gathered people in the lobby, talking softly and reverently. After a few minutes, Mayor Heinrich and Big Red came down the stairs. The mayor explained Cole was steady, but unconscious. A fever was the biggest challenge he faced. He coughed and introduced the big Irishman as the interim marshal.

Several people walked over to congratulate Big Red, including Jinette and Dinclaur. He was uncomfortable with the attention until he saw Wilomina watching him. She smiled and he left the others and walked over to her.

"How is Cole Kerry this morning?" she asked, touching his arm.

"Not good, I be thinkin'. His big brother, he be with him. An' Peaches. Prayin' be our best thing to be doin'," Big Red said, avoiding her gaze.

Jinette Six watched Big Red walk toward the jail with Wilomina on one side and Mayor Heinrich on the other. The postmistress was talking and gesturing. When Dinclaur and Jinette were alone again in the alley next to the hotel, she pressed him on taking action. "Glory, we can get both Kerrys out of the way right now—and throw in that damn Chink for good measure." Jinette was excited and waving her arms. "Both that big Kerry and the Chink are half asleep. They've been awake all night. We can slip up there and kill all of them. It'll be easy."

Dinclaur frowned and motioned for her to lower her voice. "Dammit, sis, be *quiet*. People will hear *you*."

"There isn't anyone around," she challenged, but lowered her voice. "I was trying to tell you something important. You can drop that damn minister sing-song crap."

"Just how would we explain three *killings*?" Dinclaur deliberately continued his affected manner of speaking. His eyebrows jumped in defiance.

Jinette crossed her arms and stared at him. "We can use towels to muffle the gunfire. Like you did before. Then we'd run down the stairs, yelling some guy just ran out of the hotel room. We could even fire a shot toward the back door up there."

Dinclaur grinned. "Too risky and you know *it*."

"Are you going to stand there, grinning like some sappy preacher, or tell me what's going on?" Her voice rose again.

Motioning for her to lower her voice, he stepped out of the alley and looked both ways. No one was near. Satisfied, he returned to remind her of Tiorgs's planned ambush.

"The Bar K riders will ride into a wonderful *ambush*," he declared, "and while that's going on, Tiorgs will take out Ethan Kerry—and the rest of that damn *family*. We'll have control of the place by the end of the *day*."

Jinette smiled. "I can hardly wait, my beloved brother. But we could wrap it up nice and pretty by getting rid of those three right now."

"You really want to do this, don't *you*?"

"I didn't like the way that Chink looked at me."

"You'll have your opportunity, sis. We'll *wait*."

A black cat meowed as it came into the alley. Dinclaur believed the cat brought good luck if it came toward a person and took the luck away if it turned away. He was smiling until Jinette stomped her feet and scared the cat out of the alley. Now he wasn't sure. Had the cat been coming to him or was it turning when she scared it away?

Luther was almost asleep when a knock on the door jolted him awake. It took a couple of seconds to remember where he was and why. He left his chair, next to Cole's bed, glanced at his sleeping brother and headed for the door. Then he remembered Peaches's instructions.

"Uh . . . who's there?"

"It's me, Missa Luther. Peaches."

"Hold on. I'll be right there."

Noise from the other side of the door stopped him again. Following the noise came a terse "Wait, Missa Luther."

Luther stood beside the dresser propped against the door; his Winchester lay on its scarred top. He squinted to hear what was going on in the hallway.

"You go away. You no see Cole Ker-rie-son."

"You don't understand . . . Deputy." It was Dinclaur. "I am a pastor and he is one of my . . . sheep. I am a man of God and can bring His mercy to the marshal."

Peaches turned toward the minister. The Chinaman was weary and tense.

"God no need you to help with Cole Ker-rie-son. God there now. You go away."

Some conversation followed that Luther couldn't make out, then stomping footsteps disappeared down the hallway.

"Missa Luther, you open now."

CHAPTER 32

Ethan Kerry held up his hand to halt the men behind him. A thick morning fog had created an eerie sight as they advanced, making the riders appear as half men in midair. But the fog was burning away and he was certain the outlaws could see them on this gentle rise. The only sounds were spurs and bits jingling, leather creaking, and an occasional cough.

Every sound, every sight, was a new world to the Bar K leader. He couldn't explain the feeling, but it reminded him of the old days of battle. The awesome experience of seeing again was a wonder as he saw everything they rode past as if seeing it for the first time.

The men with him were focused on the narrow valley ahead. Each man carried a rifle, laying across his saddle in front of him. All were armed with either a Winchester or a Henry, along with belted sidearms. They weren't gunmen, they were cattlemen. But they rode for the brand and would follow Ethan Kerry anywhere.

The hidden ambushers could see Ethan and his men at this point and would be waiting for them to ride down to retrieve their stolen cattle. If his plan went well, the outlaws would be surprised by the Bar K men in place above them and surrender. He hoped so. None of them were worth losing any of his men. That was the key to good leadership to achieve the goal without sacrificing any of one's men. He practiced that during the war and he had done so in building and protecting the ranch.

Astride his black gelding, Ethan waved his extended arm back and forth. The agreed-upon signal. An instant later, a roar of gunfire poured down on the waiting outlaws on both sides of the valley. Six of the Bar K men with Sotar and Dorn, three on each side of the valley, had Sharps .50's and their heavy booms were ominous within the torrential gunfire. The Rocking R outlaws jumped, yelled and many of them fell. Those not wounded scrambled for cover against the rocky edge of the valley rim. Some began to return fire. Frightened cattle bawled and began to stampede toward the far end of the valley.

"Let's go, men!" Ethan yelled and kicked his horse into a gallop. Behind him came yells of approval and challenge as the others raced to keep up.

As they entered the mouth of the valley, Ethan put his knotted reins in his mouth and began firing his Winchester with both hands. A two-gun outlaw rose next to their rock position on the valley's left side to aim at the Bar K men above them. Ethan's bullets took him chest high and the man teetered and disappeared. Other outlaws turned toward Ethan's band and began to fire, as the Bar K men continued to pour lead at them from their higher positions.

Ethan's black staggered, then stumbled and fell, hit by an outlaw's bullet. Ethan flew from the saddle and his Winchester soared ahead on its own. He hit the ground hard, stunning him. He lay there for an instant and his first thought was fear for his newly returned eyesight. His eyes opened and it was dark. Fear snapped at his courage until he realized he was lying face down in the mud. Shaking his head, he slowly stood.

In a breath, the valley became strangely silent once more as the remaining outlaws surrendered, both wounded and unwounded, standing with their hands up. Ethan wiped mud from his face and looked in both directions. Yes! They had done it. He rubbed his shoulder; it was sore, but he was fine otherwise.

How about his men?

John David Sotar reached him first. "Boss, you hurt? They gave up quick just like you said they would."

Ethan smiled. "Yeah, I'm fine. They got Jake." He patted Sotar on the shoulder. "How about our men?"

"Loop got hit in the arm. Gonna be a while before he plays with a lasso. Ramos took one in the shoulder. Everybody else looks good."

"Are they Rocking R, like we thought?"

"Yeah, they are." Sotar rolled a smoke and handed it to Ethan. "Ain't a cowhand in the bunch." He snapped a match to life on his belt buckle and lit the cigarette now in Ethan's mouth.

"You think they figured to take over the Bar K just like that?" Smoke curled around Ethan's hard face and ran toward his hat.

"Guess so."

"Where's Tiorgs? Is he with them?" Ethan rolled his shoulder to ease the pain.

"Dunno. Haven't seen him."

"You figure he's behind all this?"

"Hard to figure he's not."

"You don't think he's Glory Van Camp." Ethan wiped a remaining chunk of mud from his face. "Got a feeling there's somebody else pulling the strings."

"Dunno, Boss. But whoever won't like what happened today."

"Right."

From both sides of the valley rim, Bar K men led the surrendered outlaws down to the valley floor.

"Our beeves are scattered all to hell, Boss."

"They'll settle soon enough. We've got all winter to find them," Ethan said with a grin. "Give our boys somethin' to do."

Sotar shook his head and walked over to the gathering outlaws.

Ethan took a deep breath and took charge. "Check 'em all

for hidden iron, then tie their hands behind them. It's a long walk to town and that's where they're going."

"What? Come on, we can't walk that far. Give us a break. We were just doin' what we were paid to do." The challenge came from a lanky outlaw with a heavy beard, wearing leather cuffs, stovepipe chaps and a new, short-brimmed hat.

Ethan walked over to him and stared at the outlaw, forcing him to look at the ground.

"Your choice. We can hang you here. If you want." He jammed his finger into the man's chest. "Don't know where you're from, mister, but around here, we don't take kindly to rustlers and killers."

The outlaw shook his head negatively.

"Where are Loop and Ramos?" Ethan demanded as he spun away and walked along the line of surrendered outlaws.

"Over here, Boss." It was Loop's voice. "I'm fine."

A heavier voice with a Mexican accent followed.

"We'll get you some help," Ethan said and looked at Sotar. "Bandages an' medicine. In my saddlebags."

"Sure." Sotar said and hurried to the downed black horse.

Another outlaw stepped forward. His arm was covered with blood. "Some of us are hurt, too, Mr. Kerry."

"I don't give a damn about you. You hoped to kill us an' take our ranch."

"I-I-I. . . ."

A short, stocky outlaw, with a dark goatee and wearing a bandolier of cartridges across his shoulder, frowned and said, "Say, I thought you was blind. You are Ethan Kerry, aren't ya?"

"I am and I was," Ethan snarled, spun and went over to see how Loop and Thomas Ramos were doing.

Sotar and another cowboy were cleaning their wounds with neckerchiefs soaked in canteen. Neither wound held lead. Salve and bandage wraps from Ethan's saddlebags lay close by. Satisfied, Ethan returned to the surrendered outlaws. He ordered three Bar K men to check out their hiding places to make sure no outlaw alive was still there.

"What are going to do with the bodies, Boss?"

"I don't want them on Bar K land," Ethan growled. "These bastards here can carry them off our land—and bury them in a hole. One they dig."

Ethan walked over to the first outlaw who didn't want to walk to town. "Where's your boss? Where's Tiorgs?"

The outlaw's sneer was more than Ethan could stand and he slapped the man hard across his face.

"I said, where's Tiorgs?"

Rubbing his jaw, the outlaw said, "He's at your place with a bunch of men. They were after you. Didn't know you could see again."

"Damn!" Ethan spun away. "I need a horse."

CHAPTER 33

At the Bar K ranch house, dawn found everything quiet once more. Young Mike McCoy was dozing on the barn roof with his rifle laying across his stomach. In spite of his weight, the cowboy was agile. Below, Harold "Preacher" DuMonte had stationed himself near the shed where he could see most of the ranch yard. Rommey was inside with the family.

A rattle on the far side of the house surprised DuMonte and he decided to check it out. Shifting his rifle to a firing position, the black cowboy strode out from the tool shed. Looking up at the barn roof, he saw Mike McCoy had gone to sleep, in spite of the awkwardness of his position.

DuMonte cupped his hand to his mouth and yelled, "Hey, Mike! Wake up. I heard something. Mike!"

The cowboy jerked awake, almost losing his balance. "What are you yelling about? I wasn't asleep."

"Sure looked like it," DuMonte said and pointed to where he had heard the rattle on the far side of the house itself. "You see anything over there? I heard something. Like spurs jingling or something."

McCoy slowly climbed to his feet and stared. "There's nothing there, Preacher. You're imagining things."

Three gunshots rang out and McCoy grabbed his chest and tumbled from the roof. An instant later, DuMonte fell to another round of bullets.

"That's it, Heredith," a gruff voice called out. "The family's inside. Don't see Ethan Kerry, though. You think he rode out with the others?"

"Aye, an' a stupid one, ye be. How's a blind man going tae ride . . . like a man?" The voice was Heredith Tiorgs.

"Just sayin' . . ."

"I know what ye be sayin'. A cader's curse, it be. Check the rest of thae buildings. No surprises be bringin' me. I want thaim all."

Beside the barn, Tiorgs waited patiently while his five men searched the barn and other small buildings. He smiled. This was going to be a very special day; his stepson had promised him a share of the Bar K holdings. He was going to be a rich man. A very rich man.

His men returned and reported that there were no other guards posted and no signs of activity in the house itself.

"Did ye check thae bunkhouse?" Tiorgs asked.

"Naw. Didn't figure they left anybody there. All of 'em rode out."

"I see. An' countin' thaim ye did, did ye? Hamilton, ye check thae bunkhouse. When ye finished killin' anyone there, ye join us."

The Scotsman sent another two men to the back of the house while he and the remaining outlaw would enter from the front.

"Remember, our first job is tae kill Ethan Kerry. Then the rest of thaim. Little ones, too. Glory be plannin' tae take over thae Bar K this fine day," Tiorgs said. "Should only be Ethan . . . an' the missus . . . an' the children. Aye, but be careful in case there be others. Donna know if the big Kerry brother rode out with thae others or not." He finished by folding his arms and the three outlaws hurried away.

Tiorgs stopped in front of the porch and yelled, "Weel, Ethan Kerry, ye come out now! 'Tis a fine day tae die! Do so an' your family weel be spared!"

From the bunkhouse, three quick shots rang out and Tiorgs grinned. "Ah, one more is dead. Ye hear that, Ethan Kerry?"

As he and the two outlaws stepped onto the front porch, a woman's voice challenged them. "Ride away—or you will die."

"Aye, an' a guid mornin' tae ya, Mrs. Kerry. 'Tis your husband we seek," Tiorgs said, touching the brim of his hat with his hand. "He that dinna be seein', ye know."

"He's not here."

"Not guid enouch, Mrs. Kerry. We know Mr. Kerry be inside." Tiorgs motioned for the other man to slide toward one of the front windows. "We also be knowin' there not be any men around. Your friend on thae roof—and thae colored man—they be dead now. 'Twill go a lot sweeter if ye understand what must happen." He pulled the revolver from its holster. "Your husband, he knows what must be." He cocked the weapon and added, "Oh, an' your riders, all the fine young boys sent out this morn, they will not be returnin', ye know. A fine trap they will ride into. This day, the Bar K has new owners."

A shotgun blast from the window slammed the creeping outlaw against the porch railing and over it. He lay in an awkward pose next to the hitching post. He looked up at Tiorgs with a bewildered expression and died.

"Hauld a wee now, missy. Would ye be willin' tae listen? That will only be gettin' ye in trouble. Tell your husband to come out. Or ye can bring him since he cannot be seein'."

A young man's voice answered this time. "You heard my mother. Get out of here."

"Aye, an' a guid mornin' tae ye, young Master Kerry. It's ye we be comin' for as well, ye know."

"Guess again, mister."

From the back of the house, rifle shots rang out.

"See? Me fine boys wull be comin' in. Dinna be naught a chance for ye. Give up now an' we'll see that thae missus and thae children are spared." Tiorgs's face was dark red. "Me patience be growin' a thin."

"Oh, really. Ours already has gone." It was Claire again.

This time Tiorgs dove from the front stairs and hid against the raised porch. He fired two wild shots into the closest window and yelled for his men. "Joe! Billy! Jose! Where are ye?"

Silence. Then came a groan for an answer.

Heredith Tiorgs was stunned. How could this be? How could six gunmen be stopped by a blind man and his wife? There had to be others in the house. Had he been set up? No, they had seen a huge bunch of riders leave in a hurry.

Behind him came a faint sound, like someone crawling. He turned slowly and saw a bloody Harold DuMonte half-crawling, half-limping toward him, holding a revolver in his shaking hand.

"Hauld a wee, mister," Tiorgs said, swinging his revolver toward DuMonte.

The colored man fired an instant before the Scotsman did. DuMonte jerked as the bullet hit his upper shoulder. Tiorgs cursed as DuMonte's bullet drove into his thigh. The Scotsman tried to cock his gun and a woman's voice warned him, "Put it down. We've had enough of you."

Tiorgs glanced back over his shoulder and saw the woman pointing a double-barreled shotgun at him from the porch. In the doorway, he saw a young man with a rifle, a teenager. He looked back at the colored man, stretched out on the ground and struggling to recock his own weapon.

Shrugging his shoulders, Tiorgs tossed his gun toward the porch.

Minutes later, Rommey led two outlaws to the front, guiding them with a shotgun. One of the outlaws was limping. "The third bastard won't be doing anything again. Excuse me, Mrs. Kerry."

Eli Kerry smiled from the doorway. From behind him, Maggie asked him a question and he shook his head.

"Aye, we are stopped by a woman, a cook—an' a boy," Tiorgs grumbled.

"What did you think would happen when you tangled with the Kerrys," Claire said. "Rommey, we'll watch these three. Take a look at Harold. He's hurt bad, I think."

From the bunkhouse came J.R. Middleton holding a revolver in one hand with his other pressed against his bleeding upper shoulder. "There's one in there that won't be causing the Bar K any more trouble."

It was afternoon when Ethan rode up on a lathered horse. Behind him rode six men on equally tired mounts. His worried face became a smile when he saw his family and the attempted attackers spread out on the ground. He was down from his horse before it stopped moving and ran for Claire.

He hugged her, then Eli and then knelt to embrace Maggie and the twins. The wounded Bar K men from the range battle were slowly brought into the bunkhouse and settled. Ethan spent a half hour sitting beside the bed in the bunkhouse where DuMonte lay and sent a buckboard to DuMonte's house to bring back his wife and children.

CHAPTER 34

Three days later, Cole Kerry slipped into a deep sleep and his mind was thrown back to the end of the war. His nightmare twisted into a wild series of half memories and half imagination. The enemy was shooting at him from all directions and he yelled out for help, but no one was there. Holding his rifle, he dove toward a short row of dead grass pushing against the right side of a pile of snow. He rolled until he was lying in a long natural trench. More gunfire crackled, but none near him. Angry curses hurled through the cold snow and more faceless shooters appeared from the trench itself, shooting and grabbing at him. Ahead in the woods was Kathleen, waving for him to join her. He yelled out for her to take cover and then she was gone.

In his nightmare, he began crawling slowly along the trench. He had no idea where his brothers were. Where the trench turned sharply upward, he climbed out and looked around. Only the gray shapes of trees and rocks greeted him. A heavy fog lifted him from the trench and into the air where he looked down at the land below. From out of the fog came a chickadee. He smiled and leaned down to greet it. But a large, black hawk swooped down and tore the tiny bird away from him.

Cole blinked his eyes and saw Luther sitting next to his bed.

"Wake up, Cole. Wake up, little brother. You're havin' a nightmare." Luther moved closer and took Cole's fist holding his Colt and slowly eased the gun from his hand.

Cole's eyes fluttered and he was asleep again. Around a

newborn campfire, Union soldiers relaxed. As he walked closer, he saw there were Rebel soldiers sitting with them, laughing and talking. The Southerners were in worn-out clothes barely resembling uniforms; one was barefoot with rags wrapped around his feet. The only Rebel standing was lighting the stub of a cigar and a yellow halo outlined his frame. He smiled warmly and turned into Jesus.

"Wake up, Cole. You need to wake up."

From somewhere in Cole's tormented mind, a man in a black hat and long black coat and wearing a wooden mask emerged from the shadows and fired a double-barreled shotgun at him. A beautiful woman rushed over to him and pointed a gun at his head.

"Come on, boy, you need to wake up."

Cole's eyes opened and he saw Luther standing next to him, holding him. Nearby was Peaches. They had been taking turns giving him water—and peach juice and broth—while the other slept.

"G-Good morning, Luther. Where have you been?" he asked. "I was trying to find you."

"I was right here. Peaches an' me. Been right here all along, Cole."

"Luther, I gotta pee," Cole said and slid off the bed. He tried to stand and fell.

"Hey, you can't expect to go runnin' to the outhouse," Luther said, part excited that Cole was finally awake and part frightened by his weakness. "Let me bring over a pot."

Luther held Cole steady while the youngest Kerry brother urinated into the night pot set aside for that purpse. Then Peaches and Luther helped him walk around the room.

"They really set me up, didn't they?" Cole said, pausing by the window. "Who were those bastards?"

"Don't know, Cole. Gunmen. Nobody from around here,"

Luther answered, letting his brother study the empty streets as morning began taking its place in Uvalde.

Peaches nudged him away from the window. He was not convinced the attempts on Cole Kerry's life were over.

"Peaches an' Big Red an' other folks got all of them that you didn't get. None of them got away," Luther said, nodding to Peaches and assisting in urging Cole to move past the open window.

"Come on, Cole. You'd better get back to bed," Luther said, guiding his brother toward the bed. "Are you hungry? We'll get you somethin' to eat."

"Well, maybe so. I'm just a little dizzy right now, that's all." Cole looked at the two men. "Thank you, both of you. I'd be dead now if it weren't for you, Han Rui. I know that."

"I go get breakfast for Cole Ker-rie-son," Peaches said.

"Bring back a chaw, will you? I used up mine comin' in."

Peaches nodded and left.

"Cole, you remember when I came to town awhile back with the good news?" Luther pulled a chair close to the bed. His face was beaming and his eyes twinkled.

"You're getting married?"

Luther sputtered and laughed, shaking his head. "No sir, not your big brother. This is real big news . . . remember me tellin' you . . . Ethan can see."

Cole's expression didn't change for a moment as the importance of the statement caught up with his mind. "What do you mean . . . 'Ethan can see'?" He squeezed his eyes shut. "You were in town . . . before? And told me . . . Ethan can see."

Luther shrugged his big shoulders. "Just what I said. It'll come back to you. Our brother can see. Just like he always did. Yes sir, just like he always did."

"Luther, that's terrific! My God, when did this happen?"

Luther was still retelling the story of Ethan's sight returning when the Chinaman returned a half hour later with a tray filled with scrambled eggs and bacon, a bowl of hot oatmeal, coffee—and a fresh cut of tobacco. Luther thanked him and shoved it in his shirt pocket for later. The food was far more than Cole could possibly want to eat, but Mayor Heinrich insisted. The longer Luther talked, the more Cole recalled his brother bringing him the news before.

"Han Rui, Luther just told me Ethan can see again. His eyes healed up and he can see. Can you believe it?"

The Chinaman's face broke into a wide smile that neither Kerry brother had seen before. "Ah, 'tis the gods. It be their wish." He did not to tell Cole that he had shared the news with him before.

A short time later, they heard a noise outside the window. Coming down the street was a solemn group of nine Rocking R outlaws, walking with their hands tied behind their backs.

Pushing them along were Ethan and eight of his riders. A buckboard carried four wounded outlaws, including Heredith Tiorgs. He had long ago quit cursing in Scottish and sat in silence. Ethan had finally agreed to let the wounded outlaws ride instead of walking. Not because he cared about their welfare, but it was faster. The Rocking R dead had been buried in one large grave on Rocking R land.

The living outlaws had been given water three times and some jerky twice on their hike to Uvalde. Sleeping on the ground, without blankets, had brought groans and more cursing. Townspeople gathered on both sides of the main street to watch the unusual entry.

Big Red ran from the jail with a double-barreled shotgun. "Good day to ye, Mr. Kerry. What do ye bring to our fine town this morn?" He paused a few feet from Ethan's horse.

Ethan grinned. He was pleased not to be asked if he could see again. "These boys stole our cattle, then tried to kill us.

They murdered Orville Miller, Zeke Ferguson and Mike Mc-Coy. They shot up . . . Loop, Thomas Ramos and J.R. Middleton." He pointed at Tiorgs. "This sonuvabitch tried to kill my wife and children. I want them tried for rustling, murder and attempted murder. Oh, and my good friend, Harold DuMonte, is lying in a bed badly wounded. But I think he's going to make it."

"One of me cells be in use," Big Red said. "If your men could be helpin' meself, we'll be putting them in the other five."

"Good."

Ethan motioned for his men to direct the arrested outlaws to the jail.

Swinging down from his bay horse, Ethan said, louder than necessary so the gathered townspeople could hear, "There's somebody behind all this. And it isn't this Scotsman. He's just another hired gun—and he isn't that smart."

Tiorgs glared and Ethan stared him down.

Ethan continued, "This isn't over. There's somebody close by who wants the Bar K bad enough to murder us. That's why they tried to kill my brother, Cole." His eyes took in the townspeople on the street. 'We're going to find him. Count on it."

Sotar led the way to the jail while Ethan walked over to the hotel, leading his horse. He wrapped the reins around the hitching rack and went inside. The lobby was empty. Ethan strode over to the clerk.

"What room's my brother in . . . Cole Kerry." His voice was heavy with anger.

"I know, Mr. Kerry." The young clerk studied Ethan's face. "Uh, sir . . . uh, are you . . . seeing again . . . sir?"

Ethan realized he had intimidated the clerk unnecessarily and said with a smile, "I am—and it's great. The room?"

"Oh. Oh, of course. It's two-twelve." The clerk handed him a key and leaned forward. "Your other brother, he's up there. And, uh, the . . . Chinese deputy. We have orders not to let anyone else up." He tried to smile. "But I'm sure that didn't mean you, Mr. Kerry."

"Right."

He took the steps two at a time.

"Luther. Peaches. It's me, Ethan." He pounded on the door.

"Well, I'm comin'. Hold your horses," Luther responded from the room.

The door opened and a weary Luther welcomed him into the room, smelling of cooked eggs, urine, blood, medicine and sweat. As soon as Ethan stepped inside, Peaches closed the door, locked it and shoved the dresser back in place.

Ethan hugged Luther, then shook hands with Peaches.

"Hey, little brother, heard you stepped in front of some lead," Ethan boomed his greeting and hurried to the bed. The breakfast tray was forgotten as Cole grabbed Ethan and held his brother with his left hand. His right arm lay unmoving on the bed. And the greeting took most of his strength. Stepping back, Ethan examined his younger brother. "Damn, they were trying real hard to bring you down. Guess they don't know how tough Kerrys are."

It took awhile for everything to settle down. Cole wanted to hear more about Ethan's sight and Luther wanted to hear about the Rocking R outlaws brought to town. When all the stories got told, Luther insisted Cole eat some of his breakfast.

Ethan said, "This isn't over. Somebody's behind this. We know it's not that damn Scotsman. I think it's somebody in town. Whoever it is, he wants our ranch bad."

"Really, you don' think it's the Scot you brought in?" Luther said, adjusting the blankets and moving the tray out of harm's way.

"No, it's not Tiorgs. I'm sure of it. He knows who's behind

all this, but he won't say. Not yet, anyway."

Cole took a deep breath. "Just before Meken died, he told me his brother was in on the ambush when I was headed to the ranch. Glory Van Camp. That's who it is. He's got a string of warrants trailing him."

"I heard that from Sotar. You know this Glory Van Camp?"

Cole shook his head. "No, I don't. Nobody else seems to, either." He shook his head. "I-I almost forgot. I wired the Rangers about him. Haven't heard back."

"Missa Ethan, I think the Six woman be involved. She evil," Peaches spat. "She try to kill Cole Ker-rie-son. When bullets take him . . . to sleep."

"What?" Ethan's question was a knife.

The Chinaman repeated his allegation more intensely, leaving out the timing. Cole added to the assessment by explaining that she had come to town a month back and that she supposedly was related to someone at the Rocking R.

He shook his head. "I must've faded out. At the bank. I remember she came out of the bank with the outlaws. They were using her as a shield."

"Where is she now?" Ethan said.

"She stay in minister's house, I think. No see her since . . . bank ambush."

"Real pretty lady? Black hair. Fancy clothes?" Luther asked.

"Ah so."

"Saw her yesterday. In the lobby. She was talking to two cowboys there—an' Miss Reid."

Peaches stared at Luther, then at Ethan and was silent for a moment, then explained the cowboys were from the CW Connected and had helped bring Cole to the hotel and stood guard in the lobby.

Ethan hitched his heavy gunbelt and blinked his eyes. "Let's find this woman. Maybe she can tell us something."

"Give me a minute. I'll get dressed." Cole swung his legs off the bed. His right leg wouldn't hold his weight and he slid to the floor and sat there.

Ethan folded his arms. "Whoa, Cole. You're not going anywhere. You're gonna get back in that bed—and stay there. You're damn lucky to be alive."

Cole started to complain, but he was too weak to do anything. He couldn't even lift his arm. By the time the three men got Cole back in bed, he was sweating heavily and three of his wounds were bleeding through their bandages.

"All right, Luther, you find the doc and bring him here to check on Cole again," Ethan directed. "Peaches an' I will go find this woman."

Peaches hurried to the dresser blocking the locked door. "No. We no leave Cole Ker-rie-son alone. Not for any time."

Cole raised his left arm to protest, but no words came.

A knock at the door stopped further conversation.

"Who's there?" Ethan challenged.

"It's me, Boss. John David."

"Hey, John David. Glad you're here. Come in." Ethan motioned for Peaches to move away the dresser and let him in.

Instead of complying, Peaches drew his shoulder-holstered Webley Bulldog double-action revolver. His hard eyes flickered with intensity.

"Hey, Peaches, that's John David Sotar. Our foreman," Ethan explained. "You know him."

The Chinaman turned toward Ethan. "I see bad men shoot at Cole Ker-rie-son. I kill three. We must be of care. There are more. You not know John David alone."

Ethan grimaced. Peaches was tense and tired. The Chinaman had been a great friend to Cole and had faced danger for him.

"I'm sorry, Peaches," Ethan said, quietly. "You're the one who has kept our brother alive. I wasn't thinking." He moved to the dresser. "John David, anybody with you?"

"No, Boss. Just me. Our men are in the saloon. Bought them a round. Waiting on your orders."

After looking at Peaches for his approval, Ethan pulled away the dresser and opened the door. The Missouri foreman stood in the doorway, surprised at the slow response.

"How's Cole?" he asked.

Ethan turned toward the bed and saw that Cole was already asleep. The tall rancher told Sotar about the ambush. It was decided that Luther would go for the doctor while Peaches and Sotar would look for Jinette Six. Ethan was glad to stand guard over his younger brother.

After they had gone, Ethan returned the dresser to block the locked door and went to the window to study the busy street below. Much had happened since the fall roundup and it was only now making sense. Someone had gone to great lengths to secure the acquisition of the Bar K. The strategy depended on killing Cole and himself. Anyone less tough than Cole would be dead now. Whoever was behind the scheme hadn't figured on Peaches's fighting skill or his own sight returning.

He looked back at Cole, then walked over to feel his brother's forehead. Hot. Feverish. After putting a fresh, wet washcloth on Cole's forehead, he continued his silent assessment of recent events. Cole had lost his beautiful wife and his own sight had finally returned. Those didn't have anything to do with the attempts on their lives. Why hadn't he been more concerned when Cole was ambushed riding back to the ranch? Why had he been so caught up with running the ranch that he hadn't pressed to find the shooters?

His mind ran through what he knew. The town bum, Meken, wasn't really a bum at all. He was a gunman and the brother of another gunman. That man had tried to ambush Cole twice, once with his brother. It would seem Meken, as a bum, was situated in Uvalde to learn what was happening. Could that mean his brother, Glory Van Camp, didn't need to be in Uvalde? If so, there had to be a way Meken delivered any news. How? And what? What news would be important to Glory, assuming his goal was to take over the Bar K? What Cole was doing? Details about the bank? Details on how the marshal's office was run?

Maybe.

Ethan knew most of the people in town, but certainly not all. Uvalde was growing and he barely knew anything about the mining operations outside of town, or any of the miners.

This was a waste of time, he told himself. The person behind all of this could have come to town anytime in the last few years. If he was in town at all.

Walking over to the bed, Ethan checked on Cole again. His fever had gone down some. He rubbed Cole's right hand showing the almost healed owl cuts. Was there someone in town who hated the Kerrys? The question ripped through his mind. Triston Yankison was the bank president and he was always prickly. How about him? What about William Pottewait who owned the CW Connected? Both would benefit if the Bar K went down and the Kerrys with it.

He shook his head. He didn't know enough. When Sotar and Peaches came back with this woman, maybe he would begin to see what was really going on.

Luther returned shortly with Dr. Wright. The physician was surprised to hear Cole had been awake and had even attempted to stand. He was also pleased to learn of Ethan's returned sight.

"Well, well, Ethan. I am very pleased to hear your eyesight has finally returned," Dr. Wright said brightly. "I thought such would be the case. Given time . . . and patience." The thin physician-and-barber folded his arms triumphantly.

Ethan smiled and decided not to respond. It was Claire who

thought his eyesight would return, not this man. Dr. Wright had simply told Ethan to see a better professional in Kansas City.

"How soon before we can move our brother to the ranch?" Ethan asked, having already made up his mind to do so in the next day or two. Cole could be better cared for there—and it was safer.

"Oh, I would say he shouldn't be moved for, at least, two weeks. Maybe longer. He is very weak, you know," Dr. Wright proclaimed as he removed Cole's bandages and replaced them with new ones. Luther helped and was surprisingly adept.

"Two weeks, huh?" Ethan walked over to the window again. It hurt to see his brother so badly shot up. Deep inside, he knew Cole would make it—he had to make it. In many ways, Cole was the strongest of the three Kerry brothers.

After the physician left, Ethan said matter-of-factly, "I want you to take Cole home now. Get a buckboard. John David and the boys'll ride with you. I'll stay for the hearing. Longer if I have to."

Luther's expression was one of agreement. "Yes, Cole needs to be home."

"Can you stand watch, Luther, for a little while? I want to see Big Red and the judge. Get this thing moving," Ethan asked, then added, "Hell, we could've hanged that sorry bunch and saved ourselves a lot of trouble."

"Don't think Claire would've liked that much."

The tall rancher's eyes sparkled. "Don't be too sure. When those bastards shot up Preacher, she was ready. Right then and there. That's one tough lady."

Ethan left, lumbered down the stairs and out into the street. The town was busy again. He didn't mind having his men let off some steam in the saloon, but he was anxious to see if Sotar and Peaches had found Jinette Six. He was greeted by friends who didn't know his eyesight had returned and were eager to express their excitement in learning of it. The attention made him uncomfortable and he was glad to see Sotar and Peaches coming down the sidewalk, even though it meant they had not found the woman.

"Excuse me, folks, but the deputy wants to see me."

"Of course. Of course," a stout woman said. "We were praying for you, Ethan." The statement was echoed by her balding husband. "An' we're praying for Cole now."

Neither had asked about the outlaws his men had brought in. He shook his head and walked quickly toward Sotar and Peaches. The liveryman said she had rented a horse and left town shortly after Ethan and his men brought in the outlaws.

"That's an interesting coincidence," Ethan said. "Did he have any idea where she was headed?"

"No. Said she was in a hurry. And real snippy," Sotar answered. "Yah want us to track her down?"

Ethan pushed his hat back on his forehead. "My guess is she's headed for the Rocking R. We'll bring her back here."

Rubbing his chin, Ethan was quiet for a moment, then said, "No. Let her go. I want you and the boys to ride with Luther. He's going to take Cole home. Peaches'll stay here. The marshal'll need his help." He paused. "I will, too."

A thin smile found its way to Peaches's face.

Sotar started to leave and Ethan added, "Put my horse up in the livery. I'm staying for the hearing. Make sure Kiowa's doing good, will you?"

"Got it."

Peaches watched the Missouri gunfighter stride down the sidewalk before turning his attention to Ethan.

"Who be with Cole Ker-rie-son?"

"Luther." Ethan smiled. How like the Chinaman to focus on protecting his brother. "Where you want me to be?"

Ethan motioned toward the marshal's office, then continued

to the judge's small office, three buildings farther. A hearing was scheduled for the next morning. The session would be brief and perfunctory. The judge felt the situation demanded as early a trial as the circuit judge could make; Ethan agreed. Before he left, Judge Moreland asked if the rancher thought this rustling was related to the bank ambush on Cole.

"No question about it, Judge. Somebody wants the Bar K real bad," Ethan answered. "So far, he hasn't been successful." He stared at the youthful justice of the peace and said, "If those bastards in the jail aren't found guilty, then we'll have more of a mess on our hands." He took a deep breath. "Then . . . I don't think we'll be bringing any more of them to town."

Judge Moreland nodded and said quietly, "Maybe it's time I moved back to Grand Rapids, Michigan. Nice town, Grand Rapids."

"So is Uvalde . . . Texas," Ethan replied and left the office in time to see Sotar and the Bar K riders riding out of town, headed north with the buckboard and a blanketed Cole.

CHAPTER 35

Entering the marshal's office, Ethan Kerry asked the big Irishman a question without any other greeting.

"Marshal, how are the scum doing?"

"Aye, an' a good day to ye, too, Mr. Kerry," Big Red said, rising from his desk chair and holding out his hand to greet the tall rancher. "They've been actin' nasty. I might just be forgettin' to get theirselves suppers, if it keeps up."

Laying on the desk was a double-barreled shotgun. Over by the stove was Peaches, sipping coffee.

A voice from the center cell yelled, "Let us loose! We didn't do nothin'!"

Ethan exploded. "Give me the key to that cell, Marshal. That sonuvabitch needs to understand that you can't murder our friends and steal our cattle."

Big Red smiled and reached for the desk drawer where the keys were kept.

"You wouldn't dare," the bearded outlaw said, his eyes widening.

"Hell, he's just bluffing, Logan. He ain't gonna hurt ya none." An outlaw in the same cell pushed Logan forward.

Big Red pointed his shotgun at the three other outlaws and told them to stand back while he opened the cell door. Stepping inside, Ethan grabbed the bearded outlaw by his shirt and yanked him out of the cell.

"I-I didn't mean nothin' . . ."

Ethan's left fist exploded into the outlaw's stomach. He groaned and grabbed it in pain. Ethan slammed a haymaker into the outlaw's exposed chin and the man flew backward into the closed cell door. Staggering, the outlaw swung wildly and missed. Moving inside the errant blow, Ethan pounded him with punches to the outlaw's body and face. Blood spurted from the outlaw's mouth and a tooth followed. He sank into unconsciousness.

With his shotgun on the others, Big Red walked over to the rancher and put a hand on his shoulder. That served to calm Ethan down.

"Guess I should leave some for the hangman," Ethan said, gasping for breath.

"Aye. 'Tis a pity he wasn't more careful. Slipping on the floor that way," Big Red said. "Give me a hand an' we'll put hisself back with the others."

Shaking his right fist to clear it of the pain, Ethan stared at the cells. "Any of the rest of you sonuvabitches want a hand at this old man? I was blind, remember? You bastards thought you were fighting a blind man. Well, I can see an' you're going to hang. Every damn one of you."

Hearing nothing in return, he turned back to Big Red, rubbing his hands and his bleeding knuckles. They carried the moaning outlaw back into the cell and laid him on the floor.

"Anybody been here . . . to see them?" Ethan asked as they closed the cell door.

Big Red sat down again and explained Pastor Dinclaur had been by to offer a prayer for their poor souls, and to listen to any confessions they might want to give.

"Who'd he talk to?" Ethan asked and headed toward the coffee pot resting on the top of the wood stove.

Rubbing his chin, Big Red said, " 'Twere only the Scot. At least that all me be seein'. Workin' on some papers."

"Did they talk long?" Ethan poured coffee into a stoneware mug.

Four other cups of different designs remained on a short shelf next to the stove. Two were chipped. A spoon with a small bowl of sugar occupied one edge of the shelf.

"No sir, not long at all," The Irishman said. "The preacher told me theirselves be a sorry lot and that they deserved hangin'. That's what hisself be sayin' before he left."

Ethan tasted the coffee. Bitter and almost scalding. He blew on the remaining cupful to cool it.

"Missa Ethan, you need to put hands in hot water. Epsum salts good for hands," Peaches said, watching the rancher with his coffee. "I get Epsum salts."

"Thanks, Peaches, but I'll be fine." Ethan smiled. "I'll pour some of this coffee on them when I go outside. It's strong enough to cure anything."

Both Peaches and Big Red chuckled.

"How be Cole?" the Irishman asked, watching the beaten outlaw groan and move on the cell floor. None of his cellmates made any attempt to help him.

Glancing at Peaches before he answered, Ethan said, "He's going to make it. Going to take some time though. Even for him."

"I be lookin' forward to the day me can pin this badge on his shirt again." Big Red patted the silver star on his vest.

Nodding, Ethan asked what the Irishman knew about Jinette Six. He didn't know much, but thought she was actually quite religious, having seen her come and go from Dinclaur's church on several occasions. She often stayed in the pastor's house, too. Ethan took a long drink of coffee, deciding it was a little less hot, but no less bitter.

"I'm to going to check on something. Be back later," Ethan

took the unfinished coffee with him. "I'll bring back the cup, too."

Peaches said he was going back to Cole's room after he made a stop at the general store.

Outside, Ethan poured the rest of the coffee over his sore hands, left the cup by the door and went to the telegraph office, operating within the Hancock Lumber Company at the far end of the main block. The Chinaman headed for the general store and emerged a few minutes later, carrying a can of peaches, and walked toward the hotel.

Down the street, Pastor Dinclaur watched the two men and wondered what Ethan was doing. The fake minister had been stunned when he saw Tiorgs and his men being brought to town this morning. How could that have happened? Couldn't the damn Scot do anything right? Who would Ethan Kerry want to wire? Maybe he was wiring the Rangers. That was likely. They would come. For a man like Ethan Kerry.

Damn him.

At the jail, he had told Tiorgs to wait quietly, that he would get him and his men out in the next few days. The Scotsman made it clear that he didn't intend to hang alone. Dinclaur slammed his fist into the counter. His well-laid plans were in total disarray. Why did Ethan Kerry have to get his sight back? Definitely, the tall rancher had directed the counterattack on Tiorgs's men and outambushed the ambushers. Was the rancher ever really blind or just pretending?

He stomped through the tiny church, stopping to straighten a crooked pew bench. He prided himself on the ability to think, not just use a gun. He must really think now.

As he went to the church's door, he knocked the spoon from his coffee cup. Leaning over to retrieve it, Dinclaur warned himself, "Don't touch it. I must not pick it up. I'll leave it there. One of the church women will see it and pick it *up*." He straightened himself. "It is bad luck to pick up a utensil that one has *dropped*." He opened the church door and stepped into the street.

Maybe the smartest thing to do was to leave town now. Forget Tiorgs. The problem with that idea was it wouldn't take long before Ethan Kerry figured out he was behind the scheme—or Tiorgs talked. If he left now, the Kerrys would be on his trail quickly. To escape, he had to create a diversion, something that would occupy them for a few days. The only thing he could think of was his original promise to Tiorgs, to break him and his men out of jail.

Ethan Kerry would concentrate on recapturing them. The rancher would only have the Chinaman with him, plus any townsmen brave enough; the Irishman would be dead. Earlier, he saw Luther and the other Bar K men ride out of town with Cole Kerry resting in a buckboard. That would give him precious time to escape and cover his trail.

His stepsister had already left at his urging. Their time together had been sweet, especially at night. He shivered when recalling her enthusiasm for intimacy. They had been that way for years. That society prohibited two children in the same family having sex made their times together even more delicious. She would stop at the Rocking R for a new mount and leave for the East. She said she would wait for him in Houston. Whether she did or not didn't matter for now. She could take care of herself. And he needed to concentrate.

Nightfall brought a strange silence to the town. Dinclaur had secured his carriage from the livery earlier, telling the livery operator that he needed to see the other ranches and farms in the region and make certain his "sheep" were comfortable, especially after this "rustling and murdering." The statement was a good cover and allowed him to have the carriage behind the church for a quick getaway.

He could wait until after tomorrow's hearing, but that was a foregone conclusion, only a formality. Acting quickly was essential. The Kerrys were too important in the region to be denied. That Tiorgs and his men were guilty was immaterial. He hated the Kerrys and their growing wealth and influence. Every fiber in his being hated them. That thought gave him a new spark.

The key to freeing Tiorgs would be if the Irishman was alone guarding the jail. He had seen Ethan go to the hotel after leaving the telegraph office and a stop at the mayor's restaurant. The Chinaman was already there; he'd seen him go there from the general store. So both Ethan Kerry and the Chinaman were away from the jail.

That meant only the Irishman was in the marshal's office. Perfect. He would open the door for him. The stupid fool.

The town was dark and the night was cold. He put on his coat and hat, wrapped a thick towel around his pistol barrel and set out, keeping to the shadows. No one was out and even the saloons sounded subdued. As soon as he released Tiorgs and his men, the outlaws would be on their own. There was no way he could gather that many horses without most of the town knowing. He had already decided to fire his gun a few times, without the towel, once he was near the church. That would awaken the town and bring Ethan and the Chinaman to the jail.

He eased up to the door of the marshal's office and knocked. He had done this before, killing Marshal Montgomery. Only then he had eliminated the idiots who would have talked. He hadn't made up his mind yet if he would let Tiorgs live or not. Probably he would. But he was the only one with a direct connection to him. However, if the Scotsman was caught again, it wouldn't matter if Tiorgs talked, because he would be gone. Long gone.

Knock. Knock. Knock. He rapped on the door with his left

fist, which held a Bible. In his right was the wrapped gun.

"Who be there?" Big Red answered from inside.

"It is Pastor Dinclaur, my *friend*," Dinclaur replied. "So sorry to be calling this late, but one of your prisoners asked if he might have a Bible to *read*—and I meant to give it to him earlier. Some parishers kept me busy until now going over plans for the Thanksgiving *service*."

"Of course, Pastor."

Dinclaur heard the movement of the heavy crossbar acting as reinforcement, then a pause and finally the rhythmic unlocking of the door. He cocked the revolver, keeping it hidden under the Bible. Once he stepped inside, he would kill the Irishman. Yellow light seeped from the cracks around the door. The process seemed to take a long time, but he forced himself to be patient. Saying something right now might make the Irishman suspicious. Gradually, the door swung open and yellow light took over the doorway.

He didn't see Big Red. Probably standing behind the opened door. Dinclaur took a step inside, making certain the Bible would be the first thing the marshal saw.

"Marshal?"

"Right here I be."

Dinclaur spun to his left, but the Irishman wasn't there. He was crouched behind his desk. A rope tied to the latch led to the desk explained how Big Red had opened the door without exposing himself.

"Drop the gun . . . Glory." From the shadows came Ethan Kerry's hard voice. No one had seen him slip into the jail from the back.

From against the farthest cell, a silhouette appeared, holding a red-handled Smith & Wesson revolver. Peaches had also slipped back after dark. From the other end appeared Mayor Heinrich and Judge Moreland, both holding rifles. With Ethan's assistance, the two civic leaders had crept into the marshal's office after dark. Both had been reluctant, but Ethan wouldn't accept a negative answer. Neither could believe that their town minister was actually a known gunman and behind all of the trouble on the range. In the cells all of the outlaws were tied and gagged.

"I-I d-don't understand. I was just bringing a B-Bible to a lost *soul*. Mr. Tiorgs asked for it. Ask him if you don't believe *me*." Dinclaur held out the Bible in his left hand, leaving his right holding the wrapped gun.

Ethan moved toward him. "And just who was supposed to get what's in that gun? The one wrapped so no one could hear the noise when you fired it."

"It *ist* over, Glory Van Camp," Mayor Heinrich spat. "*Herr* Tiorgs . . . *hast* told us all of it."

Dinclaur looked down at the cocked revolver in his right hand, now at his side. "I am a man of *God*. How dare you accuse me of being a part of murder and . . . and cattle rustling. How dare *you*."

"Drop the gun, Glory," Ethan demanded again. "I invited the mayor and the judge to join us as witnesses."

The fake minister looked up again, saw Ethan's intense expression and Peaches's cold face. He eased the hammer down and leaned over to place the gun on the floor.

"Rangers are coming," Ethan said. "They'll escort all of you away after the trial."

Peaches checked Dinclaur for any hidden weapons and found a derringer in the minister's coat pocket. Big Red opened the center cell, holding the beaten outlaw and three other men.

"What happened to *him*?" Dinclaur asked as he slowly entered the cell.

"Oh, hisself fell down," the Irishman replied as he shut the cell door behind Dinclaur. "Not as careful as hisself should be."

The phony minister stared at the beaten outlaw, then the others, all tied and gagged. His shoulders sagged and he went over to one of the cots and sat. The other outlaws lay on the floor. The other jailed men were similarly tied and gagged, including Tiorgs.

"Oh, I almost forgot, Glory. There's a U.S. Deputy Marshal coming from Colorado. He knows you. Knows you well," Ethan said.

CHAPTER 36

Next morning, the town was wild as the story of the arrest of their minister hurried from person to person. By ten o'clock, it was decided to move the hearing to the mayor's restaurant so that more citizens could attend. The restaurant was rearranged for the hearing and packed with townspeople.

Twenty upset men and women had cornered the front tables. They were furious that anyone would dare think Pastor Dinclaur could be guilty of anything so evil. The front of the restaurant was lined with additional interested people, standing and waiting. Vehement denials were combined with loud statements that Ethan Kerry was trying to run the town. Near the kitchen, where the trial's action would take place, one table and chair had been set off by itself for the judge. Another chair would serve as the witness chair. Two other tables had been arranged a few feet away, one for the prosecution, one for the defense.

Ethan sat quietly at the prosecutor's table.

Judge Moreland ran through the first phase of the hearing, deciding that Tiorgs and his men should stand trial for murder, attempted murder and rustling. Ethan told the judge what had happened, the cattle rustling, attempted ambush, the killing of several of his men, and the attack on his house. The latter brought sympathetic responses even from the annoyed crowd. None of the arrested outlaws were interested in talking, except for the man Ethan had beaten yesterday. He whined about being whipped when he had no chance to defend himself.

Judge Moreland asked him one question: "Was anyone hold-ing you at the time?"

That ended the outlaw's recital.

The crowd was restless and growing angrier by the minute. Soon the outlaws were led away to the jail by Big Red. Tiorgs remained in the back, waiting to be a witness; Peaches stood with him. Big Red returned with Dinclaur in handcuffs. Judge Moreland hammered the crowd into silence as he entered and announced that he was stepping down for this hearing. He would serve as a witness for the prosecution. That brought new boos and shouts.

Taking the gavel as planned was Jimmy Victor. He was much more comfortable in this role than in his previous one as defense attorney. Dinclaur announced his intention to serve as his own counsel. The minister took a chair at the defense table and made a showing of praying. Victor was actually excited about the opportunity to preside over this hearing. He wanted to be the next justice of the peace. This would provide an excellent opportunity to display his leadership skills. He opened this phase of the hearing with a customary statement that its purpose was to determine if an actual trial was justified and that he, and only he, would make that determination.

Ethan testified first, explaining what had happened. He also said that he had contacted the Rangers with the mayor's ap-proval and they had contacted a U.S. Deputy Marshal in Colorado who knew Glory Van Camp. He would be coming to Uvalde to testify at the trial. The deputy marshal had been try-ing to find Glory since he had portrayed a minister in Leadville and had swindled several widows there. There were other instances of his using a minister's disguise for unlawful gain.

"What have you got against our preacher, Kerry?" a raw voice rang out.

The tall rancher stopped his presentation, looked in the direction of the challenge and said evenly, "I don't like people who try to kill my brother, my wife, my children, my men and try to steal my property. How about you?"

Muttering followed and Victor gaveled the crowd into a strained silence. After Ethan was finished, Dinclaur stepped up to cross-examine him.

"Let us begin this search for the truth with a *prayer,*" Dinclaur declared, motioning to the crowd. "Oh Lord, watch over us, our community, our *families;* keep us safe from misunderstanding and misguided *behavior.* Amen."

Ethan glared at Victor who shrugged his shoulders as Ethan took a seat in the chair set aside for witnesses.

"It is this court's understanding that you believe I am somehow behind the recent disasters that have befallen your *family.* Is that correct?"

"It is . . . Glory."

Dinclaur smiled. "You have made the strange claim that I am . . . what's the name . . . Glory, uh something, a notorious hoodlum from *Colorado.* Is that correct?"

"Yes, you are Glory Van Camp, gunman, murderer and crook."

The audience roared its disapproval and Dinclaur raised his arms to quiet them. It was clear a majority of the town did not believe their minister was involved in the crimes and he knew it.

"Do you have any proof of this serious *accusation?*" Dinclaur asked, putting his hands on his hips.

"We have the word of your stepfather, Heredith Tiorgs, and, as I just said, we have authorities coming from Colorado who will confirm it." Ethan didn't like the mood of the hearing.

"I see. So, one day you just decided I was this . . . wicked *person.*" Dinclaur stepped close to Ethan, sitting in the witness chair; the fake minister's eyes shone brightly with the gleam of victory.

Without waiting for a question, Ethan began explaining his hunch and that Dinclaur showing up at the jail with a gun cinched it. He said Mayor Heinrich and Judge Moreland were also there and would testify later.

"Let me get this straight. You decided I was this Glory Van Camp because I brought a *Bible* to the jail last *night*?"

"No, I decided because your stepfather told us about you, Glory . . . and you cinched it when you brought a gun to kill the marshal and spring Tiorgs and his bunch of outlaws," Ethan said and cocked his head. "I finally remembered you from the war. You pretended to be a preacher then, too. Only then you were a spy for the Union."

Dinclaur spun around and paced to the far side of the room, touched one of the moved-aside tables and turned around.

"So you took the word of a man who tried to kill your wife and *children*," Dinclaur snarled. "What did you offer him . . . to tell this, this absurd *story*."

Ethan straightened his back, his eyes narrowed. "The lies won't help you this time, Glory. We've had enough."

If the answer surprised Dinclaur, he didn't show it. Instead, he reverted to his ministerial guise. "Bless you, my son, for you know not what you *do*."

The audience murmured.

With a snort, Ethan went on the verbal attack. "Glory, your biggest crime wasn't murdering Marshal Montgomery and his prisoners to keep them from talking . . . and it wasn't having your men steal Bar K beef and try to kill my men and my family . . . and it wasn't your attempts to kill my brother." He paused for effect. "No . . . your biggest crime is pretending to be a minister, a man of God—and lying to this great town."

Dinclaur swallowed, unsure of what to say next. Ethan didn't wait.

"By the way, it was slick that you managed to arrive in Uvalde right after gentle old Reverend Joseph B. Hillas died. In his sleep. Suffocation doesn't take long, does it?"

Jimmy Victor admonished him to stay with the facts of the case while Dinclaur mumbled something about it being an unfair question and dismissing Ethan as a witness.

Stepping away from the witness chair, Ethan called Heredith Tiorgs to the stand. Tiorgs started off in a foul mood, staring at Dinclaur as he talked. His Scottish accent was thick as he explained the arrangement between himself and Dinclaur, that the minister was actually Glory Van Camp, a known Colorado gunman and his stepson, and that Jinette Six was his daughter and their goal was to kill the Kerrys and take over the Bar K. He admitted that the late town bum, Meken, was also his stepson and a criminal.

As he spoke, the crowd became incensed, with yells of "liar" echoing through the restaurant. Victor slammed down his gavel and declared that he wouldn't stand for any more interruptions.

Dinclaur chose not to cross-examine Tiorgs, so Ethan called Judge Moreland to the stand. He told what he had seen the night before at the jail and what he had heard from Tiorgs.

The audience stirred and was uncomfortable.

"Good day to you, Judge Moreland," Dinclaur stood and walked again to the far table and turned slowly toward the justice of the peace. "Let's see if I understand you *correctly*. A man of God enters the jail with a Bible and you decide he's a known *gunman*. Is that right?"

"You had a revolver," Judge Moreland replied, running a finger over his lips. "And you had a towel tied around the barrel to keep the gunfire from making noise."

Dinclaur folded his arms. "Why did I tell you I was carrying a weapon, your *Honor*?"

After clearing his throat, Moreland explained the minister had said he carried the gun for protection since Uvalde was unsettled by the outlaws brought in by Ethan Kerry and his men. The justice of the peace added in a sarcastic voice that the towel wrapping was to keep from bothering others if he had to shoot.

Dinclaur walked toward him, his eyes glaring, but he managed to soften his response. "I take it you don't believe a minister would be somewhat uncomfortable around *guns*?"

"You looked very comfortable with that Colt." Moreland folded his arms. "And I never knew anyone wrapping a towel around a gun to get comfortable."

Moreland was silent and Dinclaur decided it was best to let him go.

Next, both Mayor Heinrich and Big Red testified along the same lines as Judge Moreland. Dinclaur didn't bother to challenge them on the gun issue, but he went after Big Red on the identity issue.

"Marshal, earlier there was a claim made by Mr. Kerry that I was, what's his *name*?"

"Ye be Glory Van Camp," Big Red declared in a loud voice. "Ye be misusin' the word o' God."

"And what proof do you have of this absurd *claim*?"

Without standing, Ethan announced, "This is a hearing, your Honor. We do not have to prove every aspect of our charge. As I said earlier, there is a lawman coming from Colorado who will make a positive identification. He will be here for the trial." Ethan glared at Dinclaur. "As you know, we already have the sworn testimony of Glory's . . . un, Dinclaur's. . . . stepfather."

Dinclaur erupted, slamming his fist against the defense table and screaming, "You idiots! God damn you all!"

The crowd inhaled as one and the jabbering that followed

was intense and furious. A woman in the front row began to sob.

Someone yelled, "Hang the blasphemer!"

Big Red stood and walked to the door of the restaurant where Moreland and Heinrich stood. Moreland told him that this was the reason he wanted to move East. The Irishman didn't respond.

Peaches came alongside Ethan and whispered in his ear. Ethan nodded as Judge Victor pounded his gavel and tried to bring the audience back under control.

"I will clear this courtroom if there is another outburst."

Ethan rose from his chair behind the prosecutor's table. "There is one more piece of evidence we'd like to introduce, your Honor."

"Proceed."

The tall rancher described what Cole had told him about the two ambushers who tried to kill him on the road to their ranch. Both of the ambushers had small feet. Before Meken Van Camp died, he told Cole that he and his brother, Glory Van Camp, were the ambushers.

"Take off your boots," he said, pointing at Dinclaur.

"Take off my *boots*? Does it look like I have small feet? *This is absurd!*" Dinclaur hollered.

"Either you take them off—or I will."

"What? I will do no such *thing*. I have . . ."

Judge Victor pointed his gavel at Dinclaur. "Sit down and take off your boots or let Mr. Kerry do it. This court wants to see your feet."

Ethan strode over to the flustered Dinclaur, crouched and pulled off his boot. A piece of crumpled newspaper came out with this foot. Dinclaur's feet were those of a small boy.

Standing, Ethan tossed the boot at Dinclaur. "Your Honor, we will add the attempted murder of my brother to the charges.

We already know there was a carriage at the scene—and that this man had checked one out at the livery."

Dinclaur sat at his table, gripping the Bible with both hands. It was the only display he could think of at the moment.

Leaning over the table, Ethan said, "By the way, Glory, the Rocking R will be coming up for sale by the county soon. When the taxes aren't paid."

Dinclaur blurted, "Why would I care? I'm a poor *preacher*. I don't own anything. Except this . . . *Bible*."

"Well, our attorney will start proceedings with the county to buy the Rocking R," Ethan said and smiled. "Then we plan to help one of our neighbors take ownership."

The audience bubbled with enthusiasm.

"Oh, Glory, I almost forgot. Remember when we found the bodies of the Drako family not far from here?" Ethan growled. "After they sold their ranch . . . to your stepfather. He admitted to those murders, too."

Jimmy Victor banged his gavel. "This hearing is hereby adjourned. The defendant, known here as Paul Dinclaur, is held over for trial for murder, attempted murder and cattle rustling."

"No! No! I can't be. You fools. . . ." Dinclaur stood, red-faced, and screamed at the assembled crowd. "Can't you see? I'm just a preacher. A preacher . . . *Damn you all.*"

CHAPTER 37

As the courtroom slowly dispersed, stunned, angry and confused, Big Red and Peaches took a depressed Dinclaur and Tiorgs out of Heinrich's restaurant, reapplying handcuffs, and herded them toward the jail.

Ethan stayed behind to help Heinrich and others reset the restaurant for regular service while Judge Moreland and his replacement for the hearing, Johnny Lee Victor, conversed in the corner. On the main street, a freighter rumbled along and behind it came a hooded rider leading two saddled horses. They had just emerged from the livery.

No one paid any attention to Jinette Six, wearing a long coat with a hood as she kept her head down. A silver-plated revolver in her right hand was hidden within the coat's unbuttoned opening. She had ridden back from the Rocking R early to be with Dinclaur and heard the news. The beautiful woman rode slowly, advancing toward Big Red and Peaches as they walked behind Dinclaur and Tiorgs. The Scot was cursing in Scottish, but the minister glanced in Jinette's direction. His eyes widened in recognition. Twenty feet from where they were walking on the sidewalk, Jinette drew her revolver and fired at Peaches. Her bullet struck him in the heart. Dinclaur bolted for the second horse and Tiorgs was only a step behind as Jinette emptied her gun into Peaches and fired a last bullet at the stunned Big Red. She shoved the empty gun into her coat pocket and drew a second revolver from a holster belted around her waist.

"Hurry, Glory! Hurry, father!" she yelled.

Both men reached up with handcuffed hands, grabbing the saddlehorns of the two horses, and swung into the respective saddles. She released the reins so they could handle the horses.

Peaches fell to his knees, drew his red-handled handgun and fired, then collapsed, face down. Big Red spun with the impact of the bullet, but managed to draw his own weapon as the three galloped away.

"Stop them!" he yelled, stumbling into the street and shooting at their fleeing mounts. People up and down the sidewalk scurried for safety. Jinette fired wildly as they raced away.

At the restaurant, Ethan burst out of the doorway with a Colt in his hand. Jinette, Dinclaur and Tiorgs were nearing the end of the main street. He realized what had happened and ran for the downed Chinaman instead of firing at their fleeting images. Six townsmen had already reached the wounded men and one was running for Dr. Wright. Big Red's wound was slight and he was waving off help

Peaches was dead.

Ethan cursed the discovery of the Chinaman's passing and announced he was going after the three criminals. He picked up Peaches's Webley Bulldog double-action revolver with its red handles and shoved the weapon into his waistband.

Mayor Heinrich yelled that a posse would be formed and Big Red said he would lead it. Ethan didn't wait for the gathering, but ran to the livery for a horse. But not his, he would ride Cole's horse, Kiowa. No animal was faster and stronger. Entering the barn, he saw the liveryman staggering to his feet from within an empty stall. A bloody gash on the side of Benjamin's forehead told the story: Jinette Six had knocked him out and taken the two horses.

Ethan didn't want to wait to help him, but knew he should. Claire would somehow know if he didn't. "You've been hit hard, man. Let me help you."

"I-I'll be passable. That fancy Six woman," the liveryman blubbered. "She, she surprised me. Had a gun. Didn't . . ."

"I know. She got two of your horses. Escaped with two prisoners and killed a deputy. Our friend," Ethan explained as he helped the man to an unpainted bench near the front of the livery. "Where's some water? Clean water. That cut needs cleaning."

"A-Ain't none here, 'ceptin' what I give the hosses." Benjamin's thick stomach heaved up and down as the liveryman tried to regain his full consciousness. Ethan went to a bucket, dipped in his neckerchief and returned to clean the wound.

Benjamin straightened his back, pulling on his red suspenders. "I'll be fine. Ya need to be gettin' after them, don' ya?"

Ethan couldn't resist. "Yes. That's why I came here. I need Cole's horse."

The liveryman was surprised and hesitant. "That big sorrel, he don't like many folks a'ridin' him."

"I know, but he's faster than any horse I've ever known," Ethan said, handing the wet bandana to him. "If you're all right, I'll saddle him an' get going."

"I'll be fine. Jes' a bit dizzy. Say, Mr. Kerry . . . weren't ya blind?"

Ethan smiled. "I was. Healed now."

"Well, Lord be praised."

"That's a good way to put it."

Without another word, Ethan went to Kiowa's stall, strapped on the saddle, slipped the bit into his mouth and settled the bridle over his head. The big sorrel stood motionless as he worked, talking quietly.

"Got a Winchester? I'll bring it back," Ethan said as he

secured his canteen around the saddle horn. "Left mine at the jail."

"Got a Henry. In the tack room over there. Shoots good. It's loaded."

"Good." Ethan hurried to the crowded room, grabbed the rifle and shoved it into the saddle boot.

He turned his attention to the horse. "Kiowa, like I said . . . I need your help. Will you let me ride you, boy? I need you."

With his boot in the stirrup, he swung onto the big red horse and prayed the sorrel would accept him. He ignored the image of the horse throwing and kicking him in the head years before.

Kiowa snorted and shook his head. Ethan nudged him with his spurs and the sorrel moved out smoothly.

"He's been grained and watered good. Ride strong, Mr. Kerry!"

After clearing the barn, Kiowa was in full gallop in three strides. Ethan and the powerful sorrel thundered down the street and past the gathering posse.

Big Red saw him and shouted, "Wait for ourselves, Mr. Kerry. We be comin'!"

If Ethan heard him, he didn't react, spurring Kiowa toward the end of town. Soon Uvalde was barely in sight and Ethan was reading the trail of the escaping horses as they galloped. There was no attempt at deception; there was no time.

Kiowa ate up the open land, loving the opportunity to run. Really run. The soft dirt left clear marks of where Jinette, Tiorgs and Dinclaur had traveled. They were headed for the Rocking R, most likely for fresh horses. However, an hour later, the tracks turned northwest as if the riders were headed for the little town of Pitch. He eased Kiowa into a lope while he thought through that possibility. For the first time, he realized that Thanksgiving was two days away. A very special gathering for the Kerry clan. How different it would be this year.

He decided to head for the Rocking R. It made no sense for them to go to Pitch. This had to be a feint to lead pursuers off their track. If he was wrong, he was wrong. He swung Kiowa and spurred him into a ground-eating gallop toward the outlaw ranch. As they rounded a huge rock formation, his vision blurred and he trembled. He squeezed shut his eyes without slowing the sorrel and prayed.

"God, I need my eyes. I need to see. You know I do. Be with me."

Opening them tentatively, then fully, his vision was clear once more. He said another prayer, this one of thanks. It must be fatigue, but there was nothing he could do about that right now.

He cleared a flat mesa and saw where the three had turned back toward the Rocking R. Licking his cracked lips, he prodded the big horse into a new gallop and Kiowa responded. His hunch had gained him much precious time; they would reach the ranch no more than eight or ten minutes ahead of him. If he was lucky, they wouldn't be expecting anyone from town so soon.

Easing Kiowa into a lope, he yanked the Henry free of its saddle boot and levered the gun into readiness. Henry carbines had a tendency to jam if they were fired too fast, he reminded himself. There might be some left-behind gunmen still at the ranch, but he doubted it. Tiorgs would have thrown all his manpower into the ambush and the attack on his house. But he must be prepared. If he waited for the posse to catch up, Dinclaur, Tiorgs and Jinette would be long gone—and darkness would soon take away any reasonable chance of tracking them until dawn.

He would not wait. "The hell with being outnumbered, Kiowa."

Laying the carbine across his saddle, he slowed Kiowa into a walk as they came upon the Rocking R ranch buildings. The heavily sweating horse complied. The big sorrel was weary and Ethan knew he had pushed the great animal harder than he should have. Both Luther and Cole would be angry at him.

He patted Kiowa's wet neck. "Thanks, boy, you did good. Now we've got to be smart. Real smart. And lucky."

Ahead the ranch yard appeared deserted. Fresh tracks disappeared on the far side of the house. He figured they would switch horses first before going inside to gather food and supplies. That way they would be ready to ride out quickly if a posse appeared.

At the edge of the ranch yard, he dismounted and tied Kiowa to a cottonwood. The horse would be unseen from most places on the ranch; the big sorrel needed to cool down before drinking water. The ranch yard itself was rundown, quite different from the way the Drakos had kept it. Tumbleweeds pushed against the sides of every building. A window was broken out on the front of the ranch house and the roof of the barn needed patching. A small shed, next to the barn, was missing a door.

Long shadows were gaining ground everywhere. After removing his spurs, he advanced quickly, using them to keep out of sight of house windows and the barn. He passed their sweating horses tied to a hitch rack in the back of the house. That surprised him; he thought they would switch them first. Slipping next to the barn's open door, he listened, holding his carbine with both hands. There were no sounds, other than the pawing of a horse close to the door.

Crouching, he spun into the barn and confirmed no one was there and no fresh horses had been saddled. So they had gone directly into the house. They had to be inside.

Would Dinclaur and Tiorgs still have on handcuffs? He doubted it. Well-placed bullets would sever the chains.

Strange, Ethan thought. Why did they not go into the barn first? He ran across the open yard, from the barn to the back of the house. He tensed. Maybe his fast appearance had surprised them into a change of plans. That made sense. They would be waiting, knowing he was alone. He opened the back door, hoping it wouldn't squeak, but the door didn't agree. A long, low squeal gave Ethan a chill. He dove into the kitchen area and rolled over, bringing his carbine to his shoulder.

Nothing. No sound. Wait. A soft whimper came to him from the main room. He stood, holding the carbine with both hands, and tiptoed toward the low moaning. In what passed for a main room was Dinclaur on his knees. Beside him on the floor, Jinette Six lay unmoving on her stomach. Tiorgs was nowhere in sight. Ethan's strides were careful. So far, the house appeared empty, except for Jinette and Dinclaur. Where was the Scotsman?

Dinclaur glanced up from the main room and saw Ethan. His first reaction was as if they were old friends who hadn't seen each other in a long time.

"Good to see you, *Ethan Kerry*," Dinclaur said with a slight smile. "Figured it would be *you*."

The fake minister was still wearing handcuffs, but had broken the connecting chain. "That damn Chink got *her*." Dinclaur motioned toward a blood-stained Jinette. "She died a few minutes *ago*."

"She murdered Peaches. A deputy marshal. Our friend." Ethan's response was hard. He looked at the unmoving woman. Around her waist was a gunbelt with a holstered gun; her long coat covered most of her body. Across her cheek were three fingers of smudged blood. As far as Ethan could tell she wasn't breathing. He continued moving, changing directions every few steps. Where was Tiorgs?

Dinclaur shook his head. "I loved her. I really *loved her*." He explained.

"Where's Tiorgs?" Ethan growled, his gaze taking in the room.

"Back on the trail. Well, off it actually. We stopped to rest our horses a few miles back. Hid behind some cottonwoods. He died there. Just slid off his horse. Guess the big Mick got *him*." Dinclaur shook his head. "I knew he was hit. Didn't realize how bad he was. Didn't figure we could take the time to get him back on, bring the body here. Besides I had all I could do keeping her in the *saddle*."

Dinclaur's manner of emphasizing last words in his statements annoyed him. Ethan realized it always had.

Ethan growled, "Never mind, Glory. Take the gun out of your waistband and drop it on the floor. Real slow."

Dinclaur moved his right hand to his waistband and pulled out the revolver and tossed it toward Ethan. The tall rancher studied the main room, looking for a hidden Tiorgs. There was only a light green sofa with several torn places, a lopsided dresser and a stone fireplace, quite cold. Across the room was a closed closet.

"So you remembered me from the *war*? I was hoping you wouldn't," Dinclaur said. "That was a long time ago—and I wasn't around you much. Just a day, *I think*."

Never standing still, Ethan shifted the carbine to keep it pointed at Dinclaur as he moved. "Yeah, you were playing minister back then, too." He cocked his head. "Only then, you were also a spy for the Yanks. Got away before we could string you up." Pausing only momentarily, Ethan walked to the far corner and glanced inside a dark bedroom but kept his carbine aimed at Dinclaur.

"I told you, Kerry. Nobody else is *here*," Dinclaur said, "It's just me—and you've got me *covered*."

"Maybe I will," Ethan snapped and reversed his movement. "As soon as your sister gets rid of her guns."

"What are you talking about, Kerry? Jinette's dead, dammit. I just told you that." Dinclaur waved his arms wildly and dropped his accenting.

"I heard you. Now, you two hear me. I just saw her breathe. Tell your little sister to pull out those guns of hers. One at a time. From under her coat," Ethan growled and continued moving. "Tell her to do it with her left hand." Ethan swung his carbine toward her head. "You tell her that she wouldn't be the first woman I've killed."

It was a lie, but he wanted to force her to act. He got what he wanted.

Her eyelashes fluttered and she sat up, shrieking, "I told you it wouldn't work!" She lifted her right hand in defiance.

"Get rid of the guns, lady."

"You wouldn't shoot me."

Ethan fired and she screeched an animal sound and grabbed her arm.

Dinclaur yelled, "My God, you shot *her*!"

"I told her. Get rid of the guns. My next bullet ends this game." Ethan levered the Henry into readiness. He was glad the weapon hadn't jammed.

Glaring at him, she raised her skirt to reveal a second heavy revolver and pushed it away with her left hand as if it were spoiled food. Her holstered revolver followed. She returned her hand to her bleeding right arm; a circle of blood was widening on her sleeve. Ethan walked over and kicked both guns away.

"Satisfied, Kerry?" she said. "I'm bleeding. Look."

"Actually, no."

"What now, you sonuvabitch?"

"Shed that derringer. Under your cuff. If I don't like the way you do it, I'll put a bullet in your other arm," Ethan pointed at her right cuff. "You'll find I'm not as nice as my brothers."

Her eyes flashed hatred and she pinched her blouse cuff at her wrist and out sprang a hidden derringer attached to a release mechanism. She stared at the derringer in her opened hand.

"Now's the time to be careful. Real careful," Ethan warned. "Take that derringer with your left hand. Toss it away." He glanced at an anxious Dinclaur and kept sliding to his right, then reversing direction to his left. He was certain Tiorgs was somewhere in the room.

"Don't do anything stupid, Glory. You're the reason some good men aren't with us anymore. I can't think of anything I'd rather do than shoot you in the head." Ethan stared at Jinette, holding her bleeding arm and cursing.

"Ten years ago, I would've shot you both and left." His hands tightened on the carbine. "I should anyway. You two had my brother shot up. You killed some good men. Good friends of mine." His eyes narrowed.

Jinette hesitated, glanced at the closet door across the room and returned her attention to Ethan. Her own eyes were hot with crazed fury. But her mind was filled with the decision. The opportunity was hot in her hand. All she had to do was squeeze, aim and fire. A second and Ethan Kerry would be dead.

Biting his lip, Dinclaur pleaded, "N-No, Jinette. N-No. H-He'll kill *you*."

She blinked, grabbed the butt of the gun with her left hand and threw it. Her gaze followed the flight of the little gun.

As it flew, she yelled, "Now . . . father!"

The derringer bounced against an old sofa and plopped on the dirty, wood-framed floor. The closet door knob turned. But it was Ethan Kerry who reacted first. Not following the flight of the small gun, he fired three times as fast as he dared to lever the Henry, stepped to his left and fired once more. His bullets drove a pattern the size of a silver dollar into the middle of the closet door fifteen feet away. A groan followed, then the sound of staggering feet. Ethan's carbine jammed and he tossed it aside, drawing his long-barreled Colt in one motion. He cocked and fired the handgun, slamming bullets through the closet

306

door, a foot higher than his rifle shots.

Glancing at Jinette and Dinclaur, he saw both were stunned. The fake minister appeared resigned to defeat. Keeping his attention on Jinette, Ethan shifted the handgun to his other hand and pulled Peaches's gun from his waistband.

"Lady, open the closet and step out of the way. Your pa's coming out."

"You sonuvabitch, that's my father!" she snarled, holding her right arm with her left.

"Do it." Ethan waved Peaches's gun toward the closet door.

Reluctantly, Jinette grabbed the handle and pulled it open. She couldn't get out of the way fast enough as the dead Heredith Tiorgs fell out of the door. His Smith & Wesson revolver tumbled ahead of him and slid on the floor. Ethan pushed away the gun with his foot, then punched his boot toe into the lifeless body to make certain the man was dead.

She screamed and fell across Tiorgs's unmoving body.

"Got any more clowns around here? Any so-called family?"

"Wouldn't you like to know," she snapped, her eyes brimming with tears.

Ethan moved back, covering both Jinette and Dinclaur with his revolvers while he studied the house again.

"You know, lady, the only reason you think you're tough is that men are nice to you," he said. "My wife, Claire, is older. A grand woman with four kids—and she could whip your ass any day and twice on Sunday." He stared at her. "You're nothing but a fancy piece of crap."

Jinette looked at him, holding her bloody arm. She said nothing. Her eyes were glazed with pain and defeat.

"Now, drop the gun you took from your pappy. Or do you think I won't shoot again?"

Snarling, she tossed the derringer toward him.

Dinclaur stared across the room. A chair was turned toward

the wall. He hadn't noticed it before. A sign of bad luck. He should have known.

Ethan studied the outlaw stepbrother and -sister. "Tell you what . . . if you two want to make a former blind man real happy . . . make a move for those guns." He walked over to the scattered weapons and pushed them with his boot in the direction of Jinette and Dinclaur.

"I'll wait."

He holstered his Colt and shoved Dinclaur's gun into his waistband.

"How's that?"

Neither would look at him; neither looked at the guns.

"What's the matter, Glory? How about you, little lady? Not good at taking on somebody facing you?"

He stepped closer and pushed the guns even closer with his boot. "Come on. There are two of you. I'm just an old cowpuncher. Fifty-fifty chance, I'd say. Hell, I'd get one of you for sure, but . . ."

Staring at the floor, Dinclaur mumbled, "How come everything comes out good for *you*—and all you Kerrys? It's not *fair*." His manner of speaking had long since become a habit, regardless of the situation.

Kicking away the guns, Ethan stepped next to Dinclaur and back-slapped him with his opened hand. The blow was so hard, the fake minister rocked backward on his knees. Blood began to seep from his mouth.

"Maybe you should've tried working hard. That's what the men were doing before you killed them." He slapped Dinclaur again even harder.

The broken outlaw began to cry. His teeth were covered with blood. "D-Don't . . . please. Don't."

Ethan shook his hand to rid the sting, looked at the sobbing Dinclaur and drove his fist into the fake minister's face. The crunch of a breaking nose was loud as blood spurted over both men. Dinclaur collapsed into an awkward heap.

"That's for Cole, you bastard," Ethan growled and shook his hand again.

Jinette stared at the tall rancher. Her eyes were wide and soft. "P-Please . . . I-I don't want to d-die. I'll do anything you want." She looked down at her heaving bosom and then back into Ethan's face with eyes that invited him.

"What I want," Ethan said, "is to watch the two of you hang."

A half hour later, Big Red and the posse arrived at the Rocking R; they had followed Ethan's trail, ignoring the outlaws' feint toward Pitch. The ranch house blazed with every gas lamp and candle Ethan could find. He waited patiently on the porch, drinking coffee he had made and sitting in an old rocking chair that had once belonged to the Drakos. Jinette and Dinclaur were tied up and laid on the porch not far from him. He had gagged them after tiring of their laments. Jinnette's arm was wrapped with an old towel he had found. Dinclaur's face was a bloated red-and-purple pumpkin, his broken nose barely extending beyond the swelling. After subduing the pair, he had brought a bucket of water to Kiowa and found a bag of oats for the big sorrel. Kiowa was now standing three-legged, tied at the hitching rack in front of the house.

"Whoa, men. It be Mr. Ethan Kerry hisself." Big Red yelled to the others as they galloped into the ranch yard.

"Good to see you, boys." Ethan declared and stood. "Glory Van Camp and his sis are right here. Tied up nice and neat. Tiorgs is dead. Body's inside." He cocked his head. "They tried to ambush me. Weren't good enough."

Big Red shouted more orders and the armed men swarmed around the house, dismounted and went inside from the front and back. Casually, Ethan told him the ranch was empty.

"Got some coffee on," Ethan said and motioned with his

cup. "How are you doing, Marshal Clanahan?"

"Fine as a fiddle I be. Now," the Irishman said as he stepped onto the porch and patted his wounded arm. Only dried blood served as a reminder. "But me good friend, Peaches, he be gone." He sniffed and wiped his nose with the back of his hand. "Hisself be with the coroner when we left."

"I know." Ethan held out his hand. "We'll want . . . Shi Han Rui buried at our ranch. Luther and I will come in for the body tomorrow," Ethan said. "He was part of our family."

Big Red shook his hand hardily, thinking through Peaches's real name before understanding. "Better there be a can of peaches when ye bury hisself."

"Good idea." He wondered if they should bury the China-man's distinctive handgun with him, too, or if Cole would want it.

After a few minutes of reflection on the day, Ethan announced he was heading out to the Bar K.

"Couldna ye wait til morn? It be late, ye know," Big Red said and asked one of the men to see about fixing something to eat.

"No. Thanksgiving's just two days away. Claire'll be needin' my help," Ethan said. "We'll be expecting you for Thanksgiving. About noon."

"I do thank ye."

A few minutes later, Ethan Kerry rode out of the Rocking R ranch yard. It would be the first Thanksgiving without Kathleen, but at least Cole was there. He nudged Kiowa into an easy lope. He smiled and let his tired mind drift. Claire would have hovered around his young brother, between work on the Thanksgiving feast and caring for the wounded DuMonte and Middleton. Maggie would have bombarded Cole with ques-tions. And the twins would have demanded him to play with them. Eli would have watched his uncle as if he were a god.

"Maybe he is. Well, he is a Kerry." He chuckled to himself.

All would be asleep by the time he got home. Except for Luther. His oldest brother would be waiting on the front porch. He would be angry Ethan had left his horse in town and surprised—and worried—to see him riding the big sorrel. He laughed out loud; Kiowa's ears perked to understand. He patted the sorrel's neck. It seemed like another world since the fiery animal had thrown him.

Somewhere along the trail, a lone chickadee sang and Ethan would have sworn the little bird was saying "Cole-a Kerr-ie. Cole-a Kerr-ie." How silly, he was just tired and nudged Kiowa into a lope.

"Let's go home, boy."

ABOUT THE AUTHOR

Cotton Smith has been a writer all his life, from award-winning advertising to unforgettable Western novels. A Western historian, artist and horseman, his books have won accolades for their historical accuracy, memorable characters and intriguing plot twists. A Spur Award winner, he is a former president of the Western Writers of America and recipient of the WWA Branding Iron Award.

Roundup magazine states: "The traditional Western doesn't get much better than Cotton Smith." *True West* magazine says: "Cotton Smith is another modern writer with cinematic potential."

Jay Wolpert, screenwriter of *Pirates of the Carribean*, states: "When it came to literature, middle-age had only three good things to show me: Patrick O'Brien, Larry McMurtry and Cotton Smith."

Other books by Cotton Smith include *Dark Trail to Dodge*, *Pray for Texas*, *Behold a Red Horse*, *Brothers of the Gun*, *Spirit Rider*, *Sons of Thunder*, *The Thirteenth Bullet*, *Winter Kill*, *Death Rides a Red Horse*, *Stands a Ranger*, *Blood Brothers*, *Blood of Bass Tillman*, *Return of the Spirit Rider*, *Death Mask*, *Morning War (Way of the West)*, *Ride For Rule Cordell* and *Ring of Fire*.

His website is cottonsmithbooks.com.